FORBIDDEN

by

Victoria Taylor Murray

AmErica House
Baltimore

First printing

ISBN: 1-58851-594-X
PUBLISHED BY AMERICA HOUSE BOOK
PUBLISHERS
www.publishamerica.com
Baltimore

Printed in the United States of America

DEDICATION

I would like to dedicate my LAMBERT SERIES of books
to my amazing son,
Michael.
Without his never-ending love, support, encouragement,
and much needed assistance with this enormous project--
my four book series,
starting with book one,
THIEF OF HEARTS, and now book two,
FORBIDDEN- would still be a life long dream,
instead of the reality it has now become.
Thank you darling, (ILYTWATC).

I would also like to dedicate my Lambert Series of four
books,
to my wonderful daughter-niece,
Michelle,
who helped create a few really neat names for some of the
characters.
Thank you honey,(ILYTWATC2).

ACKNOWLEDGMENT

Others I owe a special thank you to include:
MY FAMILY "THE TAYLOR'S"
Milford, Mary, Liz,
Bradford, John, Mary V,
Joe, Tony, Dan, Lisa, TC,
Joey, Matthew, Josh,
Tim, Kay, Tonya (Cool Breeze),
Brenda, Bill Reilly, Travis Thomas,
Anita, Frank, and Pat Thernes,
Herb Murray,
Lacey and Jackie Bonner,
Diane and Brian Adams,
Millie, Andrew, Andy, and Rae McKinney,
My friends on the Covington Kentucky Police Force.
All of my Aunts, Uncles, Cousins, Nieces, and Nephews
(too many to mention by name)
Eva Taylor at Eva's Treasures – eva4350@msn.com
A Special Thanks to my friends at Fifth Third Bank in
Covington especially, Candace

A VERY SPECIAL THANK YOU to my publishers at
AmErica House/ PublishAmerica House Publishing for
believing in my four book LAMBERT SERIES- "THIEF
OF HEARTS" "FORBIDDEN" "FRIENDLY ENEMIES'
and "THE FIN".

And, to all of my OLD FRIENDS as well as NEW, too
many to mention by name.
I LOVE YOU ALL.
Oh yes, and THANK YOU to all of my FANS and
READERS of whom I love hearing from-
vtm_inc@hotmail.com
And last but not least, a few of my favorite
CELEBRITRIES who were kind enough to give me a truly

UNIQUE *(one-of-its-kind)* in the world specially
autographed item:
BILL COSBY
RICH LITTLE
BOB SIGER &THE SILVER BULLET BAND
WAYLON JENNINGS
CHUCK MANGIONE
VICTOR BORGE
JOHN DENVER

Dear Reader:

The four book LAMBERT SERIES is a ROMANTIC MURDER MYSTERY, written from the viewpoint of the colorful cast of characters. Some of the characters you will love, while others you will love to hate. Each of the four books in this series has its own story line connecting the lives of its five keys characters – NOURI ST. CHARLES SOMMERS – ETHAN SOMMERS – CLINT CHAMBERLAIN – CHARLES MASON – and GABE BALDWIN. However, to fully enjoy the overall story, I strongly urge you to read the four book series in its intended order – starting with book one of THE LAMBERT SERIES titled, THIEF OF HEARTS.

FORBIDDEN is the second book in the series, FRIENDLY ENEMIES the third, And THE FIN is the fourth.

My LAMBERT SERIES will provide its READERS with hours of entertainment with its many surprising twists and turns; PASSION & ROMANCE-MYSTERY-HUMOR-BETRAYAL-SECRETS-REVENGE-LUST-SKELETONS-SIZZLING CHEMISTRY-ENVY-DISAPPOINTMENT-REGRET-DUTY & HONOR AMONG FRIENDS-AMAZING WILL POWER & INNER STRENGTH-TWO MURDERS TO SOLVE-A KNIGHT IN SHINING ARMOR-RENEWED LOVE-LOST LOVE-REMEMBERED LOVE-AND … A FORBIDDEN LOVE!

But wait! There's still more … A FAIRY TALE MARRIAGE TURNED NIGHTMARE-CHANGES-CHALLENGES-AN UNCERTAIN TOMORROW-AN ATTEMPTED KIDNAPPING-AND … A DEATH THREAT …

The Lambert Series will take its READERS from Boston to Lambert, from Lambert to Boston, from Boston to Connecticut, from Connecticut to Lambert, from

Lambert to France, from France to China, finally returning home to where it all began in Boston. A JOURNEY YOU WON'T WANT TO MISS …

Lambert was written for everyone- both ROMANCE LOVERS, as well as MYSTERY LOVERS but its contents were not intended for anyone under eighteen …

So, RELAX, GET A SNACK, KICK BACK, and let the JOURNEY BEGIN …

THE *COLORFUL* CAST OF CHARACTERS

NOURI ST. CHARLES SOMMERS: The main character in the Lambert Series. Nouri is the heart-stoppingly beautiful, but bored wife, of one of the wealthiest men in the world, Ethan Sommers. Nouri's secret passion is romance. And her favorite pastime--writing in her fantasy journals.

ETHAN SOMMERS: A dashingly handsome and powerful, but mysterious and ruthless billionaire businessman--who seems to have less and less time for romancing his beautiful, hot-natured wife of only two years. Ethan is a man surrounded by mystery, and skeletons from his past. His secret passion is revenge. And his favorite pastime--beautiful super-young women.

CLINT CHAMBERLAIN: Ever so sexy, but hot-tempered and sometimes hard to control best friend and high-powered attorney to Ethan Sommers. Also quite the ladies' man. And secret lover from Nouri's past – that her husband was never told about. Clint holds the key to Nouri's heart. A man with a few skeletons of his own. His secret passion is Nouri. And his favorite pastime- catering to his one true weakness--beautiful women.

CHARLES MASON: Incredibly manly, but obstinate, private eye extraordinair! The best private dick in the country. Quite the ladies' man himself. Charles is also a man from Nouri's past (her first real man) that she will always have deep feelings for. His secret passion is also Nouri. And his favorite pastime--trying to win her back.

GABE BALDWIN: Not only the sexiest, but also the best homicide detective on the Boston Police Force--that is, after Charles Mason left the force. His secret passion soon becomes Nouri. And his favorite pastime--nailing the bad guys.

BECKA CHAMBERLAIN: The incredibly beautiful, but whacko wife of Clint Chamberlain. Becka is also Nouri's ex-partner in an Interior Design business--who happens to hate Nouri with a purple passion. Her secret passion is to become the next Mrs. Ethan Sommers. And her favorite pastime--to destroy Nouri or anyone else who tries to get in her way.

RENEA CHANDLIER: A seductive temptress who is hired by Ethan Sommers to help destroy someone close to him. With Renea's unbelievable beauty, she has zero problems getting close to her intended mark.

GENNA MATTHEWS: Beautiful, but wild and zany best friend of seven years to Nouri Sommers. They had met while attending the Fine Arts Academy in Boston. Genna has a dark side that Nouri isn't aware of. Genna's secret passion is Charles Mason. And her favorite pastime--to settle a score!

MAI LI: Originally from China where she worked for the House of Chin-- China Royalty. Now, she runs the Sommers' Estate. Mai Li is a beautiful, but mature woman who is as mysterious as the well-kept secrets she manages to hide so well.

STEVEN LI: A character with a lot of mystery surrounding him, one of which is his association with the Chinese mob--a.k.a. THE RED DEVIL.

TONYA DAUGHTERY: The District Attorney of Boston. She's also Charles Mason's "EX." And even though engaged to someone else now, Charles Mason is still her one true passion in life.

OLIVIA & OTTO LAMBERT: Own and operate the exclusive Lambert paradise. A truly one-of-a-kind couple, who take tremendous pleasure in *serving* themselves, as well as their guest elite.

KIRSTEN KAMEL: Ethan Sommers' super-young new mistress.

KIKI: Super-young, super-sexy special service employee in Lambert.

THOMAS: Super-sexy, special service employee in Lambert. Thomas' special skills make him and his unique service very much in demand with the island elite.

KIRT JARRET: An employee in Lambert with special connections to Otto Lambert, Kirsten Kamel, and Ethan Sommers. His secret passion is Kirsten Kamel.

STACY & STUART GULLAUME: Close friends to the Sommers, the Chamberlains, Matthews, and Lamberts. Also a couple on the rocks.

GUY MATTHEWS: Billionaire oil tycoon who is married to Nouri's zany best friend, Genna - even though he's thirty years Genna's senior.

CHRISTOPHER GRAHAM: An over-priced attorney that is engaged to the DA of Boston, Tonya Daughtery.

AL BALLARD: Young, inexperienced police detective that Gabe Baldwin takes under his wing.

LACEY ALEXANDRIA BONNER: Charles Mason's old flame. Also, ex-lover to Gabe Baldwin. Not just another pretty face. Lacey Bonner is also a Famous Star of Stage, Screen, and Television. A lady with a few skeletons and secrets of her own.

KIMBERLY MICHELLE: International Super Model. And Charles Mason's current love interest.

LISA CLAYBORNE: A front page socialite--The Baron's Daughter and police detective, Gabe Baldwin's on again--off again fiancé.

CELINA SAWYER: Gabe Baldwin's sexy new neighbor in Connecticut – where he owns an A-frame cabin in the woods--the detective's new little hideaway for a little down time between cases.

ISABELLA BEDAUX: Connecticut Police Department's new bombshell detective from France who just happens to have the hots for sexy detective, Gabe Baldwin.

JIN TANG: Ethan Sommers' Asian connection to THE RED DEVIL.

ANNA McCALL: Ethan Sommers' private secretary.

VIOLET SMITH: High-priced attorney, Clint Chamberlain's beautiful Malaysian private secretary.

TESS: Charles Mason's private secretary.

FREDRICK: The two-generation chauffer for the Sommers.

ROBERT BARNET: Stationed in Boston, Robert works undercover for the FBI.

RICK HOBNER: The young police officer in Boston.

PIERRE DuVALL: Famous French clothing designer.

HEIDI: The Sommers' downtown maid.

JAMES: The Sommers' downtown chauffer.

TALULA: Charles Mason's pet feline.

A WORD ABOUT LAMBERT

Lambert is located in the Eastern Bay area near Cape Cod and neighboring Nantucket. Lambert is isolated from the land mass of New England, where its sands are enclosed by the restless waters that both caress and influence the weather. Lambert is breathtakingly beautiful. The sea has shaped the land itself. Year by year, tide by tide, and storm by storm. Honey-suckle, wild roses, lilacs, mint, and salty sea air scent the air from magnificent sunrise to spectacular sunset!

Lambert is more than a resort on an island, surrounded by sand dunes or salty sea air. It's a hidden hideaway where the super-rich go to find solace from their billionaire empires and super-rich life styles. A quaint little village it is not! At this secret haven, guest elite come and go at will; to unwind, relax, and be pampered in every imagined way, a place where every whim is granted and every demand fulfilled. It is year-round paradise created exclusively for the wealthiest of people, a place where money is never an issue, and, of course, it's scandal free.

That is, scandal free until a double murder is discovered on the island elite, implicating the wife of one of the wealthiest and most powerful men in the world.

From that moment on, the island paradise will never be the same. Neither will the lives of the many guest elite who frequent it.

PROLOGUE

"From the windows of my eyes... I can see... that you were a part of me... why'd ya go away... and leave me... you've abandon me... love don't live here anymore..."

Nouri, the beautiful wife of billionaire--businessman Ethan Sommers, was softly singing along to the tune being played on her favorite oldies but goodies channel on the radio, as she continued to stare out of the large Victorian Bay window inside her bedroom. Her thoughts were scattered about, recalling the strange events that had taken place in her life over the past few days.

A moment later, the attractive, but mature Asian woman who ran the massive Sommers' Estate, gently tapped on the bedroom door.

Nouri cleared her dry throat, released the thin, sheer panel of window drapes, and turned her gaze to face the door.

"Yes. Come in, Mai Li." Her tone was one of distraction.

Her employee smiled affectionately as she entered the spacious, bedroom chamber.

"Excuse please, miss." She bowed politely.

The billionaire's wife, smiled in spite of her mood, slowly crossed the room, moving closer to where the tiny, Asian woman was now standing.

"What is it, Mai Li?" she asked softly.

"I fix your favorite food for dinner," Mai Li replied with a concerned expression draped across her face. "Miss not eat all day." She shook her head caringly. "Please, come eat now," she prodded, studying the tired lines now appearing around her mistress' face.

Nouri shook her head, declining. "No thank you...I'm sorry you went to so much trouble, but I'm just not that hungry right now." She shrugged releasing a soft sigh.

Mai Li objected with concern. "I know miss worried about husband and Mr. Chamberlain, but..." she was saying as Nouri cut in...

"Mai Li, I know you mean well, and are just trying to look after me, but I just don't feel like eating right now," she remarked stubbornly releasing another sigh. "Maybe I'll feel more like eating later. Why don't you put a plate of food in the microwave." She caringly patted the tiny woman across the shoulder as she turned to walk toward the over-sized, brass waterbed.

"Yes, miss," Mai Li said softly in response, turning to leave the room. Before she reached the door, Nouri spoke out...

The tiny woman turned to face her. "Yes miss," she responded, meeting her gaze.

"Thank you," Nouri said smiling. "I just have a lot on my mind," she sighed. "So much has happened these past few days..." She released another sigh, sitting down on the side of the bed. "I...I just..."

Mai Li, smiled understandingly walking over to her. "I know, miss. Try not to worry." She patted Nouri's arm affectionately. "Mr. Sommers or Mr. Chamberlain will phone soon. You'll see," she said attempting to comfort her mistress.

Nouri swallowed hard. "I wonder where they are? Why did they just suddenly vanish into thin air like they did? Mai Li...what's going on?" she asked in confusion, struggling hard to hold back her tears.

Mai Li shook her head unknowingly. "Mai Li not know, miss. But, one of them will phone soon." She smiled, patting Nouri's arm again.

The billionaire's wife shook her head, rising to her feet, and slowly walking to the large bay window. "God, Mai Li! How could Ethan do this to me? Especially, at a time like this…And Becka…DEAD! Oh, God…I can't believe it!"

She gently pulled the thin, sheer panel of the window drapes back and stared outside again. "Murdered! Who could've done that to her?" she said shaking her head in total disbelief. "And that poor young woman in Lambert…Who on earth could have killed her? I can't believe it…Two Murders! Who could've hated both Becka and that other young woman enough to kill them?

"FOR GOODNESSAKES! These past few days have been an unimaginable nightmare!" She released the curtain, walking toward the tiny Asian woman again. "God! Ethan's disappearance… Becka's death…and…now Clint has suddenly vanished off the face of the earth, too! Oh, God, Mai Li! What am I'm going to do?" she sobbed hoarsely.

The tiny woman shook her head sympathetically, crossing the room to comfort her again. She gently patted her mistress on the shoulder affectionately.

"There…There…Maybe, miss needs to try and take her mind off things for a while. How about hot bubble bath? You get journals out," she suggested in an attempt to get Noir to stop worrying over the brutal murder of her one time best friend and business partner. The sudden and mysterious disappearance into thin air of her elusive husband —and, his high-powered-attorney--the same man that secretly holds the key to her heart.

Nouri considered Mai Li's suggestion as she glanced in the direction of the bathroom. She finally conceded…

"Maybe you're right, Mai Li. Writing in my journals just might take my mind off of things for a while." She nodded. "Why don't you go pop the cork on a cold bottle of *Asti* and bring it up, while I go and run myself a hot bath." She smiled. "Oh…and then, Mai Li, you can send everyone home and take the rest of the evening off yourself."

Mai Li smiled in relief, happy to see her mistress do something besides worry. "Yes, miss…be right back," she said, swiftly leaving the room.

Nouri crossed the room, heading in the direction of a large antique dresser. She opened the over-sized jewelry box that was sitting on top of it. After a few moments of fishing around inside it she pulled out a small silver key.

She glanced at the key and smiled as though she were smiling at an old friend. A split second later, she was standing inside her room-size, walk-in closet. She flicked on the light switch and shoved aside several expensive evening gown originals by the famous French clothing designer, Pierre DuVall. She leaned down to retrieve the silver, jeweled box that housed her most intimate thoughts of passion.

"Oh, Clint, I need you," she whispered under her breath tightly clutching the silver jeweled box to her breasts. She left the closet and walked over to her dressing table, gently placing her treasured journals on top of it, releasing a sigh as she unlocked and removed her journals from their guarded domain. "Oh, Clint darling… I need you," she whispered again turning to face Mai Li as she was entering the room. "Thank you, Mai Li," she softly remarked, watching the tiny woman cross the room carrying her bubbling bottle of sparkling sweet wine. "Just set the tray on my night stand… I'll pour it myself," she said smiling. The tiny Asian woman returned the smile and left the room.

A short time later, the beautiful billionaire's wife was soaking in a silky, hot bubble bath. She laid her head back, closing her eyes and releasing a sigh. After a few moments of relaxing, she picked up her journal and pen in one hand, while reaching for her chilled glass of *Asti Spumanti* with the other. She took a sip of the sweet, fruity wine, as she opened her journal, and then set the wine glass back down.

Her mind quickly shifted from the confused and bored Mrs. Ethan Sommers …

To … Nouri St. Charles Sommers…aka *DAMSEL IN DISTRESS*!

OUT OF NOWHERE HE CAME ... JUST SIMPLY BANG HE WAS THERE ...

STANDING DIRECTLY IN FRONT OF ME ... HIS SHIRT SLUNG OVER HIS   LEFT   SHOULDER ... THE SCHOURCHING SUN BEATING DOWN ON HIS   PERFECTLY CONTOURED BODY ... HE RAISED HIS MUSCULAR ARM IN   AN   ATTEMPT   TO   BLOT   THE PERSPERATION   THAT   WAS   BEGINNING   TO   TRICKLE DOWN HIS BEAUTIFUL, BUT MANLY FACE ... HIS MOCHA   BROWN EYES GAZED INTO MINE ... SO MYSTERIOUS ... SO ...

SEDUCTIVE ... SO MESMERIZING ... I FELT PASSIONATELY DRAWN TO   HIM ... HE SMILED FAINTLY ... HIS SMILE LIT A FLAME INSIDE ME ... MY   HEART WAS UNDER SEIGE ... SUDDENLY ...

Chapter 1

HIGH-POWERED-ATTORNEY, Clint Chamberlain glanced at his watch nervously. *One hour*, he thought, reaching for his phone card. *A tight schedule, but I think I can make the next flight to France. That is, with the help of Violet Smith.* He smiled fondly, picturing her beautiful Malayan face.

Violet Smith was his private secretary, who has been in his employ for almost fifteen years. She was originally from an island between Southeast Asia and Australia.

Clint had met her while on one of his many business trips out of the country handling billionaire businessman, Ethan Sommers' bids to take over large corporations on a rapid and vast scale. As far as the high-powered-attorney was concerned, his private secretary was not only beautiful and loyal, but brilliant as well. He'd be lost without her, and he knew it.

Before dialing his secretary's telephone number, Clint asked the airline host to make the necessary flight connections for him on the most immediate flight out, if at all possible. Luckily, the airline had a last minute cancellation, and the high-powered-attorney was told he would have thirty minutes to make the connecting flight once they landed in Boston.

After endless ringing of the telephone in his ear, Violet Smith finally answered the phone with a sleepy, "*Selamat* (hello)." She yawned and tried to squint a look at the clock sitting on the nightstand beside her bed, but her eyes were too blurry.

"Wake-up sleeping beauty," he said in a soft but nervous tone. Recognizing the familiar voice on the other end of the line, Violet quickly sat up in bed.

"Clint..." She cleared her dry throat. "Clint Chamberlain, is that you? What happened? Are you all right?" Her tone rang out in panic.

"Yes Violet," he replied forcing himself to calm down. "It's me... I'm fine... Calm down... Sorry to wake you, but its almost time for you to get out of bed anyway," he said, glancing at his watch.

She threw the sheet off of her body and lowered her legs to the floor. "What is it, boss? You've never called me in the middle of the night before." She stretched and rubbed the sleep from her eyes.

"Violet..." he sighed. "... It isn't the middle of the night – It's five-thirty... almost daybreak. Come on, sleepy head, wake-up! I need a favor," he stated anxiously.

"I'm awake," she yawned again. "What kind of favor?" she asked rising to her feet and stretching.

He released a heavy sigh. "Something terrible has happened." He paused briefly rubbing his tired eyes... He went on...

"I don't know where to begin." He shook his head.

"What is it Clint? Where are you?" she asked nervously.

"I'm on my way back from Lambert. I'll be in Boston in about an hour. It's... It's Ethan. Ethan Sommers..." He swallowed. "I think he may have killed someone." He sighed deeply.

Violet's mouth flew open in shock.

"Oh my God! What happened?" she exclaimed in a stunned tone, completely awake at that point.

He released another a sigh of frustration. "I don't have all the answers yet, but I'll tell you what I know at the airport."

His secretary nodded understandingly. "Okay, I'll get dressed now. Where shall I meet you? What airline?" she asked wiggling out of her rose-pedal-pink-colored teddy.

"First, I need you to run by my apartment and pack a suitcase for me. Don't forget to bring my passport. I'll meet you inside the terminal," he said pausing briefly to think. "There's a restaurant to the right of Air France Airlines. I believe the name of it is *Michael's*. I'll meet you inside the restaurant, okay?" he sighed again.

"Sure Clint. I'd better hop to it. I don't have much time," she answered excitedly.

"Thanks, Violet," he was saying just as the airline host snatched the plastic glass from his hand.

Moments later, the aircraft was preparing to land... "Ladies and gentlemen. We are approaching the Boston International Airport. Please return to your seats and fasten your safety belts. Make sure that your trays are securely locked in place in their upright positions. Thank you," were the next words he heard. A short time later, the aircraft was gliding onto the runway.

When the plane came to a full stop, the high-powered-attorney quickly gathered his belongings, swiftly departing the aircraft in a heated rush, wanting to grab his passport and jump on the next flight to France. Glancing at his watch he hurried into *Michael's* restaurant.

When he entered the restaurant, his secretary spotted him immediately. Violet rose to her feet, motioning him to the table with a wave of her hand. His long legs were standing beside her table in no time. "*Selamat* (hi)." she said excitedly. He nodded, smiled faintly, and leaned over to kiss her on the cheek. "*Terima Kasih* (thank you) for meeting me." He sat down at the table. She extended her arm across the table to pick up the stainless-steel coffee pot, already sitting on top of the table, and poured a cup of coffee for him.

"*Kembali jsama-sama* (you're welcome). Here drink this. You look like you could use a cup." she smiled.

He returned the smile. "Thanks you must've read my mind." He rubbed his temples, waiting for her to fill his cup.

Violet curiously leveled her eyes to her his. "Now…What's this all about?" she asked studying the tired lines now appearing around her boss's eyes.

"I only have a short time until my flight to France leaves. But, I'll tell you as much as I can." He smiled nervously, glancing at his watch.

He took a sip of his coffee and began to speak… "As I told you yesterday while you were driving me to the airport, Ethan Sommers is back on drugs…and when he's on that shit he can be a very dangerous person ." He swallowed nervously, glancing at his secretary …

"Remember I told you what happened the last time Ethan was on that shit. A young woman was killed…so, I went to Lambert last night to try and get to him before he had a chance to hurt someone else…

"I think I was too late…" He hung his head briefly and then continued.

"When I arrived in Lambert, I went straight to his hotel suite. When no one responded to my knocking on the door, I tried the door handle. Surprisingly, the door wasn't locked," he explained, rubbing his chin in a thoughtful manner.

"I went inside, glanced around the room and didn't see anyone. So, I walked back to the master bedroom. When I glanced inside the room…" He inhaled deeply, slowly releasing it. "I saw a young woman lying on the floor in a pool of blood…Ethan was gone." He shook his head and rubbed his tired eyes.

Violet looked at him sympathetically patting him on the hand. *"Permisi-ma' afkan saya. Ma'af. Saya tidak fahm,"* (Excuse me. I'm sorry. I don't understand) she replied excitedly.

"I'm sorry Violet. I don't understand either. I'm just attempting to tell you what appears to have happened last night in Lambert, as best I can. *Adakah saudara faham* (Do you understand)?"

He smiled faintly after his secretary nodded her head understandingly.

He went on. "*Dengariah. Penting.* (Listen. It's important). I'm running out of time, and I have a lot to tell you, so pay close attention- Violet, I don't have a lot of answers yet," he sighed. "So try and save the questions until I track Ethan down, okay."

She nodded in agreement. "Sure Clint, you have my undivided attention. Please go on." She returned his smile.

"My Malayan is a little rusty, so I'm going to speak to you in English, okay?"

"Okay boss. *Saya Siap* (I'm ready)."

"Where was I?" He scratched his head thoughtfully.

She smiled and refreshed his memory. "The young woman was lying in a pool of blood and Mr. Sommers was no where to be found." She smiled, proud of her ability to recall most anything at most anytime. The high-powered-attorney's secretary had an incredible memory.

"I just can't believe it! Ethan's out of control again. I'm talking the heavy shit, Violet," he sighed in disgust. "I'm pretty certain Steven Li has gotten him hooked on the stuff again." He shook his head sadly.

She glanced at her boss sympathetically and patted his hand. "I'm sorry Clint," she said caringly. He went on. "I have to find him... It has to be me... It can be no one else." He shook his head...

"If the F.B.I. gets to him before I do, he won't stand a chance... They'll to have to kill him. I... I don't want that to happen... I know he's out of control, and maybe even a little crazy..." He paused to light a cigarette... "okay, crazier than most, but he's still my friend- we have a lot of issues to settle between us." He stopped to catch his breath, glancing down at his watch. He continued.

"I phoned the Lambert police before jumping on the airplane to come here. I anonymously phoned them from a pay phone outside the airport." He released a puff of smoke shrugging his shoulders defensively.

"I didn't want to be pulled into the investigation. I needed to figure things out for myself," he said, reaching for his coffee.

Violet swallowed nervously. "Why bother to phone the police at all? What if they would have traced the call to the airport and stopped your flight?" she asked with concern.

Clint shook his head impatiently and sighed. "In the first-place, Violet, I wasn't on the phone long enough for the call to be traced... And anyway, the dead body wasn't in my hotel suite so why would they..." He stopped talking.

"What is it, Clint?" she asked nervously.

He shook his head. "None of that matters now... I mainly phoned the police hoping they would get to the hotel before Otto Lambert had a chance to make another one of Ethan's little problems disappear again. Don't get me wrong Violet. I don't know for sure if Ethan Sommers killed that young woman or not...And if he did, he of course, needs to face charges for doing so. But, at this point my only concern is finding him... Before I can find out what happened inside that hotel suite, I have to locate him...Hell! Violet. Steven˜ could've killed that young woman. For all I know, Ethan's probably already in France running scared," he sighed glancing at his watch nervously for the umpthteenth time.

She glanced at her boss with interest. "France. Why France?" she questioned curiously.

"There are only two places that Ethan can hide. I mean literally disappear--without so much as a trace of him and that is in France- and the other place is in China." He paused to down the rest of his coffee.

"France? China? Wow! Ethan Sommers really is a man of mystery, huh?" Violet shook her head in amazement.

Clint nodded. "Violet, my pet, you have no idea." He smiled faintly.

"So, what do you need me to do?" she asked with concern.

He gazed thoughtfully for a moment releasing a sigh. "Clear my calendar for the next few weeksWhat can't be postponed, turn over to Nick Brewer, Ken Wilkie, and Joe Sullivan. Tell the three bums to earn some of those huge salaries I've been paying them for years, for a change," he teased.

"Next, put our recent bid to take over the Medallion Corporation on hold--I don't care how mad they get... I'll deal with them personally when I get back. Transfer that one billion dollars into a new account in Switzerland. I know you didn't have time to do it yesterday, but it has to be taken care of today, understand?" He glanced at her. She nodded. He went on ... "Make up a new name or number, I don't care what, just don't give that information to anyone except me. That includes; Ethan Sommers, the police, the F.B.I or, anyone else...Got it?"

She nervously shifted in her seat. "Yes Clint, I don't understand, but I'll do it. Of course, you realize I'll probably die from curiosity before you..."

"No time for teasing, love," he interrupted.

She nodded understandingly. "Okay. What else do you need from me, Clint?" She smiled.

"Take every single file, transcript, videotape, and computer record-- whatever we have pertaining to Ethan Sommers business or otherwise, and make them all disappear...I want it to appear as though we have never heard the name Ethan Sommers. Put everything into a safety deposit box under your name, Violet... There are only two people in the world that will have that information." He smiled when she pointed to herself and then to him.

"Exactly," he said gently patting Violet's arm, thankful that he had such a loyal friend, as well as a highly competent, secretary.

He glanced at the time again. "I have to run in a few minutes Violet, let me think," he said rubbing his eyes.

"More coffee?" she offered nervously.

He shook his head. "I don't have time. Listen, before I forget. No one at the office is to answer any questions about me, Ethan Summers or anything else, is that understood?" She nodded.

He went on. "There's one more thing, Violet. Mrs. Sommers may have hired a private dick...his name is Charles Mason." He unconsciously cringed. "Mr. Mason is supposed to be the best private investigator in the country. I don't want to make his job easy, if you know I mean..." He leveled his eyes to hers.

Violet interrupted. "I don't understand. Sounds like you don't like this guy very much." She shrugged. "Why?"

Clint rolled his eyes with irritation. "I told you, love, I don't have time for questions," he sighed in frustration shaking his head. "But, I will tell you this. You're right! I don't like the man...Mason was her first..." He caught himself and stopped talking.

Violet glanced at her boss curiously. "Her who? What?"

"Never mind, Violet." The high-priced attorney shook his head hopelessly. "Just phone Mrs. Sommers... Tell her I'll phone later." He squirmed uneasily in his seat. "Oh, the hell with it!" he impulsively blurted out an instant later, when Nouri Sommers beautiful face suddenly popped inside his mind after mentioning her name. He swallowed hard in an attempt to calm his need to see her.

"Violet... Nouri Sommers and I are in love!" he stated excitedly, not wanting to secretly hide his love for her any longer. "She's the woman I told you about yesterday over the phone. Nouri was engaged to me before she married mister impulsive. Ethan Sommers stole her from me. I want her back," he sighed.

"She wants a divorce, but Ethan won't give her one." He shook his head heatedly.

"Ethan told me yesterday that the only way she would get out of her marriage to him would be in a body bag... so, Nouri wanted to hire Charles Mason to help her get a divorce." He glanced over his shoulder after noticing a few people rising to their feet and hurrying out the door. He glanced at the time and then turned his attention back to his secretary...

"She used to live with the prick seven years ago. Mason was her first REAL MAN... whatever the hell that means ... Anyway." He shrugged, glancing at her. She smiled knowingly.

He went on. "I told her that I would handle things, but I don't think she wants to wait that long...I don't know whether she knows about her husband's affair with that young woman in Lambert or not. Or if she knows about what has happened yet, or not. I don't even know if Nouri has arrived in Lambert yet. But in any case...when all this shit hits the front pages of tomorrow's newspaper's..." He shook his head after realizing the hour..."I'm talking a few hours from now... all HELL is going to break loose!" he said excitedly, glancing at his watch, nervously tapping it with his finger.

Violet sat frozen in her chair with her mouth opened wide for several moments. Finally, after the shock of it all passed, she gasped... "Oh my Lord! Nouri Sommers is Nouri St. Charles?"

"Yes Violet... That's right, my woman!" he announced passionately.

"Oh God! Clint, I have so many questions..."

He chuckled, knowing how nosy his secretary was...especially when it concerned his love life.

"Violet, my sweet, I don't have any more time. My flight is boarding now... here... keep my cell phone with you...I'll call you on it later...Think you can handle things on this end for me for the next few weeks?" He smiled, handing the phone to her and standing on his feet.

Violet knew that her boss was aware that she was more than capable of handling most any job assignment he gave her.

She raised her eyebrow questioningly. "What do you think?" she playfully barked.

He lowered his body, kissing her on the cheek.

"That's my girl...Oh, by the way Violet...when I call you on my cell phone, don't call me Clint or boss. Call me Traz." He smiled adding, "I've got my reasons." He turned to walk away.

She teasingly stopped him... "Let me guess. You'll explain that later to me too, huh? "she mused, shaking her head in playful dismay.

Clint turned to face her without speaking. He winked and flashed her that incredibly sexy smile of his...The Very Smile most women had trouble resisting. She smiled, watching him disappear into the heavy rush of weekend travelers.

Violet Smith sat inside *Michael's* restaurant sipping on her coffee after her boss disappeared in the crowd of busy weekend travelers, pondering over in her mind a list of things she needed to do for him. She glanced at her watch, wondering what time it was in Switzerland.

Moments later, she excitedly jumped to her feet after suddenly remembering she had forgotten to shut the shower off inside her apartment.

She quickly tossed a ten-dollar- bill down on top of the table for the pot of coffee she and her boss had been drinking, and ran out of the restaurant, hoping to get home before her apartment flooded.

Chapter 2

"**Extra...Extra... read all about it! A double murder was reported this morning on the beautiful island paradise of Lambert!**" shouted the young newsstand worker on the busy downtown street corner across from high-powered-attorney, Clint Chamberlain's office.

"**Extra...Extra... read all about it! There's been a double homicide reported on the island paradise of Lambert! Home away from home to the Super-Rich People of the world!**" shouted the newspaper hustler stationed across the street from the head office of private investigator, Charles Mason.

"**Extra...Extra...read all about it! A double murder in paradise! The island of Lambert.**" shouted the newspaper boy who was selling his papers across the street from the Boston police department.

"Here boy...over here. I'll take a couple of copies please," shouted Charles Mason, waving a dollar bill high above his head trying to get the attention of the newspaper boy across the street from his office.

"Here, I'll take a copy please," said Gabe Baldwin, Chief Detective, homicide Division of the Boston police department.

"Over here mister. I'll take one," shouted the nervous, secretary to high-powered attorney, Clint Chamberlain. "Two murders! I thought there was one murder!" Violet exclaimed excitedly.

"No ma'am. The report says there were two murders." The newspaper vendor replied.

"But I don't understand," she said jerking the newspaper out of the man's hand.

"Excuse me miss?" He stared at her curiously.

"Never mind," she snipped storming away. "God! I can't believe it. Mr. Sommers must have killed two women," she whispered under her breath, unlocking the office to let herself in.

She quickly put on a pot of coffee, anxious to read the newspaper. She stood beside the coffee machine, nervously reading the Front Page Article on the Two Lambert Murders'.

An instant later, Violet uncontrollably gasped, after suddenly recognizing the high-powered-attorney's wife's picture in the newspaper.

She let out a scream. "Oh my Lord! Becka Chamberlain!" She swallowed hard. "Clint's wife! Oh, my God!" Her mind swiftly scattered into several directions at once.

She nervously glanced at her watch, realizing she had no choice but to wait until he phoned later, to tell her boss about his wife's murder.

Violet went into her office and turned on the television set to the twenty-four hour news channel, hoping to get more information on the Lambert Murders than what little bit was reported in the early edition of the newspaper.

"Ladies and gentlemen-.may I have your attention please? We are now boarding Air France flight 3170 to Paris France, The Rolssy-Charles Airport. Please bring your tickets and boarding passes to the front. We are currently seating first class passengers, and those passengers, that may need or require additional assistance. We will be departing the Boston International Airport in approximately fifteen minutes. We apologize for the delay. Thank you."

As Clint Chamberlain fastened his seat belt he could see streaks of lightning flash across the sky and hear distant muted sounds of thunder. He cringed at the thought of having to fly during the storm. But, he had no choice. He had to find Ethan Sommers. And he had to do it before anyone else, especially the F.B.I.

As the jet taxied off the runway, he glanced at the attractive young woman seated to the right of him. He smiled. Her Face... Her Smile... The shape of her eyes, and even the color of her hair reminded him of someone very special- someone who shared a similar expression. "Sweetness," he whispered unconsciously, when Nouri Sommers' beautiful face suddenly popped inside his brain.

'A Nouri Sommers look-alike', he was silently thinking when suddenly hearing the attractive, young woman sitting beside him speaking to him somewhere in the background of his mind. He jarred his thoughts back to the present.

"Hi. Did you say something just now?" she asked gazing into his melting-brown eyes with her beautiful royal- blue ones.

He felt his face slightly flush. "No. I guess I've must've been mumbling to myself." He returned her smile and mesmerizing gaze.

She shrugged her shoulders and smiled again.

"Trying to take your mind off of flying, huh?"

"I guess you could say that." He smiled again, with that incredibly sexy smile of his.

"Yeah, I know what you mean. I hate to fly too. My name is Renea Chandlier," she offered. "Nice to meet you," she said seductively, holding out her hand for him to shake, as she toyed with the top button on her silk blouse with her other hand.

He smiled approvingly after noticing the sudden, rise and fall of her large breasts through her thin, sheer, silk blouse. He swallowed nervously, quickly bringing his gaze back to her face.

"My name is Clint Chamberlain. It is nice to meet you, too," he said, gently releasing his hand from hers.

He went on..."Do you fly to France often?" His eyes slowly, traveled over her shapely figure, as he waited for her response.

She smiled. "I guess you could say that. I live there."

"Oh." He sounded surprised. "You live there, huh? You don't look French."

She laughed softly. "I guess that's because I'm not... French, I mean."

"Is your family in France, too?" he asked curiously.

She shook her head. "Oh... no, actually I don't have any family left, I'm afraid." She paused thoughtfully. "My mother and father both died three years ago and I was an only child. My mother died of cancer. A week later my father decided he couldn't live without her, so, one night he took a bottle of sleeping pills; the next morning he never woke up," she said sadly, turning to look out the window, as she continued to toy with the button on her silk blouse.

Clint extended his arm gently touching her shoulder. She turned to face him. "I'm sorry, Renea." She turned her gaze back to his sexy, brown eyes.

Thanks. But I've learned to deal with it." She paused, smiled faintly, and continued to speak...

" I just can't seem to find the courage to let the family mansion go, however. It's so beautiful," she sighed. "I just love it! It's been in our family for generations."

He released an understanding sigh nodding. "I can understand that. Memories can be hard to let go of sometimes." He smiled.

"Yes they can be, especially if there are a lot of fond memories." She returned the smile.

He swallowed nervously, again. "Renea, I was just about to have a Bloody Mary. Would you care to join me?"

"Sure." She nodded her acceptance. "But, make mine a Screw driver. I'm more of an orange juice type person. Russian Vodka, please."

"Russian Vodka, huh? I have a friend that loves the stuff," he chuckled. "I don't care for it myself. I favor the American brand Vodkas."

"I like them, too. As long as its vodka, it really doesn't matter much what flavor or country it's from," she mused playfully shrugging her shoulders.

Clint pressed the signal for the cabin steward. "One Bloody Mary and one Screwdriver. Oh, make hers with Russian Vodka," he ordered turning his attention back to the sultry, young temptress. He swallowed nervously.

The beautiful stranger instantly found herself smitten by the sexy and ever so charming high-powered-attorney sitting beside her. A seductive grin curled her lips.

"So, Clint Chamberlain, tell me about yourself." She smiled with interest. "Are you married?"

"Thank you," he said when the cabin host handed him their drinks. He sat the mesmerizing young woman's drink on the small tray in front of her, before unhooking his tray and sitting his drink down. "No. I mean yes." He felt his face flush. "I mean yes, I am married, but not for long. I'm getting a divorce. Thank God!" He shook his head and playfully cringed.

She laughed. "That bad, huh?"

He cringed playfully, again. "Renea, you have no idea!" he laughed.

"Your wife must be crazy to let a gorgeous man like yourself get away from her so easily." She began to toy with the top button of her silk blouse again. His eyes were glued to her impressive large breasts, as he continued to watch her play with the button.

The continued rise and fall of her breasts as she inhaled and exhaled slowly began to excite him. He swallowed nervously.

"Well, I don't know about that, but she was pretty crazy all right!" he said slowly shifting his gaze to her face. He pressed the signal for the cabin host, again.

"Two more, please," he said handing his empty glass to the steward.

"How about you Renea. Are you married?" He studied her beautiful face, thinking to himself how very much she looked like Nouri Sommers.

"No, I'm not," she smiled. "I guess you could say I like my freedom. Besides, I travel too much." She shrugged her shoulders. "Being away from home so often wouldn't make for very happy marriage." She began to nervously toy with the button on her blouse again. He noticed her apparent nervous habit and smiled.

"I suppose you're right. While the cat's away?" he mused... "Exactly." She returned laughing. Strangely, the beautiful, young temptress was surprisingly taking his mind off his current problems concerning his billionaire client, Ethan Sommers; the reason he was going to France to begin with.

"So, tell me, Renea, what do you do for a living?" he asked with a growing interest. After a few moments of silent thought, she answered, "Oh, ... I... work for an insurance company, Milford's of London. We insure super-expensive items like; diamonds, antiques, oil paintings. Things of that nature." She smiled.

"That sounds pretty exciting. Do you cover museums and places like that?" He smiled picking up his drink.

"Not just museums. We cover quite a few private collectors, as well as just super-rich people. I call them the rich and the shameless," she laughed. "You'd be surprised how many super-rich people there are in the world." She reached for her drink.

"The rich and the shameless, huh," he chuckled.

She nodded. "Oh yeah, the more rich they are, the more shameless they become!" She laughed again.

"So do you get to know most of your clients on a personal basis?" he asked with curious interest.

"Yeah." She shrugged rather-matter-of-factly. "Sure. A few more personal than others." She met his searching gaze with an inviting grin curling her lips.

"Personal, like in dating, AND..." He stop talking, thinking his question may have been too personal.

She chuckled knowingly. "Yes. That includes the question that you were about to ask." She blushed. "I'm afraid I don't have much of a social life and if I didn't..." She shrugged defensively and went on...

"Well, you get the idea, right?" She smiled. "And how about you, Clint? What do you do for a living?"

"I suppose you could say we're in the same type of business, sort-of. My clients are very wealthy, as well. I'm an attorney--high-powered-attorney, actually. My number one client, and of course, top priority, most of the time, is one of the three wealthiest men in the world--Ethan Sommers... Have you heard of him?" he asked curiously, as he studied her face for a reaction.

The seductive, but nervous, young, temptress began toying with the button on her blouse, again. "Ah ... yeah," she nodded. "I've heard of him. Who hasn't?" She shrugged.

"Is Ethan Sommers a client of yours too, Renea?" he asked with interest.

She was silent for a moment and then smiled. "Ah ... Not me, personally. But he may be a client. I've seen him in the home office a few times, I think." She began to toy with the top button on her blouse, again.

"Two more please, steward," Clint said handing him the empty glass. "How long have you worked for Milford's of London, Renea?"

"Renea shrugged with uncertainty. "Gee! I'm not sure ...let me see ..." she said, with a thoughtful expression covering her face. "I think about four years or so now?"

"Do you like it?" he smiled.

"Yes. I like my job very much." She returned his smile, quickly changing the subject. "Clint, could you order us another drink while I make a visit to the little girls' room?" She handed the sexy attorney her empty glass, suddenly tiring of the conversation surrounding her employment.

After the steward took the glasses away, he rose to his feet, stepping backwards in the aisle so Renea could get out. As he watched the sexy, young stranger walk to the back of the aircraft, he smiled to himself when a naughty, but nice fantasy about her entered his brain.

An instant later, a sudden twinge of guilt surprisingly engulfed him, when the image of the woman of his dreams swiftly pushed the lovely Ms. Chandliers' image out of his mind.

"How strange!" he whispered under his breath as he watched Renea Chandlier make her way back to her seat. He stood up, stepping back into the aisle so she could be reseated.

"Miss me?" she teased sitting down in her seat. He met her penetrating gaze and smiled. "You know Renea, strangely, I think I have." He nervously picked up his drink. She smiled and did the same. Nouri's image suddenly vanished from his mind.

"Where will you be staying while you're in France?" she asked as she sipped at her drink.

"The Bristol. I've been saying there for years. I guess you could say I'm a creature of habit. You know where it is." He smiled, toying with the ice cubes in his drink.

"The Bristol. Sure I know where it is." She nodded. "It's a magnificent hotel. Very posh! I drive by it on my way home." She licked her lips... "Hey, if you like, when we get to France, I could give you lift to your hotel. It would be no trouble." She smiled suggestively.

Nouri's image suddenly popped back inside Clint's brain, cautioning him to beware! He quickly blinked the image away. "That would be great! If you're sure it wouldn't be out of your way." He returned the inviting smile.

She continued to smile in a playful manner. "Trouble. No. It would be no trouble. But..." she teased.

"But what?" A curious expression crossed the attorney's handsome face.

"But, I didn't say I'd do it for free." She continued to flirtatiously tease as she toyed with the top button on her silk blouse, again, thinking to herself, 'this is going to be fun'.

Clint knew that Renea was flirting with him. He also knew she was trying to seduce him. Hey, you can't seduce the willing....

"Hum..." he playfully groaned. "And exactly how much do you intend to charge me for this lift to my hotel, Ms. Chandlier?" He flirted back. She looked so much like the woman that held the key to her heart that he couldn't seem to help himself from being attracted to her.

"How does a cozy dinner for two sound?" was her lustful response. She smiled wantonly.

He bit his lower lip, as though he was thinking. "Sounds like a fair price." He smiled seductively, aware that her eyes never left his.

After much effort she finally shifted her gaze to her empty glass. "Good," she said in response. "Do you have a favorite restaurant?" She picked-up her empty glass, and put an ice cube into her mouth tauntingly, sucking on it as she toyed with the top button on her blouse again-. Her gaze was piercing and hungry.

He noticed the sudden rise and fall of her large breast again, as his mind flashed him an image of her naked body.

"Ah. Yes. I do. How does Benoit sound?" He swallowed hard in an attempt to take his mind off her super sexy body. And what he lustfully longed to do with it.

"Sounds yummy- I like their beef a la mode." She licked her thick, full lips sensually, causing his heart to suddenly race with anticipation.

"Braised beef, huh? I like that too." He smiled.

"Yeah. Braised beef. Then it's a date?" She returned the lustful smile thinking to herself she would have him for her dessert.

"Yes. It's a date," he said pressing the signal for the cabin steward. "We'd like two more drinks, please."

As they continued to chat amongst themselves, the attraction between them continued to grow stronger and stronger...

Every once in a while, Clint would feel a sudden twinge of guilt when Nouri Sommers' beautiful face would sneak into his thoughts.

He, however, would somehow manage to replace her beautiful remembered image with a real face...the beautiful woman sitting to the right of him... Her face was not only beautiful, but she was REAL... SO VERY, VERY REAL... SO CLOSE... SO TOUCHABLE... SO SEXY... And SO AVAILABLE... Renea wanted him and, God help him! Clint found himself wanting her too.

A few drinks later, the flight attendant mumbled her well-rehearsed lines into the microphone, asking everyone to take their seats and so on and so forth...

When the airplane came to a complete stop, Clint gentlemanly stood to the side of his seat so Renea could exit first. She smiled, walking past him, impressed with his charm, manner, and demeanor, as well as his good looks, brains and an apparent class, nothing at all like the usual men she was accustomed to dating.

A SHORT TIME LATER- the seductive, young temptress pulled her lemon colored Jag in front of The Bristol hotel. She shoved the gear into park, but left the car running. She turned to face the handsome attorney...

"Well..." she sighed. "Here we are. The Bristol." She smiled, leaning over to the passenger side of the car. She glanced into the attorney's, incredibly-sexy, brown eyes as she put her arms around his neck.

"Kiss," she purred, closing her eyes and pulling him close. He gently pressed his lips to hers. The kiss only lasted a heartbeat at best. He playfully groaned, reluctantly pulling back, removing her arms from around his neck.

"I'll send a car for you tonight. Is around seven all right?" He smiled.

She nodded her agreement. "Seven it is." She anxiously echoed the time. She turned to pull the gear into drive only to just as quickly change her mind. "Oh, my address..." she suddenly remembered, reaching inside the glove compartment, pulling out a business card with her address and phone number on it, and handing it to him.

Clint accepted what was being handed to him, smiling. "I'll see you later, thanks for the lift," he said, exiting her car. He waved to her as she pulled her Jag out into traffic.

He smiled and shook his head, amused by his sudden diversion, as the bellboy quickly retrieved the suitcases sitting on the ground in front of him.

"Check in sir?" he asked, glancing at Clint.

"Yes, thank you," he answered following the bellboy inside the hotel via the revolving door, glancing at his watch as he walked past the newspaper rack with his dead wife's picture plastered across the front pages of each and every one, MISSING his wife's picture altogether. He walked up to the front desk to check in.

Chapter 3

"The rain will end by noon. Now back to you, Dave."

"Thank you Howard... And now for a recap of today's headlines across the New England states... There was a double murder reported earlier this morning on the island paradise of Lambert... The two victims were Mrs. Becka Adams Chamberlain of Boston and, Ms. Kirsten Kay Kamel of Lambert... Becka Chamberlain was twenty-six years old, and Kirsten Kamel had just turned eighteen apparently two days before her death... We don't have a lot of information yet but we do know that Mrs. Chamberlain was a member of the exclusive resort and Ms. Kamel was an employee inside the hotel... We also know that both women were brutally murdered and found nude... Stacy and Stuart Gullaume, who are also members of the exclusive resort, found Mrs. Chamberlain's body on the beach... while Ms. Kamel's body was found inside one of the hotel suites of the exclusive resort... A tip was phoned into the Lambert police department anonymously reporting one of the murders... No other information has been given to our reporters yet, but we will keep you informed as new information comes in to us... This is Dave Johnson of W.L.A.N.D. Channel..."

Violet Smith turned the news channel off and stared blankly at the darkened TV set. A few moments later, the telephone rang, jolting her back to reality. She quickly reached for the telephone for the tenth time that morning. "Hello this is Violet Smith, how may I help you?"

"Yes Ms. Smith. This is Annie Parker of the Boston Enquire. I'd like to make an appointment to speak with Mr. Chamberlain about his wife's murder."

Violet rolled her eyes with annoyance. "I'm sorry Ms. Parker, but Mr. Chamberlain isn't giving any interviews at this time."

"But..."

"I'm sorry." Violet cut in. "Have a nice day." She quickly slammed down the telephone and buzzed the receptionist.

"Peg."

"Yes, Ms. Smith."

"Please screen all my calls. If it isn't pertaining to one of our clients, or if it isn't Mr. Chamberlain, or Mrs. Sommers, just take a name and a number for me. I'm sick of all the newspaper reporters and TV reporters, and oh yes- the tabloid people, too, okay?" She sighed, shaking her head in disbelief.

After Violet Smith transferred the one billion dollars, belonging to billionaire businessman, Ethan Sommers, into a new account in Switzerland for her boss, she gathered all the paperwork connecting Clint Chamberlain and his billionaire client and swiftly made her way to the bank to put all the information she accumulated inside a safety deposit box under her own name, just as she was told to do by her boss.

She then made her way back to the office where she was confronted by not only newspaper reporters and camera crew, but also a private investigator by the name of Charles Mason.

Declining to be interviewed by anyone including the famous P.I., she quickly exited the back door of the office and quietly disappeared into the five-car pile up on the interstate

Several hours later, Violet finally arrived home only to be met by a mob of reporters, camera crews, and once again, a private investigator by the name of Charles Mason, all demanding to know where Clint Chamberlain was. As she made her way through the insistent mob of people, her throat had become almost raw from screaming: "No Comment At This Time!"

An eternity later, she escaped from the massive crowd of people and nervously locked herself inside her apartment, leaving the twenty-five phone calls from T.V. and newspaper reporters and a P.I. by the name of Charles Mason unanswered on her answering machine.

"Oh, My Lord! What A Nightmare!" she whispered under her breath, sinking down into her favorite cozy chair with a double shot of *Chivas Regal* in her shaking hands. "Call. Please call. Dammit! Clint Chamberlain... you call me this instant!" she demanded shaking his cell phone in her hands.

After several double shots of scotch, Violet finally decided to take a long, hot shower, throw in a TV dinner and check the news channel, again, hoping to hear more news about the two murder's in Lambert.

While Violet was in the shower, however, she had forgotten to take her boss's cell phone into the bathroom with her. After ten rings, high-powered-attorney Clint Chamberlain slammed down the receiver on his end and decided to wait until the next morning to try and phone his secretary again.

Chapter 4

A very disappointed Charles Mason jumped into his car, reaching for his cell phone. He wasted no time in phoning his friend, federal agent, Robert Barnet who worked for the F.B.I.

"Hello Robert, this is Charles Mason." The famous private investigator's tone was excited.

"Hey, Mason how the hell are ya?" his friend responded in a playful manner.

"Good thanks, and you?"

"Not too bad for an old fart." Robert mused.

"You've been saying that for the past ten years Robert." Charles returned teasingly.

"Is this is social call Mason?" The agent's tone took on a more serious edge.

"I need some information, Robert."

"What are you working on?"

"Three guesses and the first two don't count." Charles playfully teased in response.

"Got something to do with the two Lambert murders?" Robert asked suspecting as much.

"Maybe. I'm not sure yet," Charles shrugged unknowingly.

"I don't understand, Charles," The federal agent curiously remarked.

"There's a buzz you might be interested in."

"I'm listening."

"Does the name Sommers ring any bells?"

"Is that like in Ethan Sommers, the billionaire businessman, Mason?" He countered.

"The one and only," Charles nodded.

"What about him?" His friend asked with moderate interest.

"Like I said, there's a buzz. One of the dead women was found inside his special service suite, in Lambert."

"No shit?" The federal agent remarked knowingly. He went on... "So what do you need from me?"

"I know you're working on an investigation that involves Sommers."

"Now how in the hell would you know something like that, Mason?" Robert shook his head in playful dismay.

"I'm the best at what I do, remember?" Charles mused mischievously.

"You've been reading your own press again, huh Mason?" His friend mused in return.

"Something, like that." Charles chuckled. "All joking aside, I need to know the address of Sommers' secret office. I know it's here in town somewhere. It's important, Robert or I wouldn't ask," he sighed, reaching for a cigarette.

"Whoa! Wait a minute Charles, what's this all about?" his friend asked with growing interest.

Charles released a sigh. "I know you already have all the information that you need from that location...So, my having it wouldn't interfere with your investigation." He exhaled a puff of smoke and then continued to speak.

"I've been hired by Ethan Sommers' wife to find out things about him... Business things... She needs to find out who her husband really is... She wants a divorce but he won't give her one." He paused briefly to exhale another puff of smoke.

"So, she's hoping..." Charles suddenly stopped talking to blow his horn at the idiot in front of him for slamming on his brakes. He shook his head heatedly, pulling his car into the next lane.

He started to talk again, but the agent interrupted him. "Yeah, yeah, yeah. I get the picture. There's always a woman involved. Sounds like you've got the HOTS for this

Mrs. Sommers, Mason." He laughed, knowing his friend's reputation when it comes to the ladies.

"It's personal, Robert. Nouri Sommers and I go back a long way," Charles responded defensively.

"Like I said Mason, with you there's always a woman." The agent chuckled.

"Robert, Nouri isn't just any woman. She is THE WOMAN." He shook his head in awe.

"Sounds Serious," the agent remarked, glancing at the time.

"I wish." the P.I. sighed wishfully.

"Wait a minute Mason. Nouri Sommers--isn't that young broad that broke your heart seven or eight years ago is she?" Robert asked curiously.

Charles released a sigh of hopelessness. "I'm afraid so. I'm still in love with her, God help me!" He laughed.

"Oh shit! What about Daughtery? I thought..."

Charles rolled his eyes, released a sigh and stopped his friend. "Ah... You thought wrong, pal!" he snipped teasingly.

"When I was still with the force, you two were awfully hot together."

"Daughtery was hot... I was lukewarm!" Charles laughed.

"No shit. I thought you two made a great team. I just assumed you would wind up together."

"You and half the force," Charles replied shaking his head.

"Do you ever see her anymore?"

"No. Hell no! She..."

"She's what, Mason?"

"Never mind Robert. I need that address," he prodded switching the subject back to the reason he had phoned.

"You know that I can't give you that information, Charles." The agent shook his head.

"Not unless we are working on something together…
Right?" The P.I. remarked with determination.

"So, what are you saying?" The agent's tone was
curious.

"A pairing of sorts," Charles said tossing his
cigarette but out the window.

"A what?" Robert asked unknowingly.

"A team… I'll trade information with you… I know
the son-of-a-bitch is mixed up in a lot of shit."

"Tell me something I don't know."

"All right Robert, I will, but then you will give me
the address that I need,, right?"

"All right, but it better be good."

"Does the Red Devil ring a bell?"

"No shit!" The agent's gasp was one of both surprise
and interest.

"No shit, Robert." Charles responded smugly.

"And you can prove this?"

"Give me a little time…work with me and I'll prove
it for you."

"Well, I know you well enough to know you
wouldn't say it if it wasn't true… Okay Mason, but keep
me informed, all right?"

"Sure. The address Robert," Charles said with
insistence.

"628 Crescent Avenue… There's a hidden set of
steps along the sidewall… The hidden locks go along the
side of the fake grain in the wood… There are eight
locks… Once the locks are opened, you'll see an alarm
signal go off to the right… You'll only have ten seconds to
silence the alarm… It's not a sophisticated alarm system,
surprisingly, so the B&E shouldn't be that difficult. Getting
the alarm shut off within ten seconds will be the hardest
part. Once the alarm is shut off, walk around the hidden
staircase. You'll see a beige colored wall. The wall is really
a hidden elevator. Press the dark brown button located

halfway between the wall and the floor... Believe it or not, it's really quite obvious, if you're looking for it... The elevator door will open once you press that button... After stepping into the elevator, the door will automatically close, taking you to the top floor... Once inside the apartment go into the study. I think you'll be pleasantly surprised." The agent released a deep sigh.

"What's the combination of the alarm system?" Charles asked excitedly.

"It's a good one. I honestly believe you won't have any problem remembering it." The federal agent laughed.

"So what is it, Robert?"

"34 - 24 - 34." He sighed lustfully.

"It's easy to see what's on Sommers' mind," Charles remarked chuckling.

"Is that all you need, Mason?" The agent asked, glancing at the time.

"I think so. I'll call you in a few days. We'll meet for lunch and see what we can put together."

"Mason, I want to nail that rotten bastard!"

"And you will my friend. I promise." He sighed. "Do you have any undercover in Lambert yet?"

"Yes. They've been in place for about a month now. We've had Lambert and Sommers in our sights since their last shipment of ..." He stopped talking when his beeper went off.

" I know you gotta run, I heard your beeper go off, but before you hang up, I want to ask you a couple of quick questions, Robert... Do your undercover agents know anything about the Lambert murders?"

"Not much I'm afraid. I do know that Becka Chamberlain's husband phoned in the Kamel woman's death. He didn't kill her, though. I'm sure of it."

"How do you know?" Charles asked with surprise.

"One of our men followed Chamberlain to the airport. He jumped the next plane back to Boston. He met his secretary at the airport when he arrived this morning. She gave him his passport, and he jumped on the next flight to France. My guess is that he's trying to track down his billionaire client."

"Or leaving the country to protect his ass," Charles snapped sharply.

"I don't think so, Charles. All the undercover we've been working on lately surrounding Ethan Sommers and anyone connected with him, especially, his high-powered-attorney, has turned up clean. The fact that Chamberlain was the one that reported the murder in his client's hotel suite--it just seems to me like if he had had a hand in the dirty deed, why would he have even bothered to phone the police?" He shook his head.

"Maybe so. But why didn't he just phone the police from the hotel suite? And why did he do it anonymously?"

"I don't know for sure, Charles. But, I would guess that he didn't want to be pulled into the investigation."

"Yeah okay. I can buy that. But, what about his wife's murder?"

"I honestly don't think he knows about it, yet."

"Well, at least that theory makes sense. So, you just think he's just trying to track down his friend."

"That's the way I see it. For now anyway."

"Okay Robert, thanks. I'll phone you in a few days."

"All right, Charles, bye."

"Clean my ass!" the private investigator mumbled under his breath, as he turned his car around heading for Ethan Sommers' hidden office in the heart of downtown Boston.

He reached for his cell phone again. "Hello Tess, it's me. Have John, Brad, Joe, Tony, Danny, and Tim, meet me inside a restaurant called Mary's. It's located on Crescent Avenue downtown. I'll be in the bar. I have a job for them to do so, tell them to load up the van, okay?" he sighed.

"Sure Mr. Mason, anything else?"

"Yeah, call Violet Smith, again for me, both at home and at her office. Leave several more messages telling her it would be to her advantage to speak with me sooner rather than later about her boss. Also, send Amy out to do an in depth interview with the couple that found the Chamberlain woman's body... Stacey and Stuart something or other."

"Anything else Mr. Mason?"

"Yeah, have Beth and Randy fly to Lambert to see what all they can dig up about the Kamel woman. Have them interview the Lamberts and as many employees as they can. Oh, and Tess, I've heard a buzz or two about some special service suites inside the Lambert hotel. I want to know what the hell all that is about. I'll be in touch later."

"Okay Mr. Mason. Goodbye."

Chapter 5

"Hello. Yes. Thank you. Would you send someone up? I need my suits pressed right away. Yes, this is Clint Chamberlain, Suite 1948. Thank you," he said, glancing at his watch and redialing the phone.

The high-powered-attorney crossed the room with the telephone still in his hand. He poured himself a double shot of scotch, as he waited for Mai Li to answer the telephone.

"Sommers' residence, Mai Li speaking. How may I help, please?"

"Hi, Mai Li. This is Mr. Chamberlain."

"Oh! Mr. Chamberlain. Where are you?" The tiny Asian woman asked excitedly. "You find Mr. Sommers yet?"

"No Mai Li, I haven't. I'm looking for him now."

"I'm so very sorry, Mr. Chamberlain," she said shaking her head sadly. She was referring to the murder of his wife, of which he still knew nothing about.

"Yeah, me too, Mai Li.," he said in response thinking she was referring to his not being able to locate Ethan Sommers. He was quite certain that she hadn't heard anything about the Kamel murder yet, or she would have surely mentioned it to him immediately.

He took a sip of his scotch, then continued to speak... "Is Mrs. Sommers still in Lambert?" He sat his drink down on top of the bar.

"No. She come home, been worried sick about things." She swallowed nervously.

"May I speak with her, Mai Li?" he asked taking a sip of his drink.

"She not home. Went to town to have dinner with old friend," she offered.

"I see." Clint felt his heart suddenly drop to his feet. "Did she say who she was having dinner with?" His tone was jealous, after his mind flashed him a picture of Nouri having dinner with Charles Mason, her first real man...

"No. Not say. She just say old friend."

"Umm... An old friend, huh? Well then, did she say what time she would be in?" he asked sharply, reaching for his drink, again.

"No. Not say. I think she might stay in the city tonight, at condo. You have that phone number?"

He released a deep sigh. "No I don't have that number, not with me anyway. Will you get it for me please, Mai Li? He downed his drink and poured himself another.

"Sure. You wait a minute, okay," she said laying down the receiver. Clint nervously downed another drink glancing at his watch, again. His imagination began to run wild. He nervously began to pace back and forth while he waited for Mai Li to get Nouri's condo number.

After Mai Li gave him the number, he thanked her and quickly dialed the number. Several moments later, he angrily slammed the receiver down, after being informed the woman of his dreams whereabouts wasn't known, neither was a return schedule.

"It just isn't my day!" he groaned in complaint under his breath, as he began to rehash his last three unproductive telephone call efforts.

"A split moment later, it dawned on him. Nouri obviously didn't know about her husband's young mistress' death. If she had known, surely she would've stayed in Lambert, possibly even detained by the police. They would most certainly have tons of questions about her husband that needed to be answered...

So, if she doesn't know about the young woman's murder, yet, then just what in the hell was she doing meeting with Charles Mason again!

The more he thought about her being with her former lover, the more jealous he became.

"Well, two can play that game, sweetness!" he heatedly mumbled, carrying his drink into the bathroom with him. "I too, have a date with an old friend of about umm..." He glanced at his watch. "Of about ten hours now!"

He sat his drink down on top of the sink area, turned on the shower, and walked back into the bedroom to undress. After shedding his clothing, he jumped into the shower, pressing his arms against the tiled wall, letting the hot water pellets beat down on his back.

"God this feels good!" he moaned as the water continued to soothe his tired aching muscles. Suddenly, he heard the muffled sound of knocking on his hotel suite door. Thinking it was someone from laundry service coming to pick up his suits, he reluctantly shut off the water and stepped out of the tub reaching for a towel to put around his waist.

"Just a sec. I'm coming," he shouted making his way to the door. An instant after opening the door, his mouth flew open in surprise when he saw Renea Chandlier standing on the other side of it.

"Hi there," she whispered seductively as her gaze traveled the length of his very sexy body.

"Hello yourself," he returned, after the shock of seeing her standing there wore off. He blushed nervously.

"May I come in?" she asked, glancing approvingly at his perfect, muscular frame, again.

"Sure," he smiled, and invitingly stepped back, gesturing her inside. He shook his head excitedly when she brushed past him.

"Looks like my timing is perfect," she lustfully remarked turning to face him. She nervously began to toy with the top button on her sheer, thin, burgundy colored blouse.

"That, Ms. Chandlier, depends on what you have in mind," he teased in response. She continued to seduce him with her eyes, trying to picture in her mind what he looked like without the towel.

As he met her searching gaze, she inhaled and released it slowly, noticing that his eyes had shifted to admire the erotic rise and fall of her impressive large breasts, as she walked past him. She smiled winningly.

"Care if I fix myself a drink?" she asked softly.

He chuckled, knowing she came to his hotel suite to seduce him. *'Hey, you can't seduce the willing'! he thought to himself.* "Help yourself to whatever you like," he said walking towards the bedroom door. "I'll just hurry in and finish my shower. I'll be out in a few minutes, okay?" he smiled, glancing over his shoulder.

"Sure. Can I fix you a drink?" She returned his smile.

"Scotch on the rocks," he called out closing the bathroom door behind himself. He turned the shower back on and stepped inside. His mind began to race into several directions at once.

"Damn you, Nouri," he whispered once again picturing her in the arms of Charles Mason.

Suddenly, interrupting his thoughts, Renea Chandlier slowly opened the glass door to the shower and stepped inside to join him. She smiled.

His eyes quickly raked in her beautiful, large, round breasts. He returned the lustful smile, causing his previous thoughts of the woman of his dreams to instantly vanish.

"Well! You did say I should help myself to whatever I like, didn't you?" She curled her arms around his neck.

He put his arms around her at the same time he pulled the shower door closed pulling her tightly to him, molding her body perfectly to his.

"Wow, what a fit!" he groaned excitedly leaning his head down to kiss her open mouth. It was a very arousing, hungry kiss. She aggressively responded more than happy to be a part of the heated moment.

"Wow!" she whispered breathlessly, after he finally removed his hot mouth from her swollen lips. He greedily slid his kisses to her large, round breasts eager to taste the incredible fullness of them inside his mouth." My God, Renea! Your body is unbelievable," he breathlessly panted after tasting them. "I'm glad you approve," she playfully returned.

"Approve! That's an understatement," he teasingly moaned as he continued to kiss, suck, and lick one nipple and then the other bringing them both to large, full, puckered buds.

After he finished ravishing her breasts, he slowly made his way down the rest of her body, orally bathing her with his deep wet French kisses, anxious to make his way to the wet, heated location between her shapely thighs. The sultry temptress soon began to moan with eager anticipation as he continued to bring her to the brink of an explosive climax time and time, again- not allowing her to finish until he was ready to join her.

After an eternity of teasing and toying and tasting her body, Clint was finally ready to join his body to hers.

A short time later, he turned off the shower and led her wet trembling body into the bedroom.

"But we're soaking wet," she objected momentarily. He put his fingers to his lips. "Shhh, we'll be wetter than that in a few moments," he whispered pulling her down on top of the bed. Nouri's face appeared once again in his mind. Guilt quickly surged through him causing him to tense.

Renea caught the look of resignation in his eyes. She knew she'd better get him hot and bothered, again and fast, before he changed his mind. He's probably thinking about that woman of his again, she thought to herself, quickly planting a kiss across his lips.

The seductive beauty had no way of knowing just how close to being right she was. Clint was indeed thinking about the woman of his dreams. He was waging an inner battle within himself between hurt pride and lust.

Lust won the battle. Renea's incredibly, sexy body was more than he could resist. Clint joined his body to hers urgently- more than ready to explode inside her but he knew it was too early for his own self- gratification.

"My God! Renea, you feel so wonderful," he breathlessly groaned against the side of her throat, as he continued to move his body rhythmically to hers. She shivered excitedly, when his movements grew more demanding- more needing- more urgent.

"Please. Don't stop, Clint," she begged as each new thrust grew more intense. She dug her fingernails sharply into his bare shoulders, as he continued to ride her like a Wild Bronco…

"Ah…Ahh…Ahhh…Ahhhh!" She shouted her explosive release - an instant later they magically melted together in utter ecstasy.

Clint continued to lay on top of Renea's magnificent body for several long moments, too exhausted to move. Finally, he somehow managed to pry himself up and off of her steamy hot body. He continued to gasp for air as she continued to do the same.

"My Lord! Clint Chamberlain! She breathlessly gasped. "Your wife has got to be insane to let a man like you go! All my life, I've been searching for a lover like you!"

She released a sigh of blissful contentment. "I knew the moment our eyes met on the airplane that I just had to have you! It's almost as though I couldn't help myself. You were magnificent! Just simply magnificent!" she lustfully raved.

Clint chuckled at her words, throwing his arm over his red face, not wanting her to see him blush.

"You were pretty magnificent yourself, Renea!" He lustfully returned shaking his head in playful dismay. "Whew!" He released a deep sigh. "My Lord! Renea, It's a damn good thing that I don't have heart trouble. Your... well... your body is... uh...uh... just unbelievable!"

She laughed at his words. "Thank you. I think!"

"Oh, yeah!" he sighed deeply. "How about a drink?" He nervously jumped to his feet.

"Sure. I think I need one." she smiled, sliding out of bed and rising to her feet.

Clint went to the bathroom, grabbed a towel, and wrapped it around his waist. He walked out of the bathroom and across the bedroom floor. Renea was already in the living room beside the bar, pouring herself a shot of Russian Vodka.

"What would you like?" she asked when he entered the room.

"Scotch for me," he answered still out of breath.

"Here," she said handing him the drink. "Oh, by the way, Clint, while you were the bathroom taking a shower earlier, the laundry guy came by for your suits. I gave them to him. I hope that was okay." She glanced at him. "He said he would bring them back in about an hour." She smiled, putting the glass to her lips.

"Thanks. That's who I thought you were when you knocked on my door." He smiled nervously.

"I didn't get any calls did I?" he added uneasily, hoping no one from Boston knew where he would be staying while he was in France.

"No. No calls," she smiled, walking closer to him.

"Good." He returned her smile and sighed at the same time.

"I hope you didn't mind too much my stopping by like I did. I can be pretty aggressive when I see something I want." She placed her left arm around his neck lifting his empty hand with her right hand filling it with one of her large breasts. A naughty smile curled her lips.

Clint chuckled in amusement. "Idle hands, huh?" He gazed nervously into her hungry eyes, as he began to caress her breasts. "Umm," he groaned softly at the fill of their fullness.

"You like, huh?" she softly whispered sliding her hand under his towel.

"Oh, yeah! And how!" He heatedly returned as he lowered his head to kiss her breasts. She excitedly removed his towel.

"Humm... Let me guess... You want some more, huh?" he whispered in her ear with his warm breath.

"And how!" was her breathless response.

"No problem, Ms. Chandlier," he teasingly replied lowering his mouth to her breasts, again.

One kiss lead to another... One thing led to another... And an instant later, they were rolling around passionately on the shag carpet - sharing their passion and the present... No Questions... No Promises... And Problem Free... That is except for a few minor rug burns!
...

Chapter 6

A small group of six men, all former undercover agents with the Boston Police Department, hired by Charles Mason, carefully made their way to the privately owned apartment-complex of the rich and powerful, Ethan Sommers.

This particular complex secretly housed the hidden secrets of the real Ethan Sommers. And his many, business activities; past, present and future.

The location itself was not as much help to the F.B.I. as they had hoped for in their ongoing investigation of the mysterious billionaire, but Charles Mason knew the information housed there would prove to be a huge help to him and his very different type of investigation.

The P.I. had originally heard a rumor that inside this eight-story complex there were all types of records, files, and secretly recorded video and audio tapes on all sorts of people. These included seven of the mysterious, billionaire's ex-wives, a business associate by the name of Otto Lambert, and numerous other friends and associates, including his best friend and high-powered-attorney, Clint Chamberlain. Files might also contain information about a man named Steven Li, who was known to have ties with the Chinese Mafia a.k.a. The Red Devil, information the F.B.I. obviously overlooked during their secret break-in and search, Charles Mason, however, would not make that mistake.

Robert Barnett was right; surprisingly the alarm system was indeed not that sophisticated and easily entered after planning this covert mission with the greatest care.

The six men broke into the complex with very little effort. In total darkness, around 3:00 am, they disarmed the alarm, entered the hidden elevator, and quickly and quietly completed their paid assignment.

Once the mission was completed and everything was put back into its proper order and place, the alarm was reset and the professional team of ex-agents vanished into thin air, unnoticed. They turned over their findings to Charles Mason just before dawn.

"A job well done men," he said accepting the copies of files, tapes, and photographs.

The six men smiled as they accepted their overly stuffed envelopes from Charles Mason.

"Anything else, Charles?" John Harmon, senior covert task commander asked excitedly.

"You know me too well, John," The famous P.I. said smiling, and handing him the address of an abandoned warehouse on the outskirts of town, also belonging to Ethan Sommers.

He swiftly crossed the room and opened a file cabinet, pulling out a large 8x10 yellow envelope.

"Inside this envelope is everything you need to know. You know where to find me after the job is done," he said handing the 8x10 envelope to the lead detective. He smiled and nodded, dismissing the six men.

Charles walked over to the coffee maker and put on a fresh pot of coffee. "This is going to be a very long day," he mumbled under his breath walking to his desk and opening the extra large briefcase that the six ex-agents had left for him.

He opened it and pulled out ten videotapes, glancing at each tape trying to determine in which order they should be played. With no apparent markings anywhere on them he randomly selected one and then walked across the office floor and shoved the tape into the VCR.

He refilled his coffee cup and made himself comfortable, propping his feet up on top of his expensive antique desk. After reviewing four of the ten tapes, Charles could stand it No More! He angrily clicked off the VCR.

"That rotten son-of-a-bitch!" he heatedly spat throwing the remaining videos across the top of his desk.

The four tapes that he had viewed were pornographic- starring the billionaire tycoon in the flesh, doing the most horrible sex acts with young teenage girls. The P.I. imagined the oldest couldn't have been more than fifteen, possibly sixteen, tops. The youngest may have been twelve or thirteen.

The private Investigator- suddenly found himself longing to be alone with the billionaire-tycoon- for five or ten minutes, so he could beat him to a pulp.

On the plus side of the disgusting tapes- there was sufficient evidence to provide his client with enough information about her perverted husband to get a divorce. The dates and the times recorded on each tape would hang him in any court of law. He was without doubt married to Nouri at the time of their taping.

But, Charles Mason wanted more on Ethan Sommers. Much, much, more! His next game plan was to track down all seven of his ex-wives. That would take some doing; Two of them were French, two of them were Asian, one was from Africa. Her last known address suggested she still lived there. One was the former Miss Hawaii, whose address suggested the same, and, the elusive billionaire's seventh wife was Malian--no address posted on her at all.

Charles curiously found himself wondering if Nouri was even aware of her husband's prior wives. He pressed the intercom button and asked his secretary to step into his office.

"Tess, put seven of our investigators on this," he said handing her seven individual 8x10 envelopes.

"Inside each one of these seven envelopes is a different woman- all ex-wives of Ethan Sommers. I want each woman tracked down and interviewed. I want to know everything they can tell us about this billionaire prick.... their marriage and their divorce... I want to know everything! … How they met… When they married… When they divorced… What caused the divorce? What were the conditions of their divorce, etc. & etc … I also want their families and friends interviewed… Go back as far as possible finding out about each wife… I want to know why he chose each woman for his bride... I want to turn Ethan Sommers inside and out. Understand, Tess?" He leveled his eyes on her.

His secretary swallowed nervously. "What if they won't be interviewed?" she questioned with concern.

"Tess, you surprise me," he playfully responded, scratching the side of his head. "Everyone has a price; if it isn't money then we'll just have to find out what the weakness is. Everyone has a price, one way or another, one thing or another. I need these women to talk. Got it?"

She nodded, understanding, tightly clutching the seven envelopes to her chest and exiting the room.

Charles Mason went back to the coffee machine and poured himself another cup of strong, black coffee, then walked back to his desk. He reopened the large briefcase removing thirty roles of film and a stack of files with no labels on them.

"Yes, this indeed is going to be a very long day," he mumbled to himself reaching over and pressing the intercom button for his secretary again.

"Yes Mr. Mason." Tess answered.

"Call Jerry at the photo lab. Tell him to send someone over. I have thirty roles of film that need to be developed ASAP!"

"Right away Mr. Mason."

The P.I. opened the first file at random. "The Medallion Corporation." He began to read….

Chapter 7

"This must be it... The Sommers' Estate, sir." Young Al Ballard, the recently, assigned, inexperienced, detective said, pointing to the Sommers' logo made of cast iron stretching across the entire front entrance gate to the estate.

"Ya think, detective?" The veteran detective, Gabe Baldwin said teasingly in response, shaking his head in amusement.

"I think so, sir. 7712 Crestview Hills Lane. Yeah, this is it sir," he beamed, pointing to the address on the file cover. The veteran detective smiled to himself at the young detective.

"Good Ballard, now maybe we should pull up to the gate, huh?" He gestured to the gate with a wave of his hand.

The young detective pulled the police car up to the gate.

"Maybe I should press the intercom button, sir." He glanced at Gabe.

"Ballard, if we're going to get inside the estate sometime in the near future, maybe you should." Gabe sighed and scratched his head in playful disbelief.

The senior detective knew he should be more understanding with the young detective. After all he was once an inexperienced detective himself, many years ago. But, he couldn't seem to help himself. His young partner was so funny... A virgin to investigating... His very first case. And a high- profile, heavy media case at that... 'The poor kid has no idea what he is getting into with the press', the chief homicide detective silently mused to himself.

The press could be brutal, especially when it came to high profile cases such as this one, which the press has dubbed "The Lambert Murders." But, that could change. Just one slip of the tongue by the young detective could change the dubbing of the case in the media and possibly even affect his career in one way or another... It was no fun being a virgin, especially when it involved solving a murder.

The Two Lambert Murders were unimaginable, and so far, no one seemed to have a clue, or reasonable theory. Not even the F.B.I. Mind-boggling to say the least. Currently, everything about this case had been successfully kept under wraps. And they wanted to keep it that way for as long as possible. Even the location of the young Kamel woman's body has been successfully hidden from the press. If the press would get wind of her body being found in one of the world's wealthiest men's exclusive hotel suites--Oh, Mama Mia!

Gabe Baldwin slipped a pair of sunglasses from his pocket and put them on. The young detective noticed and did the same after rolling down his window and pressing the intercom buzzer.

The tiny Asian woman answered on the second buzz. "Yes, how Mai Li help you, please?" she answered the early morning intrusion softly.

"Yes Mai Li... I mean Hi.... I... ah... ah... mean good morning, ma'am. We're with the Boston Police Department. We need to speak with Mr. and Mrs. Sommers, please. May we be permitted to enter the estate grounds to do so?" young Ballard said, speaking nervously into the intercom. Gabe struggled to hold back his laughter at his young partner's nervousness. He cleared his throat

"Police. Oh my! Yes, come in, please. Mansion is top of driveway. Stay on driveway about ten miles. When driveway run out, you see house, okay. Mai Li meet you in front of house."

"Thank you, Mai Li," the young detective said in response, quickly heading the police car up the long winding macadam driveway after Mai Li released the lock on the gate.

The small Asian woman wasted no time in making her way to the master bedroom to get her mistress out of bed. "Miss. Wake please. Police want to talk to you. Come quick, please," she said nervously, gently shaking Nouri's shoulder. Mai Li curiously wondered if the sudden visit from the police had anything to do with Mrs. Chamberlain's death.

"Mai Li. What is it? What were you just saying?" Nouri stretched, yawned, and sat up in bed.

"Police want to see you. Come quick, please." The tiny Asian woman repeated, gently pulling the sheets off her mistress' body.

"Did they say what they wanted to see me about?" Nouri yawned again, wondering if the visit had anything to do with Becka Chamberlain's death. Or possibly their visit might have something to do with the sudden disappearance of her mysterious and elusive husband. Mai Li handed Nouri her housecoat and slippers.

"I not know miss, police not say. Please. Hurry, okay?"

"Wait a minute, please...Mai Li, slow down. I need to brush my hair and my teeth. I'll be down in a few moments. Give the police officers some coffee or something. I don't know. I think they like doughnuts, rolls, toast... Maybe some juice," she added standing to her feet. "Just tell them I'll be down in a few minutes, okay?" she smiled.

The small woman nodded respectfully. "Yes miss." She crossed the bedroom and opened the door to leave, glancing back over her shoulder to make sure her mistress wasn't going to jump back into bed.

Nouri knew the look. "I'm up...I have no intention of going back to bed...don't worry...I'll be right down," she said, smiling.

Mai Li returned the smile, gently closing the bedroom door behind her, quickly heading to the kitchen to make a fresh pot of coffee and put a tray of fresh Danish together.

'Oh, yes! And juice, the miss said', she thought to herself, opening the refrigerator door.

Chapter 8

Admiring the massive estate grounds, the two detectives wondered enviously about how one family could afford to live in such splendor. They were even more curious about where the money to support such a life style must have come from. They continued to chit chat between themselves, as they drove slowly up the ten mile stretch of driveway leading to the estate mansion.

"This place sure is something, isn't it sir?" young Ballard said, shaking his head in amazement. The veteran detective smiled, "Yes, it is, Ballard." They drove past the servant's living quarters and tennis court.

He went on..."I bet the two old fogies that live here are too old to really appreciate what they have here. This place has probably been in the family for generations. I think they call it old money, sir." The young detective sighed.

They drove past Mai Li's house and a separate swimming pool that wasn't part of the actual mansion itself.

"Yeah, its something all right. Just look how expertly the grounds are maintained; the trees, the flowers, the plants... look over there Ballard... would you call that a small river or a pond?" Gabe mused fumbling inside his shirt pocket for a cigarette.

The young detective turned his head to check out the scenic view of the pond.

"I think it must be a pond, sir," he offered.

"I know it is a pond For Chrissakes! Ballard. I was only trying to be humorous." The veteran detective barked in response, rolling his eyes.

"Humorous, sir?" The young detective looked puzzled.

"Never mind, Ballard." Gabe shook his head in playful dismay as young Ballard continued to glance around the estate grounds in envy.

"Ya know, sir, this place is enormous! I bet you could house a small country of people on this property," he sighed. "I could sure get used to living in a place like this, how about you, sir?" He smiled.

Gabe shrugged rather-matter-of-factly. "Yeah, it's huge all right. But, it's too big for me, I'd feel uncomfortable." He shook his head.

The young detective glanced at his partner curiously. "You mean you're a city boy, sir."

"I suppose you could say something like that, Ballard," Gabe responded as he continued to glance around his surroundings.

"I'm a born and bread city boy too, sir," the young detective returned, smiling.

"I'm not exactly a born and bread city boy Ballard. I just simply meant that a place this large is almost obscene. It's too big for someone like myself. I prefer more intimate surroundings. I don't want to impress anyone. Nor do I need to, that's all." He shrugged defensively.

Young Al nodded. "I understand sir. Ya know I look around this place and it's hard for me to imagine anyone that could afford something this magnificent to be mixed up in a murder. I just can't imagine anyone being stupid enough to want to risk losing something like this. It doesn't make any sense to me. You know what I mean sir?" He glanced at Gabe.

"And that's your thought on the Lambert murders, kid?" Gabe exhaled a puff of smoke.

"Yes sir. I've given the murders some thought, and if two people like the Sommers can afford to live like this, why would they want to risk losing it all by murdering two people? I just can't see it, sir. What you think?" He glanced at the senior detective.

Gabe released a sigh. "Detective, it's really too early to say. We were just invited to join in on the investigation yesterday. But, I've given the case an early thought or two myself, Ballard... All we have to go on so far is a few pieces of circumstantial evidence...It's too early to hear from the lab boys yet, or any of the other experts, as far as that goes. We've just begun the investigation process. But all that aside Ballard, to me, it looks like someone is trying very hard to frame the Sommers'." Gabe took a long drag off his cigarette before releasing it.

"A deliberate frame up, sir? I don't understand." The young detective glanced at his partner, again.

"Well Ballard, we have the private hotel suite belonging to one of the wealthiest men in the world- with not one single fingerprint inside of the place to be found. But, yet we find a dead woman lying right in the middle of the floor, wearing only a diamond necklace around her lovely neck. We also find an antique hairbrush, supposedly belonging to Mrs. Sommers, and once again not a single fingerprint to be found on it, that we currently know of anyway.

"The Lambert police talked to Mr. Lambert and he told them that Mr. Sommers left a few days before the murders, and to his knowledge neither, Mr. or Mrs. Sommers even knew the Kamel woman. Right?" Gabe shrugged his shoulders and continued to speak...

"Then we have the other woman--Becka Chamberlain. She was also found naked. But, instead of a diamond necklace wrapped around her neck, she had an expensive leather whip wrapped around hers. There was also an antique lipstick holder supposedly belonging to Mrs. Sommers lying right beside the dead body. Once again, there was not a single fingerprint on anything, including the body, at least that we know of. Right?" He stopped talking to take a drag off of his cigarette.

"I don't know, Ballard, I just think someone wants us to believe that somehow the Sommers' are involved in these two murders. It just feels like a frame job to me. I could be wrong. Only time will tell, son."

"I see, sir, but maybe whoever killed the two women just didn't have time to get rid of the bodies yet. After all, the police zoomed in the moment they received the anonymous telephone call about the Kamel woman. Right, sir?"

"Well, Ballard, that's also a theory we'll need to consider. But, if that were the case, why would someone bother to remove any of the prints at all? Removing the fingerprints would have taken quite some time. So, if someone wanted to get rid of the bodies then why bother, right? Removing the prints would've taken too much time. It would've been easier and less time consuming to just dispose of the body... And, as far as the mystery caller, hell, Ballard, the killer could've been the caller himself for all we know. It's just too damn early to say yet."

"Yeah, I see what you mean." Young Ballard nodded. "We sure have our work cut out for us, don't we, sir?" He glanced at the senior detective again.

"Yes Ballard, we certainly do. Anytime we get a high-profile case we have our work cut out for us. I knew the moment the DA's office called me at home yesterday morning, and invited me to join the Lambert police department in their investigation, that this case was going to be something." Gabe lit another cigarette.

"What all did Ms. Daughtery say, sir?"

"Not much. Just what I've already told you, that and she didn't want any screw up's! ... She also said that if we need to have the Sommers come down to headquarters for questioning, she wanted someone from the DA's office to be present during their official statement." He exhaled a deep breath mixed with the smoke from his cigarette.

"This is my first case, sir." The young detective remarked nervously.

"I know Ballard, remember? This high-profile case is a hell of a way to start your career, son. The media will make or break you," he teased, not being able to resist the temptation. "Just make sure you know what you're saying before you open your mouth, son. I wouldn't want you to have to pull your foot out of it later. Know what I mean?" Gabe smiled releasing a few rings of smoke from his cigarette.

"Oh, I won't open my mouth sir. My mouth is sealed." Young Ballard offered nervously.

"All joking aside, Ballard, we need to keep as much of our investigation under wraps as long as possible... The moment the wrong info is leaked to the press, all hell is going to break loose... There's a lot more to this case than meets the eye... We will be working with numerous branches of law enforcement, so stay close to me and watch your P's and Q's, okay?" The senior detective smiled protectively.

"Thank you... I will... I...I appreciate the opportunity to be working with you sir. I'm aware of your history... I mean that's ah..ah... all the cases that you've solved, sir... You're the best, I hear." He glanced at Gabe nervously.

The senior detective laughed amusingly. "Well detective, thanks for the complement. I really don't know how much truth there is to my so-called history, as you so delicately put it, but... but I've done all right for myself with the department." He returned the smile.

"Just all right, sir? Your record says otherwise! Like I said sir, you're the best. You've solved every case you've ever worked on."

"All except one case, Ballard." Gabe shook his head and removed his sunglasses.

"I don't understand sir. I was told you..." he was cut off sharply.

"Listen Ballard, that was a long time ago. I'll tell you about it sometime. Right now, let's just stick to the Lambert Murders. Okay?" He pulled another cigarette out of his pocket.

"Oh look, detective! That must be Mai Li." The young detective pointed to a small Asian woman standing in the doorway of the huge mansion.

"I better wait to light this one." The senior detective said sliding the cigarette back inside its pack, before reaching over to remove the young detective's sunglasses and shoving them into his pocket. He smiled fondly and shook his head again.

Chapter 9

The two Boston police detectives jumped out of their car, quickly making their way to the front of the huge mansion where Mai Li was anxiously waiting for them.

The young detective fumbled with an ink pen that was stuck inside the breast pocket of his suit jacket, as he continued to follow the seasoned detective to the front door. He finally managed to get the pen out of his pocket, but he had forgotten his pad to write on. He swallowed nervously while tugging on the senior detective's jacket.

"Sir. Excuse me sir. I... I seem to have forgotten my notepad."

The senior detective turned to face him, sighed deeply, reaching inside his jacket pocket and pulled out a pad of paper, handing it to him without saying a word. He then reached inside his jacket pocket again and pulled out his identification and badge.

"Hello. You must be Mai Li," He nodded. "I'm detective Gabe Baldwin and this is detective Al Ballard," he said, flashing his badge and a small grin.

Mai Li smiled nervously, stepped back and motioned them inside the house.

"Yes, detectives, please come in. Mrs. Sommers will be down in a minute," she said closing the door behind them.

"Come," she said walking past them- showing them into the living room. "Danish. Doughnut. Raisin Toast," she offered picking up the silver tray.

The hungry, young detective quickly snatched up a fruit Danish before the senior detective had a chance to decline. "Thanks," he said, deliberately avoiding eye contact with his partner.

"No thanks." The veteran detective responded, glancing around the elegantly furnished room, silently admiring the super-expensive oil paintings, and priceless antiques.

"Coffee or juice, maybe you like some black rum tea." Mai Li smiled.

"Coffee will be fine ma'am, thank you," Detective Baldwin said reaching for a cup.

"You sit please. Mai Li will pour coffee." She smiled, gesturing towards the couch and two chairs.

"I'll have the black rum tea please, Mai Li." Al Ballard said with his mouth still full of the fruit Danish he was chewing on.

The veteran detective smiled, shaking his head at his funny partner. A split moment later, the young detective choked on a bite of his fruit Danish, and Gabe's mouth almost dropped to the floor, after noticing the breathtakingly, beautiful, billionaire's wife standing on the bottom step of the spiral staircase.

Gabe jumped to his feet nervously, while the young detective continued to sit with his mouth still opened wide, too stunned to move.

Nouri instantly noticed the clumsiness of the two detectives and chuckled to herself.

"Good morning, gentlemen," she said in a cheery tone, crossing the room to join to them. Her gaze quickly zoned in to the senior detective's incredibly handsome face- thinking silently to herself--'Wow! What a gorgeous man', as she continued to gaze into his melting teal-blue eyes.

Gabe stood in stunned silence, mesmerized by Nouri's unbelievable beauty, while young Al Ballard slowly jarred himself back from the shock of it all. He nervously cleared his throat and started to speak. "Mrs. Sommers good morning, I'm..."

Gabe swiftly jumped in, taking charge. "He's detective Al Ballard." He smiled seductively and continued to speak, aware that the billionaire's wife's gaze had not left his. "And I'm detective Gabe Baldwin. We're with the Boston Police Department, Homicide Division, ma'am." He smiled again, secretly trying to regain his composure, nervously swallowing as they continued to gaze into one another's eyes.

As he continued to stare into Nouri's eyes, he suddenly felt as though he had been struck by a bolt of lighting. He swallowed hard, again.

Nouri slowly lowered her eyes to his sexy, full lips as she spoke. "I'm Nouri Sommers. How may I help you, detective?" She returned his seductive smile, causing Gabe to suddenly eyeball the nearest chair, seeing how his legs suddenly felt as though they were about to buckle right out from under him.

He slowly managed to calm himself after noticing the odd expression covering his young partner's face.

An instant later, his gaze fell victim to the breathtaking beauty again when she walked past him to sit down. He released a deep silent sigh, and then cleared his throat.

"We need to ask you a few questions ma'am," he answered nervously, quickly stealing a moment to admire her shapely figure. He smiled approvingly.

Nouri could tell right away that the veteran detective was smitten. She noticed his eyes traveling the length of her body, as she walked past him. She smiled knowingly.

"What about, detective?" she asked after sitting down in her favorite cozy spot on the sofa.

Gabe cleared his throat in an effort to snap himself out of the hypnotic spell he seemed to have fallen back into when she walked past him on her way to the sofa.

"Uh...Uh..." He cleared his throat, again and then continued. "There was a double murder reported in Lambert over the weekend, ma'am."" He swallowed hard and released another deep sigh in an attempt to clear his head. The young detective noticed and shot him a questionable look, as he fumbled inside his pocket for his pad and pen.

"Thank you Mai Li." The billionaire's wife said accepting the cup of coffee the tiny Asian woman was handing her. She smiled. "Please sit down detective. Join me in a cup of coffee. Mai Li, please." She gestured towards the two detectives. "I'm sorry, detective, you were saying." She turned her attention back to the handsome detective.

"Thank you, Mai Li." Gabe nodded accepting what was being handed to him. He sat the cup down glancing at Nouri. "I was explaining to you that there had been a double murder in Lambert, Saturday morning ma'am."

Nouri's gaze slowly traveled the length of the detective's muscular frame as he sat down. She smiled approvingly as she attempted to speak between her lustful thoughts.

"I know, detective," she responded gazing back into his sexy eyes.

The young detective grew tired of watching the senior detective and the beautiful billionaire's wife making Goo-Goo eyes at one another so he cleared his throat and impulsively blurted out…"Would you mind telling us, Mrs. Sommers, how you knew about the two murders, ma'am?" He glanced at his partner nervously, after realizing his mistake.

Gabe rolled his eyes and shook his head in embarrassment.

Nouri chuckled to herself, suddenly realizing how inexperienced the young detective must be.

"No. Not all detective Ballard. You mean besides the newspaper headlines and the news channels, and radio news cast?" She playfully remarked quickly adding… "I'm sorry detective. Actually, the valet in Lambert told me." She smiled sympathetically.

The two detectives quickly shared a glance.

"Oh, so you were in Lambert when the murders were reported?" Gabe's tone was one of surprise.

"In a way, detective," she replied reaching for her cup of coffee. The senior detective glanced back at her with a nervous expression running across his face.

"I'm sorry ma'am. I don't understand the contradiction."

"Contradiction? What contradiction detective?" She questioned curiously.

"We were told by Otto Lambert that you hadn't been in Lambert in over a month."

Nouri smiled. "That sounds about right." She nodded.

"I'm afraid I don't understand ma'am." The detective shot another curious glance at his partner.

"Maybe I can clear the contradiction up for you detective." She smiled and then went on... "Of course, you'll stay and join me for breakfast while I attempt to explain. Won't you detective?" She gazed into his beautiful eyes again and smiled as she waited his response.

Not even knowing this mesmerizing woman, Gabe Baldwin, not knowing why or even how it happened, suddenly felt as though for some unexplainable reason, he would not be able to deny this woman anything now or ever...

He responded after several unaccountable moments of silence. "I'd love to," he said in response after much thought, suddenly realizing his slip of tongue he quickly added... "I mean yes, thank you, ma'am. My partner and I would love to join you for breakfast and give you an opportunity to explain the contradiction." He squirmed uneasily in his chair, when he caught the odd expression still plastered across his young partner's face.

Oddly, Nouri couldn't explain her impulsive attraction to this handsome detective, either. She also squirmed uncomfortably, as she asked Mai Li to serve breakfast out on the south lawn.

"It's such a beautiful morning detective. I hope you don't mind having breakfast outside." She smiled, rising to her feet. "It's this way, gentlemen," she said, leading the way.

Nouri glanced over her shoulder, as she walked past the handsome detective. He turned a bright shade of red when he realized she had just caught him checking her out, again! She smiled knowingly, giving him a quick once over in return. Their eyes met briefly. The young detective noticed and shook his head in total dismay, wondering to himself what the hell is going on with these two?

Gabe unknowingly found himself wondering the same, while on the other hand, Nouri Sommers found herself wondering what the sexy homicide detective must look like under the awful suit he was wearing.

As they walked outside, everyone seemed to be lost in their own thoughts…

The south lawn offered a spectacular scenic view of the very large pond off to the left, where a few ducks and swans were busy playfully taking their morning baths.

Off to the right of the south lawn was a picturesque view of a dozen or so century-old trees busy at work, swaying their full budded leaves proudly to the quiet sounds of music being played to them by the comforting warm breeze of the late spring morning. Such a glorious day!

To the rear of the mansion, Gabe could see an elderly gentleman busy at work detailing a beautiful white Rolls Royce, and a much younger gentlemen detailing a very impressive Bentley. The shiny black limo and candy-apple red Corvette appeared to have already been detailed.

"Nice cars, ma'am," Gabe remarked when he noticed Nouri patiently waiting in front her chair. He approached her chair, smiling. "May I?" he asked placing his hand on her chair. Their eyes locked again, causing them both to swallow hard. Gabe cleared his throat and pulled out her chair.

The young detective smiled, shaking his in amusement, as he waited for the detective to take his seat.

"Would you care for a Bloody Mary, detective? I'm going to have one." She smiled at the tiny woman, as she stood beside her, waiting to hear the two detectives drink orders.

"No thanks ma'am. We're on duty," he replied. "Coffee for myself, and...." he gestured to the young detective... "What for you, Ballard?"

"Juice, please," the young detective responded as he once again reached inside his jacket pocket for his pen and note pad.

"Where were we sir?" the young detective asked, fidgeting with his pen.

Nouri quickly jumped in. "Detective Ballard, I think I was about to thank detective Baldwin for admiring our automobiles before I began to explain..."

"The contradiction," the young detective nervously cut in. "Yes, I wrote it down right here, see," he said nervously, pointing to the pad of paper.

Gabe and Nouri smiled at one another, knowing the young detective's eager response was meant to be helpful.

"Yes, that's right, detective Ballard," she said winking at the senior detective. He smiled.

"Thank you, Mai Li," Nouri said when Mai Li sat her Bloody Mary down on the table. She went on. "It's true, I haven't been in Lambert for about a month now, I guess...

"Saturday morning, when we arrived, the valet in Lambert, Veda, explained to us that there had been two women murdered...

"Everything in Lambert was in such a mess that morning," she shook her head, reaching for her drink. "That we decided not to check in....

"The last thing we wanted to see was our faces plastered all over the front pages of the newspapers and television sets for the next six months, or so." She smiled at Gabe as she took a sip of her drink.

"I see, ma'am." Gabe said, releasing a sigh of relief. The young detective noticed and frowned. He quickly added... "You said 'we', ma'am. Who is 'we'?" He stared into her eyes as he studied her expression.

"Yes, detective Ballard, you're right. I did say 'we'... my longtime friend, Genna Matthews. She rode with me to Lambert... We were originally going to fly to Lambert Saturday morning, but after I found out that my husband was already there, and had been there for several days, I wanted to surprise him... Anyway, we would've arrived in Lambert Friday night, but Genna and I decided to spend the night in Mason, instead... There's a nightclub in Mason Genna likes to go to from time to time...

"As for me, there are a few little country- type shops that I like to go to... They make the cutest..."

The young detective interrupted her again.

"What's the name of the club in Mason, ma'am?"

The senior detective shot young Ballard an angry look, quickly cutting in the conversation...

" That's not important at this time," he stated picking up his cup of coffee and nervously taking a sip. He shot his partner another warning glance.

"Sorry ma'am. I was just trying to keep your statement straight," he remarked nervously.

A curious expression subtly crossed her face.

"My statement, detective. I don't understand?"

"I'm sure the young detective meant to say notes, not statement... If we were taking a statement from you, ma'am, we would have to ask you to come down to the station with us, and someone from the district attorney's office would have to be present... But of course, that isn't why we're here today... We just have a few questions to ask you... Nothing more. You understand?" He smiled.

"I see, detective Baldwin. But I still don't understand what the two murders have to do with me," she said in response reaching for her drink

"I'm sure the two murders have nothing to do with you, Mrs. Sommers... Like I said, we're just here to ask a few questions. Okay?" He smiled again and the young detective shot Gabe another questionable glance.

"All right, detective, what else do you need to ask me?" She met his searching gaze and smiled.

"Can you tell us anything about the two murders, ma'am?"

"No. Only what I've read in the newspaper, seen on TV, or what the Lambert's valet has told me." She shrugged.

"All right ma'am. Did you know either victim?" He studied her expression, as he waited for her to respond.

"Yes detective, I did. Becka," she offered, lowering her eyes long enough to place her empty glass down on the table. "Becka Chamberlain."

"And the Kamel woman?" he asked.

"No, detective. I don't believe so, but then again Lambert is always hiring new people all the time," she answered taking the last sip of her drink.

"What do you mean, ma'am?"

"I don't mean anything, detective. It's just every time that I go to Lambert, I notice a lot of new faces, that's all." She motioned for Mai Li to bring her another drink

"I see, ma'am. I had almost forgotten to ask where your husband is?" Gabe studied her face thoughtfully.

"To tell you the truth, detective, I'd like to know that myself," she said taking the Bloody Mary from out of Mai Li's hands.

"Thank you, Mai Li," she smiled.

The two detectives exchanged suspicious glances at one another.

"I'm not sure I understand ma'am. Are you saying that you don't know where Mr. Sommers is?"

"Yes, that's right. When I arrived in Lambert Saturday morning, Veda told me that Mr. Sommers was no longer there. Or at least that's what he was led to believe." She shrugged with uncertainty.

"Did he say what time Mr. Sommers may have left, ma'am?" He waited patiently for her response, while Mai Li sat their plates of food down in front of them.

"Thank you, Mai Li." Gabe said glancing at the young detective.

"Oh yes. Thank you, Mai Li." Ballard quickly added.

"Looks good, Mai Li, thanks. Yes, detective. I believe he may have said something to that effect." Nouri picked up her fork and put a bite of food in her mouth.

"Do you remember what he said, ma'am?" Gabe picked up his fork.

Nouri nodded as she swallowed her bite of food. "I believe he said someone thought they may have seen him leave around midnight, detective, why? She looked in his direction.

"You say midnight, Mrs. Sommers?" The two detectives glanced at one another again.

"Yes, that's right," she nodded, picking-up her drink.

"When was the last time you saw or heard from your husband, ma'am?" The senior detective continued to study Nouri's facial expressions while listening to her remarks.

"Well, I'm not sure. Let me see..." She paused as though she were trying to remember. "I was still asleep when he left to go to his office... I believe it was Tuesday morning... Ethan phoned me later that night to tell me that he was going to stay in town, at our condo.... But..." she suddenly stopped talking, again.

"But what, ma'am?" Gabe asked with growing interest.

"Oh, nothing detective. Forget it," she said picking up her drink again.

"So that was the last time you talked with him?"

"Yes, that's right detective... You see we had an argument that night, nothing really... Anyway, my husband promised to take me to lunch at the new French restaurant that just opened downtown *Le Massionette's*... Anyway, he had his private secretary phone me at the restaurant to cancel yet, again... She also reminded me that my husband expected me to join him in Lambert for the weekend... Originally I wasn't going to meet him after breaking another date with me... I was still angry at him, but after pouting for a few days, I decided to go to Lambert anyway..." She stopped talking and reached for her drink.

"I see. So you talked to your husband Tuesday night... pouted at him on Wednesday and Thursday night... and left Friday to drive to Lambert, but decided to spend the night in Mason instead.... And you arrived in Lambert on Saturday morning with your friend Genna Matthews only to change your mind and turn around and come right back home to Boston. Is that right ma'am?"

"Yes detective. That sounds about right. Please eat, detective. Your food is getting cold." She smiled, gesturing to his plate of food.

"Mrs. Sommers, this is a very personal question, and you don't have to answer it if you don't want to, but I'd appreciate it if you would." He paused to clear his throat before continuing...

"Could you tell us what you and your husband argued about on Tuesday night?"

"You're right detective, it is a personal question." She paused sitting her drink down.... "But, I don't mind telling you... It was, well detective, I was just... uh... tired of him standing me up all the time... For the past several weeks Ethan just hasn't seemed much like himself... I hardly see him anymore... And when we do talk it's always him phoning to tell me that he isn't coming home, or else it's his secretary breaking another dinner date with me... I guess I was just getting tired of it so, we had a few words and I pouted." She shrugged defensively.

"I can certainly understand your point of view, ma'am." Gabe said, as he gazed into her incredible hazel-colored eyes.

She motioned for Mai Li to bring her another drink.

"Thank you, detective," she responded, as she stared back into his mesmerizing teal-blue eyes. She smiled.

"So you have no idea where Mr. Sommers may be?"

"No, I'm afraid not."

"Mr. Lambert said that Mr. Sommers left several days before the two murders."

"Yes, so?" She shrugged unknowingly.

"You tell us that the valet in Lambert said that your husband had been seen leaving the island resort around midnight .... That, Mrs. Sommers, would make it right after the murders."

"I suppose that's something you will have to work out with Mr. Lambert and his employees, detective... I wouldn't know... All I do know is the last time I talked to my husband was on Tuesday night, when he phoned me to tell me that he wouldn't be home that night... I will tell you this however.... it was very late when Ethan phoned... Actually, his phone call woke me up... Anyway, I did catch my husband in a lie... It was a stupid lie, but nonetheless, a lie... He told me that he was phoning from the city... He wasn't ... I glanced at the caller ID when I answered the phone...

"I recognized the area code that he was actually phoning from... He was in Lambert... I was going to ask him about it at lunch the next day, but he stood me up...

That's all I know detective." She sighed, reaching for her drink again.

"I see ma'am ... There's a few more questions that I'll need to ask you pertaining to Mr. Sommers, but I can do that at a later date... Now, Mrs. Sommers, I'd like to ask you a few questions about Becka Chamberlain, if that is okay, ma'am?"

"All right, detective."

"How well did you know her?"

"Well enough not to like her much. Don't get me wrong, detective, I wouldn't wish death on anyone. I'm very sorry that Becka's dead. Its just Becka was a very disturbed person. Very beautiful to look at but, just plain nuts!" She sighed sadly.

"In what way?" Gabe asked curiously, as young Ballard sat quietly, attempting to take notes as best he could.

"I used to be in an Interior Design Business with Becka. At one time I thought we were best friends. I found out that we were far from it." She shrugged her shoulders defensively. "Our friendship turned sour. I sold the business, and only saw her on occasion; after that, socially, mostly." She paused briefly to sit her glass down. "Becka was a real wacko! Extremely obsessive- Becka wanted to be me, quite frankly! She copied everything about me. The type of automobiles I drove. My hairstyles. Even the type of clothes I wore. Everything I had, she wanted. Including, a few of my former dates. When I told Becka she should seek counseling, she turned on me. The rest is history, I guess." Nouri shook her head with sadness and regret.

"When was the last time you saw her or talked to her?" Gabe asked with interest.

"Tuesday night as well. She phoned late, looking for her husband, which is my husband's best friend and high-powered- attorney."

"I see, Mrs. Sommers. Can you think of anyone that would want to kill Mrs. Chamberlain?"

"There were a lot of people that didn't like Becka," she sighed. "But as far as someone wanting to see her dead, I don't think so, detective. I just can't imagine that." She shook her head with sadness, again.

"Is there anything else that you might be able to tell us about Mrs. Chamberlain that might help us in our investigation ma'am?" Gabe glanced at Nouri's beautiful face finding it harder and harder to keep his mind on business…Yes, the beautiful billionaire's wife was quite a distraction to be around.

"No detective, not that I can think of. Can you tell me, detective if Mr. Chamberlain knows about his wife's murder yet?" She asked nervously.

Gabe shook his head with uncertainty. "I don't think so, ma'am. We haven't been able to locate him yet. From what we've been able to find out, Mr. Chamberlain may be out of town."

"I see. I'm sure once Clint finds out, he'll be devastated. I feel so sorry for him. I'm surprised Becka's name was released without her husband being notified first." She glanced at the handsome detective.

"One of the Lambert employees mentioned it to the press before he was informed not to."

"I guess that happens, too bad, really. Poor Clint…" She stopped talking to wipe a teardrop from her eye.

"Well, I guess we'd better get going, ma'am. I'll be in touch with a few more questions later, if it's all right." He smiled, standing up.

"You know where to find me, detective." She smiled. "Oh, by the way detective Ballard, good luck."

The young detective was stunned that she somehow seemed to know that this was his first case. Or maybe she was only guessing, he thought. "Thank you, ma'am." He returned her smile, rising to his feet. Thanks for breakfast ma'am."

"Yes, thank you ma'am," Gabe offered. Nouri smiled and nodded, reaching for her Bloody Mary. An instant later, she eagerly glanced over her shoulder for one final glimpse at quite possibly the sexiest looking guy on the face of God's green earth. "Whew!" she quietly sighed, trying to slow her heartbeat. She swallowed hard when he disappeared out of her sight.

As the tiny Asian woman, escorted the two detectives to the front door, Gabe glanced back over his shoulder for the one final look at the breathtakingly beautiful Nouri Sommers, wondering to himself how a man, any man, could ever ignore such an amazing woman. Her husband must be insane, was his final thought on the subject, as Mai Li smiled, and shut the large, double doors behind them.

The two detectives entered their car in silence. Gabe Baldwin was lost in thought about his confusion and attraction to Nouri Sommers. And his younger partner was lost in thought wondering just what had happened to his partner inside the Sommers' estate.

A moment later, the young detective broke the silence between them.

"What happened back there, sir?" He glanced at the senior detective with curious eyes.

Gabe returned the quick glance, knowing good and well what the young detective was referring to.

"What do you mean, Ballard?" He answered coolly. The young detective sheepishly grinned at his partner. "Duh!" he playfully mused.

Both detectives looked at one another and laughed uncontrollably. After several long moments of laughter, Gabe defensively responded. "I don't know exactly Ballard." He shook his head in disbelief. "Wow! When I saw her standing on that step, and our eyes met for the first time, it felt as though a lightening bolt shot through my body." He shook his head in amazement. "I've never experienced anything like that before in my life!" He confessed, shrugging and turning red in the face.

"She certainly is beautiful isn't she sir?" young Al smiled, and then glanced back at the detective to see his reaction.

"That, Ballard, is an understatement if I ever heard one," Gabe remarked, before shaking his head, attempting to get his emotions back under control.

"Well, what do you think sir? Think Mrs. Sommers is capable of two cold blooded murders?" Having difficulty getting the image of Nouri Sommers' beautiful face out of his mind, he answered disbelievingly. "If she is, Ballard, there is something terribly wrong with the world as we know it." He sighed.

"Which head are you thinking with, detective?" the young detective asked, before realizing that what he had said to the senior detective completely caught the senior detective off guard.

After several moments of silence, Gabe responded. "Probably a little of both." He glanced at the young detective with a look that they both understood. Meaning, lucky for you, kid, I decided to let that remark slide. The detective knew that his young partner probably had a point, though. He also knew that for reasons that he couldn't explain, he was somehow strangely attracted to a possible murder suspect; an experience he had never known before.

After several moments of silence, the young detective asked his boss, "Sir, why didn't you tell Mrs. Sommers about where the Kamels woman's body was found? Or about her lipstick holder, or her hairbrush lying beside the victims' bodies?" He shot another curious look at his partner.

Gabe took a deep drag off of his cigarette and released it before answering.

"Too early, Ballard. Why do you think we didn't feed that information to the press?" he sighed impatiently.

"I don't know sir, why?" Al shrugged unknowingly.

The detective smiled at his inexperienced, young partner. "You'll see, son, just be patient." He shook his head, trying to recall if he was ever that inexperienced. The young detective shrugged his shoulders, again, at his partner's remark. "Where to Sir?" he asked glancing in Gabe's direction.

Still trying very hard to shove the beautiful Nouri Sommers out of his thoughts, he answered half- heartedly, "I don't know Ballard, let's go see if we have any news from the medical examiner in yet." He sighed, as they made their way back downtown.

Chapter 10

After the two detectives left, Nouri Sommers walked to the bar to pour herself another Bloody Mary. As she mixed the ingredients together, her mind was racing in several directions at one time.

It wasn't bad enough her elusive husband had suddenly disappeared off the face of the earth, but now it appears that the man of her dreams had suddenly vanished into thin air as well.

"Where are you, Clint?" she whispered under her breath, as she circled the bar carrying her drink in one hand and the morning newspaper in the other. She put her drink on top of the coffee table and removed the rubber band from around the newspaper. She was anxious to see if there had been any new information reported on the two Lambert murders.

"Oh my Lord!" She groaned after, noticing two of her husband's closest friends faces plastered across the front page of the morning newspaper. The headlines read: 'Wealthy couple find friends nude body on beach'. The article went on to explain how the two women were best friends while both husbands were close as well.

"What a crock of..." Nouri was mumbling to herself as Mai Li entered the living room.

"Excuse, miss."

"Yes, Mai Li. What is it?" She smiled putting the newspaper down on the coffee table and picking up her drink.

"Telephone, please."

"Thank you Mai Li. Who is it?"

The tiny woman shrugged unknowingly. "Caller not say, miss."

"I see. Okay Mai Li, I'll take it, anyway. Thanks." Nouri took a drink of her Bloody Mary and then put it back down top of the coffee table, standing up, on her way to the hallway to answer the telephone.

"Hello, this is Nouri Sommers."

"Yes, Mrs. Sommers, I just phoned to ask you something."

"Who is this? What do you want?" she asked curiously.

"My name isn't important. But, what I want is very important, Nouri Sommers." The mystery caller replied smugly.

"What are you talking about?" she nervously snapped.

"I'm talking about you, Nouri."

"If you don't tell me what you want this instant, I'm..."

"Calm down Nouri The caller quickly silenced her. "It's too early for me to tell you what I want from you, but I will be in touch. You can count on it." The voice on the other end snipped coolly before slamming the phone down in her ear.

"Hello... Hello!" she shouted into the receiver, before putting it down.

The tiny Asian woman came running into the hallway when she heard her mistress raise her voice. "Is everything all right, miss?" she asked with concern.

Nouri released a deep sigh. "I think so." she sighed again and went on. "That was an odd phone call. I have no idea who it was." She shook her head in a disbelieving manner, as she walked back toward the living room.

Mai Li followed. "What you mean, miss?"

Nouri sat in her cozy spot reaching for her drink. "I'm not sure what they wanted. I mean what the caller wanted. He made no sense at all," she said again, shaking her head. The tiny woman glanced at her with a puzzled expression covering her face. "What did caller say, miss?"

"Not much really. He just said that it didn't matter who he was, but what he wanted from me was very important. He went on to say that it was too early for him to tell me what he wanted from me. That he would be in touch." She nervously downed her drink.

"Maybe we should call the two police detectives back, miss."

"I don't think so Mai Li. I'm sure it was nothing. It was probably someone just playing a joke or perhaps a wrong number. I don't know." She shook her head, nervously jumping to her feet.

"No, miss. The caller asked for you by name. I think we should call the police."

"I appreciate your concern Mai Li. But, no need to worry so much. I'm fine. If he calls back again maybe I'll call detective Baldwin then. But, for now, I really don't think it's worth worrying about, okay?" she smiled.

"Yes miss, as you wish," Mai Li responded turning to leave. She hurried to the hallway and quickly wrote down the telephone number that was on the caller ID machine to be on the safe side.

"You can't be too careful these days," she quietly mumbled to herself, making her way back into the kitchen.

"Clint Chamberlain, where the hell are you?" Nouri whispered under her breath, as she made herself another drink.

Longing to hear a strong, powerful voice of reassurance to comfort her, Nouri decided to call her P.I. friend, Charles Mason and invite him to her house for lunch. She was curious as to what he may have found out about her mysterious husband so far. She slowly made her way into the study with her drink in one hand and Charles Mason's business card in the other. She had hidden the famous private investigator's business card under the Ming Vase in the hallway. She took a sip of her drink and then dialed his office.

"Charles Mason Investigations, how may I direct your call please?" A polite young receptionist said on the other end of the telephone line.

"Yes, I need to speak with Mr. Mason, please. This is Nouri Som... I mean Nouri St. Charles," she responded, not wanting to use her married name.

"Yes, Ms.St. Charles. One moment please. I'll connect you."

"Thank you, miss."

A few moments later, an excited Charles Mason responded with an eager, "Hi, sugar."

"Hello yourself, Charles." Her tone was one of nervousness. The P.I. noticed right away.

"Are you all right Nouri?" he asked with concern.

"Yes Charles. I'm fine. I... I just need to talk to you."

"Okay sugar. Want to meet me for lunch?"

"I... I was hoping you would drive out here to see me. I could have Mai Li fix us something before I send her home." Nouri swallowed hard.

"Sure I can't talk you into driving into town, sugar. I'm awfully busy today," he sighed.

"Please, Charles, you come here. I... I need you." She crossed her fingers hopefully.

"Nouri, are you sure you're all right?" he asked with concern again. She tugged nervously at the phone cord and sighed.

"Yes Charles. I'm fine. I just need to see you, please, Charles."

"Okay, sugar, but I can't make it for lunch. How about an early dinner? I'll stop by and pick up Chinese food. How's that sound?"

"That sounds just fine, Charles. Thanks." Her sigh was one of relief.

" I'll be out around five-ish. All right?"

"Perfect. Bye, Charles," she said softly, quickly hanging up the phone, not giving the private investigator a chance to say goodbye.

As Charles Mason put down the receiver, he couldn't help but wonder what was bothering her. He knew Nouri well enough to know something had happened to upset her. It was in her tone.

After Nouri replaced the receiver on its hook, she released another sigh, this time the sigh was one of nervousness. She couldn't help but feel as though something terrible was about to happen.

She didn't know what exactly, but she sensed whatever it was had something to do with her. She released a deep sigh and stood up.

She wanted to go upstairs to shower and dress, after suddenly remembering she hadn't had her morning shower yet. The two humorous detectives had interrupted her morning routine. She smiled without realizing it when she thought of the handsome detective. The telephone suddenly rang, jolting her back to the present. She hesitantly picked up the receiver after glancing at the caller ID machine.

"Hello," she said softly, but with concern, not recognizing the phone number.

"Hi sweetness, it's me." Clint Chamberlain said on the other end of the telephone wire.

"Oh, darling! Thank God!" she sighed in relief.

"Nouri, I... I miss you so much. I'm in France trying to track Ethan down. He's gone crazy I'm afraid," Clint sighed.

"I don't understand darling. What are you talking about?" she asked nervously.

"Ethan. He's..."

Suddenly, there was a knock on the high-powered-attorney's hotel suite, interrupting him.

"Hold on a second sweetness, someone's at my door," he said, walking to the door and opening it, nestling the phone between his ear and neck.

"Oh, Clint darling. I've missed you too much to wait until tonight!" Renea Chandlier said loudly, jumping into his arms and snugly wrapping her legs around his waist. She kissed him.

Nouri overheard every word that Renea had said to Clint. A tear fell down her cheek.

"Clint! Who the hell is that? And what the hell did she mean, she's missed you too much to wait until tonight?" she shouted into the phone. Clint was still in shock, but somehow forced himself to push Renea away from him. He knew Nouri had heard every word. Still stunned, he responded in a 'guilty as sin' tone of voice. "Oh God! Nouri, please, baby, wait. Let me explain. It's... it's not what you think!" He lied.

Nouri instinctively felt her heart drop to the floor. She could no longer fight back the tears. She could no longer deny what the man of her dreams really was. She shouted hoarsely into the receiver: "Clint Chamberlain! You two-timing bastard! You'll never change. How could I have been so stupid? So blind! I never want to see you again!" She cried hysterically slamming the phone down in his ear.

She began to cry uncontrollably; her heart broken in two. After a few moments of feeling sorry for herself, she stopped crying.

"Damn! I forgot to tell him about Becka," she mumbled out loud, wiping the tears from her eyes. For the next few moments, she silently fought with herself, wanting desperately to call him back. Her stubborn pride and hot temper kept getting in the way every time she reached for the telephone.

"Damn you, Clint!" she moaned hopelessly, staring blankly at the telephone, one final time, before rising to her feet. She departed the study and made her way to the bar where she poured herself a double shot of Cognac and swiftly downed it. She poured herself another, telling Mai Li to take the remainder of the day off, before going upstairs to shower and dress. A short time later she made her way back downstairs to wait for Charles Mason.

"Two can play that game, Clint Chamberlain, you skirt chasing jackass!" she mumbled drunkenly to herself, as she poured herself another double shot of Cognac.

Chapter 11

"Son-of-a-bitch!" Clint Chamberlain shouted, slamming the telephone against the wall of his luxurious hotel suite, barely missing Renea Chandlier's head by several short inches.

He stormed to the bar, grabbed a full bottle of *Chivas Regal Scotch*, quickly opening it, and downed several long drinks of the strong, but smooth tasting liquor, before coming up for air. He spilled liquor down his throat and chest. After wiping the spilled liquor from his mouth with the back of his hand, he shot Renea Chandlier a chilling look that needed no words.

With a shocked expression still masked across her face, she swallowed hard and tearfully responded, "What is it, Clint? What's wrong?"

When he didn't answer, she tried again. "It's me. Isn't it? Oh God! I've done something really stupid, haven't I?" She bit her lower lip nervously.

He shot her another disbelieving look. Still too angry to speak, he shook his head and stormed to the bedroom with his bottle of scotch in his hand. An instant later he threw his body across the bed, covering, his eyes with one of his muscular arms.

Bravely, she followed after him. She stood beside the bed, looking down at him, quietly studying his hurt expression and full pouting lips.

"Clint. What is it? What's wrong with you?" she sighed. "How can I help if you don't tell me what's wrong?" She leaned over and tried to touch him. He jerked away from her touches.

"You've all ready done enough, thank you very fucking much, Renea!" he snapped as he sat up. He downed several large shots of liquor.

"Clint, please! I... I don't understand. What have I done that's so terrible?" she pleaded.

He shook his head in despair.

"Just get the hell out of here, Renea! Go on! Get the hell out!" He motioned in the direction of the bedroom door with his hand that held the liquor bottle.

"No. I won't leave, Clint. At least not until you tell me what I've done to you that is making you act this way!"

He swallowed hard, trying to stop the tears that were running down his handsome face.

"Please Renea. Just leave. I'm... I'm in too much pain to talk about it right now. It's better if you just leave." He wiped the tears from his face with his forearm.

"I'm not leaving, Clint. Not until you tell me what's wrong!" Her tone was filled with stubbornness.

He looked up at her hurt expression, wondering why he was so angry with her. After all it wasn't like she just ruined his life on purpose.

'Hell! Poor Renea didn't even know about Nouri. This whole thing had nothing to do with her. It had everything to do with me not being able to keep it in my pants long enough to...'

His thoughts were interrupted when he heard Renea talking to him somewhere in the background of his mind.

"Please don't send me away like this, Clint," she was saying disappointedly.

He swallowed hard. "I'm sorry Renea. It's just..." he stopped talking and shook his head again in despair.

"Please Clint. Let me..." she suddenly stopped speaking and dropped to her knees. She positioned herself between his muscular legs and gently curled her arms around his neck.

"Please Clint," she begged softly, as their eyes met. She wiped away a tear with her thumb. He lowered his head to meet her open mouth. They kissed... Deeply- Hungrily- Passionately.

"Oh, God, Renea!" he whispered hopelessly when he stopped kissing her to catch his breath.

"I know, baby. Please, let me make love to you," she whispered in response, releasing the towel that was snuggly wrapped around his waist.

"I want to make love to you, Clint," she breathlessly gasped lowering her eager kisses to the location between his muscular thighs.

The bottle of scotch dropped from his hand to the floor as she lustfully sent his body into oral orbit.

"Oh, God, Renea!" he groaned with an urgent need for release. Soon after his explosive climax, he collapsed on top of the bed.

Renea quickly shed her clothing and joined him in bed, where they spent the next several hours making love until they both fell asleep from exhaustion.

Chapter 12

Nouri Sommers impatiently glanced at the antique clock, sitting on the mantle above the fireplace. She squirmed uneasily on her barstool, as she reached for the half empty bottle of Cognac, quickly pouring herself another shot. Even though the alcohol was strong, it felt smooth going down.

"Hmm … that tastes nice," she mumbled pouring herself another shot of the auburn-colored liquor, desperately attempting to remove Clint Chamberlain from her thoughts. As far as she was concerned, he was no longer a welcome person in her life, her heart, or her thoughts. The high-powered-attorney was history!

"To hell with you, Clinton Jerome Chamberlain! I hope I never see your two-timing ass ever again! Not now! Not ever!" she drunkenly spat under her breath, reaching for the liquor bottle again.

After finishing her shot of cognac, she circled the bar and crossed the room, pulling back the drapes and sheers from the large bay window, and began to stare blankly into space.

She was soon jolted back to reality after becoming lost in thought when the loud buzzer from the front entrance gate intercom demanded immediate attention. It was Charles Mason, seeking permission to enter the estate grounds.

Nouri walked to the front door, with a fresh drink in her hand to wait for him.

She was leaning selectively up against the frame of the door with one arm and holding her drink with the other hand, as he quickly made his way to the front door.

A surprised look suddenly masked his face after quickly noticing her obvious drunken condition.

"Sugar," he said disappointedly. "I see you started without me, huh?" He forced to smile. She drunkenly tossed her empty brandy snifter out on the front lawn and grabbed him by the necktie, playfully pulling him inside the mansion. With her index finger gently pressed against her lips. "Shhh... Big guy," she whispered playfully, as she continued to pull him into the living room, giggling like a mischievous child. She finally shoved the private investigator to the sofa playfully jumping onto his lap.

"What's this all about, Nouri?" he asked in a stunned tone.

"Kiss me, Charles," she whispered in his ear with her warm breath.

"My pleasure sugar," he hoarsely whispered in response, lowering his head to meet hers. They kissed and kissed and kissed again, Charles not wanting to stop, and Nouri not wanting him to. Finally, they were both forced to stop kissing to come up for air.

"It's been a long time since I've been welcomed home like that, sugar," he breathlessly remarked.

"So, what did you stop for?" she breathlessly responded.

"I'm not sure, sugar. But as long as we have, why don't you get up and pour us both a drink, and tell me what this is all about, okay?" he said halfheartedly.

A surprised look of rejection crossed her face.

"Oh, God, Charles! I'd almost forgotten. You're married. I'm so sorry," she responded jumping up off his lap.

"Married!" he exclaimed before remembering that he told her a little white lie a few days earlier to secretly hide his hurt pride.

"Oh, that." He swallowed nervously. "No sugar it's not that... It's just I want to talk first... I know something has happened, this... well this behavior... is out of character for you." He stood to his feet crossing the floor to join her.

"Sugar, what is it? What's happened?" he asked gently pulling her into his arms.

"Oh God Charles! It's Clint... he's... he's..." She suddenly stopped talking and began to cry.

What's his face! I knew it! The private detective silently thought, gently patting her across the shoulders.

"Shhh sugar. It's all right. Tell me, what has that pompous jack-ass done to you?" he remarked, shaking his head in disbelief.

"I hate him, Charles. I just hate him! I never want to see his two-timing ass ever again, as long as I live!" She continued to sob.

"I see. Well sugar, I wish I knew what to say to make you feel better. Unfortunately I don't." He released a sigh of frustration. "Come on now, let's have a drink and forget all about him, okay?" he said releasing his arms from around her.

"Come on, sugar, let's sit down." He ushered her to a barstool.

"Cognac, right?" He smiled dangling the bottle in his hand playfully.

"Yes, thank you, Charles." She forced a grin.

"I'll have the same, only I'll have a double, no make that at least a triple. After all, I need to catch up with you." He smiled before belting down his drink, quickly helping himself to another.

'If I'm going to have to spend the biggest part of the night listening to her cry about what's his face, I'd better get drunk first', he silently thought, quickly downing another shot.

"Sugar, I know you must not feel like talking about business right now, but..."

She cut in.

"Oh Charles! I don't feel like talking about business, I mean Ethan's business, I mean Ethan. Oh, Charles, you know what I mean, right? I've had a terrible week and it only seems to keep getting worse!" she cried.

Shaking his head in dismay, he heatedly responded. "Is that why you made me drive all the way out here? To listen to you cry about what's his face!" His tone was noticeably jealous.

She shook her head. "No, of course not, Charles. But now, I just can't seem to help myself," she sobbed.

"Nouri... news flash..." Charles leveled his eyes to hers. "I didn't drop everything that I was doing to drive all the way out here to listen to you cry over some son-of-a-bitch that I can't stand to began with, okay. Pull yourself together and tell me why you needed to see me." His tone was stern and impatient.

She cleared her throat pushing her drink to the side and the hair from out of her eyes.

"You're right Charles. I'm sorry. Didn't you say something earlier about bringing some Chinese food?" She forced the tears back down to her stomach and forced a slight smile.

He nodded excitedly. "Yes, I did, sugar. I'll run out to the car and get it." He kissed her on the cheek and darted across the room, making his way to the car and back.

No sooner than he was gone, Nouri laid her head down on top of the bar and passed out.

"Well, here we are, sugar!" Charles was saying when he entered the living room. He instantly noticed she was asleep.

He walked over to her, shaking his head.

"Poor baby," he whispered under his breath, picking her up in his arms. He carried her up the long, spiral staircase, to the master bedroom where he undressed her and put her to bed.

"I love you sugar," he whispered, leaning over to kiss her gently. He closed the bedroom door quietly behind him swiftly making his way back downstairs, where he had every intention of heating up his Chinese food and eating it.

He was in no hurry to leave. With Nouri sound asleep, it gave him an opportunity to do a little detective work. A.K.A.: a little snooping!

After the private detective warmed up and ate his dinner, he checked on Nouri, wanting to make sure she was still sound asleep before he started snooping around the Sommers' Mansion.

Several hours later, the private investigator had accumulated numerous listening and taping devices along with videotapes taken by secretly hidden cameras. He was certain that Nouri knew nothing about them.

Charles Mason quickly put his secret findings inside his car before going back inside the mansion, where he had every intention of waking up and making love to the beautiful woman of his dreams.

"How are you feeling, sugar?" he asked softly, as he continued to blot the throbbing temples of the incredibly beautiful woman lying in front of him with a cool damp cloth.

"Here, sugar take these two aspirin with this orange juice; it'll help." He put the two pills into her mouth and held the glass of juice, while she swallowed them.

"You'll feel better in a few minutes." He leaned over and kissed her on the cheek.

"Ugh! You mean I'm still alive!" she teased in response, pulling him back down to her.

"I'm afraid so, sugar," he mused gazing into her sexy hazel-colored eyes.

She smiled lustfully. "Good, now you can make love to me," she seductively whispered across his lips with hers.

Her former lover didn't need a second invitation. He kissed her with an urgent need of his own, a deep routed passion that never died, even after seven years.

"God, sugar! How I've longed to hear you say that," he finally responded, removing his lips from her.

"I've missed you too, Charles," she whispered in response as she began to unbutton his shirt. He stopped her, jumping to his feet.

He eagerly shed his clothing and hurried back to the waiting arms of the woman he would always be in love with.

"Nouri, I've dreamed of this for the past seven years," he confessed excitedly.

"Oh God, Charles. You feel so wonderful. So familiar," she panted breathlessly as he entered her body. Entering her magnificent body made him eager to come, but Charles forced himself to hold back, slowly moving his body to the sensual movements of hers. Each time movements increased so would his. His body solidly molded to her body, as one. Every time he'd bring her to the brink of an explosive climax he would withdraw suddenly causing her to cry out in protest.

"Oh, God! Oh my God! Charles, please don't stop!" She begged breathlessly. He silenced her with a kiss, as he brought his right hand around to cup her right breast. She opened her eyes when he slowly began to caress her.

"Oh God, I've missed you- missed your body, sugar." He smiled and shook his head lustfully.

"I've missed you too, Charles. I had no idea!" she whispered in response.

Her hardened nipples continued to stand at attention, as he gently, softly, lovingly kissed, caressed, and suck them- time and time again, causing her to moan deep with desire.

He slowly lifted his body up off of hers, while his lips stayed busy showering her incredible body with hundreds of passionate, wet kisses, anxious to taste her again, after all this time.

After bringing her to several oral completions, Charles eagerly entered her body again- anxious to reclaim the body of the woman that stole his heart seven years earlier- soon after, they passionately melted as one in utter ecstasy.

"Oh my God! Sugar! You have no idea what it is that you do to me. Do you?" he panted, rolling his body off hers, only to gently pull her back into his arms again.

"Oh, I don't know about that. Big guy," she teased in response, rubbing his muscular, manly chest.

"God!" He paused, sighed and shook his head.

"I thought I lost you forever, Nouri." His gaze lowered to look at her beautiful flushed face.

Looking up to meet his gaze, she smiled and continued to rub his chest.

"I'll always love you, Charles." She paused. "You do know that, don't you?" She smiled lovingly. It was her expression that disturbed him.

Charles suddenly realized disappointedly that Nouri did love him, but obviously she just wasn't in love with him. Longing to tell her that he really wasn't married in the moment of heated passion earlier, he was suddenly grateful that he had held his confession, for the time being, anyway.

"I know sugar." He smiled gently pushing a strand of hair from her face. "Hey, how about we get up and you make us a cup of coffee?" he said, lazily sitting up in bed.

A confused expression crossed her face. "Charles, what is it? Did I say something wrong?" she asked nervously.

He shook his head and kissed her hand. "No sugar," he lied. "I just thought we both could use some coffee. I have a few things I need to talk to you about. That is..." he paused, as he turned to face her. "If you're up to it. She smiled, lovingly pulling him back into her arms.

"No. Actually Charles, I'd rather stay in bed and make love to you all night. We can talk tomorrow. I don't feel much like talking tonight. I need to be held, okay?" she said softly.

Charles smiled and nodded, and without speaking leaned over to kiss her. He was fully aware that Nouri was using him or rather his body, to vent her frustration over Clint Chamberlain. After several hours of making love, they both dozed off, tightly embraced inside one another's arms--a familiar feeling for both of them.

Chapter 13

Clint Chamberlain was jolted from a restless sleep by the throbbing pain inside his head.

"Oh shit!" he moaned, grabbing both sides of his head, slowly sitting up in bed removing Renea Chandliers' arms, which were snuggly wrapped around him.

He walked over to the dresser and pulled out a small leather zipper case that he stored a few different types of medication in. He dumped out the contents of the case, quickly locating the bottle of aspirin. He popped several aspirins into his mouth and went to the bathroom for a drink of water.

After digesting the aspirins, he glanced at his reflection in the large mirror. Dark circles were beginning to form under both of his eyes from lack of proper sleep, and they were still red and swollen from crying half the night over the woman of his dreams.

"Nouri," he whispered softly shaking his head in frustration.

"God! How could I have been so damn stupid? How could I do this to her again? What the hell is wrong with me fucking anything that comes my way with big tits and..."

He suddenly stopped scolding himself after realizing he had to talk to the woman of his dreams.

"Oh God! Sweetness..." he sighed hopelessly.

Clint walked out of the bathroom and glanced over at Renea. She was still very much asleep. He leaned down and replaced the sheet over her that had fallen off onto the floor. He silently stood beside the bed for a few moments, staring down at her. How beautiful she was. Maybe if she hadn't looked so damn much like Nouri... 'I wouldn't have gotten involved', he thought to himself before he turned away from her.

Quietly leaving the bedroom, he closed the door shut behind him and went straight to the telephone to call Nouri before he lost his nerve again.

He prayed silently to himself that she wouldn't slam the phone down into his ear again. '*God! I'm so sorry, sweetness*! He was thinking silently as he continued to listen to the endless ringing of the telephone in his ear.

Finally, after eight or ten rings, the phone was answered by a surprising hoarse, very masculine voice. Immediately recognizing the unexpected voice of Charles Mason, Clint angrily shouted into the receiver: "Charles Mason, you son-of-a-bitch! What the hell are you doing..."

"Swell," Charles Mason mumbled under his breath before interrupting him.

"Oh, Chamberlain. It's you." He rolled his eyes and sighed deeply. "What the hell do you think you're doing phoning here this time of night?" He grinned with pleasure knowing his being with Nouri must be driving the high-powered-attorney to the brink of insanity.

Clint was hurt, heart broken and *still* very much in shock. After several moments of uncomfortable silence, he shook himself back to reality and responded with a threat.

"Charles Mason, you low life fuck!" He raved. "Put Nouri on the goddamn telephone before I catch the next airplane out of here and beat your goddamn brains out!"

"Charles laughed in amusement.

"Yeah, right... Like I'm scared of the likes of you." He chuckled again, making Clint wish that he could reach his hands through the phone lines and choke the life right out of the arrogant private investigator.

"I'm serious, Mason. Put Nouri on the goddamn telephone!"

"No can do asshole! She doesn't want to speak with you! As far as that goes, Chamberlain, she doesn't want to ever see... and I quote, 'his two- timing ass ever again!' Unquote... Got it?"

"It's not your place to tell me that, Mason! Put her on the phone and let her tell me herself!" Clint's tone was desperate.

"Listen Chamberlain... Nouri is asleep and I don't intend to wake her. I do, however, need to talk to you. It's about your wife," he sighed deeply, standing to his feet. Charles crossed the floor with the telephone and quietly made his way out onto the terrace. He didn't want to wake Nouri from her much-needed sleep.

"What the hell are you talking about!"

"Your wife, Becka."

"Not that it's any of your business Mason. But, what about her?"

"Umm... it's true then." Charles sighed.

"Like I said before Mason, just what the hell are you talking about?" Clint snipped with an attitude.

"She was found murdered in Lambert Saturday morning." Charles swallowed nervously. He hated being the bearer of bad news, especially, when it involved the death of someone's husband or wife!

After several long moments of eerie silence, Clint finally responded. "There must be some mistake, Mason." His voice shook with disbelief.

"No, I'm afraid not, Chamberlain. Actually, there were two dead bodies found that morning. But, then you already know about the Kamel woman, right?"

"What the hell is that supposed to mean, you prick?" Clint snapped heatedly.

"Cut the bullshit, Chamberlain. I also know that it was you that made the anonymous phone call to the police that morning from the airport on your way back to Boston. So don't deny it!"

"I'm half afraid to ask you just how the hell you would know something like that." He paused, still stunned by Charles' accurate account of what had transpired in the early hours of that morning. If the high-priced private investigator already knew that much, Clint began to wonder just how much more he actually knew about things- And just how in hell he found out about them so quickly.

"Okay, Mason, for the sake of arguing, let's say you're right. I did phone the police about the young woman's dead body. But I swear I know nothing about my wife's death. What happened?" Clint sighed deeply.

"Too early to say yet, Chamberlain. All I can tell you right now is that she was found murdered down on the beach. Her body was naked and she had a whip wrapped around her neck."

"Oh God no!" Clint whispered hoarsely. "Do they have any ideas on who may have done it?"

"You get my vote, Chamberlain," Charles said with an attitude.

"Cut the shit, Mason. I told you, I honestly don't know anything about it. I'm sorry Becka's dead." The attorney's voice cracked as he fought back the tears that were beginning to form in his eyes.

"For the time being, Chamberlain, lets just say for the sake of argument, just quoting you of course..." he paused. "I believe you. We still have a more serious issue to worry about right at the moment."

"What is that, Mason?" Clint asked with growing interest.

"Nouri." Charles answered in response.

"What has she got to do with it?"

"Evidence linking her to both murders was found at both crime scenes."

"That's impossible. Nouri couldn't hurt a fly."

"Yeah, that's true enough. You know that and I know that, but we still have to prove her innocence."

"Oh my God! You mean they're going to charge her with both murders?" Panic quickly filled Clint.

"Not if I can help it." Charles sighed again.

"Son-of-a-bitch! I'll catch the next flight out."

"Hold it, Chamberlain. I don't think that's such a good idea right now." Charles cut in.

"What the hell are you saying, Mason?"

"From what I can gather right now, you're in France trying to track down Ethan Sommers. Is that correct?"

"What is it, Mason. You got a microscope stuck up my ass or what?" Clint said angrily.

"Something like that," Charles mused teasingly.

"I'm serious as hell. How in the hell would you know something like that? Nouri, did she tell you that?"

"No. She didn't." Charles shook his head in amusement, knowing he was driving the arrogant attorney nuts. He continued. "I have my ways. Anyway, I need you there. We have to track down Ethan. You got any leads yet?"

"No. I sort of got side tracked, if you know what I mean." Clint shrugged defensively.

"I can only imagine. You want to talk about it?"

"With you, Mason? Yeah, sure. Like that's going to happen." Clint rolled his eyes.

"All right, then. Tell me what you do know. Tell me about the dead woman that was found in Ethan Sommers' hotel suite."

"I don't know anything. I went to Lambert to speak with Ethan. I knocked on his hotel suite, and when he didn't answer I turned the doorknob. It wasn't locked, so I went inside. Not seeing him, I walked into the master bedroom and saw the young woman lying on the floor, apparently in her own pool of blood. I checked to see if she was breathing; she was not. I left the room and walked through the hotel suite looking for Ethan. He was nowhere to be found... That's pretty much it." Clint swallowed nervously.

"Was there anything lying around the Kamel woman's body?" Charles asked lighting a cigarette.

"Like what?"

"Like anything that could connect Nouri to the murder?"

"No Mason. Of, course not. And even if there had been, I would have removed it." Clint shrugged defensively, again.

"That's what I thought. I would have probably done the same thing myself.... God help us!" Charles sighed.

"You're still in love with her too, huh?" Clint remarked knowingly.

"I'm afraid so. I always will be," Charles admitted.

"Me too, Mason."

"Nouri has always had that affect on men." Charles shook his head and smiled.

Clint shook his head. "Like I needed to hear that shit, Mason."

"Sorry, Chamberlain. I just don't understand men like you and her perverted husband. You get a woman like Nouri, most every man's dream girl and you screw around on her. I just don't get it." Charles Mason shook his head in disbelief.

"Listen, Mason. No matter what you must think of me, I do love her. Nouri's everything to me and I do intend to get her back."

"Not if I can help it." Charles remarked sharply.

"Tell me something, Mason. Have you been seeing her all along?" Clint asked jealously.

"I only wish, Chamberlain. Sadly, she's in love with you. Oh, yeah, sure she loves me. She always will, but... she's in love with you. How could you hurt her like that? I just don't understand."

"I'm a fucking idiot. I admit that, but God... I do love Nouri, I honestly do. Please, Mason let me speak to her," Clint pleaded as he wiped a tear from his eye.

"I'm sorry Chamberlain, I can't. She's had a really rough night. She phoned me this morning, and said she needed to talk with me. That it was important. When I arrived late this afternoon she was drunk and crying over you. Like I said, she needs to sleep."

"Will you at least tell her that I phoned?"

"Now why in God's name would I want to do that?"

"Okay. Fine. Have it your way, Mason. I'll catch the next flight out and tell her myself."

"I'm telling you, Chamberlain. Right now you're the last person she wants to see. You're better off staying in France and trying to locate Ethan. We need to find out what really happened in Lambert. If we don't, the DA might..."

Clint cut in, stopping Charles from finishing his sentence. "I get the picture. Okay, I'll stay. I'll find Ethan. I have to. If he isn't in France, he'll be somewhere in China. I may have to go there."

"I don't understand," Charles stated with growing interest.

"It's a long story, Mason."

"All right. Are you sure there wasn't a hair brush or her lipstick holder around the Kamel woman's body?"

"I'm positive," Clint nodded.

"Do you think Ethan killed the Kamel woman?"

"I honestly don't know. Maybe. It also could have been..." Clint caught himself and stopped talking.

"Who? Who could it have been, Chamberlain?"

"Never mind Mason. I'm not sure. It could have been any one of at least a hundred people. Ethan has a lot of enemies."

"Okay. How about your wife? Could Ethan have killed her?"

"Maybe. I just don't know, Mason. He might have tried to frame me and Nouri for the murders if he was the person who killed the two women."

"So he did know about you and Nouri."

"Apparently."

"What does that mean, exactly?"

"What part of apparently don't you understand, Mason?"

"Cut the shit, Chamberlain. I need to know everything. I'm trying to protect Nouri here."

"All right, Mason. He did know."

"And he was okay with that?"

"Apparently not!"

"For Chrissakes, Chamberlain, can't you complete at least one entire sentence without making me drag it out of you!"

"All right, shit-head. He was not okay with it. We had an argument on the phone Friday night. He was strung out. Apparently, back on drugs, the heavy shit. Anyway, he seemed to know about the two nights we spent together at the old Fantasy Suite Hotel. He must have had us followed. Anyway, he went ballistic on the phone with me. I immediately caught the next flight to Lambert. By the time I got there, he was apparently already gone.

"Now why do I get the feeling that you're not telling me everything, Chamberlain?"

"Oh, I don't know, Mason. Maybe it's the line of work you're into or something," Clint mused.

"Funny. Listen you arrogant prick! I know that Ethan Sommers is into a lot of shit. I also know that he has ties with the Chinese Mafia..."

"So you think that you are all that, huh Mason?"

"Yeah." Charles nodded. "As a matter-of-fact shit-head, I'm all that and more. I'm the best there is in my line of work, and before this is all over, I'm personally going to take Ethan Sommers down. And take my word for it, Chamberlain, if you are tied into any of his illegal activities, any at all... I'll take you down, too."

Clint chuckled sarcastically. "Whew! I'm scared of you, mister. All that and more!" he mused.

Charles Mason scoffed, "You better be. You have no idea."

"Very funny, Mason. Now, tell me exactly what it is that you want me to do to help Nouri?"

"If Ethan Sommers is that dangerous, and if he is the person that is behind trying to frame Nouri, then I'm very worried about her, and her safety. I'm going to phone a friend of mine to look after her. I need to meet with you in person. So, I'm coming to France. I'll get in touch with you when I arrive. It might be several days before I get there." He paused to put out his cigarette. "In the meantime, do your best to track down Sommers before he hurts or possibly kills someone else. Maybe even Nouri. Okay?"

"Wait a minute, Mason. I don't even like you. What makes you think I..."

"Listen asshole... You will talk to me. You will see me. You will even work with me if I ask you to. We both have one interest and that is to help Nouri. She needs us both right now, and there's someone out there who's trying hurt her, or worse. Got it?"

"All right Mason, I'll do it for Nouri, but first you have to promise me that you'll at least tell her that I phoned, and what she is thinking right now, well... it just isn't so. I swear!" He lied.

Charles shook his head once again in dismay and released a deep side.

"Liar!" He said in response to Clint's statement after a few uneasy moments of silence, "All right, I'll tell her, but you understand this Chamberlain. I love her too. It's far from over between Nouri and me. I have no intentions of backing away from her that easily, her love for you or not. I intend to try and win her back. Got it?"

"Fine. Give it your best shot, Mason. But you will tell her what I said, right?"

"Right. That is, right after I finish making love to her again in the morning." Charles couldn't resist driving Clint crazy with jealousy.

"When this is all over Mason, I intend to beat your goddamn brains out. You got that?" Clint snapped into the receiver angrily.

"Goodbye, Chamberlain." Charles Mason hung up the phone, grinning triumphantly."

Chapter 14

Clint Chamberlain poured himself another shot of Chivas Regal, crossed the floor, and sank down into an overstuffed chair in the living room of his posh hotel suite.

"Oh, God! Becka! I can't believe it. She's dead," he mumbled under his breath, shaking his head sadly. 'Ethan, you sick bastard! If I find out that you had anything to do with her death, I'm going to kill you with my own two, goddamn, bare hands'! He was saying to himself as Renea Chandlier entered the room.

Still naked, she slowly walked over to join him. She smiled longingly, as she opened his arms so she could sit down on his lap.

"Who were you just talking to? I thought I heard voices," she said softly wrapping her arms around his neck.

"Myself." Clint's one word reply.

"Do you go around talking to yourself often?" She teased.

Apparently more often than I had realized," he smiled back.

"Clint, what is it? You're shaking," she asked with concern. He handed her his empty glass and gently pushed her off his lap.

"Here, Renea, fix us a drink. Make mine a double."

"She looked at him curiously, shrugged her shoulders, and went to the bar to fix their drinks. After handing him his drink, she sat down on the floor in front of him. She glanced up at him and smiled. "Now can we talk?"

"Oh, God, Renea. You have no idea what I'm going through right now." He sighed deeply.

"No I don't, Clint. How could I possibly?" She shook her head sympathetically. "Why don't you tell me?

Maybe I can help in some way." She rubbed his muscular thigh.

"Renea, last night when you knocked on my door, I was…was talking to the woman that I'm in love…"

Without meaning to, Renea chimed, "Nouri." She swallowed hard, quickly realizing her mistake. A stunned expression quickly crossed Clint's face. He leveled his eyes to hers.

"I never told you her name." Renea blinked several times and swallowed hard again.

"Oh, so, her name is Nouri?" She faked a smile.

"Yes it is. But how would you know that Renea?" he asked sharply.

She was silent for several moments before answering. "You talk in your sleep. I don't suppose you knew that, huh?" She smiled nervously and rubbed his inner thigh softly again.

He studied the expression on her beautiful face for several moments, finally sighing out loud.

"I suppose I'd better watch doing that sort of thing in the future, huh?" he smiled.

"So you're saying what, Clint? That Nouri overheard me talking to you over the phone." She bit her lower lip nervously.

"Exactly." He downed his drink and handed her his empty glass again. A small frown crossed her face. But she stood and walked over to the bar again, pouring them both another drink.

She handed him his drink and sat back down on the floor in front of him.

"I'm sorry, Clint. I didn't mean to cause you any trouble with your woman," she lied.

He smiled and gently rubbed her arm.

"I know, Renea. It was my own fault, or rather my apparent uncontrollable lust for beautiful women, especially with a body like yours." He smiled again.

"Oh, so you've hurt her like this before, with other women?"

"I'm afraid so. But this time it's different. I don't think she'll forgive me so easily." He downed his drink again.

"I'm sorry, Clint. I can see how hurt you are. You really do love her, huh?"

"More than life itself," he sighed, handing her his empty glass again.

"I'm sorry, Clint. I just don't get it. If you love her so much, why am I here?" She shrugged, standing, and walking to the bar again.

"Truthfully, Renea?" He glanced at her from across the room.

"Yeah." She smiled, walking back across the room. "Truthfully."

"You look just like her. I couldn't resist. I miss her so much." He hung his head.

"A Nouri Sommers look-alike, huh?" A slip of the tongue, again. *'Damn it, Renea'*! she thought to herself, hoping he hadn't picked up on her mistake. Too much to hope for. He leveled his eyes to hers again.

" Don't tell me. I called out her last name in my sleep too?" A confused look crossed his face.

She smiled innocently. "Yes. As a matter-of-fact, you did. If Sommers is her last name. Is it?"

Maybe you should tell me everything I said in my sleep last night." The attorney's tone was questioning.

Renea downed her drink nervously and reached down to toy with the top button of her blouse, suddenly remembering she didn't have any clothes on. Deciding to try and trick him into answering a few questions, she decided to go for it. She stood and walked to the bar for another shot of Russian Vodka.

"All right, Clint. You also mentioned the name 'Charles Mason', I believe. Who's he? Her husband?" She said, trying to play dumb.

"Wow! A man I can't stand. And I'm dreaming about him too." He mused. "Are you sure you didn't listen in on one of my phone conversations, Renea?" he asked nervously.

"Your phone conversation. I don't know what you mean. I thought you said you were mumbling to yourself when I walked in a few moments ago."

"I'm sorry, Renea. I suppose I'm just feeling a little paranoid, lately." He forced a smile, but was still uncertain about her at this point.

She didn't want to seem too curious, so she decided not to push her luck with questions about Ethan Sommer's wife or the P.I. she had hired. She sat back down in front of Clint.

"So now what? Do you want me to phone the love of your life and smooth things out for you?"

"Yeah, right. Like you could do that. You don't know Nouri. It's not going to be that simple. But it was nice of you to offer." He smiled.

"Okay, then Clint. Tell me what I can do for you to make you feel better, then." She smiled, rubbing his inner thigh again.

"Just having you here with me right now helps." He smiled. "There's something else I just found out." He downed his drink. "I phoned Nouri while you were asleep. A man answered."

He looked at her. "Charles Mason, apparently Nouri was mad at me and invited him to spend the night, knowing that it would tear my goddamn heart out." He swallowed hard and wiped a tear from his eye. He went on... "After the private dick told me that he was fucking her, because of me, and my own fucking stupidity, he informed me that my wife was found murdered Saturday morning."

He stood to his feet and walked to the bar.

"Oh my God, Clint! I'm so sorry. What happened?" She stood to her feet and walked over to the bar to join him.

"Do they know who killed her?" Renea asked excitedly.

"Naturally, I'm a prime suspect. From what I understand, husbands usually are." He downed another shot and refilled his glass.

"I don't understand." You were here in London with me. How could they even suspect you killing her?"

"Apparently, she was murdered Friday night, possibly early Saturday morning. I'm not sure. Anyway, she was in Lambert." He paused, taking a sip of his drink. "Apparently, the same time that I was there." He downed the rest of his drink.

"And you didn't know that your wife was in Lambert at the same time?"

"No I didn't. I went to Lambert to talk to a friend. Well…An ex-friend."

"I sorry, Clint."

"Yeah, me too."

"How was she murdered?"

"I'm not sure yet. Mason didn't say. He was apparently in too much of a hurry to get back to what he was doing before I called."

"And what was that?" She jealously inquired; knowing exactly what Clint meant. She just wanted to hear him say it. She was hoping to get him angry at Nouri all over again, so she could have her lustful way with him again.

"Why fucking my woman, of course." He snapped, reaching for the bottle of scotch again.

"Doesn't sound like there is any love between you two men."

"There isn't. Mason was Nouri's first real man. Whatever the hell that means," he remarked sarcastically, downing his drink.

"It means that he was the first man that showed her how to enjoy being a woman," she blushed.

Clint arched his eyebrow and sighed hopelessly.

"Oh, Clint. Honestly. He gave your woman her first climax." She giggled, deliberately making him crazy with jealousy.

"Oh that's just great, Renea. Like I really needed to hear that!" He cringed at the thought.

"I'm sorry Clint, but you said —and I quote, 'whatever the hell that means...' unquote!"

"Thanks for the goddamn help." He barked with disgust.

"Come on, baby, take your anger out on me, rather my body. I love the way you feel inside me. You make my knees go week just thinking about you making love to me."

"Not now Renea. I'm not in the mood."

Renea unwrapped the towel from around his waist and gently squeezed his testicles.

"Are you sure?" She whispered playfully.

'*God I'm such a whore-dog*', he thought, feeling himself grow hard again because of her erotic touches to his body.

An immediate reaction to a sudden surge of shame and lust quickly swept through him. He pulled her to the floor and quickly mounted her; thinking only of his own urgent need for release. The next instant they were rolling heatedly across the thick shag carpet, as the hidden camera continued to roll.

Chapter 15

A pre-dawn chill caused Charles Mason to shiver slightly, as he dialed the telephone number to the Boston Police Department while he was standing outside on the terrace at the Sommers' Estate.

He was trying very hard not to wake the beautiful woman who was only a few short feet away, sound asleep in her warm bed. He could hardly wait to get his call over with so he could join her. His body was aching to make love to her again. He smiled at the lovely thought.

"Boston Police Department, how may I direct your call?"

"To Gabe Baldwin. This is Charles Mason calling."

"Oh, hello Charles. This is Cool Breeze; Spike's wife, remember me?"

"Hey, Cool Breeze. Are you kidding? Have you forgotten just who it was that gave you that nickname to begin with?" He chuckled.

"Oh, Charles. It's been so long that I'd almost forgotten. By the way, I'd always wanted to ask you something and never got the chance. After your breakup with the DA...I thought I'd never get to see you again."

"What's that, Cool?" he laughed.

"I'd like to know why you branded me *for life* with such a silly nickname like that?" she laughed.

"Think about it, Cool. When you got that damn Irish temper of yours all riled up, that's exactly what it took to get you to cool back down again. A Cool Breeze." He laughed again.

"Oh Charles, I miss you around here. Hell, we all do!"

"I've missed you too, Cool. How's Spike doing these days?"

"Oh, I guess you haven't heard. Of course you haven't. What am I thinking? He's coping, as best as he knows how. He took a bullet through his spine. He may never walk again. Hard to say."

Oh God, Cool. I'm sorry. I didn't know. Where is he?"

"Dullard's in Carlisle. He was transferred there last week. I couldn't afford to send him to Corona for surgery. The specialist there said it would take more surgeries than we could pay for. So Spike said forget it. He's pretty depressed."

"Hey Cool. Don't worry about it. I'll take care of it. What's the surgeon's name in Corona?"

"Oh thanks Charles, but we couldn't possibly let you do that. You're talking hundreds of thousands of dollars. Spike won't stand for it. Neither will I. But the offer was very sweet."

"Like I said, Cool. What's the surgeon's name?"

"Jonathan D. Lira. Why?"

"At least let me talk to him, okay. Spike doesn't have to know."

"Okay Charles. Talk to him. I won't mention it to Spike. But you will go see Spike, won't you? I'm sure a visit from you would make him feel better."

"Of course I will, Cool. You have my word on it. Can I talk to Gabe now? He's in isn't he?"

"Oh yeah, sure. I'm putting your call through right now. It was great hearing from you again, Charles."

"You too, Cool. I'll call you after I talk to Lira, okay."

"Thanks, Charles."

"My pleasure, Cool."

"Mason, you son of a…"

"I've missed you too. My old partner in Crime Fighting."

"God, is that really you, Charles?"

"In the flesh."

"What do I owe this pleasure? Oh! Wait just a minute. Let me guess. This call from you doesn't have anything to do with the Lambert Murders. Does it Charles?" The homicide detective mused.

"I see you've been working with those crime busting psychics again, huh, Gabe?"

"It shows, huh, Charles?" he chuckled.

"Speaking of showing, how about you meet me for lunch today and fill me in on what you have on the Lambert Murders."

"Technically, I can't do that Charles, as you damn well know, but seeing how I owe you one and all, how about we meet at *Caproni's* Restaurant, downtown-- Northside, around one o'clock."

"Sounds good. Oh, and Gabe, you're right. You do owe me. This case isn't just any case. This case is important to me. Real important."

"I figured it must be for you to be interested in it."

"You have no idea, Gabe."

"I suppose you'll fill me in at lunch, huh?"

"You bet. Oh, by the way, sorry to hear about Spike, they get the bastard who shot him?"

"Not yet, but we're working on it."

"Mind if I poke my nose around a bit?"

"I'll bring what we have on it, too, okay?"

"Good. Tomorrow at one then Bye, Gabe."

"Bye, partner." The police detective said, hanging up the phone.

Charles glanced at the antique clock sitting on the nightstand beside Nouri's bed. He wondered if he had time to make love to her again, take a shower, have some coffee, and talk to her before all the hired help started arriving for work.

"I'll risk it," he mumbled under his breath, climbing back into bed with the woman of his dreams.

He removed the sheet and began to nibble up and down her incredibly sexy spine with hundreds of tiny little kisses, causing her to stir.

He gently turned her body over to lie on her back, lowering his kisses even further - to the warm area between her sexy thighs. She moaned as his kisses continued to tease her- she invitingly opened her legs to him.

"God, you taste wonderful, sugar," he whispered breathlessly, putting his hands under her shapely bottom and pulling her towards him, closer and more intimately. "I want you, Nouri," he whispered as he watched her eyes slowly open.

She responded by running her fingers threw his hair and opening her legs wider still. She arched her back to meet his mouth, pushing herself against him. He groaned with desire burying his face between her thighs. The strokes of his tongue soon became more demanding.

She squealed in surrender as he continued to pleasure her with his hot tongue and even hotter kisses. "Oh God, please!" She grasped. "I need to feel you inside me, please Charles. Now!"

He shifted his position lowering himself on top of her – jerking her hips towards him, urgently ramming his hardness inside her.

She shuttered and moaned, spreading her legs even wider, running her hands over the well built muscles of his back and broad shoulders frantically. As she closed her eyes tightly enjoying the sensations of pleasure that he was so graciously bestowing upon her. He lifted her shapely behind higher, increasing the depth of penetration so deep he felt the top of her womb, driving them both lustfully out of their minds.

Moments later, she felt him grow even harder, as he pulsed his hot release at just the same moment she released hers. He collapsed on top of her too weak to move.

"Oh God sugar! That was incredible," he whispered in her ear with his hot breath.

"Oh Charles! I don't remember it being quite so wonderful between us. After we catch our breath, can we try that again?" She laughed.

"You can count on it. But first sugar, I need some coffee, a hot shower, and..."

"I know that tone, Charles."

"I know you do, sugar, but it's important. We need to talk."

She released a deep sigh. "Oh, all right Charles. I'll race you to the shower. The last one in has to wash the other's back," she teased. They both laughed and sat up in bed.

"This feels so right, sugar," he said, as he continued to lather her satin-soft body with the bar of soap.

"Umm, this does have a familiar feel to it." She smiled lovingly, enjoying his touches.

"And that's it?" he asked teasingly.

"Oh please, Charles. You know what I mean. Us bathing together is one of my fondest memories of us together."

"Thank you. I think?" he chuckled.

"Honestly, Charles. You seem so moody tonight."

"I've got your moody, Nouri!" He gently squeezed her right breast playfully.

"I saw that you rolled your eyes at me." She playfully arched her eyebrow in a questioning manner.

"Teasingly, I assure you, sugar. You're the one that seems sensitive tonight. And rightfully so, I might add." He chuckled.

"I'm sorry Charles. Without you tonight, I don't know what I would have done."

"Nouri, I'm glad I was here with you, too." He pulled her soapy body close to him. "Tell me sugar, without Ethan in your life and What's His Face out of the picture, where does that leave us?"

"Charles. I can honestly say that at this particular moment, there is no other man in my life well, that is except for my father." She smiled. "Charles, I need you." She turned herself to face him.

"Come here, sugar," he said molding his body to hers. He kissed her deeply. Passionately. Urgently.

She opened her eyes and blinked back the water from them. "Oh Charles, I do love you, you know," she breathlessly whispered.

The private investigator was instantly aroused again. He continued to caress her slippery body with his large hands; making her moan with desire. She watched his hands through her water soaked eyes, gently massaging her shoulders... breasts... stomach... and hips. He pulled her to him again, sliding his hands over her shapely bottom.

"Why should I let you have all the fun?" She playfully whispered running her hands over his masculine body in return – So Powerful... So Muscular... So Very Manly... She gasped, as she continued to longingly touch him. There wasn't an ounce of fat on his body. Her hands slid over his hairy chest, flat, muscular stomach and hips, down to his muscular thighs.

Charles Mason was a very attractive and manly man. Nouri loved his body- loved touching him- loved him making love to her- the thought of his manly body making love to her, made her feel weak in the knees – she suddenly leaned against him.

"Oh God Charles," she breathlessly whispered in his ear. She could feel him shaking with desire. He wanted to make love to her again. She was completely engulfed with lust for him, for his body.

He tightened his embrace on her slippery wet body. Her breasts crushed against his strong chest. She glanced up to look at his handsome face. He hungrily kissed her, his hot tongue plundering inside her mouth their tongues so intimately embracing, swirling around and around.

"Oh God sugar!" He groaned needingly against her throat. "I want you sugar!" He moaned, as he positioned her against the wall. He eagerly spread her thighs. She felt his hardness rub against her.

"I want you too, Charles," she responded half-unconscious from her need to be fulfilled. "Please Charles, now!" she softly begged.

More than happy to oblige, he entered her – more slowly this time.

"Please Charles! Please!" She begged for deeper penetration.

"Slow down sugar. I want to make it last forever," he whispered in response to her desire for him.

"Oh please, Charles, I'm so…so…"

He stroked her wet hair lovingly. "Shhh, sugar. Relax. You feel so wonderful. I don't want it to end," he panted in jagged breaths, as he continued to slowly pleasure her with his hard body.

Thrust after deep thrust, he would plunge in and slowly pull out. The affect on her was almost maddening. Finally, after not being able to control himself any longer, they both shuddered and came together – magically melting their body's together as one.

When it was over, she collapsed in his arms. Too drained to move, they stood inside the shower holding one another tightly.

After several long moments, Charles released her from his powerful arms reaching for the bar of soap, again quickly lathering himself and then her- just as quickly rinsing them off. He shut off the water and stepped out of the tub reaching for two fluffy over sized terry cloth towels.

He took great pleasure towel drying her magnificent body. Her cheeks were still flushed from the glow of their magical moments together.

"God, sugar. I have to tell you something." He smiled lovingly.

She returned the smile. "What's that, Charles?"

"I...I don't know if I will be able to let you get away from me so easily this time around." His voice shook.

"Oh Charles," she sighed. "Maybe I won't want to let you go so easily this time either." She curled her arms around his neck pulling his head down to meet, her kiss. He picked her up into his arms and carried her to the bedroom.

"Nouri, if we don't get dressed and go downstairs this very instant, and have some much needed coffee, I don't think I will have the strength left to make myself leave before your hired help arrives this morning," he sighed pulling her hand over to feel his new arousal, causing her to giggle.

"Wow! You are unbelievable Charles! What a man. I had to have a screw loose to leave a man like you," she said removing the towel from his body. "Charles. I... I..."

She stopped speaking and lowered her head eagerly, showering his hard body with her warm, wet French kisses anxious to make her way down his body to the stiff rod of hardened flesh dangling between his muscular thighs.

An instant later, her mouth opened wide, taking the huge mass of hardened flesh deep inside her throat.

Charles couldn't believe what was happening to him. "My God sugar! Where did you learn to do that?" He exclaimed. A split second he groaned the words, "never mind. I don't want to know, and it feels too good to make you stop... what am I saying? ... Listen Nouri," he moaned but forced himself to finish what he wanted to say. "It will be light soon- we have to talk before the hired help arrives- please stop, while I have enough will power to ask you to." He swallowed hard gently running his fingers through her thick, reddish- brown, curly hair.

"Shhh, big guy," she whispered giggling childishly. "Relax, I want to do this, please... I don't care if the help would walk in right this minute... I just don't care anymore... Now relax, it's something I've wanted to do since last Wednesday when we had dinner at *Pompilleao's.* Okay?" She said gently stroking the shaft of his hardness with her soft hands.

"God! That feels good sugar," Charles said in response closing his eyes tightly only to just as quickly snap them open again- when Nouri briefly stopped pleasuring him- and stood to her feet dropping her bath towel. An instant later, she dropped back to her knees.

Without saying another word Charles moaned and thrust his groin toward her. He closed his eyes when she put his manhood into her mouth. She cupped his testicles with her soft warm hand and felt them tighten at her touch. She slowly took him deep inside her mouth.

He gripped the sides of her head to help guide her mouth movements to his body rhythmically. He slowly began to move his hips, drawing himself in and out of her hot, slippery, wet mouth, long slow stroke after stroke. She loved the way his body felt inside her mouth.

A passing thought quickly entered her brain as she continued to lick, suck, and kiss his huge, stiff rod of hardened flesh ... My Lord! I never knew I enjoyed sex this much before. She continued to silently think ... Maybe because I've been starved for it for the past two years with Ethan ... That was her last thought on the matter as she switched her attention back to what she was doing- which was treating herself to Charles Mason's manly body.

His manly scent exciting her more- she tightened her suckling hold to him driving him mad with desire. He began to move his body more urgently, not thinking about anything but his own satisfaction at that point using her mouth as a tool to achieve oral gratification- she actually savored the thought of being used- maybe I'm just trying to impress him with how much I've grown up, after all I was only nineteen when I met him, she forced her thoughts back to his delicious body.

"Oh, God, Nouri!" He moaned. "That feels so…so…Oh, God! A sudden grin curled her lips, as the unexpected thrill of power surged throughout her body- a feeling she had never experienced before.

She concentrated on the sensual sensation of having him in her mouth - the exciting tickle of the tip of his glands at the back of her throat.

"Oh, my Lord! I'm actually enjoying this she silently mused to herself as she tightened her hold gripping his buttocks. When she dug her fingernails into the flesh of his rear, he began to stiffen, approaching release. He shouted moans of ecstasy exploding deep inside her mouth. Too weak to stand he braced his body against her holding onto the sides of her head with both of his hands to balance himself.

"Oh, God, sugar. That was incredible!" He breathlessly panted, pulling her up to his arms.

They deeply and passionately kissed. After several moments of kissing, Charles took Nouri by the hand and walked her back to bed.

"It's my turn to pleasure you," he whispered in her ear.

"Oh, but you already have, big guy," she responded excitedly.

"Oh, no! You aren't getting by that easy, sugar. Lay down," he playfully ordered, but a serious expression ran across his flushed face.

She shivered with anticipation, knowing the sexual pleasure her first real man was capable of giving to her.

An hour or so later, Nouri was sipping coffee with Charles in the kitchen; still basking in the glow of it all.

"My Lord! Charles Xavier Mason, you were magnificent! I still can't believe I let you go so easily seven years ago," she said smiling contentedly.

He pulled her over onto his lap and kissed her.

"Listen sugar, there's nothing that I would rather do more than to sit here with you, having coffee and making love to you all day, but I have to go; and I need to talk to you before I do." He kissed the palm of her hand.

She released a sigh and another sexy smile. "Okay, you talk and I'll listen while I warm up our coffee." She kissed him again before standing.

"Nouri... to put it bluntly, I'm worried about your safety," he said sharply reaching for his coffee cup.

"What do you mean, Charles?"

"I don't have time to get into everything that I had originally intended to with you, but I've learned enough about your husband to know that he is a very sick and dangerous person," he sighed, reaching over to pull her back down on top of his lap.

"What do you mean?" She put her arms around his neck.

"Sugar. I know you don't know this, and I'm not really sure if I should be telling you this yet or not. But the truth is I have reason to believe that you might be in some serious danger."

"I'm sorry, Charles. I still don't understand what you mean by danger." She kissed his cheek lovingly.

"Sugar. One of the murdered women in Lambert was found inside your husband's hotel suite. The young woman, Kirsten Kamel."

Nouri's mouth instinctively flew open in utter disbelief. "You can't be serious, Charles." She leveled her eyes to his.

"I'm sorry, Nouri. It's true and it gets worse."

"Worse!" A curious expression crossed her face.

"Yeah! A hairbrush and lipstick holder belonging to you were found beside both of the dead women's bodies." He shook his head and sighed.

"Charles, that's impossible! How can that be?" She jumped off of his lap and stared at him blankly.

"I'm sorry, Nouri. It looks as though someone is trying to pin both murders on you." He shook his head.

"Ethan!" She cringed at the thought.

"Possibly. He knows about you and Clint." Charles shook his head again.

"That's impossible!" She exclaimed.

"Sorry, sugar. He knows. He had you followed. He's had you followed for the past two years." He paused to light his cigarette. " I noticed a black sedan following you and Chamberlain last Wednesday night after you left *Pompilliao's*."

Nouri shook her head in disbelief. "I still don't see why he would want to frame me for a murder. He's been having an affair with a young woman, himself."

"Probably the Kamel woman," Charles said shaking his head.

"Oh, my God!" Nouri gasped in dismay. She went on… "From what I've found out on my own, Charles, Ethan has been sleeping with a lot of women all along. The entire two years of our marriage."

"And you and Chamberlain?" Charles asked jealously.

"No. I've never cheated on Ethan. Well, that is until last Wednesday night. I spent both Wednesday and Thursday nights with Clint." She swallowed hard. "We stayed at…"

Yeah, I already know. The Fantasy Suite Hotel. A real classy man, huh?"

"You followed us, Charles?" Nouri asked in a stunned tone.

"No, of course not. Chamberlain told me."

"Clint told you that we spent two nights together. When?" A puzzled look crossed her face.

"Yes, Nouri. That's right. He told me last night when he phoned you." He studied her expression.

"He called last night?" Her face lit-up unknowingly.

"Yes. You were asleep. I had no intention of waking you. After all, you said you hated him and never wanted to see or talk to him ever again, as long as you live. That's what you said, isn't it?"

"Yes, of course, Charles. I did, and I mean it!" She reached for her cup of coffee nervously.

"So you say now. But, what about when you two decide to kiss and makeup again?"

"I have no intention of making up with him, as you put it. It's over between us. I said it last night, and now I'm saying it again today." She walked over and sat back down on his lap, again. They kissed. She could feel Charles' body trembling. She knew he was afraid of losing her again. She also knew that she still loved Clint Chamberlain hopelessly. God help her.

"Nouri, in all fairness I promised Chamberlain two things. And you know me, I always keep my promises." He smiled nervously, angry at himself for being such a man of his word.

"What two things, Charles?" she asked curiously.

"To tell you, that he phoned, and that he is innocent. What you apparently were thinking about him and some other woman wasn't true. He called to explain." Charles released a frustrated sigh.

Nouri giggled, covering her face with both hands and shaking her head in disbelief. "I'm sorry Charles. I just find it hard to imagine you promising Clint anything." She removed her hands. "Or even him talking to you, having nerve to ask you to relay a message to me. You have to admit the sound of it even sounds strange." She giggled again.

Charles chuckled too, as he began to caress her firm, round breasts. "Yeah, you're right. But, stranger things have happened." He shook his head.

"I bet Clint about died when you answered the telephone." A childish grin curled the corners of her lips.

"Yeah, he was pissed all right." Charles smiled, knowing she was pleased at Clint's jealously of her and Charles spending the night together. " I'm sure he wanted to crawl through the phone, but enough about Chamberlain. You are sure that it's over between the two of you, right? I'd hate to get completely lost in you again, only to have you rip my goddamn heart out again, Nouri." He swallowed hard.

"Charles, I honestly don't know what will happen between you and me, but I will tell you this. It's over with Clint and me."

"Fair enough, sugar, but remember this. I don't have much of a heart left, so be easy with me, okay?" He began to tremble again.

"What ever would I do without you, especially right now Charles?" She swallowed nervously.

"Nouri. I have to go out of town, maybe as soon as this evening or at the latest tomorrow. I want to have a friend of mine to stay here with you, and protect you. I'm honestly worried about your safety."

Nouri stared blankly at him. "What! A babysitter right here in my own home. I don't think so." She shook her head in disagreement.

"Okay, at least let me put a few men around the estate."

"Why can't I go with you Charles?" She pouted.

"I think we both know the answer to that question, don't we?" he sighed, taking the carton of orange juice from her unsteady hand. After sitting it down, he pulled her into his arms.

"Nouri, you would be a major distraction for me. I'd never get anything done." He sighed, again. "We wouldn't be able to get out of bed long enough to do anything except make love. I'm sorry, you'll have to stay here."

"All right, Charles, you can put in a few men, but I don't want to cause any unnecessary stresses for the employees. Oh! And Charles, they wont be that obvious, will they?" She frowned.

"Sugar, you won't even know that they are here, promise." He lifted her chin. They kissed.

The telephone rang, jolting Nouri and Charles' apart, "You want me to get it sugar?" he asked thinking it might be the high-powered-attorney again.

"No." Nouri answered turning to go answer the phone. "It might be Ethan. I'd better get it."

As she was getting ready to exit the living room, she heard Charles's sarcastic response. "Or Clint Chamberlain!" His tone was jealous. She smiled, rolled her eyes and continued to walk down the hallway deliberately ignoring his jealous words.

"Hello," she said softly.

"Hello, Nouri. It's me again." The voice on the other end of the wire said in an eerie tone, quickly giving Nouri the chills.

"Who is this?" she demanded nervously.

"I told you already. I'm not going to tell you until I'm ready to tell you." The caller's voice was icy and sharp.

"Listen, if you don't tell me this instant who you are, and what you want I'm going to phone the police. Do you understand?" Her voice was loud and shaky.

The private detective came running down the hallway when he heard the fear in Nouri's voice. " Who is it sugar? Give me the phone," he said quickly noticing the scared look on her face.

"Who the hell is this? What the hell do you want?" Charles shouted into the receiver.

"Who I am is not important, but what I want is very important. Put Nouri back on the phone."

"Listen, you sick fuck," Charles spat angrily. "Call this number again and I'll rip your goddamn lungs out with my bare goddamn hands! "He snapped heatedly.

"Bark! Bark! I like that in a man." The caller laughed in a dark, wicked tone.

"What the fuck do you want?" Charles shouted angrily, causing his face to flush.

"I told you. I want you to put Nouri back on the telephone." The mystery caller said insistently.

"I'm having your number traced as we speak, and when I get your location, I'm going to come down there and rip your goddamn..."

The mystery caller interrupted him in mid sentence. "In vain! In vain!" He chuckled, shaking his head in amusement. "Just tell Nouri for me. I'll be in touch!" He laughed, slamming the telephone down hard in Charles' right ear, leaving a deafening echo sound.

"What the fuck!" Charles shouted excitedly, nervously placing both hands on his hips.

Nouri, still in shock of it all, stood staring blankly at Charles for several long moments, too stunned to speak. Finally, she felt the blood slowly flow back into her body. "Oh God, Charles! That was him, again!" she cried.

"What? What do you mean him again? You mean he's called before?" A shocked expression quickly crossed his face.

Nouri nodded. "Yes. That's what I needed to see you about yesterday. That's why I asked you to drive out here. He called and said pretty much the same thing--right before I phoned you. It gave me the creeps!" She shivered.

Charles pulled her into his arms. "God... Why the hell didn't you tell me right away?" He paused, shaking his head in disbelief. "Never mind. You were too busy getting drunk over Clint Chamberlain! What a childish thing to do!" he lectured hurtfully.

Nouri pulled free from Charles' embrace and stormed into the living room, quickly making her way to the bar and making herself a strong vodka and orange juice.

She turned to face him. "So, you want to talk about being childish, huh? You have some nerve!" she snapped. "How dare you judge me! You don't know anything about it! You think you can just come back in here, after all these years, make love to me a few times, and completely take over my life again! How dare you! Maybe you should leave before I really say something that I might regret!" she hurtfully shouted, as tears began to run down her beautiful face. She quickly turned her back to hide her tears.

Charles was too hurt to speak and too stunned to move. He just stood in silence for several moments; wondering to himself if, in fact, he should leave. He turned to leave, but suddenly stopped, when he realized she was trying to hide her tears. He quickly changed his mind and went to her, and without speaking gently turned her to face him. He lifted her chin and wiped the tears from her soft face.

"God, sugar. I'm sorry. I was such a jerk. And you were right... About the Chamberlain thing, I mean." He nodded. "I was being childish. I'm sorry. I think jealous is probably a little more like it, though. Can you forgive me?" He leveled his eyes to hers.

Nouri threw her arms around his neck hugging him tightly. "Oh, Charles! I need you so badly right now," she sobbed.

Charles kissed her deeply as he slowly removed her bathrobe- once again their needs for one another raging out of control...

After the private investigator left the mansion, Nouri flew upstairs to shower and change, knowing it was time for Mai Li and the rest of her staff to arrive.

"Whew! That was close," she mumbled under her breath, glancing at the clock on her nightstand.

Suddenly, she was wondering what was taking Mai Li so long to enter the house.

Nouri had spotted her car around back by the employee's parking area when she had glanced out her bedroom terrace before jumping into the shower. "Hmm," she sighed making her way downstairs.

Mai Li was just entering the living room as Nouri was circling the bar.

"Oh, there you are, Mai Li. I was beginning to wonder where you were." she smiled.

"Good morning, Miss. You okay today?" She returned the smile.

"Yes. Thanks. I'm starved, for some strange reason." She sheepishly smiled, as she turned to walk to the sofa, eager to sit in her cozy spot.

"Be ready in a few minutes, miss. Oh, by the way…"

"Yes, Mai Li." Nouri glanced at her from where she was sitting.

"That Mr. Mason… Nice man. Very nice man." Mai Li turned to leave the room, supporting a knowing smile plastered across her attractive Asian face.

Stunned and not knowing what else to say, Nouri softly replied, "Yes, Mai Li, he's a very nice man." She shrugged her shoulders, watching the tiny Asian woman slowly disappear around the hallway entrance.

Chapter 16

Charles Mason's mind was racing in several directions at one time, as he reached for his cell phone.

"Good morning, Tess," he said to his private secretary after his receptionist sent his call through.

"Oh, hello, Charles. Where are you? You must have at least a hundred messages waiting on your desk. Not to mention six ex-agents waiting in your office to see you," she sighed.

"Swell," he sighed shaking his head. "All right, Tess, I won't be able to get to the office until after lunch. I'm on my way home right now. I have to shower and change. Oh, don't bother to ask, Tess. Anyway, tell John and company to stop in after lunch. I have something special for them to do, and to leave whatever they have for me on my desk. I'll answer my message after lunch. I also need you to phone a doctor for me. He's at Corona. His name is Lira, first name John, I believe--yes that's it. John ... John D. Lira . Tell him who I am--and I want him to take care of a police detective friend of mine, Spike Lauer. He'll know whom you're talking about. Tell the good doctor I don't care what it costs. Money is not an issue. I want my friend to walk again. Also tell Dr. Lira not to let Spike know that I'm flipping the bill. I don't care what he tells him, but not to use my name. Got it?"

"Yes, Mr. Mason. Is there anything else?"

"Yeah, tons, I'm afraid. But most of it can wait until this afternoon. I do, however, need you to book me on a flight to France tonight, if possible; if not, then first thing in the morning. Call Franco in Paris and have him make reservations for me at my usual hotel. I'll need him to meet me at the airport; give him the time and flight number. Also tell Franco a man by the name of Clint Chamberlain is in France. Find out what hotel he is staying at for me. I'll need all the information he can track down on a man by the name of Ethan Sommers, and his activities there. Have him call Robert Barnet with the F.B.I. and get a few names of the local Feds that will be able to assist us while we're in France. Put a tail on Chamberlain. Stay close, but don't get spotted. I don't want him to know he's being followed. Also, tell Franco to search Chamberlain's room. I want to know if he's hiding anything, and whom he's been shacking with, if anyone, and put a tail on her, too. Lastly, tell Franco I'll need all the current info the local authorities have on The Red Devil.

He pulled a cigarette out of his shirt pocket and lit it.

"The *what*, Mr. Mason?"

"The Chinese Mafia, Tess."

"Is that all, sir?"

"Call Holly and tell her I'll need her to go to my house and pack a suit case for me. Tell her not to forget my passport and Visa. I'll also need her to drive me to the airport and I want her to stay at my place and take care of Talula until I get back. She knows the routine. Give her the flight info so she can check my bags in ahead of time. That should cover it, Tess. I'm going to make a quick stop to see Spike at Dillard's and then I have to run home and change. I'll meet detective Baldwin for lunch at *Caproni's*. I'll be in after that.

"Yes, Mr. Mason. Goodbye."

"Bye, Tess."

Charles lit another cigarette and inhaled deeply, as he glanced into his rear view mirror. He spotted a black sedan three cars back that looked like the same sedan that was following Clint Chamberlain and Nouri the night he had met her for dinner at *Pompilliao's*.

He deliberately took the next exit ramp off the freeway to see if the sedan would follow. It did. "Swell," he mumbled after realizing he was being tailed. He reached for his cell phone.

"Hi Tess. It's me again. I'm on my way to Dillards. Have Joshua Wynn jump in the van and get the license number of the black sedan that is following me. I believe it's the same sedan from the other night. I'll go as slow as I can to Dillards, so tell Joshua to hurry. Have him buzz me when he gets the number."

"He's on his way, sir."

"Good."

Charles shut off his cell phone. *'Damn. I hope Nouri is all right',* he thought, quickly dialing her number. A brief silence crossed his ear as Mai Li went to get Nouri. An instant later she answered the phone with a cheery, "hi big guy." She released a contented sigh and smiled at hearing his voice.

"Hi sugar. I just called to say I miss you."

"How sweet Charles. I miss you too." She smiled, again.

"Are you all right, sugar?"

"Besides being worn out, you mean," she teased.

"A tiredness well worth it, sugar." He smiled blissfully.

"Oh, yeah. You got that right! Are you going to spend the night again, big guy?" She crossed her fingers hopefully.

"I'm not sure, sugar. I might be leaving for France tonight. I'll have to phone you later and let you know. Nouri, you know I want to spend the night don't you?" He sighed.

"So you say," she teased again.

"Nouri."

"Oh, all right. Yes I do know. I wish you could, too. You were wonderful last night Charles, thank you. I really needed to be held. Lately I've felt so lonely. So neglected and so confused." She took a sip of her Screw Driver.

"I know, sugar. How about you stay at my place while I'm gone? It would make me feel a lot better…"

"Oh yeah, like that's going to happen. I'm sure your wife would just love that!"

"My wife... Oh...Umm... Nouri, there's something I need..."

Suddenly his other line beeped. "Sugar that's my other line, I gotta run. I'll call you later. Hey, behave yourself. I love you."

He quickly changed lines. "Yeah."

"It's me, Joshua. We got the tags. Want us to trace it?"

"No. Just give it to me. I'm meeting Gabe Baldwin for lunch. I'll have him do it. He can get the address a lot faster. Thanks... What's the number? Boston tags... DAR 124 okay, got it!. Yeah, that's the same sedan that was following Clint Chamberlain and Nouri Sommers Wednesday night, probably her husband spying on her. Thanks Joshua, see ya later."

Charles made a quick stop by to see his friend Spike Lauer at Dillards and then ran home to shower and change.

As he pulled his Mazaradi into the garage and parked it snuggly between his Jaguar and his Mercedes, he noticed his frisky feline, Talula, catnapping on the cushioned seat of his Harley that was parked between his Caddy and his prized antique Model T. Ford convertible.

After getting out of his car, he walked over to pick up his loyal feline, talking to her as though she could understand every word that he was saying.

"Come to daddy, Talula. I've missed you. How's my pretty lady today? Hungry? I bet you thought I had forgotten all about you, huh? Sorry Talula, but I was busy cheating on you with the beautiful Nouri St. Charles Sommers. I hope you aren't too angry with me." He kissed her fur, gently carrying her into the house.

After letting himself into his house via the garage entrance, he sat his cat down on the floor, turned on his answering machine, made himself a bourbon and water, and glanced through his mail.

Carrying his drink to the kitchen, he fed Talula and pulled out his wallet, pulling out ten crisp one hundred dollar bills. He laid them on the breakfast counter with a scribbled note to Holly, asking her to pick up some more cat food and to restock the kitchen and bar for him. He then went back to the bar and poured himself another bourbon and water to take upstairs.

As Charles reached the top of the staircase, he heard the shower running. He instinctively reached inside his jacket and pulled out his revolver.

Cautiously he entered the bathroom, quickly putting his revolver back into its holster when he recognized the shapely-silhouetted form showering in the tub.

Suddenly remembering his scheduled date with the ever so lovely Kimberly Michelle, top model for *Play House Magazine*, he cringed. She once displayed a terrible temper after Charles stood her up before. He quietly walked back into the bedroom, debating with himself on whether he should face her like a man, or run like a coward. Being much too tired and drained, after making love to Nouri all night, he decided to stay and face the music, as well as ask for his house key back. Their breakup was long overdue.

He walked over to the bed, picking up the drink he had set down on the nightstand after entering the room, and propped himself upon the bed, as though he was preparing himself for battle.

Much to his surprise, the Super Model was not angry. She had heard him enter the bedroom earlier. Walking over to him with a towel wrapped around her shapely body, she seductively smiled. Taking his drink from his hand, Kimberly took a sip before speaking, not taking her eyes off of his.

"Why didn't you join me Charles? I heard you come in. I was hoping you might be in the mood for a shower."

Her eyes lustfully traveled the length of his very masculine frame.

Caught off guard, he swallowed hard and reached out to retrieve his bourbon and water from the lovely woman standing in front of him.

"Listen Kimberly. I'm sorry. I just thought you might still be angry with me for standing you up last night. It wasn't intentional, I can assure you." He attempted a smile.

"So you stayed out all night long to do what?" She shot him a hurt look.

"Listen Kimberly, I really don't have time for this. I'm sorry. I have to be somewhere in an hour so, I have to shower and change."

"So. I'll shower with you," her tone determined.

"No, I'm afraid not. You're going to have to leave. I'm sorry."

"What is it, Charles? You're trying very hard not to tell me something." She smiled faintly.

"I don't have the time to explain. I'm sorry." He glanced at his watch nervously and walked away from her and into the bathroom thinking to himself: '*Charles Mason, you're a coward! Tell her you're in love with someone else. Ask for the key and be done with it'!*

Determined to have her way with him, she dropped her towel, and went into the bathroom, and slid the glass shower door open and stepped inside.

Having soap in his eyes and shampoo in his hair with the water running full force, he didn't know Kimberly was behind him.

She lathered her hands and reached around his stomach, rubbing the soap across his manhood.

"I want you to make love to me, Charles," she whispered insistently.

"Kimberly, please stop," he whispered. "I don't want to hurt you."

"Please Charles, I've been waiting all night long for this," she pleaded.

"Kimberly, I'm not going to make love to you. It's just not going to happen right now."

"There's someone else, isn't there?" Her voice cracked.

"Kimberly, please. The shower isn't the place we should be discussing this." He swallowed nervously.

"Answer me, damn it!" she demanded.

Charles gently lifted her right hand and kissed the palm of it. "Please Kimberly, you're trying to force me to do something I don't want to do."

"What? Make love to me?" She jerked her hand away from him.

"No. You're trying to make me tell you what it is that I have to say to you, like this. Please, just let me take my shower, and we'll talk later." He leveled his water soaked eyes to her beautiful emerald green ones.

"There is someone else! Isn't there?" She slammed her back against the wall of the shower in a pouting manner.

Charles stubbornly rinsed his body and shut the water valve off, stepping out of the tub as fast as he could. '*I guess I'll use my electric razor in the car*', he thought to himself, opening the bathroom door and walking into the bedroom.

"Goddamn it, Charles! Talk to me!" she shouted to him, still standing in the shower.

Ignoring her demands, he walked to his large walk-in closet and selected a charcoal gray suit, a crisp white shirt and a pale blue tie (with specs of charcoal) to wear.

Next, he went to his shoe rack and selected an Italian pair of loafers. As he turned around, he didn't notice the

Super Model standing so close behind him; he almost knocked her over.

"Oh, God! I'm sorry, Kimberly. Are you all right?" he asked noticing a tear fall from her eye. Feeling sorry for her, he pulled her into his arms. "Please, don't do this. Not now."

I love you, Charles," she cried.

"Kimberly, stop it!" he responded in a hoarse whisper. He went on.

"You knew going into our relationship that I refuse to…"

She quickly interrupted, "I know Charles, you're right. But I just can't seem to help myself when it comes to you."

Charles swallowed hard and shook his head, hopelessly. "I'm trying very hard here not to hurt you anymore than I already have. Listen, Kimberly, you're going to have to leave. I need to shave and get dressed. You're going to make me late." He stepped back and turned away from her.

"Fine, Charles. I'll leave, but I won't be back! I'll leave your goddamn key on the bar when I go!" she snapped angrily.

She stormed over to the dresser and grabbed her clothing, bent over to retrieve her high heels and huffed out of the bedroom, slamming the door behind her.

"Swell," he mumbled shaking his head in aggravation, as he released a deep sigh. "Well, that went well," he muttered darting back into the bathroom to shave.

He quickly dressed and ran down stairs glancing at his watch, glad he still had enough time for another bourbon and water to calm his emotions.

After fixing another drink, he picked up the spare key off of the bar and studied it thoughtfully. He shook his head in dismay, when he suddenly realized that Kimberly had left him *her* house key- not his. *Intentional? Who knows*? He shrugged his shoulders walking back into the kitchen to add a small message to Holly, asking her to change the locks on the front door, the garage door, and to also change the security code-- Holly would know why-- she'd had to do it many times in the past! He laughed at himself.

'*Women! Go figure. You explain right up from you're not interested in marriage, or exclusive relationships; And after a few dates they think they own ya*', Charles thought to himself, as he walked back into the living room. "Swell."

"Here kitty-kitty... Talula, come to daddy. Come kiss me goodbye."

The furry feline came running into the living room, purring loudly.

"Now you be a good girl while I'm away. Holly will be staying with you again. Bye, pretty lady," he said to his fluffy white, emerald-green eyed cat, as he made his way down to the garage.

Remembering he had forgotten to fill the gas tank of his Mazaradi, he quickly jumped inside his forest-green Mercedes.

As he was pulling out of the driveway, he spotted the mystery sedan parked a short distance down the road, obviously still under the watchful eye of Nouri's elusive husband.

Charles jumped onto the freeway and headed into the direction of *Caproni's Restaurant* to meet his friend and ex-partner in crime fighting, Detective Gabe Baldwin.

Chapter 17

"Hello, this is Renea Chandlier. I need to speak to Ethan Sommers. He's expecting my call, thank you," she said nervously, hoping the high-powered-attorney wouldn't wake up and catch her talking to her boss.

"Yeah, it's me. It's about goddamn time you called. What the hell took so long?" he snapped sharply.

"I'm sorry, Mr. Sommers. It's the first time..."

"Yeah, yeah. Forget the chit, chat. How's it going?" he cut in rudely.

"Great! Everything is going exactly like you said it would. It appears that you know Mr. Chamberlain better than he knows himself."

"And he doesn't suspect anything?"

"I don't think so," Renea replied, shaking her head.

"I'm not paying you to think, Renea. That's my fucking job. Now you're sure Clint doesn't suspect anything!"

"Yes sir. Clint doesn't suspect a thing."

"Good. Let's keep it that way," he barked coolly.

"Yes, sir." Renea swallowed nervously.

"Are you getting everything on tape, Renea?"

"Yes Mr. Sommers, starting at the airport."

"Good. When are you going to fax everything to me?" he asked excitedly.

"The report will be faxed to you today. The courier will drop off the tapes, recordings and photos in a few days or so. We don't have a lot on him yet."

"No. I want to see the tapes today. You have been fucking him, haven't you?"

"That's what you're paying me for, isn't it, sir?"

"Don't get smart with me, bitch! Just answer the goddamn question."

"Yes, but he hasn't been going out of his room much. He's terribly upset. Stays pretty drunk over Nouri," she sighed.

"How the fuck am I going to hurt my wife without them? I wanted to send her the first sex scene between you and Clint today, damn it!"

"I'm sorry, sir. All he wants to do since she overheard me sweet-talking him on the telephone last night is stay drunk." She shrugged.

"All right, Renea. I'll wait a few more days for the tapes, but I need them."

"He seems to be really obsessed with her."

"Well, of course he is Renea, you idiot! The man is in love with her. Why the hell do you think I married Nouri? I wanted to hurt him, or have you forgotten that!"

"Sorry sir. I'll try to get him out of the room today." She shook her head.

"Good. Let me know so I can send in the surveillance team to get the tapes. Got it?

"Yes, I will, Mr. Sommers."

"Now, about my wife. What's she been up to?"

"I put a surveillance team on her last Tuesday, remember, sir?"

"That's right, you did. Has she been seeing anyone other than Clint?"

"I don't think so, sir. But then I haven't called Boston in a few days. I'll call this afternoon if I get a chance."

"Wrong answer, Renea. Make the time, understand!"

"All right, but it's hard for me to find the time to do anything but baby sit Clint Chamberlain. He's really emotional over your wife... Oh, wait a minute. I've just remembered something."

"What Renea?" The billionaire asked with growing interest.

"Late last night Clint got out of bed. He thought I was still sleeping. I listened in on a conversation he was having with someone. I think the man's name was Charles Mason. Anyway, I think Mason may have spent the night with your wife in the mansion."

"Bloody Hell!" Ethan exclaimed excitedly.

"It's true. Clint was phoning Nouri and a man answered, said he was making love to the woman he has always been in love with, which of course, is your wife, sir. From what I gather, he was her first real man!" She laughed.

"Get the fuck out of here!" Ethan chuckled.

"That's what Clint said. Anyway, he's very jealous of this Mason character."

"Honey, Chamberlain is jealous of anyone that even looks at Nouri. He gets all crazy over it! Worse than me if you can imagine."

"No, I couldn't possibly," she responded, rolling her eyes in disgust.

"So my wife is turning into quite a little slut, huh?"

"I don't know, sir."

"Umm. Maybe I might enjoy fucking miss goody-goody again after all. Here I always thought she was so goddamn prim and proper. Bloody Hell! I don't know, maybe she'd like to join you and me in the sack sometime. I'd love to fuck that little virgin rear of hers- something I've always dreamed of doing but never had the balls to try with her. Think she might enjoy something like that, Renea?" He chuckled, again.

"I'm sure I wouldn't know, sir." Renea frowned.

"Speaking of sex, Renea- all this sex talk has got me all worked up. I want you to forget Clint Chamberlain for a little while, and bring that tight little rear of yours over here. I need some release."

"Oh, I'm sorry, Bonnie..." Renea cut in. "It completely slipped my mind. I was in such a hurry yesterday afternoon. A friend of mine had just arrived from Boston and I was anxious to meet him for dinner. You do understand don't you?"

"Bloody Hell! The prick just walked into the room, right?" Ethan asked with a frown.

"That's right." Renea answered in response.

"Okay, call me later," he said slamming down the phone.

"Bye, Bonnie." She smiled up to Clint.

"Hi. I hope I didn't wake you. I suddenly remembered a phone call I needed to make." She stood to her feet and walked over to where he was standing.

"I rolled over; you weren't in bed." He pulled her into his arms and kissed her." An odd expression crossed his face.

"You want to go back to bed?" She smiled.

"Yes, but I need a drink first." Clint released his hold on her and walked over to the bar.

"Want one, Renea?" He glanced at her.

"Sure, why not?" She walked to the bar and slid on a barstool.

He poured them both a drink and then turned to face her. "God, Renea, you're so beautiful." He closed his eyes and began to slowly run his hands across her large breasts. He sighed lustfully, but was still picturing Nouri in his mind.

He lowered his head to her stomach- kissing her- licking her- tasting her- she ran her fingers through his thick head of hair gently nudging his head lower, guiding him to the location between her curvy thighs- he eagerly slid his tongue inside her kissing her heatedly.

Moaning with desire, she opened her legs to him- he slowly slid two fingers inside her- she arched her back wanting more. "Please, baby," she begged breathlessly.

He didn't need to be asked twice.

"Come here, baby," he said hoarsely, pulling her to the carpet with him. He urgently mounted her, anxious for release.

Thrust after thrust, she met him begging for more. He excitedly pulled her legs up over his shoulders, allowing for even deeper penetration in a moment of passion.

"Oh, my God!" She gasped needingly, as he continued to slam into her savagely. Finally, when he couldn't hold back any longer, he pulsated his hot release deep inside her womb- drunkenly sobbing out Nouri's name.

Several silent moments later, Clint rolled off her hot sweaty body trembling violently, gasping for breath. "God, I hope I just didn't knock you up just then," he whispered hopelessly.

Still out of breath, she glanced at him. "Would that really be such a terrible thing?" she said in response- but after noticing the look of horror suddenly masked across his face, she quickly added, "only kidding." She turned her head to hide her hurt.

Clint jumped to his feet. "Good!" He snapped. "That's the last fucking thing in this world that I need right now. And you too, right?" He glanced down at her and noticed her hurt expression, but chose to ignore it.

Forcing herself to stay focused on her real mission, instead of how her heart was really feeling, she quickly pulled her emotions back under control.

"Oh yeah, Clint. That's the last thing in the world either one of us need." She faked a smile, forcing herself to her feet.

"Got any vodka left?" she asked fighting the urge to run into the bedroom and cry her heart out.

'God. I can't believe it! I'm actually falling in love with this jerk', she thought, when she suddenly heard Clint repeat himself to her.

"Renea… I was trying to apologize to you. I said I was sorry that I called you Nouri's name while we were making love." He released a sigh of frustration.

"Oh, no problem. I've been called worse." She shrugged and then downed her vodka, quickly reaching for the vodka bottle again helping herself to another.

"I think I'm going in to take a shower now," she said clearing the tears from her throat. She quickly left the room not even waiting for him to respond.

Clint knew that he had hurt Renea's feelings. He didn't mean to, but he was feeling so miserable about losing Nouri, and the thought of her sleeping with Charles Mason again was driving him over the edge. He couldn't seem to force himself to stay focused on anything else.

It wasn't like him not to use any protection during sex, but at that particular moment he didn't care. It was almost as if he was deliberately trying to hurt his drunken self. Aware of his mistake, he kept trying to push the thought of possibly getting Renea pregnant out of his mind, but the thought kept creeping back into his brain.

"God! What if I did get her pregnant? Nouri would die. I know she's mad at me right now, but surely she knows how much I love her-I always have been and I always will be- goddamn it! … And I know she loves me. Mason says he knows it too." He was still mumbling under his breath- to himself, when the telephone rang.

He forced himself up to answer the phone with a cranky, "Hello."

"Hello, ol' buddy of mine." The elusive billionaire said in a sarcastic tone.

Clint shook his head not believing the voice on the other end of the phone. "Ethan?" he said in a stunned tone, shaking his head in an attempt to pull himself together.

"Yeah. How's it going ol' buddy?" Ethan chuckled mischievously.

Clint swallowed nervously. "Where are you?"

"Closer than you think, my friend."

"I need to see you, Ethan. It's important."

"Yeah. I bet," Ethan responded sharply.

"Please, Ethan. I'm here in France looking for you."
Clint's tone was desperate.

"Tell me something that I don't know, Clint ol' pal."

"I need some answers," Clint said instantly.

"No shit!" Ethan spat heatedly.

"I'm serious!" Clint remarked sharply. "Did you kill
that young woman in your hotel room? Please, Ethan. I
have to know. It's important. What happened?" Clint asked
excitedly.

Ethan released a sigh. "I didn't mean to, that's the
truth! I was strung out bad...And after finding out that
Kirsten was fucking some other guy, I got pissed and
knocked her across the room. When she fell, her head hit
the corner of the coffee table. Blood started squirting all
over the place. I panicked and high-tailed my ass out of
Lambert." He released a sigh of regret. "Why? What's it to
you, Clint?"

"You didn't shoot Kirsten in the heart?" Clint asked
with surprise.

"No. I knocked her across the room! What are ya
deaf?" He snipped with annoyance.

"Something is fucked up here, Ethan. The young
woman in your room was shot right through the heart."

"Bloody Hell!" Ethan remarked with surprise.

"It's true." Clint said, paused and went on... "The
gun was lying beside her body. Cops think that Nouri may
have murdered her."

"What the hell are you talking about?" Ethan asked
with interest.

"They also found a hair brush or something that
belonged to Nouri lying beside the body."

"No shit!"

"That's not all, Ethan." Clint swallowed hard to force back his tears. "Becka was murdered, too. Did you have anything to do with it?" Clint stopped breathing for a moment as he waited for his former friend's response.

"Of course not! Why would I kill Becka? I liked fucking her too much!" The billionaire said questioningly.

"I don't know, Ethan. To punish me and Nouri maybe?"

"You mean frame you and her. Revenge?" Ethan chuckled.

Clint released a frustrated sigh. "Something, like that."

"I really don't think so, ol' buddy. That might have been amusing, though, watching you two sweating it out in court, maybe even getting the chair. Yeah, that would have been something to see, but not my style. I like more of a cat and mouse chase," he mused. "Know what I mean ol' pal? Naw..." He shook his head. "I have something else in mind for you, something more entertaining. I've been looking forward to hurting you for a very long time now. I'm going to make you suffer and suffer, and then suffer some more, my friend." He smiled wickedly.

"What?" Clint asked in dismay. "What have I ever done to you to warrant so much hate? And don't tell me it has anything to do with Nouri. After all, you stole her from me. Remember?"

The billionaire inhaled his joint deeply, coughed and then answered. "Naw. I just married her as a part of my plan to hurt you. The bitch is too moody for me, too prim and proper, a real pain in my ass." He shook his head. "But that aside, she still my property- at least until I choose to let her go. She's so goddamn beautiful--not to mention classy--good for my public image. Know what I mean? I can't see me letting her go anytime soon. She might turn *you* loose soon, however. I hear there's another rooster in the hen house." He chuckled. "Doesn't sound like she loves you too much anymore." The billionaire's tone was cold and bitter.

"Oh, you must be talking about Mason." Clint sighed in disbelief.

"Who?" Ethan asked as he tried hard not to laugh.

"Charles Mason, talk about a pain in the ass. He's looking for you, Ethan, and from what I hear about him, he always gets his man." Clint's tone was serious. "Ethan, if you didn't have anything to do with the two murders in Lambert, I suggest you let me take you back to Boston. I'll help you work it out. you won't stand a chance with Mason on your ass. Do you understand?"

"Sounds like you're part of Mason's fan club, ol' pal," Ethan said inhaling deeply.

"Hardly. I can't stand the prick. But I'd turn in the Pope himself, if it would clear Nouri of these two murder charges."

"So, you think by bringing me in over Kirsten's death, it would clear Nouri?"

"That's right ol' pal. Mason is out to take you down. And take my word for it, Ethan, he's the one man that can do it. That man is one impressive fucker! No wonder Nouri is so attracted to the bastard. He's one macho son-of –a- bitch." He shook his head. "He's the only man I've ever met that makes me jealous when it comes to Nouri."

"So you've lost her to him?" Ethan sneered.

"I hope not! You Ethan, I don't give a damn about. She belongs with me. You know it. I know it. And, so does she, but Mason, he's still in love with her. And now that I've fucked up with her again, I very well may have lost her to him. But as God is my witness, I won't give her up without a fight!" Clint shouted with passion.

"Love. It makes you sick doesn't it, ol' pal?" Ethan's laugh was cold and uncaring.

"You ought to try it sometime. You might become a nicer person."

"You think so, huh?" Ethan quickly downed his double shot of Russian Vodka. "So tell me something, Clint. If you're in love with Nouri as much as you say you are, how come she caught you dipping your weenie into someone else's bun?" He laughed.

"Because, Ethan, I'm a goddamn idiot!"

"Who are you kidding, Clint? You've always been a goddamn pussy hound!" Ethan's tone was cruel and sharp.

"Fair enough. In the past, maybe." Clint shrugged and went on. "But this time with Nouri, it was going to be different. I thought I had truly changed, but then Renea came along out of nowhere." He stopped talking to down his drink.

"Who?" A devilish grin grew across Ethan's face.

Renea Chandlier- Nouri's twin- can you fucking believe it! A goddamn Nouri Sommers look-a-like. I swear, goddamn spitting image of her!" Clint shook his head in disbelief and poured himself another drink.

"Bloody Hell, you say!" Ethan chuckled and lit another joint laced with cocaine.

"Too much temptation for any goddamn red-blooded man to refuse himself!" Clint shook his head again and closed his eyes tightly.

"If you can't be with the one you love, right?" Ethan laughed amused by it all.

"Something like that, I guess. Especially if the bitch happens to look exactly like the woman you're in love with! Where's the goddamn justice in it?" He downed another drink and reached for the scotch bottle again, not aware that Renea was standing in the doorway of the bedroom listening to every word.

"You, have to at least ask yourself what's the odds on something like this happening to you, hey ol' pal?" Ethan snickered, as he poured himself another drink.

"Yeah, well you're right, of course! But that's how it happened, Ethan. At first, I must admit, I thought that maybe, just maybe, you might have had some type of role in all of this. But then I realized that you're just not that clever, and anyway, how could you have possibly had the time to line all of this up with Renea, where could you have found a woman like her-- Nouri in almost every physical way?" Clint shook his head and sighed. "Well, that is, except the eye color. Oh yeah, and Renea's goddamn big tits. Jesus! They're magnificent! She brings out the animal in me." He stopped talking and belted his shot of scotch.

"Yeah, I see your point, Clint. That would have been some kind of master minding, I must admit." Ethan chuckled mischievously and then went on... "Plus, you would've had to consider how could I have possibly predicted each and every one of your moves. Oh yes, and there would have been a time schedule of sorts to consider; timing would've been everything in a scam of this nature, right? Yeah, you're right. I'm just not that clever." He laughed and inhaled his joint.

Clint chuckled in spite of his mood. "Yeah, Houdini himself couldn't have pulled a stunt like that off. That's why I dismissed the idea. However, I must admit after our conversation a couple nights ago and after hearing your confession about some of the tricks and stunts you have pulled on me for the past fifteen years, it wasn't easy for me to rule it out." He released a deep sigh.

"You know, Clint, as much as I hate you, I have to admit at times it wasn't easy for me to continue hating you. I actually miss some of our so-called bonding moments together. Like us being able to confide in each other; especially our talks, ya know what I mean, ol' pal?"

"Yes I do, Ethan- sort of like now. Here I come to France as a friend, to try and help you. Even after our fight over the phone Friday night, still, something inside me felt sorry for you--well at least the man I thought you to be. Sure, I've always known about your dark side, but I had no idea how deep that dark side really was." Clint shook his head sadly and sighed.

"I see what you mean, pretty fucking deep, huh?" Ethan chuckled.

"That, Ethan, is an understatement if I ever heard one!"

"Disappointed?" Ethan asked, reaching for his drink.

"Hurt would be more like it. I honestly thought we were friends all of these years." Clint reached for the scotch bottle.

"Well, we were- at least until you…Whoop! I almost let the cat out of the bag! You, my little mousy friend, aren't quite ready for…" He stopped talking to pour himself another drink.

"Goddamn it, Ethan! What the hell have I done to you? I've racked my brain trying to figure out what exactly it was that I have done that is so terrible, at least bad enough for you to harbor such hidden hatred for the past fifteen years. I just don't get it!" Clint's tone filled with hurt and betrayal.

"I told you, Clint. When I'm ready to explain it to you, I will. And, quite frankly, I'm just not ready. I haven't made you suffer enough, yet."

Clint shook his head in disbelief. "For fifteen years, you tell me you have been secretly plotting things…events…and God only knows what else… pulling the strings from behind the scene…all to entertain you, and I haven't suffered enough!" He shouted. "Ethan, you are truly one sick fuck!"

"Well, ol' pal- at least I'm good at it."

"More like master of it!" Clint snipped with an edge.

"True. But then again, I've never been one to toot my own horn," Ethan chuckled.

"Ethan, please. Tell me what it is that has made you hate me so. We can make it right. Then I'll take you back to the sanitarium, here in Paris. We'll get you better, again.

I'll get you away from Jin Tang and the Asian Mob, again, and we'll all just start over. What do you say?" He walked around the bar to open a fresh bottle of scotch.

Renea quickly backed inside the doorway so Clint wouldn't notice her.

"Sorry ol' pal. It's not that easy. Too much has been done. it can never be made right." Ethan sighed.

"Ethan, if you don't let me help you, you're going to die. Don't you understand? If the Fed's nail you over your illegal activities, and believe me they will, you'll spend the rest of your life behind bars. Same thing as being dead. Or the goddamn Chinese Mafia will get to you. But in all honesty, it will probably be the goddamn drugs you're hooked on again that's going to do you in! Can't you understand that, for Chrissakes!"

"Whoops! There you go, trying to act like my friend, again." Ethan chuckled.

"I suppose I'm trying my best to be a friend. Won't you let me help you?"

"I thought you said you were tired of cleaning up my messes!" Ethan remarked coolly.

Clint sighed. "I did. And I am. I want out. I'm getting out. But first, I want to set things right between you and me. And to do that…" He sighed. "I'm willing to clean up one last mess."

"Wow! That's pretty fucking generous of you, Clint. But, that my friend would take some doing. This time it's a pretty big fucking mess. Know what I mean?" Ethan chuckled again.

"Goddamn it, Ethan." Clint shook his head heatedly. "Every time you get involved with Steven Li, look what happens! Aren't you ever going to learn? I know he's your half-brother, but goddamn it, he hates you! Why can't you understand that?"

"That little prick has helped me make billions! How can you say that about him?" Ethan said sharply.

Clint shook his head hopelessly. "Because you idiot! He's the reason you're sleeping with the Chinese Mob, again."

"Well maybe so, but it's too late now. I can't get out. They pretty much own my ass now. Know what I mean?"

"Only too well." Clint shook his head heatedly. "You can turn. Work with the government on bringing them down. They'll protect you. Hell, would it be so terrible to do something right for a change?" The hot-tempered attorney shook his head, reaching for his drink.

"Are you nuts? Give up all my power? My billions? All that young pussy! Like that's going to happen! Sounds like all that goddamn salty-sea air is starting to affect your brain." Ethan barked, nervously lighting another joint. He inhaled deeply.

"Ethan, just listen to yourself, your brain is fried! All the alcohol, drugs and young pussy has made you insane. You need help! Let me help you. I'll call your shrink- she'll know what to do. What do you say? Can I call Ms. Shaffer?"

"Naw. Last time you put me there look at all the young ass I missed out on. Besides, when I got out I had nothing to look forward to. Everything was all cleaned up. It was boring. That's why I decided to help Lambert out of his financial crunch. Why should I let him have all the fun? All those young, virgin asses to himself." The perverted billionaire sighed lustfully.

"What the fuck are you talking about, Ethan?"

"Oh, that's right. You don't know. You thought I just gave Lambert the money as a loan, huh?"

"I don't understand."

"Business. Big business. That's what I'm talking about, Clint."

"I don't know, Ethan. When I blinked just then, I must have missed out on something. What the hell are you rambling about?"

"Young, tight virgins! That's what I'm talking about. The goddamn children of the world!

"So you're saying what exactly, Ethan? That you and Otto Lambert are running whorehouses now...with children? God, please tell me that's not what you're trying to tell me!" Clint cringed.

"Well. Why should I let Lambert have all the fun? He needed the money, and you know me- I love that young pussy- It seemed like the right thing to do at the time." Ethan sighed blissfully at the thought reaching for his drink.

"You're even sicker than I thought. Where in God's name are you and Lambert getting these kids from?"

"Where the hell do you think?"

"If I knew that, Ethan, why the hell would I be asking?"

"God, Clint! You're just no fun anymore, at all. So Clean- So Straight- So Goddamn ..."

"Where do you get the children, Ethan?" Clint asked in disgust.

"Schools, street corners, runaways, playgrounds, sockhops, gimmicks in the news papers. You name it!"

"I just can't believe what I'm hearing. Where are these children kept?" Clint asked with growing interest.

"Yeah, right, Mr. Clean. Like I'm going to tell you that!" The billionaire laughed wickedly.

"All right then, tell me who furnishes the kids to Otto Lambert?" Clint insisted.

"Like I'm going to tell you that, too, huh!" Ethan chuckled again.

"Why did you bother mentioning it to me at all then?" The high-powered-attorney snapped.

"To drive you crazy, of course. I know how righteous you've become these past few years. Like I said, ol' pal...no fun anymore!"

"Ethan, you have gone over the edge. You need help. Please let me help you."

"I don't think so, ol' pal. You know, Clint, you're sitting there in your hotel suite, sipping on a few drinks, fucking some bimbo that reminds you of my wife, and you're passing judgment on me. What gives you that right? Just who in the hell do you think you are?"

Clint swallowed hard and released a loud sigh. "You know something, Ethan? You're right. Now that I've lost Nouri to Charles Mason, my life isn't worth living anymore. I don't give a fuck about you or what you do. I don't give a rats-ass about anything, anymore. And as far as that goes, I just very well may have knocked up the sexy bitch that's in my bathroom, taking a shower right now. And I don't even give a shit about that. How's that grab your sick ass?" Clint downed another drink.

"Whoa! Back up slick! What did you just say? You of all people, Why, Clint Chamberlain, I can't believe what I just heard! Bloody hell, you say! You think you just got Nouri's look-alike with child? This is too good!" Ethan chuckled.

"Yeah, I think so. I was so goddamn upset over Nouri- half drunk- not thinking clearly or just plain not giving a shit. I honestly don't know which. Renea was so hot--wouldn't stop begging me for it this morning. I was on fire, way the hell beyond hot! The wild animal in me went crazy. I pulled her goddamn long legs up over my shoulders and slammed into her--couldn't help myself--It was almost like I was possessed. I slammed inside her body so hard and so deep, I could actually feel myself inside her womb pounding and pounding her goddamn brains out! Her screams of passion made me pound that much harder inside her. Best goddamn fuck I've ever had in my life! And like you, my friend, I've certainly had my fair share of ASS! And what do I do the second it's over? I treat the beautiful woman that just gave herself so completely to me like a piece of shit! You're right, Ethan. I'm no better than you. I'm worse than you. Look how many times I've hurt Nouri, the only woman I will ever love, and because of my own lack of self-control, I have probably just ruined another beautiful woman's life! I'm no one to be passing judgment on anyone!" A tear ran down his face, as he poured himself another drink and quickly downed it.

"Bloody Hell, ol' boy! If I didn't hate you so goddamn much, I would actually feel sorry for your sorry-ass right now. So, what are you going to do now?"

"Like, I really give a shit! I don't know. If Renea isn't on some type of birth control then I guess I'll blow my goddamn brains out!" Clint belted another shot of scotch.

"You can't do that ol' pal. Killing you is my job. I've looked forward to it for years. You can't rob me of my pleasure, now can you? Anyway, you don't own a gun." Ethan mused.

"Very funny, Ethan. Well, I guess I could take the billion dollars I've taken from you and just simply disappear into thin air."

"What the fuck are you talking about, Clint?" Ethan swallowed hard and nervously sat up straight, gripping his drink tightly.

"Your money, ol' pal." Clint remarked coolly.

"Ya know Clint. I have to give you a lot of credit on this one. Fifteen years of planning your next move, next adventure, next mistake--and after all the master minding and time I've put into hurting you, making you suffer, it seems as though I may have overlooked one small thing." The nervous billionaire shook his head in total disbelief.

Clint chuckled sarcastically. "Allow me, ol' pal. Your recent bid to take over The Medallian Corporation, right?"

"A billion dollars worth of over looking." Ethan replied hoarsely. "Clint, you clever son-of-a-bitch!"

"Next, you're going to tell me that I won't live long enough to spend it. Correct? Clint sighed reaching for the bottle of scotch again.

"Exactly! That money belongs to my Chinese connection." Ethan responded nervously.

"Like, I give a shit Ethan! I told you Friday night, I don't give a goddamn about dying. You can send your boys over here right this minute and blow my goddamn brains out. I just don't care! And now that I've lost Nouri, I care even less. I'll leave my goddamn door unlocked. Send them over!" Clint drunkenly snapped.

"All right, Clint. What do you want?" Ethan asked, as sweat beads slowly began to roll down his face.

Clint sighed. "There are five things I want. Give me those five things and I'll return your billon dollars to you," he said coolly.

"You drive a hard bargain, attorney man."

"I'm serious, Ethan. If you don't give me these five things, I'll burn every last dollar, and then I'll blow my own goddamn brains out. I've got nothing else to lose since I lost my reason for living. What's it going to be?"

"All right, I'll listen. What are your five demands?"

"Tomorrow, Charles Mason will be arriving in France. I want you to agree to talk to him. He's only trying to help Nouri. There is no way in hell I'm going to let her face those two murder charges. Agree to give Nouri a divorce. Ethan, she doesn't know what kind of animal you are, let her go; she deserves better. Next, I want to know why you hate me so. I want you to let me check you back into the sanitarium. And lastly, I want out! I don't want anything to do with you anymore." Clint sighed. pouring himself another drink.

"No can do, ol' pal. What you're asking is impossible."

"Well then, kiss you goddamn money goodbye. Go ahead and send your red brothers over."

While Clint had his back turned facing the bar, Renea softly tiptoed out of the door, quickly disappearing into the elevator.

"I tell you what, Clint. I'm going to give you a few days to reconsider. But just in case I should happen to change my mind on your grace period, I suggest you start watching your goddamn back. I'll be in touch."

The next sound that the high-powered-attorney heard was a loud click inside his ear. He stood to his feet and stretched, yawned, and then reached for his bottle of scotch. After retrieving the bottle, he walked toward the bedroom, calling out to Renea.

When she didn't answer, he walked into the bedroom- quickly realizing she was no longer there. "Damn it!" He muttered angrily at himself knowing that she had just disappeared out of his life forever. And even worse, she may now be carrying his child!

"Clinton Jerome Chamberlain, you are without a doubt one serious fucking idiot!" he scolded himself as he threw himself down on top of his bed, blankly staring at the ceiling.

Chapter 18

"Yo! Over here, Mason." The homicide detective said loudly, rising to his feet and motioning the private investigator over with a wave of his hand.

Charles Mason nodded quickly darting across the restaurant floor.

Gabe smiled at his friend, as he sat down in a chair across from him.

"Gabe." Charles returned the smile. "Good to see you. Thanks for finding the time to meet with me."

"My pleasure, Charles. How's the PI Business?"

"It pays the rent," Charles smiled, knowing he had the most successful PI Business in the country. So successful, in fact, that it had made him an extremely wealthy man, and then some!

The homicide detective laughed at his friend's modesty. "Yeah, right, Charles. I've heard it does a little better than that. Hell! You're a goddamn celebrity. I've seen your face plastered all over the goddamn place. I can't even pick up a newspaper or a magazine without your face being on it some goddamn place!" he mused.

"Swell," Charles said teasingly. "Oh, I do all right I suppose, but I still miss working at the station sometimes." He smiled.

"We miss you too," Gabe smiled as the memory.

"Yeah, we sure had some cases, didn't we?" Charles nodded.

"Remember the DA, Tonya Daughtery?" Gabe grinned wickedly.

"Oh shit! You could've gone all day without mentioning her name!" Charles playfully cringed.

"She became a bloody tyrant after you quit seeing her." Gabe shook his head teasingly.

"Gabe, my dear friend, Tonya Daughtery was a bloody tyrant *before* I stopped seeing her." Both men laughed at the memory of her heated temper.

Gabe leveled his eyes to his friend's. "You know Charles, the woman is still madly in love with you, don't you?" He grinned.

"Yeah, so I've been told. How come I always seem to have that affect on the women I'm not in love with?" Charles said in response, rolling his eyes playfully.

"That's always the way, isn't it?" Gabe nodded in agreement.

"Seems to be anyway." Charles briefly glanced around the dining room of the restaurant. An attractive blonde met his roving eye. She smiled. He blushed and glanced back at his friend.

"Last time you and I saw each other, you were still carrying a torch for that young broad you lived with. That was a long time ago. Still carrying that torch?" Gabe smiled. "Is that why you never married? God knows you have had your fair share of women and opportunities."

Charles smiled shrugging. "It's been exactly seven years...two months...and one week." He glanced down at his watch and added, "as of yesterday. As a matter of fact..." He smiled and went on..."I can't seem to help myself. I'm still hopelessly in love with her. I always will be, I'm afraid." He sighed.

"Ouch! That's some torch, my friend."

"Yeah, but a heat well worth the pain." The P.I. smiled. "What about you, Gabe?" He glanced at his friend. "Ever met a woman like that? I'm sure as many hearts as you have broken, being a half-Greek God and all, there must be at least one special gal that has touched you to the core, huh?" he smiled.

"I'll have another beer, please. And my friend will have...what are you drinking, Charles?"

"The same is fine."

"What were you asking me, Charles?"

"I was asking you if you had ever met a woman that was so special, she touched the very core of your being!" he laughed.

The police detective turned an amazing shade of red and nervously reached for his beer. "I don't think so, Charles. Do they really make women like that?" he teased, playfully scratching his head. He shot a quick glance at the attractive blond.

"You mean to tell me as many women as you have dated, that there hasn't been one of them that has taken your breath away just by looking at her?" The P.I. downed a half a glass of his beer.

Gabe slightly blushed when the beautiful face of Nouri Sommers surprisingly flashed inside his head. His hand slightly wavered as he reached for his beer. "Well, I never said that, exactly. As a matter of fact, there was one such creature just recently. She was the most beautiful woman I'd ever seen in my life." He sighed. "When our eyes met for the for time...I don't know...It felt almost like a bolt of lighting had shot right through my goddamn heart. I had never experienced a feeling quite like it before in my entire life." He shook his head. "Charles, it was so...well so...fucking weird, I couldn't believe it!" The detective chuckled at himself. "Damn I was embarrassed. I felt all..." He suddenly felt embarrassed and stop talking.

"Go on...tell me, Gabe. You 'felt all'...what?"

"Oh Charles, this is ridiculous." Gabe nervously drank his beer in one long swallow, turning red in the face again. "We'll have a couple more please," he said, waving his beer bottle at the waiter.

"Go on Gabe, please. I'm trying to make a point here. Bear with me," Charles smiled downing the rest of his beer.

"All right. I can't explain it really. I just melted. That's all. I felt as though my legs were going to buckle right out from under me. My heart felt as though it were going to sprout wings and zoom right out of my chest. It was like I was a teenage boy all over again, but with a bigger hard on!" he laughed. "I could actually feel my dick throbbing for this woman." He shook his head in amusement. "God! I was so fucking embarrassed I thought I was going to die. Once I came back to my senses and saw the expression plastered across poor young Ballard's face..." He laughed loudly, shaking his head in dismay at himself and his lack of self-control around Nouri Sommers.

"Who is Ballard?" Charles wiped a tear from his eyes from laughing so hard at his friend's colorful description of his sexy fantasy woman.

"The young detective I'm trying to break in. He thinks I'm some sort of God or something--I don't know-- It's really weird."

"Oh, you mean he's gay?"

"Fuck you, Mason. No, I mean he thinks I'm sort of goddamn legend or something. The kid is still growing pubic hair for crissakes. He just never pictured someone like myself turning to mush over some woman, that's all. I have a news flash for the kid--I never thought I'd see myself acting that way over some broad either." The detective chuckled again.

"I see your point. Now here is mine. Whether or not you ever see this woman again isn't important. What is important is that, for the rest of your life, even if it's just from time to time, you'll think about her--about her beautiful face- how she made your heart pound- how she took your breath away--how she made your dick throb...get the picture? That's how I feel about the lovely Ms. St. Charles. Every time I make love to another woman, it's really her that I'm making love to... well, at least until I open my eyes. That's when I come to my senses and run like hell. Especially once they start hinting about the '*M*' word, heaven forbid." Charles laughed.

"I understand that, I guess, but I'll never see this woman again, at least not the way I would have liked too. She's married. What's the point? I'm not a fantasy kind of guy. I don't need a woman inside my goddamn head. I need a hands-on kind of gal, one I can actually touch. And anyway, I've had my fill of married chicks. Too dangerous! I gave that shit up a long time ago.

"I'll bet you anything that you will not only see this beautiful fantasy woman of yours again, but in fact, you'll make love to her before it's over with. I know, Gabe. I also know that look on your face while you were telling me about her." He teased, knowing his friend's reputation as being quite the ladies man. And rightfully so. Gabe Baldwin was an incredibly sexy man- not to mention an extremely handsome one, as well.

"Charles, you know me too well. Truth is, I 'd give one of my kidneys to make love to her just one time. I'd gladly die a happy man," Gabe mused.

"Well, at least now you know how I feel about the woman of my dreams. Who knows what the future holds? I just very well may win her back someday. She is, I'm sure, getting to the age where she just might appreciate an overly sexed manly type such as myself. You know how it goes. The older they get the more sex-crazed they become." The private investigator teased.

"We can only hope," Gabe smiled as he ordered two more beers.

"You know Gabe, when I first started dating her, she was so young and inexperienced. I think she had only been with one guy before me- another college kid like herself. Remember our college days? Wham! Bam! Thank you, ma'am!" He chuckled at the thought. "She had told me that the poor kid barely knew where his zipper was. Well...I took my time with her...teaching her.... guiding her. God! She was so eager to learn. I taught her how wonderful it was to be a woman. But she was so young. She had a lot to learn about enjoying herself. She still hadn't learned to tell me what she wanted me to do to her. God, she was hot–blooded, even back then. I bet she'd be a remarkable lover today. And I would like to be the man with her ten years from now, just to see how much she has learned to enjoy herself."

"Damn Charles. You'd actually wait ten more years just to have sex with her again? Unbelievable! She must have been one hell of a lay!"

"It wasn't that, Gabe. She was only nineteen back then. She was only as good as I was teaching her to be. I wanted to take my time with her; she had a long way to go. Oh, don't get me wrong; she was extremely eager to please me. I'm talking about her learning to accept and truly enjoy receiving sex. Not just spreading her legs just to please me. I'm talking about the feelings and emotions in a woman that get better and better with age. That's what I'm talking about. Haven't you ever..."

"Damn Charles! What the hell have they been putting in your beer? You've got me so damn horny right now--talking about all this sex stuff, that I'm about ready to pull out my little black book and call it a day. What is it, Charles? Have you seen this woman of your dreams again?" Gabe asked suspiciously.

Charles chuckled. "I'm sorry, Gabe. I get started talking about her and remembering--I just can't help myself."

"Hey, forget it. I don't mind listening, but to be honest with you, I've been trying very hard lately to behave myself. You know what a hound dog I am. And all this talk about sex and beautiful woman is causing me a lot of stress here." He cleared his throat. "I can tell you right now, Charles, there's no way in hell I 'm going back to the office today. The way I feel right now, I just might go look up my fantasy woman and have my evil way with her." Gabe laughed teasingly.

"I know what you mean, my friend. I'm suddenly feeling a little warm myself. I may just have to call a phone number or two myself before I leave for France tonight," Charles mused. "Hell! I turned some down this morning, already. Maybe I should've nailed it instead of sending it away."

"The model I saw you with in the newspaper?"

"Yeah, Kimberly Michelle. Incredible body. Good in the sack, but trying to force me into a commitment. You know the routine. I had no choice. I sent her packing." Charles shrugged defensively.

"Yeah, I just cut one loose myself. Lisa Clayborne-Daughter of Walter and Winnie Clayborne- Society front pagers. Know whom I mean?" Gabe frowned and downed the rest of his beer, ordering two more.

"Oh, sure. The Baron! He has a beautiful daughter," Charles replied.

"Yeah, but too, needy--too, pushy--and too, much like her damn mother!" Gabe cringed playfully.

"Been there. Done that!" Charles laughed.

"Me too. Too many times I'm afraid. I wish my mother would stop trying to fix me up! I don't like that type of lifestyle! I left it behind me when I joined the force. My father and mother about died, remember?"

"Oh yeah! He disowned you for a while, didn't he?" Charles replied.

"He tried to for a long time, but blood being thicker than water and all--plus my mother hounding him to death--he finally got over it," Gabe laughed.

"Ya know Gabe, there has always been something that I've wanted to ask you. Do you mind?"

"No, of course not. What is it?"

"You are worth hundreds of millions of dollars. You're the only police detective that I've ever known that has his financial advisor call him religiously at the station.

Why do you do it? And why in God's name did you want to become a cop? I just don't get it."

"It's simple really." Gabe laughed. "At first, I probably wanted to be a cop to just piss off my father. But in all fairness, I was young and liked the thought of danger, I think." He shrugged.

"If danger was what you were looking for, you should have married one of those little prim and ever so proper socialites! That would be staring danger right in the face. The thought of that scares the hell out of me." Charles shook his head playfully.

"Yeah, me too." Gabe chuckled. "Too stuffy for my taste. I don't enjoy that type of life. Never did. Even as a child. My father swears that I belong to the mailman. I'd probably believe him except that I look exactly like him." He laughed.

"Yeah, but all that money, Gabe?"

"Well that amount is highly exaggerated, I can assure you. Anyway, it's my family's money, not mine. Money never did impress me. I enjoy letting most people assume that since I'm just a cop, I don't have any money and, anyway, I honestly don't have all that much." He smiled and downed the rest of his beer.

Charles shook his head in dismay. "Bullshit! I know for a fact, Gabe, That last year you were the sole benefactor of your Grandmother's Ten Million Dollar Estate, and you own shares of…"

The police detective quickly interrupted his friend. "All right already! So I have a few bucks--look who's calling who rich! I bet you're worth at least close to a billion dollars by now, true!"

"Maybe. Give or take. So why do we do what we do?" Charles shrugged.

"For the action…For the romance…For the danger…For the chance to give back a little, maybe?" He smiled and toasted his friend.

"I suppose a little of all the above. But now that we're knocking forty- don't you think that little cottage beside the bay is sounding better and better, Gabe?"

"Well, I must admit, I have given it a thought or two lately. I have actually considered it more than that. And you?"

"Only with the woman of my dreams."

"You are impossible, Charles! Give it up. She walked out on you seven years ago for crissakes! I was there. I remember the pain. It almost killed me to see you suffer so much. I hate her for what she has done to you. She damn near destroyed you!"

"Oh, but she didn't! See, I'm much better off now. I've achieved tremendous success. If she hadn't left me, I might not have made it. Instead of just getting by, barely paying the bills, look at all I have achieved. I have her to thank for it. She gave me a reason to throw my lazy ass into my work. Now I'm a successful workaholic with a fortune," he mused.

"Give me a goddamn break, Charles. I know it's been seven years since she broke your heart, but if she walked into this restaurant this very minute, I'd probably knock her right on her ass for all she put you through."

"I don't think so. You know I would never let something like that happen to her. Just as surely as you know you'd never hurt any woman, including her. Anyway, you wouldn't recognize her if she were standing right in front of you. You two never got around to meeting for some odd reason."

"Yeah, that's true enough. But still I'd at least give her a piece of my mind."

"That, my friend, I could live with," Charles laughed.

Charles and Gabe continued to go down memory lane while they ate lunch. After lunch they both ordered coffee and began to discuss the reason for their getting together.

"So tell me Charles, why did you insist on buying me lunch today, besides wanting to know what's going on with the Lambert murders, which you probably already know more about than I do, and of course, you wanted a file on Spike. That aside...I know you...there's something else, isn't there?" The detective smiled knowingly.

"You know me too well. All right, I confess. I need a favor."

"I know that tone, Charles. Who is it this time?" Gabe smiled.

"Nouri Sommers." Charles said in response.

Gabe almost spit out his coffee, glad his friend hadn't noticed.

"The billionaire's wife? I don't understand, Charles." He swallowed hard, trying to pull himself together. Just the sound of her name sent a surge of excitement through his entire body.

"She's a personal friend, Gabe."

"No shit!" Gabe exclaimed.

"I've known her for a long time."

"Tell me Charles, is she capable of two cold blooded murders?'

"No way in hell!" Charles shook his head. "She's innocent, Gabe. Nouri couldn't hurt a fly."

"All right. What about her husband?" The police detective asked with growing interest.

"I think so. Ethan Sommers is a very dangerous man. The Fed's already know about him. He's into a lot of shit. They've had his organization under their secret eye for quite awhile now. He's apparently in France. That's why I'm going there tonight--to track his ass down. We have a few leads on his high-powered-attorney and best friend, too. He's there supposedly trying to locate him."

" Becka Chamberlain's husband?'

"Yeah. F.B.I. doesn't believe he's involved with the Lambert murders. They think he's in France trying to track down his friend."

"This case keeps getting better and better." The homicide detective shook his head in disbelief.

"I'll put a file together for you this afternoon, and all that I have about Ethan Sommers, Clint Chamberlain, and the Lambert murders."

"Wow! You are an amazing man, Charles. You just cut my workload down to almost zip! Thanks, I owe you one," Gabe chuckled.

"I'm glad you said that, partner. I need you to personally look after Nouri Sommers while I'm gone. I'm worried about her safety. I don't know who's trying to frame her for the two murders in Lambert, but if it is her husband, he has enough money to buy anyone, for any purpose he chooses. He might want her dead. Even if he doesn't, I do know that someone is trying to hurt her. She received two mysterious phone calls--one last night and one this morning. It scared her half-to-death. She could very well be in danger-possibly the next person murdered. I can't let that happen. I don't trust anyone but you. I've got a bad feeling about this, Gabe. She's in danger--serious danger!"

"I'm going to send a surveillance team to the Sommers' Estate, and call Barnet for a wire tap on the mansion; condo; apartment; and office, as well, just to be on the safe side."

"Have you run this baby-sitting thing by the DA yet?"

"Are you nuts? Daughtery would have me for lunch! I thought I'd leave that up to you," Charles smiled wickedly.

"You'll get me the proof I need to clear Mrs. Sommers and Clint Chamberlain of the two murders?" Gabe raised his brow in a questioning manner.

"Yes. I'm working with the F.B.I. all the way on this one. They're already convinced of Nouri's innocence, as well as Clint Chamberlain's."

"What make you think that Daughtery will let me babysit Mrs. Sommers?"

"Show her everything I send to you. Tell her what the Fed's said. Explain the danger Nouri is in, and if that doesn't work, make up something. You'll figure it out, right?"

"I'll do my best," Gabe remarked nervously.

"Thanks. I knew I could count on you. You know Gabe, Nouri Sommers really is in danger. Watch her as well as your own back, okay?"

"I will, Charles. How will I get in touch with you?"

"I'll send over the phone number to where I'll be staying in France- as well as the local numbers you might need there. And of course I'll be getting in touch with you, too."

"Anything else?"

"Yeah. Run this license plate for me. Call me at my office later. I'll be there all afternoon. My flight doesn't leave until this evening."

Gabe's heart began to race madly, sending shivers up his spine. Why, just the thought of being that close to his fantasy woman was more than he could bear. He released a sigh of excitement.

"So, tell me Charles, how does Mrs. Sommers feel about me babysitting her?" he asked with his curiosity getting the better of him.

Charles shot him a questionable look. "Oh, she hates the idea."

The homicide detective's heart suddenly crashed heavily to the floor of the restaurant. He was taking his friend's remark personally, though he knew he had no right to.

"Oh, I didn't mean she hated the idea of *you* personally looking after her, Gabe. I just meant she didn't like the idea of *anyone* having to keep her under a watchful eye," Charles added after noticing the uncomfortable look on his ex-partner's face.

"Great," Gabe mumbled in response. "You mean to tell me you expect me to keep this woman under lock and key against her will!" He threw his hands up in the air.

"No. Of course not," Charles chuckled. "I have a feeling that the next time she gets another scary phone call from her mystery admirer, she'll be more than happy to invite you over." He chuckled again. "I've talked to this psycho. He's a real scary guy, not to mention determined!" Charles shook his head excitedly.

"Oh, so you were at the Sommers, mansion when this fruit cake called?" An unexpected streak of jealousy suddenly surged through Gabe's body, confusing him. He quickly caught himself and pulled his emotions back under control, praying his friend hadn't noticed the jealousy in his tone.

"Yes. She phoned me about the phone call the night before and asked me if I could stop out to see her. I was there this morning when the bastard called again. Hearing the fear in her voice after she answered the phone, I ran over and grabbed the receiver out of her hand."

Gabe was grateful that his friend hadn't noticed his jealous tone of voice, and responded this time with his emotions completely back in tack. "So, what did the mystery man have to say?"

Charles sighed deeply, as he glanced at his watch. "We have time for one more cup of coffee. Want a refill?"

Gabe nodded and Charles held his empty cup up to get the attention of the busy waiter. The waiter acknowledged Charles with a nod of his head.

"It wasn't so much what he said. It was his tone of voice--goddamn eerie. He sounded arrogant and sure.

Extremely domineering and articulate, probably well educated. He was very sure of himself and seemed quite used to getting his way. He told me to put Nouri back on the phone. When I asked him who he was and what the fuck he wanted, he laughed, as though he was amused by my anger. He remarked, 'Who I am is not important, but what I want is very important.' I was hot at that point. I cursed and threatened to rip his goddamn lungs out, and etc…and so forth. The fucker laughed again, but this time his laugh was evil…chilling… It gave me the goddamn creeps. He then went on to tell me to tell Nouri that he would be in touch. The next thing I heard was the loud click of the phone slamming in my ear." Charles sighed deeply, fumbling inside his pocket for a cigarette. He offered Gabe one and they both lit up.

"Yeah, he sounds like a real psycho, all right. Does Mrs. Sommers have any idea who it might be?"

"No," Charles shook his head.

"Wonder what the fuck he wants?"

"Who the hell knows? Could be her incredible body," Charles playfully teased.

"I can understand that. Whew! Who wouldn't?" Gabe fanned himself teasingly. They both laughed.

After their playful remarks, a tone of seriousness set in again.

"All joking aside, Gabe; She and her husband are worth billions of dollars. Could be the money. Perhaps someone wanting to frighten her for whatever their sick reasons." Charles shrugged unknowingly.

"Her husband?" Gabe leveled his eyes to Charles'.

"Could be. He's certainly capable of something like that."

"Was there anything unusual about the caller's dialect? Maybe an accent or something distinguishable?"

"To tell you the truth, Gabe, I was too pissed off to really pay attention…but now that you mention it, he did seem to be trying to camouflage it somewhat. I don't know, maybe I did pick up on something…Maybe Chinese. Not heavy Chinese, but definitely Asian, at least a touch of it, I think." A confused look crossed The P.I.'s face. "Could be something to do with the Chinese Mob. Her husband is somehow involved with them. It will all be in the file I send over."

Gabe released another deep sigh and shook his head. "Like I said, Charles, this case just keeps getting better and better."

"Yeah. I really hate having to go to France right now. There's so much going on around Nouri… I'm really worried about her." Charles sighed again.

"Don't worry, Charles, I'll take very good care of your friend."

"I know you will, Gabe. I appreciate that."

"Hey, what are friends for?" Gabe smiled. "Besides, I owe ya one, remember?"

"Yeah, you do. Don't ya?" And you know what, Gabe…after this is all over…" Charles smiled teasingly, "you'll still owe me."

They both laughed again, then Gabe glanced down at his watch.

"Listen Charles, I have to go and I know you do, too. But first tell me. Should I just stop by the Sommers' Mansion, or give Mrs. Sommers a call? Have her picked up? What would be best?" Gabe asked nervously, as he tapped on his watch.

"No." Charles said shaking his head. "I'll just tell her to call you personally if her mystery caller phones back. In the mean time, I think she'll be safe enough with the surveillance team looking after her. And don't forget Barnet will tap into her phones."

"How long are you going to be gone?"

"Hard to say. Maybe a week or two, could be less, could be longer. I'm just not sure." Charles shook his head.

"Anything else I should know before you leave?"

"I don't think so. But if I should think of anything, I'll give you a ring. Oh, by the way, Gabe, I'll assign a few men to look into Spike's shooting while I'm gone. When I get back, I'll take it back over myself. I appreciate the file you put together for me." Charles shook his head sadly. "It's a shame what happened to Spike. He's a good man with a nice family. What's he got now, four...maybe five kids?"

"No. Six. Cool Breeze gave him a set of bookends after you left- boys. I think they're about four or five years old, by now." Gabe smiled fondly.

"Damn! I want the shooter. I want him real bad! Robbing the kids of their dad like that. Any ideas off the top of your head whom it might have been that nailed him?"

"Hard to say, Charles. Like any cop that's put a lot of scum away, he's got his fair share of enemies, but at the time of the shooting, he was working undercover." Gabe lit another cigarette.

"What was he working on?"

"The Papas brothers."

"Lou and Marko out of Miami?"

"Yeah. They took over the Westside about a year ago...a real pain in our ass since they moved here." Gabe exhaled a puff of smoke from his cigarette. "They get my vote."

"Swell! Another crime family. Just what our city needs."

"It's a bitch, isn't it? Hey, listen Charles. I offered to pay for Spike's surgeries, but he's too damn proud. He wouldn't hear of it. I want to help, but I don't know how. Got any ideas?"

"I've all ready taken care of it. I had Tess call Doctor Lira over at Corona and set it up. I told her to tell him not to mention my name, but to think of something. I'm sure the doctor will know how to handle it," Charles smiled.

"That was really nice of you, Charles. Thanks. What ever it costs, I got half."

"That's not necessary, Gabe."

"No. I insist."

"Swell." Charles mumbled teasingly.

"But you are getting lunch, right?" Gabe teased.

"Unless you want to flip for it." Charles chuckled, standing up. .

Gabe rose to his feet, pulling out his wallet, tossing a ten dollar bill down on the table for the tip.

Charles glanced over at him, shaking his head amusingly. "Swell," he mused walking to the front of the restaurant to pay the tab.

After saying their good-byes, both Charles and Gabe headed back to their offices, with a full day's work still facing them.

Chapter 19

Nouri walked over to her secret hiding place to retrieve the silver jeweled box that housed her most intimate thoughts of passion. After unlocking the jeweled box, she pulled out her latest unfinished journal entry. She smiled and clutched it tightly to her breast as though it were an old friend.

She glanced at the clock on her nightstand. *'Too early for a hot bubble bath and some Asti'*, she thought. But, yet, she still felt the need to do something to take her mind off of things for a while. She released a sigh of frustration and made herself comfortable on the bed.

With her pen and journal in one hand and her vodka and orange juice in another, she made a clumsy attempt to open her journal with one hand, splashing the drink on her expensive silk blouse. "Damn!" She mumbled under her breath, setting the drink on top of her nightstand in front of the antique clock.

She began to read:

"Out of nowhere he came. Just simply BANG, he was there. Standing directly in front of me. His shirt slung over his shoulder. The scorching sun beating down on his perfectly contoured body. He raised his muscular arm in an attempt to blot the perspiration that was beginning to trickle down his beautiful, but manly face. His mocha-brown eyes gazed into mine. So mysterious. So seductive. So mesmerizing. I felt passionately drawn to him. He smiled faintly. His smile lit a flame inside me. My heart was under siege...

"Humm." She sighed softly. "Not bad, but I think I'll change the color of his eyes to...let me see... Ahh...oh yes! I've got it! Teal- blue. Perfect. Now let me read it.

"His teal blue eyes gazed into mine. So mysterious. So seductive. So mesmerizing. I felt passionately drawn to

him. He smiled faintly. His smile lit a flame inside me. My heart was under siege...

"Oh, yes. That's much better...now, let me think... Oh, I've got it!" She eagerly continued to write:

"Suddenly from out of nowhere, a large black cloud appeared, threatening to create a downpour at any moment. 'Oh my!' I said, afraid I would be stranded in the desert with a car that wouldn't start. The sexy stranger removed the shirt from his shoulder, handing it to me. 'Hold this. Maybe I can help,' he said seductively, gazing into my eyes. He raised the hood of my car. Just as he did, the wind began to blow savagely, snatching his shirt from my hands. 'Oh, my!' I said, glancing at his face for a reaction. "Quick! Jump inside the car before you get soaked!' He shouted, as he continued to tug at the cables under the hood of my car. The rain began to fall fast and furious. He walked to the side of the car and knocked on the window, waiting for me to roll it down. He looked so beautiful standing there with the rain beating down on his beautiful long lashes. He looked at me longingly through his water soaked eyes. 'I need a rag or something. The wires are wet.' he said, not taking his gaze from mine. I quickly glanced around inside my car, to no avail. 'Oh, dear.' I said, wondering what I should do. He licked his lips sensually, not realizing the affect his closeness was having on me, as he continued to lean against the side of the car looking at me. 'Would these do?' I said softly, slowly sliding my panties down past my hips. 'Oh, yeah.' He whispered seductively in response, accepting the white cotton panties from my trembling hands. His eyes gazed into to mine for what seemed like an eternity. Finally, he swallowed hard and blotted the rain from his face with my panties. Lifting his head, he smiled, after noticing my skirt was still pushed up to my thighs. Without speaking, he opened the door and slid inside. A few raindrops had splashed against my throat and down the cleavage of my

blouse. I could feel the drops of rain slowly begin to sizzle against my scorching hot flesh. I released an unconscious sigh. He smiled knowingly, as he gazed into my eyes, gently pushing me back against the passenger side of the door. I was spellbound, unable to move. I inhaled deeply, watching as his eyes traveled slowly to my lips...my throat...my shoulders...and finally, resting on my heaving breasts. I felt his gaze burn into my flesh, as he watched my breasts rise and suddenly fall again, through my sheer, silk blouse. I could feel the reckless lust slowly surge throughout my body, as he gently lifted my hand and began to kiss my fingers one at a time- slowing inserting them into his mouth, sucking on one and then the other gently. I released a sigh and swallowed hard. He smiled knowingly, moving closer and suddenly leaned over to kiss me. I could barley feel his lips brush across mine. I moaned softly. He smiled, moving his kisses to my neck...down to my cleavage and then back up to my lips. 'Do you want me to make love to you?' he whispered wantonly with his hot breath across my lips. Unable to speak, I nodded, reaching for his hand, placing it on my breast. He smiled and began to slowly unbutton my silk blouse. I was so light-headed at that point, I felt I was going to faint. His touch was so..."

Suddenly, the bedroom door opened.

"Excuse please. You not answer my knock. You okay, miss?" The tiny Asian woman smiled with a concerned look on her face.

"I'm sorry, Mai Li. I was writing in my journal. I must have gotten carried away. I didn't hear you. What is it?"

"Telephone call, miss."

"Who is it?"

"I not know. He wouldn't say. I think it's the same man from yesterday. You want me to phone handsome detective?" Mai Li smiled nervously.

"Damn!" Nouri paused, shaking her head. "No, Mai Li. Just hang up the phone. I think it's just someone goofing off. I've got too much on my mind right now to worry about this mystery caller. Just ignore it. If we ignore him, maybe he will get bored and go away."

"Are you sure, miss?"

'Yes. Mai Li. Listen, have Fredrick bring my Corvette around. I feel like taking a drive, okay?" she smiled.

"Maybe Fredrick go, too. Maybe not good idea to go out alone right now." Mai Li shook her head in objection.

"Oh, Mai Li, you're such a wonderful and caring person. But please don't worry about me. I'll be fine, I promise. I just need to get out for a while. I'll be home by dinner. I'll phone if I'm running late, okay?" she smiled, with an insistent expression on her face.

Nouri quickly changed clothing and was out of the house in no time. Driving was one of her favorite things to do when she was upset, feeling blue, or just plain bored. Today it was probably a combination of emotions.

She enjoyed the way the wind ripped through her thick head of hair while driving with the top down. With her favorite radio station blasting in her ears, and the wind ripping through her hair, it didn't take long for her to forget all about her problems.

Heading nowhere in particular, she put the pedal to the metal, and began to sing along with the radio.

"Oh, God! I love this song!" She squealed excitedly and quickly began to sing:

"Ah, ah, ah, ah- Staying Alive! Staying Alive! Ah, ah, ah, ah- Staying Alive…God! I haven't heard that one in ages." She sighed. "John Travolta, What A Hunk! God, talk about a girl's fantasy guy! Fabio hasn't got a thing on you, LOVE!" She giggled mischievously.

"God! I just love this oldie but goodie channel. I was born too late. I would've loved to have been around back

then instead of being just a twinkle in my daddy's eye!"
She giggled, not realizing just how tipsy she had become
from drinking all morning, as well as, most of the early
afternoon.

"Mary Mack, all dressed in black...bum-bum-bum.
With silver buttons all down her back... bum-bum-bum-
bum. I know tippy-toe. She broke her needle, now she can't
sew- walking the dog - just walking the dog - well if you
don't know how to do it, I'll show ya how to...walk the
dog- do-do-do-do, bum-bum-bum-bum. I ask my daddy for
fifteen cents- bum-bum-bum-bum. To see the elephants
jump the fence. They jumped so high, they touched the sky
and they never got back until the Fourth of July... Walking
the dog, just walking the dog...well if you don't know how
to do it- I'll show you how to walk the dog... Here fido,
come to your mama, baby- bum-bum-bum-bum.

She was so lost in her singing, actually enjoying
herself, problem free from her current situation, that she
didn't hear the police siren closing in behind her.

Not aware that she was speeding near a hundred
miles per hour on the freeway, she continued to zoom
closer and closer to town. Suddenly, with one police car
pulling directly in front of her, one to the side of her, and
one on her bumper, she was jolted back to reality.

"Oh my God!" she squealed, finally pulling her shiny
candy-apple red Corvette convertible over to the side of the
freeway.

Six police officers quickly surrounded her car.

"Oh, my goodness!" she gasped when she saw the
stern expressions on all of their cute faces.

"Would you please step out of the car, ma'am?"
asked the nearest officer.

She blinked, still stunned by it all.

"Why officer? What have I've done?" she asked,
slightly slurring her words.

"I need you to get out of the car ma'am." The cop's tone reminded her of her father, except the police officer was a lot younger, not to mention a lot cuter.

"I don't understand. Why do you want me to get out of my car?" she repeated nervously, shaking her head and shifting in her seat.

"Have you been drinking, miss?" the officer asked, leveling his eyes to hers.

"I've had a few vodka and screwdrivers..." She snickered, quickly adding: "I mean vodka and oranges.... I mean, ah... ah... juice." she giggled.

All six of the officers smiled in amusement.

"I need to see your driver's license, ma'am." The young officer smiled and gazed into her beautiful hazel colored eyes.

"Whoops! I think I may have left my purse at home." she shrugged defensively.

"I'm sorry ma'am, but we'll have to take you to the station."

"For what? I didn't do anything For Crissakes! Why don't you go catch a bank robber of something?" Her faced flushed, as she continued to tightly clutch the wheel of her car with both hands.

"Ma'am, you've had too much to drink, I'm afraid. You'll have to come with me." He looked at her with an apologetic look on his face. He added, "I'm sorry, ma'am. I'm just doing my job."

"So, you're saying what? That you're going to arrest me?" Her eyes widened in disbelief.

"I'm afraid so, ma'am. I really have no other choice."

"Oh, my Lord! You can't do that. I don't want my face plastered all over the front pages of the newspapers tomorrow morning, for crissakes!"

"What's you name, ma'am?"

"I'd rather not say. If you don't mind." She cringed.

"I see. Well, you'll have to tell us sooner or later, ma'am. Why don't you tell us now, and make it easier on yourself?"

"I don't think so," she said smugly, still sitting in her car.

The police officer reached inside her car and turned off the keys, as well as the radio.

"I'm sorry, ma'am. You really are going to have to come with me to the station."

"You aren't going to have to put those ugly handcuffs on me, are you officer?" she smiled, causing the officer's heart to almost leap out of his chest. He swallowed hard.

"It's policy, ma'am." He smiled sympathetically again.

"Oh, dear! Can't we talk about this guys?" She smiled again, causing all six of the officers to break out in a cold sweat.

"Ma'am, are you aware that you were going a hundred miles per hour in a sixty-five mile per hour zone?" The young cop's tone was stern again.

"I... I didn't mean to, officer. I guess I just got carried away. See, I was singing along with the radio and I guess I must have forgotten what I was doing for a minute. That's all," she pouted.

"Ma'am. Do you know how dangerous that could have been? You might have been hurt--or worse. Maybe even hurt someone else. Do you understand?" He shot her a serious look.

"I'm sorry. I honestly am. I really don't drive all that often," she said, shaking her head. "I guess I just got carried away. You understand, don't you?"

"Yes, I do. But I still have to take you in, ma'am. I could lose my job if I didn't." He shrugged his shoulders apologetically.

"Can't I just have someone come and get me?" She swallowed hard, fighting back her tears.

"It doesn't work that way, ma'am. Sorry."

Nouri thought for a few moments. Suddenly Gabe Baldwin's handsome face flashed inside her brain.

"Not even if it's detective Gabe Baldwin?" she asked smiling hopefully.

Nouri overheard an officer in the back loudly whisper: "Oh, shit!" Curiosity surged through her.

"What is Detective Baldwin to you, ma'am?" The young officer asked nervously.

"Nothing really." She sighed. "But can I at least talk to him before you arrest me?"

He smiled. "This is highly unusual, ma'am." He paused, as he considered her request. "You'll still have to tell me what your name is, ma'am."

"All right. She bit her lower lip nervously. "It's... It's..." She swallowed hard. "My name is Nouri Sommers." She cringed, waiting for a response.

She overheard the same police officer in the back whisper the word 'shit' again. She smiled nervously.

"All right. Follow me. I'll call Detective Baldwin, ma'am." He smiled.

"Oh, officer. You can call him on my cell phone," she said smiling, while offering the phone to the officer.

All of the police officers looked at one another, shrugged their shoulders, and began to pace nervously back and forth.

The young officer nervously cleared his throat, and accepted the cell phone from her shaking hand.

"That might be best," he said regretting even pulling her over.

He quickly dialed the number and waited for a response. "Hi, Chaz... Is Gabe around? This is Hobner."

After a few moments of silence, Gabe shouted into the receiver. "Yo, Hobner. What do you need?"

"I… I…" he stuttered nervously.

"Well spit it out, Hobner. I haven't got all day." The homicide detective's tone was tense and preoccupied.

"I have a problem, sir." He sighed. "I pulled someone over for speeding- going a hundred in a sixty-five. Anyway, she's apparently had a bit too much to drink. I was going to bring her in, sir, but she insisted on talking to you first." The young officer swallowed hard.

"Hey, Hobner. So what are you wasting my time for? Do your job."

"Yeah, well don't you even want to know who it is? The young officer glanced at her sympathetically.

"Not really. It doesn't matter. Bring the goddamn broad in."

"I'm sorry, Mrs. Sommers. He doesn't…"

After recognizing the name, the detective screamed into the cell phone: "Wait a Goddamn minute, Hobner! Did you say Sommers?" Panic engulfed him.

"Yes sir. That's what I said."

"It fucking can't be!" he exclaimed, as he tried to think. "What does she look like, Hobner?"

"She's sitting right here, sir." he whispered, not wanting Nouri to overhear him.

"All right. Let me describe her to you then. Is she like fucking drop-dead gorgeous? Reddish-brown hair? The most incredible body you've ever seen? I'm talking perfection, Hobner." He swallowed hard, as his heart raced madly.

"Yes. That sounds about right, sir. What should I do, sir?" He blushed.

"Where are you, Hobner?"

"On west twelfth. Getting ready to take the next ramp to…"

"I know where you are. You're about five minutes from the station, aren't you?"

"That's right, sir. Are you coming to pick her up?"

"Yeah, I'll be right there. Oh, wait a minute, Hobner. On second thought, I want to teach her a lesson. Bring her in, but don't use cuffs. Don't arrest her and for crissakes don't let her know what I'm up to."

"Sir, please. She looks so pitiful. I don't know if I can, sir." The young cop cringed, glancing at the other five officers, who were all suddenly anxious to know what was going on between Gabe Baldwin and Nouri Sommers--one of the wealthiest women in the world--not to mention one of the most beautiful they had ever seen.

"Have one of the officers drive her car to the station with her in it. Tell her I'll talk to her here. Think you can handle that, Hobner?"

"Yes, sir. We'll be there in about ten minutes."

The young police officer glanced excitedly at his fellow officers and winked. He then turned back around and opened Nouri's car door.

"I'm sorry, ma'am. You'll have to get out of the car." He tried his best to be stern.

Nouri blinked back a tear of frustration. "I don't understand, officer. What did the detective say?" Her voice was shaking nervously.

"He said to bring you to the station, ma'am. Sorry." He shrugged his shoulders again.

Nouri shook her head in disbelief. "All right." She said with dread, slowly sliding out of the car. She stood to her feet and extended her arms to him so he could cuff her.

All six officers fought back their grins.

"Ah, I don't think that will be necessary after all, ma'am." He smiled when he noticed her frown turn upside down.

"I'll have to drive your car, ma'am. I'll help you in the other side." He smiled again, when he heard her sigh from relief.

"Thank you, officer. You'll never know how much I truly appreciate this. I know it was a huge effort on your part."

"I'm glad I was able to help, ma'am." He smiled, turning to face her.

Releasing a frustrated sigh, she responded: "God! I've just had a week you would not believe, officer... Hobner. I said that right, didn't I?" she asked, glancing at his nametag.

"Yes, ma'am. That's right," he responded, glad to have an excuse to look in her direction, knowing the other officers were dying of envy.

"Call me Nouri, please." She smiled.

"Then you can call me Rick." He returned the smile.

"Tell me, Rick..." She paused, then added: "What kind of man is Gabe Baldwin?" she curiously asked.

"What exactly do you want to know about him?" he asked sensing her interest in the detective.

"Oh, never mind, Rick," she blushed. "That was a stupid question. I guess it's the vodka and oj talking." She laughed amusingly at herself.

"No it wasn't. I just don't understand what it was that you wanted to know about him, that's all."

She shrugged her sexy shoulders. "Is he a good cop-- bad cop--grumpy cop?" she smiled, trying to hide her personal interest.

"He's a great cop! The best we have on the force, ma'am. A remarkable cop, actually. He always gets the bad guy." He smiled again, glancing her way.

"The very best, huh?" She seemed impressed.

They drove in silence for several moments. Suddenly, with the curiosity getting the better of her, she turned to face the handsome young officer again.

"So tell me, Rick..." She swallowed. "...Is...ah... The detective married?" She shifted uneasily in her seat.

The young officer smiled knowingly. The detective had a reputation of having that affect on most women. "Oh, look…" He pointed to the station, glad he could now avoid answering her question about the detective. "Well, here we are, ma'am," he said, quickly reaching for the door. "I'll be right around to open your door." He smiled nervously, jumping out of the car.

Nouri sensed the young police officer was trying to avoid her question about the handsome detective, so she decided it might be too embarrassing for her to repeat herself. So, she let it slide.

"Ma'am," He smiled while opening the door. "Follow me, please," he said, jumping in front of her to take the lead.

As the young officer opened the door to the police station, Nouri released a final sigh of embarrassment, but suddenly felt as though her legs were going to buckle right out from under her when she spotted the handsome detective walking toward her, glancing into a file folder.

She inhaled deeply, hoping the young officer hadn't noticed the affect the handsome detective had on her.

She felt her face flush with disappointment when Gabe disappeared into a room before he had a chance to see her. He shut the door behind himself.

Nouri was suddenly grateful when the young officer pulled out a chair for her to sit on.

"You can wait in here, ma'am. I'll tell the detective you're here. Can I get you something to drink? Maybe some coffee or…"

She interrupted him. "Do you have any hot tea?" She smiled that incredibly sexy smile of hers.

"I'll try to track some down for you. How do you take it?" He returned her smile.

"I usually like flavored teas- Black-Rum is my favorite. But if you don't have any, regular tea will be fine.

Thanks. I drink it plain." She glanced up at the young officer and smiled.

"It may take me a bit to track some down." The young officer scratched his head, wondering where the nearest store was. "I'll be back as soon as I can." He turned to leave.

"Oh please, Rick! Don't go to any trouble on my account. I'm sure I won't be here that long." She glanced at her watch. "Oh, my goodness! I can't believe it. It's almost four o' clock, all ready. Mai Li must be wondering where I am about now." She sighed again.

The young officer nodded and walked out the room, leaving the door open behind him.

For the next fifteen minutes, Nouri continued to fidget in her chair, glance at her watch impatiently, and tap her long fingernails nervously on top of the desk in front of her. She suddenly rose to her feet to stretch her legs. In no time, she was walking around the office reading the captions posted under the framed photographs, plaques, and newspaper headlines:

"THE DYNAMIC DUO SRTIKES AGAIN!" Was the caption under the front-page photograph of Police Detectives Charles Mason and Gabe Baldwin, of the Boston Police Department.

Another posted headline with another color photo read: **"BOSTON'S VERY OWN TANGO AND CASH!"**

POLICE DETECTIVE'S CHARLES MASON AND GABE BALDWIN WALSE RIGHT IN AND RELEIVE BOSTON'S BAD BOYS, ANTHONY SHAPIRO, BRUNO RIVERA, AND SAMMY 'FACE' EISNER, OF OVER $500 MILLION DOLLARS WORTH OF ILLEGAL GAMBLING MONEY AND DRUGS. A MAJOR BLOW TO BOSTON CRIME FAMILY, THE ALTUS BROTHERS..."

She continued to stroll about the room reading the captions...

**"FROM SUPER COPS TO SEXY COPS –
BOSTON'S VERY OWN BOYS IN BLUE – WHAT A
TRANSFORMATION!**

*POLICE DETECTIVE'S CHARLES MASON AND
GABE BALDWIN ATTEND A BLACK TIE AFFAIR WITH
SUPER MODEL CARLEY NELSON AND MOVIE
ACTRESS MILLIE RENEE..."*

**"DETECTIVE OF THE YEAR: GABE
BALDWIN"** She read on a wood and brass plaque.

**"DETECTIVE OF THE YEAR: GABERIAL A.
BALDWIN"** The second of many 'Detective Of Year'
plaques.

**"POLICE DETECTIVE'S GABE BALDWIN
AND CHARLES MASON TIE** *FOR THE FIFTH
STRAIGHT YEAR IN A ROW!"*

"Impressive!" Nouri whispered to herself, as she
continued to read the headline captions and plaques.

"What a couple of hams!" she giggled after noticing
the photograph of both Charles Mason and Gabe Baldwin
with not just one, but two, incredibly beautiful women, one
on each arm. The headlines playfully labeling them:

**"FROM COPS OF THE YEAR TO PLAYBOYS
OF THE YEAR"**

"Oh, Please!" she mumbled jealousy quickly
glancing at the next article…

"AND THEN THERE WAS ONE."

It was an article, saying goodbye to Detective Charles
Mason as he leaves the police Department to start his own
P.I. Business, accompanied with a photo of the two super
cops shaking hands on a job well done together.

Chapter 20

Gabe Baldwin originally had every intention of having a little fun with the beautiful billionaire's wife--at her expense of course. He wanted to teach her a lesson, give her a taste of the real world, outside the realm of her superrich lifestyle, with her billionaire husband. Introduce her to a world with rules--ones that everyone had to obey, not just common folk, but the rich and famous, as well.

But, when he entered his office and their eyes met again, something unexplainable happened, something he seemed to have no control over... *He Melted*... A shiver of excitement ran through his body. The palms of his hands began to sweat and he felt his legs suddenly turn to rubber. If he didn't sit down quickly, he knew she would surely pick up on the *affect* she was having On him--And His Body...

"Sorry to keep you waiting, ma'am," he said, forcing himself to remember just who, and where, he was, not to mention being aware of all the curious eyes behind him, in the outer room, staring in at them... He quickly added, "Please...sit down." He motioned her to a chair, anxious to sit down himself.

He deliberately left the door open to his office, not trusting himself to be alone with her.

After shaking himself from the hypnotic spell he seemed to be under, he suddenly lost the urge to teach her a lesson. It was all he could do to control himself...His Thoughts...His Urgent Need To Have His Way With Her... He released a frustrated sigh and tried to keep his words and actions all business.

He forced himself to look at her again, fighting his urge to pull her into his arms.

"Now, Mrs. Sommers. What seems to be the problem? I understand that you asked speak to me, personally." He gazed helplessly into her hazel colored eyes, and swallowed hard.

Nouri, shaking herself from a fantasy or two of the handsome detective, forced herself to respond. She blinked backed to reality and swallowed hard.

"Oh, yes. Thank you for seeing me. I… I appreciate what you have done for me." She smiled, once again causing the mesmerized detective to melt inside.

He swallowed again, deciding to play dumb. "And what might that be, Mrs. Sommers?" He leveled his eyes to hers, causing her to blush in embarrassment.

"Oh, Please Detective! They would have arrested me for DUI, if it wasn't for you." She rolled her eyes impatiently.

"Well, Mrs. Sommers, I must tell you, I was surprised. I'm one for playing by the rules. But, I understand some of what you have been going through lately, with your husband missing, your former associate's murder several days ago, and now I'm told that you have been receiving scary phone calls. I guess you could say that I just felt sorry for you. That's all." He glanced down at the file folder on his desk, trying to appear detached.

Nouri suddenly felt her blood pressure begin to rise. She glared hurtfully at the handsome detective.

"Sorry for me!" she snapped. "So this is why you wanted to see me? To let me know that you feel…feel sorry for me!" Her face flushed with anger.

Gabe quickly realized that his words had made her angry. He silently studied her expression for several quiet moments- After all, she was very attractive…even when she was mad. He smiled longingly before responding to her outburst.

"Mrs. Sommers. I, just simply meant that it was understandable why you had apparently had too much to drink, perhaps even rightfully so. But, next time, don't drive! The outcome of such… well, such… foolish behavior could have been very dangerous. You might have been killed. Maybe, you might have hurt or even killed someone else in the process. And from what I can tell about you, you wouldn't want to do that, would you?" He smiled faintly, causing Nouri to suddenly forget her anger.

She swallowed hard. "I see, detective. I'm… well, I'm very sorry. Of course you're right. Can I go home now?" She forced a smile.

He rose to his feet, aware that she was admiring his manly form. He smiled knowingly to himself while walking to the door and closing it. He heard the men sigh disappointedly in the outer office. He smiled to himself, knowing his co-workers were dying of curiosity.

He crossed the room and sat down on top of his desk, facing her. He smiled and looked down at her.

"Not just yet, please," he said in response to her question, shifting his weight to one leg. "I need to ask you a few questions." He smiled, realizing his presence was disturbing her.

She slowly bit her lower lip, causing him to get excited all over again. He quickly hopped to his feet and made it to his chair, glad to be behind his large desk and silently hoping she hadn't noticed his excitement in the lower region of his dress slacks. He cleared his throat… "Like I was saying, Mrs. Sommers, I need to ask you a few questions. That is, if you don't mind." He smiled again.

She returned his smile and crossed her legs. "Under the circumstances…" She smiled. "How can I refuse, detective."

"I've been asked to look after you while Charles Mason is in France. He's worried about you. I understand you have received several frightening telephone calls. Is that correct?"

Nouri nervously shifted in her seat. "Well, yes. Yes, I have, detective. But, I honestly don't believe it's really anything to worry about." Her smile was forced and nervous.

"I see. Well, Mrs. Sommers, just to be on the safe side…"

Nouri quickly interrupted. "I don't need a baby-sitter, detective." Her was tone insistent.

"Fine, ma'am- but what I was going to say before you jumped in…" He paused to scribble something down on a business card. "Here. Take this. It has my phone numbers on it. Home, office, pager, answering services and etc…" He blushed when he realized how his words must have sounded. He quickly added: "I mean if you should need to talk to me, please feel free to call anytime of the night or day. Okay." He smiled.

Nouri accepted the business card and returned his smile. "Now can I go detective?" She swallowed nervously.

"Sure, but you'll either have to let me phone someone to come and pick you up, or if you rather, I'll have someone drive you home."

"May I borrow your ink pen, detective?" She asked gazing into his mesmerizing teal-blue eyes, causing him to break out in a cold sweat. He leaned over his desk to get it and handed it to her with a note pad. They both swallowed hard when their eyes met. She quickly scribbled a number on it, as she cleared her throat. "Here is my down town apartment number. Ask my driver, his name is James, to come and get me, please, detective."

Gabe picked up the telephone and dialed the number, asking her chauffeur to come and pick her up at the police station.

"Thank you, detective."

"You're welcome, Mrs. Sommers. Would you care for something else to drink while you're waiting?"

"No thank you, detective. I still haven't touched the black-rum tea that Rick was nice enough to get for me."

"Rick?" The detective said sarcastically shooting her a look that Nouri could've sworn was one laced with a touch if jealously.

"Yes, detective. Rick." She smiled.

"You mean officer Hobner?" Gabe's tone was curious.

"Yes, I believe that's what his last name is." She smiled teasingly.

Gabe glanced at his watch. "Oh, damn! It's after five. I have to run." He reached for the folder that was lying on top of his desk. He glanced at her.

"Sit here as long as you like. I imagine your driver should be here any time. By the way, it was nice to see you again." He smiled, lowering his eyes to her thick full lips. "Don't forget. If you need me for any reason, you know how to reach me." He turned to leave the room.

As he opened the door to his office, he turned to face her, as she spoke to him from where she was sitting. "Detective, by the way…" A grin curled her lips. "…Thank you."

Feeling himself getting aroused, he simply nodded and hurried out the door.

'*Damn! That woman will probably be the death of me*'. he thought lustfully to himself, quickly turning down the hallway.

"Mrs. Sommers, your driver is here, but…" The young officer said in a nervous, but concerned voice.

"But *what*, Rick?" She smiled rising to her feet.

"But you might want him to pull your white stretch limo around to the back of the station to pick you up. There are a few paparazzi in the front, waiting for you."

"Oh, my. Thank you, Rick. Would you have someone tell James and would you be kind enough to show me how to find the back way out of here, please." She smiled, as she walked closer to him. "I wonder how they knew I was here?"

"I don't know, ma'am." Young police officer Hobner shook his head, as he replied in a curious tone. "Somehow, they always seem to know when we have someone rich or famous, such as yourself, here at the station. I can never figure out how they do it. Of course, having a white stretch limo pick you up here has its disadvantages. A car like that…well, you know what I mean, right?"

Nouri sighed and nodded. "I see your point, Rick."

Chapter 21

Nouri swiftly made her way down the long, dimly lit hallway of the Boston Police Department, being led by Rick, the cute, young police officer that she had made friends with a few hours earlier.

"I can't begin to tell you how much I appreciate all of your help, Rick." she smiled.

"My pleasure, Nouri." He returned her smile. "But, please, don't drive if you have been drinking, okay?"

"I won't. I promise. This whole thing has been very upsetting to me, not to mention embarrassing," she sighed. "I would have died if my picture had been plastered all over the front page of the newspaper tomorrow morning, with some ugly or humiliating caption beneath it." She shook her head again, relieved that things hadn't gotten that far.

After the young officer opened the back entrance door for Nouri, she glanced outside, thankful that there didn't appear to be any newspaper reporters or paparazzi at the station's back entrance driveway waiting for her.

Suddenly, as though from out of thin air, several flashes went off- right into her eyes. She quickly covered her face, as her driver swiftly ushered her into the limo, while ignoring all of the questions that were being hurled at her.

"Can you tell us why the wife of one of the wealthiest men in the world has been caught sneaking out the back of The Boston Police Department?"

"Why are you here, Mrs. Sommers?"

"Are the rumors true, Mrs. Sommers, that one of the young women that was murdered in Lambert over the weekend, was actually found inside your husband's hotel suite there?"

"The public has the right to know!"

"Is it true that your husband has left the country because of…"

"Hurry, James. Get me out of here! I can't stand listening to any more of these ridiculous questions," Nouri whined angrily.

James jumped inside the limo, turned on the engine, and zoomed out of the back entrance. He glanced into the rearview mirror nervously.

"Are you all right, Mrs. Sommers?" His tone was nervous and shaky.

"I… I'm fine, James. Are you?" she asked after, noticing how shaken he appeared to be.

"Ah… Ah… Yes, madam. I was only… I mean I was worried about you." He paused and quickly glanced into the rearview mirror again. "You're sure you are all right?"

Nouri responded with a nod of her head, but sensed that there was more to James' nervousness.

"Are you going to the apartment or to the estate, madam?"

"Take me back to the mansion, James. And arrange for someone to pick up my Corvette."

"I all ready have, madam." He smiled nervously, again.

"Thank you, James. I need to make a few phone calls, now. Is there anything else you need to discuss with me before I do?" she asked hoping he would change his mind and tell her what it was that was making him so nervous.

"Ah… No, madam." He shook his head, adding, "except that you have received several odd phone calls; both here and at the apartment, as well as the condo, Mrs. Sommers."

Nouri had an idea what James was talking about, but decided to inquire anyway.

"Odd, in what way, James?"

"Well, it was more of the callers tone of voice, than his actual message, madam." He shifted uncomfortably.

"Sounds like the same man that has been phoning me at the mansion. Did he say what he wanted?"

"No, madam. The mystery caller just wanted us to answer a few questions about you, but, of course, we slammed the telephone down in his ear."

"I see. I'm almost certain that it's the same man." She bit her bottom lip nervously.

"Has this been going on long, madam?" The driver asked with concern.

"He's called maybe three times, I think..." She paused, as though she were lost in thought for a brief moment. "I wonder how he got a hold of my phone numbers! They're all private."

"It's hard to say. Have you lost your wallet or purse. What about your check book, madam?" James offered to be helpful.

"No, I don't think so, James." She shook her head.

"Maybe we should report this to the authorities, madam."

"I don't think so, James. I've had enough police for one day." She reached for the telephone. "You'll excuse me, James, won't you? I have a few calls to make." She smiled, as he closed the window that connected them.

"Hello, Mai Li. I'm on my way home... What? I see ... He's apparently been phoning the condo and the apartment, as well ... What? ... Don't worry about it right now, Mai Li. We can talk about it when I get home, all right? Good. Oh, by the way, have I had any other calls? What did Mrs. Matthews want? I see. No thanks, I'll phone her later, okay ... If Mr. Mason phones back, tell him I'm on my way home ... I'll see you in about forty-five minutes," she said glancing down at her watch.

After Nouri called Mai Li to let her know that she was on her way home, she made herself cozy on the soft leather cushion of the back seat inside the long limo. Soon after downing a double shot of cognac to help calm her nerves, she laid her head back and closed her eyes to rest them.

The music being played inside the limo was soft, and relaxing. In a matter of moments, she dozed off.

In her dream state she was trembling with fear, as she continued to be chased by a person who seemed familiar, but had no face. She began to scream, but could hear no sound. Nothing but eerie silence surrounded her. She stumbled to the ground- too afraid to try and pick herself up. Forcing herself to lie on her back, she prayed silently that the faceless person couldn't find her in her hidden location, where the tall grass and beautiful weeping willow trees seemed to connect themselves from tip to tip.

As she glanced around the trees, they suddenly seemed to have faces smiling at her. One face was her elusive and mysterious billionaire husband, Ethan. Another tree appeared to have the face of Clint Chamberlain, the high-powered attorney that secretly held the key to her heart. And a third tree had the face of Charles Mason, her first real man, a man from her past that she would always have deep feelings for. All three trees with faces were trying to talk to her at the same time. But the tree closest to her, an old solid oak, beautiful in its stature, with full budded leaves on it, wouldn't let them. It was as though the oak tree was trying to protect her from the other trees. His face she knew, but couldn't remember who it belonged to … She could hear the pounding footsteps of the faceless person closing in on her. She covered her eyes, not wanting to see the person who had no face. As she heard the foot steps run past her, she opened her eyes to peak through her shaking fingers- But all she could see now was the three yellow rosebuds that were lying across her heaving bosoms.

She quickly sat up, removing the three tiny rosebuds, tightly clutching them in her shaky hands. Somehow, the magic of the three rosebuds made her fears seem to vanish. Her hands stopped trembling, she felt reborn, unafraid, and happier than she had ever felt in her life.

Suddenly, James gently called to her, forcing her to open her eyes.

"You're home, madam." He smiled, but the nervousness was still very much apparent on his face.

"Thank you, James," she said in response, stepping out of the car.

"Are you okay, miss?" Mai Li asked, as Nouri walked past her.

"I'm fine, Mai Li. But I do need a drink. Would you, please bring me a cognac in the study. I need to phone Genna Matthews and Charles Mason," she said, as she continued to walk down the long hallway leading to the study.

Chapter 22

A special delivery courier pulled his small delivery truck along the side panel of the viewing monitor and intercom that leads to the main entrance to the Sommers' Estate. The young driver rolled down his window, and while half leaning outside his truck, he firmly pressed the intercom buzzer and smiled at his reflection inside the camera monitor.

A few moments later, Mai Li answered the buss with a soft: "Hello." Quickly adding: "Sommers' residence. How I help, please?" She glanced at the viewing monitor.

The thin young driver politely responded, "I have a special delivery telegram for a Nouri Sommers."

"Wait please. I send Fredrick to gate for telegram, okay."

"I'm sorry, ma'am. Mrs. Sommers has to sign for it personally." The currier's tone grew impatient.

After a few moments of thought, Mai Li released the lock on the front gate.

"Okay. You bring telegram to mansion. Ten mile straight up driveway." She sighed.

"Thank you, ma'am." The driver said, quickly entering the estate grounds.

Around ten minutes later, the driver was asked to wait while Mai Li went to the study to get Nouri.

"Excuse please, miss." The tiny woman said softly, as she entered the study. She pushed the door open a little wider and glanced around the room.

Nouri turned her swivel chair to face the tiny woman behind the soft voice.

"Yes, Mai Li. What is it?"

"Special delivery telegram, miss." She smiled.

"Umm. Wonder who it's from?" She glanced at Mai Li. "Go ahead and sign for it," she said, turning herself

223

back to her phone conversation with Boston's most in demand private investigator.

Mai Li shrugged her shoulders and shook her head. "Sorry, miss. I can't. Man said it have to be you."

A surprised expression crossed Nouri's face.

"I see. All right. Tell the courier I'll be there in a moment." She turned in her swivel chair.

"All right, Charles. I understand. Listen, I have a telegram to sign for, so I better run. Make sure you phone me tonight after you check in. And please be careful- I would hate to hear that something happened to you, okay... Me too, Charles... Bye."

Nouri released a sigh, downed the remainder of her cognac, rose to her feet, and exited the study.

After signing the telegram and shutting the door behind the courier, she went to the living room, wondering what was inside the telegram, and who might have sent it.

"Mai Li, would you please pour me a shot of cognac? I'll be over here." She gestured toward the sofa.

"Yes, miss," Mai Li responded curiously.

Hoping the telegram might have been from her husband, or Clint Chamberlain, Nouri anxiously opened the telegram.

After the shock of reading what was written inside, she let out a terrifying scream, and began to uncontrollably shake with fear.

"Miss! Miss! What is it? Are you all right, miss?" Mai Li shouted in panic, quickly running to her side.

Too frightened to speak, Nouri stood frozen, with the telegram clutched in her hand tightly. Mai Li pried the piece of paper from her trembling hands and began to read it:

HOW DOES IT FEEL NOURI SOMMERS-
TO FIND OUT THAT YOU ARE GOING TO BE
THE NEXT PERSON TO DIE?
I TOLD YOU-

WHAT I WANTED WAS IMPORTANT.

The telegram was not signed.

"Oh my God, miss! Must be the same man that has been trying to scare you on the telephone!" Mai Li responded in panic.

Nouri ran to the bar to pour herself another drink and quickly downed it, reaching for the bottle again.

"I don't know," She shook her head in disbelief.

"Maybe... What am I going to do, Mai Li? Who could possibly want to see me dead?" She began to cry.

The tiny woman walked over to comfort her mistress- gently patting her on the shoulder. "There. There, Miss. Everything will be okay. I call handsome detective, okay," she said, waiting for approval.

At a loss for words, Nouri simply nodded giving Mai Li permission to phone for help.

She poured herself another drink and walked over to her cozy spot, where she sat down and began to stare blankly into space, her mind trying to search for some type of reasoning as to why this was happening to her. She stopped thinking when Mai Li came back into the room.

Mai Li went to where Nouri was sitting and sat beside her, placing her small arm comfortingly around her shoulder.

"Now. Now. Miss. Everything going to be all right. You see. Handsome detective on his way. He say helicopter will fly him here plenty fast!" She smiled.

Nouri smiled faintly. Why just the thought of herself running into the handsome detective's arms for protection, was the reason behind the smile. Danger or not- the sexy detective was very exciting to look *at*.

Nouri jarred herself back to reality.

"Mai Li. What else did the detective say?" Her tone was curious.

"He say not to let anyone inside estate grounds or inside mansion 'til he got here."

"I see." Nouri sighed. "All right then, Mai Li." She paused, trying to get up enough nerve to ask her a few questions about her mysterious husband.

After clearing her throat and downing another shot of cognac, she asked, "Mai Li, you have known my husband for a long time. And I want you to know that you don't have to answer my question if you don't want to, but…" She leveled her eyes to hers and swallowed hard. "Do you think my husband has ever really been in love with me?"

Mai Li shook her head sympathetically. "I not know you know me that well, miss…I did know Mr. Sommers for long time… In China. I knew his father first." She bit her lip nervously.

"Please… go on, Mai Li." She smiled and then patted the spot on the sofa next to her for Mai Li to come and sit beside her. "Okay." She said, sitting beside Nouri. "At the time, I thought Mr.
Sommers' father, Steven, was most pretty man I had ever seen in entire life." She smiled at the memory.

"So you were in love with Ethan's father?" Nouri asked curiously.

Mai Li nodded. "Yes. Very much so," she confessed.

"And Ethan didn't mind?"

"Not know. Never said really." Mai Li shook her head. "But I knew his father would never leave his American wife."

"I see… Ethan's mother?"

"Yes." Mai Li sighed.

"And after Mrs. Sommers died?"

"Steven had many…many women." She hung her head as though she were ashamed of loving a man like Steven Sommers.

"So you're trying to tell me that Ethan is like his father when it comes to many woman?"

"Yes. Sorry, miss." Mai Li's tone was filled with sympathy.

"So you don't think Ethan is capable of loving any *one* woman?"

"Mr. Sommers like his father- only love self."

"All right," Nouri nodded. "So, I wonder why Ethan married me?" She leveled her eyes to Mai Li's.

"Miss very beautiful. Very." Mai Li said, shaking her head approvingly.

"So you think it's because of how I look? Perhaps good for his public image."

Shrugging her shoulders, Mai Li responded: "Maybe, but I also think Mr. Sommers really cares." She smiled.

"So, do you think Ethan may be behind the attempts to scare me?"

"Mai Li not know." She shook her head.

"I see. Is Mr. Sommers a jealous man?"

"Don't know about jealous, but he has plenty big temper."

"Mai Li, are you afraid of Ethan when he gets angry?"

"Mr. Sommers never mad at me." Mai Li responded, shaking her head.

"That's not what I mean. I wanted to know if you were ever afraid of Ethan's temper?"

"Not for myself. No."

"For someone else?"

Mai Li nodded her head 'yes'.

"Do you want to tell me who, Mai Li?"

"No." Mai Li hung her head.

"That's okay. Really. I understand and I don't want you to answer anything that you don't want to." Nouri smiled and put her arm around Mai Li's shoulders.

"Mai Li. Do you know anyone that might want to hurt me?"

Mai Li shook her head as she answered. "Not anymore."

"What do you mean, not anymore?" The surprise in Nouri's voice was noticeable.

"Nothing, miss. Sorry. I shouldn't have said anything about your friends." Mai Li's face suddenly flushed.

"My friends. What friends?" she exclaimed with persistence.

Mai Li swallowed nervously. "Mrs. Chamberlain." She paused. "She acted like your friend, but I don't think she really was."

What do you mean, Mai Li?" Nouri gently tilted Mai Li's face up to hers.

"When Mrs. Chamberlain stopped by a few days before her murder, she acted very strange. I called for you at the downtown apartment, but was told you not there yet. I called later, but you was already gone. I forgot all about her visit, later."

"I don't understand, Mai Li? Why did Becka stop by without phoning first?

She told me she was supposed to meet you and Mr. Chamberlain here at the mansion that morning, but was running late. She wanted to know what time you and Mr. Chamberlain had left."

"And then what?"

"Wanted to come inside mansion to leave note."

"What note?"

Mai Li shrugged her shoulders in an unknowing manner. "She changed mind. Made a few phone calls instead and then stormed out of mansion, after shouting at me and threatening to tell Mr. Sommers on me for my rudeness to her.

"I'm so sorry, Mai Li. I don't know what she yelled at you about, but I know you well enough to know you certainly didn't deserve that type of treatment." Nouri shook her head heatedly.

"That's okay, miss. I never pay her any mind." She smiled.

"I'm glad, Mai Li." Nouri returned the smile and patted her hand fondly.

"Wonder what Becka really wanted?"

Shaking her head, Mai Li responded. "Not know, miss. But she was acting very crazy that morning."

Nouri shook her head defensively. "Mai Li. Poor Mrs. Chamberlain was crazy." She sighed. "Mai Li, you said friends. Was there someone besides Mrs. Chamberlain that you didn't care for?"

"Mrs. Matthews." She nodded.

"Genna? Why, Mai Li? She's been my friend for a very long time now. Why don't you like her?"

"I overheard her call you nasty names on the phone a few times after she phoned you and you weren't home."

"Genna has a sick sense of humor. I'm sure she didn't mean it like it sounded. Okay?" Nouri chuckled knowing her friend's weird sense of humor.

"Yes, miss," Mai Li said nervously.

"Thank you for looking after me, Mai Li. I honestly appreciate it," she said, and gave her a hug. "Now back to my current problem. Who could possibly want me dead?" she said and then suddenly began to cry.

"Now, Now, Miss. Handsome detective will be here anytime now." The tiny Asian woman said trying to comfort her mistress, as she gently patted her across the shoulder again.

Moments later, the lights from the police helicopter popped in brightly through the large bay window, scaring Nouri off her feet.

Mai Li jumped to her feet. "It's only the police, miss," she said, attempting to calm her mistress, down again.

"Please, Mai Li. Go let the detective in," Nouri said crossing the floor, heading to the bar again.

Chapter 23

"Ma'am," Detective Gabe Baldwin said, as he approached the bar where Nouri was busy downing another shot of cognac.

After hearing him call out to her, Nouri turned to face the handsome detective, impulsively running into his arms, wrapping her arms around his neck tightly.

"Oh, detective! Thank God you're here!" she said excitedly.

The detective glanced at his young partner, Al Ballard, and turned deep red in the face trying desperately to hide the grin that was beginning to curl at the corner of his lips.

The young detective rolled his eyes, knowing the senior detective had a huge crush on the beautiful woman that had just thrown herself into his arms.

Detective Baldwin, secretly enjoying having his fantasy woman mold herself to his body so snuggly, returned the embrace and gently patted her across the back.

"It's going to be all right, Mrs. Sommers. I'll see to it myself," he whispered protectively.

"The young detective stood frozen, where he continued to roll his eyes and shake his head.

After several silent moments, young Al Ballard, cleared his throat in an effort to separate the tightly embraced couple. The senior detective smiled knowingly and took a small step backward, attempting to separate himself from the beautiful woman so safely wrapped inside his arms.

Nouri glanced up at him surprisingly, suddenly remembering whose arms she had been so intimately embraced in.

"Oh, I sorry, detective," she remarked turning back around to face the bar.

"I... I'm just so upset. I hope I didn't embarrass you." She nervously glanced around to look at his handsome face again.

Gabe smiled longingly and released a sigh, silently hoping she hadn't noticed the affect her closeness was having on him.

"Where is the telegram ma'am?" he asked, ignoring her remark.

She motioned to the coffee table with a wave of her hand. "It's over there, detective," she said nervously, pouring herself another shot of cognac.

The senior detective nodded to the young one.

"Go get the telegram, but don't use your bare hands. Use a napkin or ink pen--something to pick it up. The lab boys don't need to be wasting their time on our prints," he said using a tone of authority.

The young detective nodded. "Yes, sir. I'll be careful."

Gabe turned to face Nouri and smiled at her. She returned the smile, knowing that the detective was teaching the young detective as they went--on the job training.

"I've got it, sir," The anxious detective responded, carefully balancing the telegram on the side of his pen.

The detective carefully took the telegram from the young detective's hand by using the corner of a handkerchief. He carefully examined the telegram for any unusual markings before reading it.

"Here, Ballard. See if Mai Li will find something we can put this in to protect it," he said handing the telegram to his young partner.

"Yes, sir," Young Ballard responded eagerly as he followed the tiny Asian woman into the kitchen for a plastic bag.

Gabe crossed the room to join Nouri and gently took her by the arm.

"Let's sit in the living room. We'll be more comfortable there. I need to ask you a few questions, okay?" He smiled, gesturing toward the living room.

Nouri sat down in her favorite cozy spot, still shaking from fear. She sat her cognac down on the coffee table and turned to face the handsome detective.

Mai Li and Al Ballard returned, carrying a tray with coffee, tea, coke-a-cola, and Nouri's favorite gingersnap cookies.

The senior detective smiled as he watched his young, eager friend swiftly help himself to a coke and a few cookie treats.

Mai Li handed Nouri a hot cup of black-rum tea, hoping she would drink it in place of the strong cognac she had been rapidly digesting.

She smiled to herself when Nouri shoved the brandy snifter aside and put her cup of tea in its place. The handsome detective smiled and secretly winked at Mai Li after realizing her good intentions.

"Thank you, Mai Li," Gabe said, accepting a cup of coffee from her shaking hands.

Gabe sat down in the overstuffed chair opposite to where Nouri was sitting. He cleared his throat. "Like, I was saying Mrs. Sommers. I need to ask you a few questions. Are you up to it?" He gazed into her beautiful eyes and smiled.

Nouri's returned smile sent a surge of excitement through his body. He quickly glanced away from her to regain his composure.

Nouri lowered her gaze to her cup of tea.

"I… I think so detective." Her response was nervous. She reached for her cup of tea.

"Good. Now tell me, Mrs. Sommers, what time did the telegram arrive?"

"I'm not sure, detective. You'll have to ask Mai Li."

"Mai Li?" He glanced her way.

"Not sure. Around seven-thirty, I think." She answered, glancing at her watch.

"All right. What did the driver look like?"

"Gee. I'm so upset, detective, I don't remember. Maybe you should ask Mai Li." Nouri shrugged her shoulders and took a sip of her tea.

"Mai Li?" The detective glanced her way again, with his brows raised.

Mai Li drifted in thought for a moment before answering. "White-- early twenties, maybe tall, thin brown hair. Oh, yes…he was wearing a uniform."

"Did his uniform fit properly?" The detective asked with growing interest.

"I think so," Mai Li nodded

"Would you know him if you saw him again?"

"Yes, I would know him," the tiny woman nodded.

"All right, Mai Li. What else can you remember about him?"

"What do you mean, detective?"

"Did he seem nervous? Happy? Angry? Impatient? Fidget a lot? Did he look around suspiciously? Maybe he had an accent or something… Anything like that?"

"He seem okay, I guess. We have him on video camera," she smiled.

"Great! Get the tape, Ballard. Replace it with a new one." He nodded excitedly.

"Mai Li, would you recognized the driver's voice again?"

"I think so," she nodded.

"Good. Now think carefully, Mai Li. Was his voice the same voice that has been placing the scary calls to Mrs. Sommers?"

"No. Not same voice." She shook her head.

"You're sure?"

"Yes. Not same voice."

"Can you describe the voice of the man that has been calling?"

"Can do better than that, detective," she smiled excitedly.

"What do you mean, Mai Li?" He leveled his eyes to hers.

"Mai Li save tape from answering machine." She smiled brightly again.

"Oh great! Good job, Mai Li," he smiled. "Would you give it to detective Ballard, please."

Gabe glanced at Nouri.

"Are you feeling any better, yet?" he asked sympathetically, longing desperately to run over and pull her safely back into his arms.

"I'll be all right, detective." She reached over to pick up the teapot and poured herself another cup of black-rum tea.

"Mrs. Sommers, can you tell me something..."

"What?" she answered curiously.

"Never mind ma'am," he said, shaking his head when he noticed Mai Li and Al Ballard walking back into the living room.

Nouri looked at the detective in wonder, leveling her eyes curiously to his.

She felt as though she suddenly wanted to run back into the protective embrace of the handsome detective. But she just couldn't imagine why . After all, he was a stranger.

Gabe smiled at her as though he could read her mind. He suddenly stood to his feet, and walked over beside her, and sat down on the couch, gently patting her shoulder and giving her right shoulder a slight squeeze.

"I promise you. Nothing is going to happen to you. I won't leave your side until this is all over."

She looked at him appreciatively and slowly slid her hand underneath his.

"Thank you, detective. I have no one else to turn to. Now that Charles isn't here, I don't know what I'm going to do," she sighed.

The young detective and Mai Li both noticed the caring exchange and smiled awkwardly at one another.

As Mai Li and the young detective walked closer to them, the confused couple quickly removed their hands.

"Here's the tape from the answering machine. Would you like to listen to it, sir?" The young detective said, offering the tape to senior detective.

"No, Ballard. We'll listen to it later. I have a few more questions for Mrs. Sommers, first."

"Yes, sir. I'll check on the video tape," he said, swiftly turning to leave the room.

The detective glanced at Mai Li. "Mai Li, would you be kind enough to make some more coffee? It's going to be a very long night. And there are a few questions that I need to ask Mrs. Sommers in private." He smiled.

"Sure thing, detective. I'll be in kitchen," she said, leaning down to pick up the silver tray.

"Thank you, Mai Li." Nouri said, placing her empty teacup on the silver tray.

"Mrs. Sommers. I need to ask you a few personal questions. Do you mind?" Gabe leveled his gaze to hers.

Shaking her head, she responded. "Not at all, detective. I'll do my best to answer them." She smiled nervously, pulling her long legs up and underneath herself.

The detective's gaze followed her every movement lustfully. He swallowed hard when she turned her attention back to him.

"Mrs. Sommers, do you know anyone who would want to see you hurt, possibly even see you dead?" He studied her expression.

"No, detective, I can't. I usually get along quite well with most people I meet." She shrugged defensively.

"I'm sure you do, but…"

"But what detective?"

"But obviously..." He shook his head. "There's at least one person out there that wants to harm you, possibly even more than one person. It's my job to find that person or persons before they get the opportunity. Do you understand?"

"Yes, but like I said, detective, I can't imagine who would want to see me dead."

"Mrs. Sommers, in order for me to keep you as safe as I possibly can, I need for you to be completely honest with me about everything. I need to find out as much as I can about you. Some of the things I may need to know about you are going to be extremely personal, but it's important that I know about them anyway. Do you understand?"

Nouri shifted uneasily in her cozy spot.

"All right, detective. I'll be as honest with you as I can."

"I realize at times some of the things that I need to ask you might even be embarrassing for you. But it's part of my job. Please don't think of me as anything but a professional doing that job. I'm not here to pass judgment on you, your friends, or your lifestyle. Understand?" The detective smiled.

Nouri gazed into his eyes.

"Strictly business, detective. I understand." She continued to stare into his beautiful teal-blue eyes.

"Good. I just want you to know that at times there are things about my job that I don't like. And, well, Mrs. Sommers, I wouldn't deliberately hurt your feelings or try to embarrass you in any way. I suppose you might say, I'm apologizing ahead of time," he mused.

"Thank you, I think, detective," she mused back.

The detective shifted his position and continued to question the beautiful billionaire's wife.

"Mrs. Sommers, am I correct in assuming that you still haven't heard from your husband yet?"

"Yes. That's correct, detective."

"Have you heard from Mr. Chamberlain?" He leveled hid eyes to hers.

Nouri swallowed hard and shifted uneasily. "Well, detective. I… uhh… uhh… I…"

Suddenly the telephone rang startling both the detective and Nouri. They glanced nervously at one another.

"Excuse me, detective." Nouri said, rising to her feet.

Gabe quickly jumped to his feet and grabbed Nouri by the arm.

She glared at him with a surprised expression.

"Wait! It could be your mystery caller. I don't have time to explain right this minute, but keep him on the phone as long as you can. Try to get him to open up to you more. Flirt with him a little if you have to." He sighed. "He can't get to you through the phone line. Okay?"

"But I don't understand. He gives me the creeps. I don't want to talk to him," she objected.

"It will be all right. I promise. I need to know if your mystery caller is the same person that has sent the telegram to you Okay?"

"All right, detective. I'll try to be brave." She bit her lower lip nervously and walked to the hallway. She ran into Mai Li who was on her way to get her.

"It's him, Miss. That scary man again. What should I do?"

Gabe glanced at Nouri again. "Mrs. Sommers, take it. Please try to keep him on the phone for as long as you can," the detective insisted.

"All right detective." She released a deep sigh, and began to mumble the words… "Be Brave Nouri." She reached for the receiver with her trembling hand.

After clearing her throat, she responded with a nervous, "Hello, This is Nouri Sommers."

"Hi, Nouri Sommers. It's me again. I just phoned to see if you received my little love letter yet?"

Nouri swallowed hard before answering. She glanced at detective Baldwin nervously.

"And what love letter might that be...ah...ah... I'm sorry. I seem to have forgotten what you said your name was."

"Nice try, Nouri Sommers, but no cigar. You think I must be pretty stupid, huh? Tell me, Nouri. Is that loud mouth boyfriend of yours still there? Or has he found out where I am- so that he could..." He paused. "What was it he said that he was going to do to me?" He laughed sarcastically.

"Oh, yes. I remember now. He was going to rip my goddamn lungs out." He laughed amusingly. "Now you have to admit something like that might be mildly entertaining to watch. Sounds like your boyfriend has been watching too many Arnold Schwarzenegger movies. Tell me, Nouri, does that kind of rough stuff turn you on?"

Nouri choosing to ignore his remarks, responded:

"Well, it appears that I have a mystery admirer. Tell me, mister mystery man, just how did you get my phone number?" She inhaled deeply and released it slowly trying very hard to be brave.

"He laughed again. "Well. Well. Well! Maybe Nouri, I know more than that about you. For starters, I know that you think by keeping me on the telephone line this long, you might be able to track down my location. But I imagine right about now the F.B.I. are just about ready to pull their hair out." He glanced at his watch and began to count the seconds. "Ten. Nine. Eight. Seven. Six. Five. Four. Three. Two. One." He mused. "Whoops!"

"What the hell are you talking about?" she snapped.

"God! I'm truly insulted, Nouri. Not to mention hurt. You really do think I'm stupid, huh?"

"Like I said, mystery man I have no idea what you're talking about."

"Oh, I suppose you aren't aware that your loud mouth boyfriend had a wire tap installed on your phone early this afternoon?"

"No. Obviously I did not." She swallowed hard.

"Charles Mason. That's his name, isn't it Nouri?"

"Who the hell are you? Do you work for my husband?"

"Ethan. Give me a break. Me work for him! I don't think so."

"So you do know my husband?"

"Intimately, I'm afraid."

"What the hell does that mean?"

"Enough about your husband. This call is about my love letter to you. Did you like it?"

"I... I don't know what you're talking about."

"Nouri, my love, you're such a terrible liar. I watched the courier enter the estate grounds myself."

"Oh, I suppose you're talking about the telegram I received?"

"I honestly thought you were brighter than this, 'ol girl."

"I'm afraid I never got around to opening it yet," she lied.

"Pity. I was looking forward to... Oh, all right. I'll just have to give you time to read it. And when do you think you might be of a mind to do so?" He sighed disappointedly.

"Gee. I'm not sure. I hadn't given it much thought."

"I see," he said turning his head away from the mouthpiece. "Did you hear that, darling?" He paused and sighed deeply before continuing. "Disappointed!" He barked angrily.

Nouri continued to keep her eyes glued to the handsome detective, as he continued to silently coach her on her replies.

"Try to keep him talking," he whispered.

"I... I heard you call someone 'darling'. So you're not alone?"

"Nouri. Really! I send you one love letter. Make several calls and you think that gives you the right to question me about my love life! Women!" He laughed.

"Listen. I don't know who you are. Or what you want, but..."

"Ah-ah-ah. Temper. Temper. You are in zero position to be talking to me that way. Listen, I've decided to give you some time to digest my love note. I'll call you back--shall we say...around midnight? That should give you enough time to ... Well, we'll talk about it then. Tell your F.B.I. friends and Mr. Mason that they're only wasting their time. Bye, Nouri."

The next thing Nouri heard in her ear was the clicking sound of the receiver being put back in its place.

She slowly blinked herself from a dazed state and returned the receiver to the phone stand. "Oh, God!" she mumbled hopelessly, turning to walk back in to the living room.

Gabe Baldwin pulled young Al Ballard into the kitchen.

"Listen, Ballard. I have to get Mrs. Sommers out of here tonight. Get a hold of the F.B.I. Ask for Robert Barnet. He was supposed to put a wiretap on this phone. See if they got anything on this call. Take the videotape and the answering machine tape, along with the telegram down to the station."

" Have Charles Mason's men hang around here for a few days or so. Ask them to detain anyone that looks suspicious."

"Have the captain call the DA first thing tomorrow and fill her in on what happened here tonight. Tell Tonya I'll check in as soon as I feel safe enough, hopefully sometime tomorrow."

"Have the captain fill her in on everything that Charles Mason has shared with us. Tell the captain, if he has to, to tell Tonya that Charles Mason left a message for her, and I'll give it to her tomorrow. That should put her in a good enough humor." He released a deep sigh and fumbled inside his shirt pocket for his cigarettes, glancing around the kitchen for an ashtray.

Young Ballard swallowed nervously. "So, where are you going to take Mrs. Sommers, sir?"

"I think it would be a lot safer if I'm the only one that has that information right now, Ballard." He lit his smoke.

"Maybe I should go with you, sir."

"I need you here, Ballard. You're going to be my legs here. Do you understand?"

"Yes, sir. But…"

"I need you here, Ballard. Now go pull Mai Li to the side and tell her I said to go pack Mrs. Sommers a suitcase of things. I'll explain things to Mrs. Sommers."

"Anything else, sir?"

"Yes Ballard. Get a statement from all of the estate employees. You'll need to ask them about the Sommers' relationship. Get as personal as they let you. Find out about their friends, family, and so forth. Don't forget to ask about all the delivery companies, anyone that has come and gone in the past month. We're looking for anything unusual. Run a background check on the estate employees. Don't forget to get the new tape out of the answering machine. We'll need the other one, too, if the mystery caller phones at midnight like he said he would. And assign a couple of people to stay inside the mansion with Mai Li for the time being.

"Is that all, sir?"

Gabe nodded thoughtfully. "For now, anyway. I'll borrow one of the estate cars and rent one later. I'll in constant touch, Ballard, so don't worry. okay?"

"Yes, sir. Whom should I work with?"

"I don't know, Ballard, that will be up to the captain. You might tell him I said to put Brady with you, if he's available. If not, maybe Finemann. Both men are good teachers. One last thing, Ballard. Don't talk to the press! Let the captain worry about that end of it." He smiled and nodded.

"Yes sir. I'll get on everything right away." Ballard smiled nervously.

"You'll be fine, Al," Gabe smiled and patted the young detective across his shoulders as he walked past him, anxious to get back to Nouri.

Chapter 24

After driving in silence on the freeway for what seemed like an eternity, Nouri Sommers, still shaking from fear, glanced in the direction of the handsome police detective.

"So detective, where are you taking me?" she asked, squirming uncomfortably in her seat.

Without looking at her and trying very hard to keep his mind on her safety, instead of his ever-growing lack of self control to have his way with her, he answered. "I have a small cabin in Connecticut, Mrs. Sommers. You'll be quite safe there for a while." He fought the impulse to pull her close to him.

"Connecticut!" She gasped nervously. "Who will be staying in the cabin with me. I... I don't think I'm brave enough to be alone, right now." She swallowed hard.

Gabe continued to struggle with himself- his emotions going wild.

"I will, ma'am. Protecting you is my job."

"I'm frightened detective... Very frightened!" she whined.

"I know." He shook his head understandingly. "Being threatened like that is very frightening thing, ma'am. But try not to worry too much. I won't let anything happen to you. I'm very good at what I do, Mrs. Sommers." His tone was comforting.

Still looking at his handsome face, she asked in disbelief: "Who could possibly want to harm me?" She sighed hopelessly.

She sounded so pitiful he couldn't bear not to look at her a moment longer. He extended his right hand to gently pat her shoulder, attempting to comfort her. He smiled as their eyes met, quickly pulling his arm back, not trusting himself to touch her any longer.

"I don't know." He shook his head. "…Yet, anyway. But I intend to find out ma'am." He glanced at her beautiful face again.

"Detective, will Mai Li or Charles Mason know how to reach me while I'm in Connecticut? They…" She paused. "They might need to get in touch with me about Ethan or Cli…" She stopped talking, not being able to bring herself to say Clint Chamberlain's name quite yet.

She swallowed hard in an attempt to fight back her tears over Clint, staring blankly out of the window in front of her. Her mind soon wandered away from her current problems when the handsome detective's face, sexy smile, mesmerizing teal-blue eyes, and sensuous full lips suddenly entered her brain, Her mind desperately tried to figure out what he looked like under that godawful suit he currently had on.

She smiled to herself when she suddenly pictured him kissing her. She quickly blinked the image of them embracing away and began to silently scold herself for such uncontrolled urges.

'*Why shame on you, Nouri Sommers! He's a cop For Goodness-sakes! He's probably married anyway. If not married, I'm sure he has someone special. With that incredible build of his and that beautiful face …and, oh God… Those eyes. He probably has at least a hundred women. Remember those newspaper clippings posted in his office For Chrissakes! Oh…Good Lord…not another skirt chasing Clint Chamberlain'!*

She shook her head still lost in thought.

'*For Crissakes, Nouri – get a grip! The handsome detective is a stranger. You don't know the first thing about him. And anyway, he made it a point to let you know that he was a professional, that he was only doing his job…a job that your own friend Charles Mason asked him to do. And speaking of Charles…What the hell are you going to do with him in your life, again? You know you aren't in love with him. His body...maybe? But the man--it just wouldn't work. He's too fatherly. Too possessive. Too...Well, too...'*

She suddenly jarred herself back to reality, when she heard the detective ask the same question to her for the second time. She cleared her throat. "Excuse me detective. My mind must have wondered. I'm sorry. What were you saying to me just then?" She forced a smile.

"I was asking you if you are all right?" A concerned expression covered his handsome face.

"I'm fine, detective. I was just...Never mind." She shook her head.

"You asked me a question. Would you like for me to repeat my answer to you, ma'am?" He glanced at her from the corner of his eye.

She nodded.

"I was explaining that, at least for the time being, no one except myself, and of course you, will know where we're at. It's safer that way, ma'am."

"I see. So you're telling me that I can't..."

He interrupted her. "Yes. That's what I'm saying. You cannot contact anyone for any reason. Is that understood?" He looked at her sternly.

"Yes detective, but I don't understand what it would hurt for me to..."

He interrupted her again. "No phone calls. Got it?" His tone was stubborn and authoritative.

She nodded. Her expression was so innocent--so childlike--he felt his heart melting inside. He quickly began to stare out of the front window.

They drove for a while when suddenly Nouri began to cry. "Oh God, detective! This entire week has been like a horrible nightmare for me." She covered her face with her hands and continued to sob. After a few moments, she tried to calm herself.

"I keep praying that everything that has happened this week has been a dream- an unimaginable dream. And at any moment I will wake up and…"

Gabe leaned over to comfort her by gently patting her on the shoulder.

"Mrs. Sommers, it's going to be all right. I promise you. Maybe if you talk about it, you'll feel better. After all, we are going to have to discuss this week in great detail sooner or later. So right now is just as good a time as any. What do ya say?" He smiled, removing his hand from her shoulder.

"I don't think we have that much time. It's a very long story, detective." She forced another smile.

He glanced at her and smiled. "Well, Mrs. Sommers, we have a very long drive ahead of us – About one-hundred-fifty miles, I believe, ma'am." He nodded rather matter-of-factly.

"Oh my! That far, huh?" She squirmed uneasily in her seat.

"Maybe talking will help pass the time between us." He continued to stare at the road in front of him.

She sighed deeply. "I should've brought my bottle of Cognac." She shrugged her shoulders helplessly and sighed.

The detective shot her a concerned look. "No offense, ma'am, but don't you think you have had enough to drink for one day?" He leveled his eyes to hers.

"Oh, please, detective! First Charles and now you! Don't tell me you intend to act as my father too? I just couldn't bear it." She shook her head.

The detective smiled seductively. "Your father, ma'am? Hardly!" he said slowly lowering his eyes to travel the length of her incredible body.

She noticed and smiled.

'*I just know he feels something between us… Or am I just imagining it'?* She thought to herself.

"You know, detective. You have a very sexy smile," she said trying to get a reaction out of him.

He swallowed hard, fighting the urge to pull her into his arms and kiss her.

"Oh really, ma'am. I guess I'll have to watch that, then, won't I?" he remarked in an unaffected manner, blushing profoundly, knowing she was intentionally flirting with him.

"Did my remark embarrass you, detective?" she asked gazing into his searching eyes, arching her eyebrow, waiting for his answer.

"No." He shook his head, lying, hoping she hadn't noticed the affect she was indeed having on him. '*Please don't look down*', he silently prayed.

Suddenly feeling rejected by the handsome detective, she responded in a disappointed tone. "Good. I'd hate to think you would be personally affected by anything that I would say or do, detective Baldwin." She quickly glanced out her window, not quite sure why she was acting this way.

Gabe quickly realized that it wasn't his imagination. Nouri Sommers was just as confused about her attraction to him, as he was about his attraction to her.

He smiled to himself, happy to know that this incredibly beautiful woman felt as he did. But how could he allow himself to show any interest in her? After all, not only was he a professional that had a job to do, but probably more important, this lovely creature was a friend of his friend, Charles Mason, who was no ordinary friend. He was his best friend. Well, at one time, anyway. And, of course, there were other reasons he couldn't get involved with her, as well. Such as she was married to one of the most powerful men in the world, and more importantly, she was a prime suspect in a double murder investigation.

'*Oh sure, Charles believes in her innocence, and he explained that Nouri Sommers wanted a divorce from the unimaginable bastard she was married to, but what about Charles? Could he have more than a friendly relationship secretly going on with her? After all, Nouri Sommers isn't just any woman. She is special. Remarkable, actually – not to mention beautiful'.* He glanced over at her, as he continued to be lost in thought.

'Could Charles not be telling me something about this beautiful woman'?

He shook his head in confusion. *'He also said he was at her house when the mystery caller phoned that morning. Could he have spent the night? Could he have been making love to her? After all, he also said that he had to turn the request for sex down from his current squeeze, super model Kimberley Michelle. As a matter of fact, he even said he had to cut Kimberly loose after he got home that morning. Humm... This Nouri Sommers is a curious one'.*

He released a deep sigh, as his thoughts continued to run together, one right after the other.

'Charles had also said that he and Nouri Sommers had been friends for a long time. If they're not romantically involved now, it's very possible they had been at one time. Why did he ask me to personally look after her? There is only one answer to that question. Because he knew that he could trust me with her. He didn't trust any other man around her. Jealousy? Maybe. He knew I'd take great pride in keeping her safe. But how could he have possibly known I wouldn't sleep with her? Because of friendship? Maybe? Or perhaps he just decided to take a risk. Humm...I wonder how far back their friendship goes? After all, she's not that old. Maybe twenty-five...possibly twenty-six'.

He looked at her.

'Oh my God! It can't be... His thoughts running ramped. *Naw, of course not. What the hell am I thinking'?*

Suddenly, Nouri noticed a shocked look plastered across the handsome detective's face, and asked curiously: "Detective. What is it? Are you okay?"

Forcing himself to draw his attention back to her he responded: "Yes, I'm fine. Why do you ask?" His tone was professional and unaffected.

"Well, detective, you had this odd expression plastered on your face. Sort of like a light bulb was going off inside your brain or something." She shrugged her shoulders.

He glanced at her. "I guess I just had a few things on my mind, that's all. It's been a very long day for me. You know what I mean...So much to do--so little time..." He smiled.

'*God! I wonder if he knows just how lethal that smile of his is*'? she thought, as she continued to study the features of his handsome face.

"Tell me, detective. Does anyone know about your hideaway in Connecticut?" Her tone wasn't as friendly as it was before the handsome detective rejected her attempt to flirt with him.

He glanced at her. "No. Actually, ma'am, I just got it several months ago, sort of a get away spot between cases." He smiled and turned to stare blankly out the front window again.

"I see, detective. So tell me about your cabin in the woods. Is your wife going to be there?" She surprised herself by her impulsive question to the handsome detective.

Fighting back a smile, he answered, "In answer to your first question about my cabin..." He looked at her. "I'll just wait and let you tell me what you think about it when we get there." He smiled knowingly.

With a curious look on her face and eagerness in her tone, she remarked, "And my second question, detective?"

He kept his eyes focused on the highway. "The answer is no." He shook his head. "My wife won't be there."

She released a disappointed sigh. "I see. So detective, you…are married?" She glanced out the window, as the feeling of disappointment surged through her body.

"Yes. In a way, ma'am." His tone was one of amusement. He turned to look at her.

Knowing he was watching her, but too disappointed to return the glance, she continued to stare out of the window.

"I don't understand, detective. One is either married or not married. How can you be married 'in a way'?" she stated coolly, turning to look at him.

"Well Mrs. Sommers, I am married, but only to my job. I do not have a wife, however." He smiled when he noticed a relieved look suddenly cross her beautiful face.

"Good." She blurted out without thinking, quickly adding: "I… I mean it's probably a good idea in your line of work. But, of course you have a girl friend?" Her tone was still curious, surprising herself and amusing the detective.

He smiled and blushed at the same time. "I date, of course." He paused, giving his grin a chance to fade. He glanced at her. "I seem to be sharing the details of my love life with you, Mrs. Sommers. Would you care to share the details of your love life with me?" he remarked, surprising himself and delighting her by his obvious interest.

She blushed and squirmed uneasily in her seat.

"I'm sorry, detective. I didn't mean to pry," she lied.

He looked at her and smiled again. "Yes, you did," he said piercing her flesh with those incredibly penetrating eyes of his.

She blushed again and then giggled. "Okay. So you caught me. But I really didn't mean to pry. I… Well, I was only curious. Do you mind?" She smiled and then shrugged her shoulders.

"No. I don't mind. But turn about is only fair play. I'd still like to hear about the life and loves of the beautiful Nouri Sommers. If you don't mind." He smiled, making her feel weak in the knees.

She cleared her throat. "Not much to tell detective, really." She shifted uneasily in her seat again, and then continued to speak. "Especially these past two years of my life... Well, except for this past week," she said without thinking. She released a sigh and glanced over at the handsome detective.

"All right. Then lets start there," he said nervously tapping his fingers on the steering wheel.

"Where? she asked curiously.

"The past week. We need to go over it anyway, remember? And it's very important that you don't leave out a single detail."

"Every single detail!" she exclaimed.

"Yes. No matter how intimate or how embarrassing, okay?" He smiled, longing to know both on a professional basis, as well as a personal one, about the men in her life, and secretly praying that his friend, Charles Mason wasn't one of them romantically.

"I honestly can't understand how my sex life has anything to do with this whole thing, detective," she pleaded.

He smiled. "You'll have to let me be the judge of that, I'm afraid, ma'am."

She blushed as her eyes widened. "Oh, dear. I... I don't know if I can be quite that open about my... Well my..."

"Sex life, Mrs. Sommers?" He smiled knowing it was his turn to embarrass her.

"God! You make it sound so...So..."

"So what, Mrs. Sommers?" he commented studying her expression.

She glared at him heatedly. "Well to be honest with you, detective. You make it sound as though my sex life this week was about nothing!" she snapped.

"Well, was it or wasn't it?"

"Quite the contrary, detective. I've had more sex in the past week than I have had in the past two years." Suddenly realizing how she had just made herself look to the handsome man sitting next to her, she quickly added: "Now, see what you made me go and say!" She shook her head in dismay and hid her face with her hands, dying of embarrassment.

"Me? What have I got to do with anything? It's not like you've got to explain anything to me about who you have been sleeping with... or, even why. I'm just trying to get to the heart of the issue here, ma'am!" He snipped heatedly.

"So you're saying what exactly, detective? That my sex life is now the heart of the issue here!"

At a loss for words, the confused detective snapped back. "No, Mrs. Sommers! I'm just saying what I'm saying." He was suddenly angry about who she had been sleeping with for the past week, but not understanding why.

"Well detective, if you're saying what you're saying, then I'm saying what I'm saying!" She folded her arms stubbornly and turned to stare out the window. She released a sigh of frustration.

"Which means what?" he asked sharply.

"Which means my sex life is off limits!" she snapped.

"Oh, I get it. You think that I'm judging you on a personal basis. Is that it?"

"Well, detective, aren't you?" She glared at him again.

He released a deep sigh and reached for a cigarette. "Do you mind?" He said not waiting for her to respond he lit up.

"I guess not! Far be it from me to try and offer you any advice on what the hazards of those god-awful things do to your lungs, detective!" She remarked sarcastically, rolling down her window and faking a cough.

"Oh, so I guess soaking my liver in alcohol would be healthier for me. Huh?" He returned her sarcasm.

"Point well taken, detective. Some choices we have, huh? Carbon monoxide or alcohol. Game. Set. And match." she mused, shaking her head in amusement.

The detective rolled down his window and removed the cigarette from his mouth.

"Listen, if smoking really bothers you…" He stopped talking and started to toss his cigarette out the window.

Nouri quickly reached for his arm. "No. That's all right detective. Far be it from me to come between The Boston Police Force and their smokes!"

"I'll have you know, Mrs. Sommers, that statement is highly exaggerated. The fine young men in blue today take great pride in keeping their bodies healthy, and while we are on the subject of exaggerated myths, the one about cops and doughnuts isn't true either." He chuckled and then took a puff of his cigarette.

She returned the detective's smile. "The statement about doughnuts…I can believe that one is exaggerated. You couldn't possibly eat all those donuts and look as well as…Ah…Ah…Well, you know what I mean, don't you detective?" She blushed.

Aware that she was checking out his body, the handsome detective decided to toy with her, to lighten the mood between them.

"Ah, no…" He shook his head. "I don't believe so, ma'am. Maybe you should tell me exactly what it is you were trying to say about my body." He gazed into her beautiful hazel-colored eyes.

"Honestly, detective! You are such a ham. I knew it!" She smiled seductively and bit her lower lip. "The moment I saw that photograph of you and Charles Mason in your office, the one where you both had not one, but two, beautiful women on each of your arms that…"

He teasingly cut in. "Okay…All ready. I don't suppose you would believe those four women were our sisters, huh?"

She laughed loudly. "Next I suppose you will want to be selling me the Brooklyn Bridge, huh?" she said, shaking her head playfully.

"Well, ya can't blame a fella for trying, right?" he laughed.

"No. I guess not, detective." she smiled and glanced at him again. "So tell me. How much farther do we have to drive before you plan to feed me? I'm starving."

"Oh, I'm sorry. I had forgotten to ask if you had dinner yet. I know a wonderful seafood restaurant not far from here. That is, if you don't harbor any dislikes for fish, ma'am.." he smiled.

"You mean like my dislike for cigarettes?" She shot him a playful look and added, "The only dislike I harbor for fish, detective, is when my plate is empty." she mused. And they both began to laugh.

"Good. Then seafood it is. And if you like, they even have a well stocked bar, you can have a few Cognacs while I enjoy a few cigarettes. Deal, ma'am?" He smiled.

"Deal. But, of course, you'll join me in a drink won't you, detective? I do hate drinking alone," she said looking his way.

"Well, Mrs. Sommers, for the next few days or so, it seems as though we have nothing but time on our hands. So I see no reason why I couldn't join you for a drink or two." He smiled and went on. "Well, Mrs. Sommers, I've shared some of the details of my love life with you and I'm still waiting for you to do the same with me. What do you say? We have about twenty more miles to drive before we get to the restaurant." He began to nervously tap his fingers on the steering wheel again.

"Oh all right, detective. Where would you like me to begin?" she smiled.

"Well first of all, you can start by calling me by my first name, which is Gabe, in case you had forgotten it. And secondly, you can start by telling me every detail of your life, starting with this past Tuesday night. That seems to be the night your entire world got turned upside down, right?" He smiled.

"All right, Gabe. But you'll have to start calling me by my first name, as well, deal?" She returned his smile.

"All right, Nouri. Please..." He gestured with a wave of his hand. "Tuesday night. Remember I want every action, every word, everything. Got it?"

He leveled his eyes to hers and smiled.

She nodded reluctantly and began to tell him about her previous week, starting with the phone call that interrupted her journal writing- and ending by telling him about her two night make up session with Clint Chamberlain, forgetting to mention her argument over the phone with Becka Chamberlain, and the short conversation she had had with her husband's mistress, Kirsten Kamel. She deliberately left out the part where Charles Mason made love to her the night before.

She was grateful when he finally pulled into the parking lot of the Bay Shore Seafood House.

"Well, here we are, Nouri. Sit tight, I'll be right around to open the door," he said, nervously quickly sliding out of the car and swiftly rushing around to the other side.

Nouri smiled as he helped her out. She eagerly glanced around her surroundings. "Oh Gabe, this place is charming. The landscape...The flowers...The ocean! Umm...And the salty sea air. I love it!" she exclaimed excitedly.

"I'm glad you like it. Wait until you taste the food. I hope you're really hungry..."

"Oh, I'm starved!" She cut in.

"Good." he smiled, as he held the restaurant door open for her to enter.

They were seated at a cozy spot with a breathtaking view of the beach.

"Shall we have a few drinks before we order, Nouri?" He asked nervously.

"Yes, thank you, detective. That would be nice."

"What would you like?"

"Cognac, please." She smiled.

"Make that two," he said nodding to their server.

"Now, where were we? Oh, yes, you were telling me about your relationship with Clint Chamberlain, I believe." He smiled, waiting patiently for her to continue.

After Nouri explained how they met and fell in love, Gabe began to ask her about their break-up.

"So, if you were so desperately in love with him, why did you leave him?"

"Because, I knew Clint would never change." she replied in a sad tone.

"What do you mean, you knew he would never change?"

"He likes beautiful women too much, can't seem to help himself." She shook her head. "I guess you could say I turned a blind eye, until I just couldn't turn anymore." She paused thoughtfully.

"You know detective, I just told you that he didn't really love me. The truth is, I believe Clint honestly does...I mean did. The other women meant nothing to him. I knew that. But when he finally broke down and gave me an engagement ring, he refused to set a date. I then realized

Clint would never settle down. He simply just didn't want to get married. The ring…" She shrugged her shoulders, as she ran her index finger around the rim of the glass.

"He gave it to me, hoping it would pacify me, he was afraid of losing me. I think the funny thing was that I really wanted to marry him and have his babies. I think I wanted that more than anything at the time." She sighed, as she picked up her drink.

"And now?" Gabe asked curiously.

"What do you mean?" She asked, glancing at him.

"Marrying Clint Chamberlain and having his babies." His tone was laced with jealousy.

"No. It's over between us." She shook her head in a determined manner. "He's cheated on me for the last time. When I overheard that other woman last night on the phone call him 'darling', and say she couldn't wait until that night to see him again… I knew exactly what was going on. I was devastated. We had just spent two of the most erotic and passionate nights that we had ever shared in our lives together. He was magnificent, as a matter of fact. I fell hopelessly in love with him all over again." She sighed and downed the rest of her drink and then went on…

"And then he does this to me." She shook her head in utter disbelief.

"And you're still in love with this jerk?" Gabe sighed leveling his eyes to hers.

"I told you, detective. It's over between Clint Chamberlain and I," She stated with stubbornness.

"So the phone call the night before last from the high-powered-attorney was the first time you had talked to him since the Lambert Murders?"

"It was last night, detective. And yes, that was the first time I had talked to him since early Friday morning, actually.'

"Did he mention the Lambert Murders to you during your phone conversation?"

She shook her head. "No. All he had an opportunity to say before miss thing buzzed on his hotel door was that he was in France looking for Ethan. He said something about Ethan being out of control, and he had to find him before anyone else did." She shrugged her shoulders unknowingly. "He didn't say why. I didn't even get a chance to tell him about Becka's murder." She shook her head in dismay.

"I see..." Gabe responded, as he glanced at her. "...And when did you call Charles Mason?"

"You mean after I hired him to find out who my husband really is?"

"Yes," the detective nodded.

"I phoned him before Clint called me yesterday. I called him right after the weirdo phoned me for the first time."

"That was yesterday too, right?"

"Yes. That's right. So much has happened since then that it seems longer."

"What did you and Charles talk about?"

"I asked him if he would join me for lunch at the mansion. He said that he couldn't make lunch, but he would stop by around five and that he would bring some Chinese carry out," she said reaching for her drink.

"You didn't tell him why you wanted to see him?" He asked with interest.

"No. I thought I would wait until he came out later in the day."

"So what happened then?"

"I gave the staff the remainder of the day off and then I got drunk." She started playing with her drink again.

"Why did you give the staff the remainder of the day off?"

"I didn't want them to know that I hired a private investigator to look into matters concerning my husband."

"I see. And you were drunk by the time Charles arrived?"

"Yes. He was disappointed, I'm sure, making him drive all the way out to the estate and all."

"What happened next?"

"Charles put me to bed... Heated up his Chinese food and had dinner by himself, I'm afraid."

"Did he spend the night?" He swallowed nervously as he waited for her response.

"Detective, please. Aren't you going to feed me? I'm starving half to death," she smiled nervously.

"Yes, of course. I'm sorry... Waiter...Please." Gabe motioned for the food server with a wave of his hand.

Both Nouri and Gabe ordered the House Special, which was an overstuffed platter of ten different types of seafood specially prepared tableside.

"Oh, this is wonderful, Gabe. I don't know when I've enjoyed dining out more," Nouri said smiling.

"I'm glad you like it, Nouri. I stop by here every time I visit my little get away in the woods. The food is always superb," he smiled.

"I can't believe how much food they put on the plates. If I ate here once a week for a month I'd probably gain at least twenty pounds!" she teased.

"Even so, I'm sure you would wear it well." He smiled lustfully and then added: "Wait until you taste their flamed liquored coffees, and another house specialty-- Flamed Drambuie."

"Sounds wonderful. Which one shall we have first?" she laughed.

"We better go with the Drambuie first- save the coffee for last."

****

About an hour later ...

"Oh, Gabe, dinner was wonderful. Thank you for bringing me here tonight. I've really enjoyed myself." She reached for her drink. "I have to admit, though, I'm beginning to feel a little tipsy. I can hardly feel my toes." She giggled. "Maybe we should take a walk along the beach. I could use a little fresh air. Would that be all right?" She gazed into his eyes.

"Sure." He nodded in agreement. "I could use the walk to stretch my legs a bit. We have a rather long drive still ahead of us," he smiled.

"Great. But first I need to stop by the little ladies' room. I won't be but a few moments," she smiled, sliding her chair back.

"Fine. I'll wait for you here." He returned her smiled and rose to his feet to pull out her chair.

Chapter 25

The police detective nervously rose to his feet when he spotted the billionaire's wife walking back through the dining room toward their table.

"You were gone so long, I thought about sending someone in to check on you," he remarked in a protective tone of voice.

"Oh, I'm sorry detective. I just had to make a ..." She suddenly stopped talking when she realized she had almost told on herself for sneaking a quick phone call to Genna Matthews, her best friend in the world.

She wanted to tell her what had happened and where she was heading. Plus, she could hardly wait to tell her friend about spending the night with her old flame, Charles Mason. She also wanted to tell her about her secret attraction to a handsome detective named Gabe Baldwin.

She quickly added..."I had to make a few touch ups with my make up. You know how we women are when it comes to make up and looking into the mirror." She laughed nervously, hoping the detective had bought her story.

"I see..." He said in a disbelieving tone. "...Ready for that walk now?" He gestured to the side door of the restaurant leading to the beach.

"You bet," she said smiling.

They walked in silence for quite some time, enjoying the salty sea air, the silent rumbling of the waves and the picturesque atmosphere surrounding them.

'*Most of the couples have gone away – probably back to their hotel rooms to make love*'. Nouri enviously thought, releasing a deep sigh.

"What's the deep sigh for?" Gabe asked, stopping to turn her around to face him.

"Oh, nothing… And possibly everything," she replied, looking into Gabe's hypnotic teal-blue eyes.

"Yeah… I understand. You've had some kind of week, all right." He sighed, quickly removing his jacket when he noticed her shiver.

"Here, let me put this around your shoulders. The air is starting to have a chill to it…Is that better?" he asked, as he rubbed her upper arms through his jacket, more out of a habit gesture than actually realizing what he was doing.

"Umm…Much better, Gabe, thank you," she said feeling the warmth of his large hands on her.

Longing to pull her into his arms and kiss her, he suddenly felt the need to put a slight distance between them. He lowered his hands with a great deal of effort and stepped back a few safer inches.

"Well, shall we continue our walk along the shore line, or is it too chilly for you now?" He smiled.

"I'm fine, detective. Let's walk and instead of me talking this time, why don't you tell me a little about yourself? I'd really like to get to know you better…After all, it looks as though we're going to be living together for a while." She smiled lustfully, deliberately trying to get a reaction out of the handsome detective.

He swallowed hard, trying to fight the feelings of excitement flowing through his body.

'*Please not now, damn it*'! He silently scolded himself, deliberately dropping a step behind her, hoping to calm himself down before she noticed the slight bulge rapidly growing in the front of his trousers.

He released a sigh of frustration. "I do wish you would watch how you phrase things, ma'am. After all, I'm only human, contrary to what you might think."

Nouri glanced around to sneak a quick peak at the blushing detective, noticing his slight problem. She giggled mischievously.

"And would you mind telling me just what it is that you seem to find so darn amusing?" he questioned silently thinking; '*God this woman is going to be the death of me... I just know it*'!

"You are, detective." She giggled again.

"Well, you just try and behave yourself, ma'am!" He blushed again. "...You're making it very difficult for me to keep my mind on what it's supposed to be on." He cleared his throat.

"And that is exactly what, detective?" She teased.

"Well... It's... Ah...Ah... The issue at hand. Remember?" He responded nervously.

"Oh that. Yes, detective, I remember now..." She nodded in agreement. "...The issue at hand. Which is my sex life, correct?" she mused, knowing she was driving the poor frustrated detective nuts.

"You like to play games don't you, Nouri?" he asked in an accusing tone.

"Not usually, detective. But with you, I can't seem to help myself." She giggled again.

"Very funny... Just try and behave yourself. My job is difficult enough." He shook his head.

"Meaning what, detective? You didn't want the job of babysitting me?" she remarked in disappointment.

"Nouri, your friend, which happens to also be my friend, asked me to do him a favor, and look after you while he is away, and..."

She quickly interrupted him. "Oh don't bother, detective!" She snapped, suddenly feeling rejected again by the handsome detective.

Gabe wanted to explain to her how he really felt about her. He would give anything to pull her into his arms and have his way with her, but he couldn't. It wasn't proper or even possible. Until he knew for sure just what her relationship with Charles Mason was, he couldn't possibly even consider continuing his lustful thoughts about her, much less anything else.

"Listen, Nouri. I didn't mean to hurt your feelings. I told you right up front that there were things about my job that even I hated. I need for you to stop behaving this way with me. I have a job to do...And part of that job is protecting you. And to do that properly, I explained to you all ready, that there are certain things I need to know, and..."

"Forget it, Gabe. You're right." Her tone swiftly mellowed surprising him.

"I am?" he remarked curiously.

"Yes. I'm sorry. I'll try my best from now on to behave myself for you," she smiled.

What's up? This is too easy'. he thought to himself, not quite sure how to respond to her. Suddenly, he noticed two lovers making love on the beach. Not wanting to intrude on the couple's magical moment, he put his index finger to his lips and softly whispered. "Shhh..." pointing to the two lovers. "We wouldn't want to disturb them," he whispered quietly, taking her by the hand and attempting to walk in the opposite direction.

"No!" Nouri pulled her hand from his. "Let's stay and watch." She sighed lustfully, shocking the detective.

"Why shame on you, Nouri Sommers. How would you like someone spying on you while you were making love with someone?" he remarked reaching for her hand again.

"Well, detective, if this couple wanted that much privacy, they would have surely gone back to their hotel room. Don't you think?" she said playfully.

"This is another silly little game of yours, isn't it? To try and get a rise out of me... Well let's get out of here before the two love birds notice us. Your game isn't working...And play time is over." He pulled her to him, almost losing what little self control he had left, when she flew into his arms.

They stood frozen, locked inside one another's tight embrace for and eternal moment. Their bodies tightly molded together, their eyes gazing into one another's longingly, and their lips only a heart beat away from touching.

Nouri seductively licked her beautiful, full lips, anticipating the detective's next move. She moaned softly when she felt his warm breath brush across her lips.

He lowered his head, his lips now less than a breath away. Nouri felt faint when his instant arousal pressed gently against her thigh, causing her to moan again.

"Oh God!" he groaned, desperately wanting her, but forcing himself, out of duty, to break himself free from the spell she seemed to have over him.

'She's going to be the death of me. I just know it'. he thought, clearing his throat and releasing a frustrated sigh. "I… I think we should start back to the car," he said with a great deal of effort, deliberately avoiding contact with her spell binding eyes.

Unable to speak, she just nodded hoping her legs were strong enough to move. She released a disappointed sigh.

After walking a few moments in silence, Nouri turned to face the visibly moved detective. She smiled knowingly.

"Tell me, detective, are you always so detached with the people you are protecting, or is it just with me?" She leveled her eyes to his.

"Nouri, please. I've explained to you that I have a job to do for a friend, and I intend to do it, as detached as possible."

"Fine detective. Have it your way, but you still didn't answer my question, now did you?" She forced a smile, as they began to walk.

"All right. The answer is 'yes'. I try to stay as detached with my assignments as possible."

"So, that's what I am... An assignment?" She snapped coolly.

"Yes. That, as well as a murder suspect."

"How shocking! Me... A Murder Suspect! If that statement wasn't so insulting, it would be quite amusing, detective." She giggled. "Why, I couldn't kill anything. Once I found a small family of spiders webbing their way inside one of my jewelry boxes, you know, the kind that looks more like a small dresser? Anyway, I couldn't bear the thought of hurting one of them. So I had Fredrick take the spiders outside and put them on a tree," she said smiling thoughtfully.

"You know, Nouri, I believe you. I've never really thought you had anything to do with The Lambert Murders, but still...It's my job to clear you or arrest you." He smiled enjoying watching her squirm.

"I still don't understand how my antique hairbrush and lipstick holder..."

Gabe stopped walking and turned Nouri around to face him quickly interrupting her. "You know about your hairbrush and lipstick holder being found at the scene of the two murders?" He swallowed nervously.

"Yes, detective. Charles Mason told me yesterday morning while we were having coffee."

"I guess Charles does care a great deal about you. Doesn't he?" He released a sigh of relief.

"Yes. Charles is worried sick about me, detective..." She sighed. "...Tell me something, what kind of a woman is his wife?" She glanced at him curiously.

"His what?" Gabe chuckled.

"His wife... Talula," she said in response. glancing at him curiously again.

"You must be joking... Charles married! That's a laugh." Gabe shook his head. "Charles has had women trying to tie his ass down for the past seven years. He's had women across the country chasing after him... From Movie Stars to Super Models... even the damn District Attorney, Tonya Lee Daughtery," he mused, shaking his head.

"The DA of Boston?" Nouri huffed disbelievingly.

"The one and only. She's still madly in love with him. Charles doesn't know this, and I probably shouldn't be telling you this, but..." He caught himself. "...Never mind. If Tonya found out that someone told Charles about her secret, she'd have their head on a platter...Forget I said anything!"

Nouri impulsively grabbed Gabe's arm and tuned him to face her. "Wait right there, mister detective man! You can't start to share something with me like that and then suddenly change your mind. You don't know very much about women, do you?" She released his arm.

"I know enough." He smiled arrogantly.

"Oh really!" She rolled her eyes.

"I've had my fair share of women," he grinned.

"I bet you have, detective!" she snapped jealousy.

The detective smiled knowingly. "Tell me, Nouri, how long have you been friends with Charles Mason?"

"Oh no you don't, mister!" She said shaking her head. "You're not changing the subject that easily on me! Now why in the world would Charles Mason tell me that he was married? And that his wife's name was Talula?" She put her hands on her hips stubbornly.

"Now, how in the world would I know something like that? All I do know about Talula is that she's his cat," he chuckled.

"I see. So he lied to me... Wonder why?" She turned red in the face.

"I'm sure he had his reasons," he said shrugging his shoulders. "See, there was once this woman about seven years ago, who stole his heart, only to break it into a million pieces. He's never gotten over this little *Thief of*

Hearts. Maybe he uses Talula as a safety shield to protect his heart or something. To keep women like you from throwing yourselves at him. I don't know," he said teasingly, shaking his head in an unknowing manner.

In an insulted tone of voice, she responded, "Throwing myself at him! "Why you…"

"Calm down! I was only kidding for goodness sakes!" he chuckled.

"Okay, detective, enough about Charles Mason… That is, unless you want to tell me about Tonya Daughtery's secret," she smiled.

"Lets just say…I hope they get back together someday." He smiled hopefully. "I think she holds the key to Charles' happiness. Even if he doesn't know it yet."

"I don't understand, Gabe."

"Nouri, I think Charles stopped seeing Tonya because he was actually falling in love with her."

"And, detective?" She motioned for him to continue, with a roll of her hand.

"He thinks he's still in love with his little *Thief of Hearts* from yesteryear. He desperately wants her back, and I honestly believe that he thinks someday she will come back to him."

"And if she did, detective? That would be a bad thing?" Nouri swallowed nervously.

"In my opinion, yes," he nodded.

"Why?" she asked nervously.

"When she left him, it almost destroyed him. I was there. It wasn't a pretty sight. After a while of feeling sorry for himself, he threw himself into his work and became a workaholic… Not necessarily a bad thing, but it kept him from really living life. Today his heart still belongs to the young broad that broke it!" He released a deep sigh.

"Gabe, you say she was a young broad. Maybe she was too young back then. Maybe she…"

Gabe heatedly cut her off in mid-sentence. "She destroyed him, damn it! Age doesn't have a damn thing to do with it!" he snapped excitedly.

"And you resent her for it?"

"No. I hate her for it! Do you have any idea what it's like to watch a person that you love as a friend, a partner that you respect and admire, self destruct like he did?" His tone was sharp and angry.

Nouri shook her head, unable to speak.

"It wasn't a pretty sight, let me tell you! I'm only thankful I never got around to meeting the bitch! I probably would have hurt her real bad," he sighed angrily.

"Gabe, I understand how you must have felt, but I'm sure there are two sides to every story. This little thief of hearts, as you refer to her, surely must have had her reasons for leaving him. Don't you think?"

"Maybe..." He raised his brow. "... But she still should've checked on him from time to time. She knew that she was his world!" He shook his head.

"Oh cut the shit, Gabe! " Nouri said with annoyance. " He was a grown man. What... Maybe ten--fifteen years her senior. Give me a break! She had the right to leave and grow up. Don't you think she was entitled to a life, as well?" She swallowed hard, glancing at the police detective angrily.

"The bitch shouldn't have been with him to begin with!" he remarked heatedly.

She grabbed his arm, turning him to face her. "What right do you have to make a remark like that to begin with, Gabe? Who died and made you Charles' father?" she snapped with an attitude.

"He was my partner. We were closer than brothers, for crissakes!" he snapped in return.

"And that gives you the right to run or dictate your brother's life!" she responded leveling her eyes to his.

"Well..." he remarked, shaking his hand in confusion.

"Well what, Gabe? We don't have any control over the people we love or who we are in love with. These two types of love are not the same. Maybe this little *Thief of Hearts* did love Charles. Maybe she would even love him forever, but maybe...just maybe, she wasn't in love with him at all. Now, would you want to stay in relationship like that? One where the person loves you, but you don't truly love them? What would you do? Especially at nineteen..." she said. Quickly catching her slip of tongue, she quickly went on ..."Or how ever old she was. Think back at yourself at that young age. Didn't you want to go out in the world and conquer it? Or would you have been happy just staying home with someone that had already lived a full life and..."

"All right, all ready!" the confused detective cut in excitedly. " I get your point. And right now I don't have an answer for you..." He turned away from her. "I need to have time to digest what all you have just said to me...So, for the time being, lets just change the damn subject, okay?" His tone was laced with confusion and bitterness.

"Fine. What subject would you like to chop away at now, detective?" she smiled sweetly.

Gabe began to walk heatedly ahead of her, his breathing so heavy, she could hear it several long steps behind him. He was still very sexy, even angry. She smiled to herself.

"Tell me detective, what else does it take to bring out that kind of passion in you?" she said, amused.

The detective ignored her remarked, but finally slowed his pace, and deeply sighed as he glanced at his watch. "How about we go back inside the restaurant and have a nightcap?"

"What detective? And soak our liver with alcohol, for crissakes?" she mused.

"Yeah, why not." He shook his head half-heartedly. "Suddenly, I feel as though I honesty need a drink to calm myself." He released another sigh of frustration.

"All right, detective," she said, glancing at the handsome detective's face under the moonlit sky.

Chapter 26

In total silence, Gabe and Nouri finished their second nightcap. Gabe was lost in thought, trying to digest everything that Nouri had said to him on the beach. Nouri was lost in thought, scolding herself again over her confusing attraction to the handsome detective.

Finally, the detective glanced at her, after glancing down at his watch. "I guess we had better get started. We have a long drive ahead of us."

He released a frustrated sigh, reaching for his wallet.

"Maybe we should get a hotel room for the night and start fresh in the morning, detective." she smiled melting the very core of his being.

God, how he wished he could do just that.

He returned her smile. "I'm sorry, Nouri. We've been here too long as it is. Someone might have spotted your car by now. It's hard to say what goes on inside the mind of the type of person that I'm trying to hide you from. I don't think we've been followed, but to be on the safe side we'd better go, okay?" He patted her hand.

"All right, detective. But this time in the car, it's your turn to talk. I want you to tell me all about yourself...starting, shall we say...from birth." she teased, flashing him a mischievous smile.

On their drive to the homicide detective's A-frame cabin in the woods, Gabe shared most of his life story with Nouri. He deliberately left out the parts about his family's money, his money, his family's background pertaining to the passing of money down from one generation to the next, his private boarding schools, and his recent breakup with the Baron's beautiful daughter, Lisa Claybourne.

"Well, it's sounds as though you have lived a very normal life, with a loving family. That's nice, Gabe. But you still haven't told me a lot about your relationship with

Charles Mason… Or as far as that goes…you haven't told me about any of the woman you date either," she smiled.

"You're sure you aren't writing a book about me, now are you?" he teased.

"I promise I'm not…" she giggled. "…Please continue, detective."

"I know. I'll tell you something that detective Ballard is dying to find out."

"Really! And what would that be, detective?"

"About the only case that I've ever worked on that I didn't solve." He glanced at her to see her expression.

"You! Well, I was under the impression that you were the best detective on the force, and I quote…'He always gets the bad guy'…unquote," she teased.

"Don't tell me…your new cop friend, Hobner. Right?"

"Yes, that's right, except he asked me to call him by his first name."

The detective laughed. "Rick." He rolled his eyes.

"Yes, Rick. What a super nice guy. He's pretty darn cute, too." She smiled teasingly.

"Yeah, he likes to think so," Gabe chuckled, shaking his head.

"Why, detective, is that a slight tone of jealousy I hear in your voice?" she mused.

"Hardly, ma'am." He glanced at her with one of his eyebrows raised.

They both laughed, and Gabe told Nouri that he would tell her about the only case he never solved after he made a quick pit stop. But by the time he had retuned, Nouri was asleep.

He smiled and shook his head lustfully, secretly wishing that he could stop and get a room and make love to the beautiful woman that had been able to distract him so easily, which was usually a hard thing for anyone to do.

He slid inside the car and quietly closed the door, trying hard not to disturb the sleeping beauty.

Closing the door jarred her awake, but she decided to pretend to still be asleep, wanting to tease with the detached detective.

She was curiously wondering how long it would take her to get him to seduce her. After all, she was pretty much a free woman now, with her elusive husband cheating and disappearing on her, her skirt chasing fiancé cheating and also disappearing on her. And well, quite frankly, even Charles Mason had a harem of woman. So why not? 'Why shouldn't she have her way with the handsome detective from the Boston Police Department'? she silently thought, faking a seductive stretch, slowly bringing her left arm down and gently running it across her left breast.

She overheard the detective release a frustrated moan. She smiled inwardly and seductively bit her lower lip- slowly releasing it, as she watched the lustful expression of the handsome detective through her squinted eyes.

Several moments later, she slid her head down to his lap. She stretched one arm over his lap and placed her other hand to rest on his bulging zipper. She smiled to herself again, as she felt his aroused state grow even larger.

She heard him mumble the words 'Oh God!' It took everything she had to keep herself from laughing out loud.

The detective swallowed hard and broke out in a cold sweat. She deliberately turned her face to lay her mouth on top of his hardness- smiling to herself, as he continued to groan helplessly.

Several stretches later, the detached detective was about mad with want for her. He swallowed hard again, as he gently tried to sit her up without waking her, mumbling words she couldn't make out.

She laid her head on his shoulder, and squinted a look at his still aroused condition. She almost giggled.

Several moments later, she seductively stretched again, letting her head fall across his throat and cheek- gently wrapping her arms around his neck. She could feel him swallow, and feel his burning flesh against her face.

He moaned again, as she slowly ran her hand down his chest, squinting another look, this time at his flushed face.

Detective or not, this man wanted her and he wanted her bad!

'*Detached...my fanny*', she thought to herself, faking another stretch, this time leaning her body away from his... This time his moan was one of protest. She smiled winningly, as she pretended to remain asleep.

A short time later, the excited detective pulled the Mercedes that belonged to Nouri into the gravel driveway to his hidden cabin in the woods.

He took one last lustful look at the beautiful woman asleep beside him, before attempting to wake her.

He released a frustrated sigh and glanced down at his trousers to make sure his hardness had disappeared.

'*God this woman is going to be the death of me... I just know it*', he silently thought, before saying her name.

When she didn't respond, he opened the car door and slid out, walking over to her side of the car and opening the door.

"Nouri, we're here," he said. Still she didn't move.

"Poor baby," he whispered, picking her up into his strong arms.

She faked a stretch and hugged him tightly, positioning her lips very close to his ear, knowing that when she breathed, she would blow warm air into his ear, and drive him lustfully crazy.

"Damn it!" He mumbled to himself, angry that he was becoming filled with desire for her again.

She fought back her laughter, lowering her head so her lips would brush against his.

"God, give me strength!" he begged softly, standing her to her feet. Not being able to control himself any longer, he knew he had to put a little distance between them.

"Nouri... wake up. We're here." His tone was frustrated and sharp.

"What? What did you say, detective?" She stretched and faked a yawn.

"I said we're here...We're at the cabin. Can you stand on your own yet?" he asked pulling his hands away from her.

"I think so." She faked stumbling up three small steps.

"Come on...let's go inside," he said putting his hand inside a large plant stand sitting on the porch, and pulling out a spare key. "I didn't feel like fumbling for my set of keys in my pocket," he said, smiling and waving the spare key playfully in her face.

"Wonder what he's trying to hide?" she whispered under her breath, amused.

"Did you say something?" he asked, looking back at her while he continued to fumble with the lock on the door.

She cleared her throat. "No. I didn't say anything," she answered, following him inside.

"Come on, I'll show you around, and then I'll bring in your suitcase," he said, leading her to the kitchen.

"Well, it's still sort -of a work in progress, you might say," he said, gesturing around the kitchen with a wave of his hand. "But it's doable." He added, smiling at her.

"I like it. It's sort of cozy. That's what cabins are supposed to be, right?" She smiled.

He shrugged his broad shoulders, thoughtfully trying to picture in his mind's eye her perspective on a kitchen being labeled cozy.

He scratched his head, not seeing her logic. "Come on. The living room is in here," he said, leading the way down a short hallway.

"And this is the living room. A bit larger, huh? The bar is over there. I think it's pretty well stocked. I'll start the fireplace after I show you the upstairs. Ready?" He said leading the way.

"Watch the third step... It's a little shaky, but safe enough, I think. I'm going to have the steps rebuilt, but like I said, I just bought the cabin a few months ago... Actually, this is only my third time here since I bought the place. It needs a lot of work, but unfortunately, I don't take that much time off," he smiled, as he continued to lead her up the flight of steps.

"Shall I take you to the bedroom next?" he said teasingly blushing after he said it.

"Why detective, I thought you'd never ask," she mused, causing him to instantly blush.

"Well, here it is. There's only one bed..."

She playfully interrupted. "Oh goodie. We get to share?" She teasingly jumped up and down, clapping her hands.

He blushed again. "Behave yourself!" He glanced longingly at her and shook his head.

He cleared his throat nervously. "I'll be sleeping on the couch, ma'am," he said, attempting to act unaffected.

Nouri leveled her eyes to his. "Pity," she said, as she enjoyed watching the *detached* detective squirm.

'God, please give me the strength to behave myself', he silently thought, crossing the bedroom floor. "Well, here is the bathroom, there's only one. So I'll try hard not to disturb you too much when I sing in the shower," he mused.

Nouri laughed out loud. "Oh God! You're not one of those are you?" She glanced at him still giggling.

"What would that be?" His tone was innocent.

"A singing in the shower type person." She giggled again.

Without speaking, he slowly moved close to her. She swallowed hard when he gazed seductively into her eyes. It looked as though he was going to pull her into his powerfully strong arms. She swallowed wantonly, excitedly anticipating his next move, but instead, he reached above her head. He knew what she was thinking. He smiled knowingly. Knowing she was hot for him both pleased and frightened him at the same time. He swallowed hard.

"Excuse me," he said, reaching into the upper closet for a spare blanket and pillow.

"No, I was only teasing," he finally said in response to her last remark.

"What?" he responded not quite sure what he had meant. His closeness caused her to lose her train of thought.

"Singing in the shower, remember? I said I was only teasing. I'm afraid I can't carry a decent tune," he chuckled.

He laid the pillow and blanket down on the bed.

"I'll get these later," he said walking to a walnut cabinet positioned along the side of the wall.

"In here are extra towels, wash cloths, stuff like that, okay?" He glanced at her, smiling.

She nodded glancing around the room.

"It gets pretty chilly in here at night, even in the summer months. Over there is the fireplace, I'll light it up for you later if you like." He glanced at her.

"That would be great! I love fireplaces. The flames are relaxing to me," she smiled.

"I like them, too. Well, that's pretty much the grand tour. Any questions?" He gazed into her beautiful hazel-colored eyes.

She melted, suddenly finding herself longing to fall into his muscular arms. She swallowed hard.

"No, I don't think so. Shall we go back downstairs and have a drink?" she smiled.

He shook his head playfully. "You and your booze," he said, gesturing towards the door.

Suddenly, the phone rang. Gabe glanced at it and then ignored it.

"Aren't you going to answer it?" Her tone was curious.

"No phone calls, remember? We don't want anyone to know where we are. You haven't forgotten, have you?" He questioningly leveled his eyes to hers.

"Ah... Ah... No detective. I haven't forgotten," she smiled.

"Anyway, I have an answering machine downstairs. If it's important, I'll get the message."

"Shall we?" he said, gesturing towards the door again.

"Sure," she whispered seductively in response, brushing past the detective, knowing every time she touched him, even in the slightest way, he would get excited. She smiled knowingly.

"Watch for the third step," he reminded her, glancing back over his right shoulder.

"Well, detective, you go start our fire. And I'll fix us a drink."

The detective shook his head hopelessly. "Nouri... I do wish you would watch the way that you phrase things," he said, glancing at her beautiful face.

"Whoops! I guess I should've said fireplace, huh?" was her playful response.

Without speaking, he shook his head at her remark, and went over and lit the fireplace.

"I'll be right back. I have to run out to the car and get your suitcase," he said, anxious to put distance between them again... So he could calm down.

Nouri brushed up against the detective on her way to the sofa, causing him to get excited again.

"Detective," she said, glancing at him from where she was sitting.

"Yes," he responded as he reached for the doorknob.

"I like your cabin. It sort of suits you," she smiled.

"In what way?" he glanced over his shoulder.

"It's sort of rough on the outside, but surprisingly nice on the inside. Quite nice, actually." She glanced at him from where she was sitting.

"Thank you... I think?" he smiled.

Nouri returned his smile. "It was meant as a compliment. I just meant you're not as tough as you would like people to think," she mused lightheartedly.

"I'm tough enough," he arrogantly responded, pulling back his jacket and patting his holstered revolver.

She shook her head amusingly. "Very funny, detective."

"Excuse me," he said, walking out the front door, happy to get a few minutes to himself, needing to pull his ever failing emotions back under control.

"Calm down, Gabe. She's just another woman..." he whispered under his breath. His next four words were..."Like hell she is." He shook his head hopelessly and released another sigh of frustration.

While Gabe was outside getting Nouri's suitcase, the telephone rang again. Nouri heard the answering machine click on. There was no prerecorded message- only a loud beep that immediately began taping.

"Hi darling. I don't know if you're there or not, but I've been phoning every number I know of to try and track you down. I miss you, Gabe... And I love you. I'm sorry about the other night. It was my fault. Don't worry about

Daddy. Mother will take care of him. Please call, darling... Bye." The next thing she heard was another loud beep, followed by Gabe kicking the door shut with his foot.

"I'll just run these upstairs for you. I'll be right back," he said, running up the stairs, taking two steps at a time.

"So, what are we drinking?" he asked, entering the living room.

"I hope Cognac is all right," she smiled, handing the drink to him.

"Perfect. Please sit down. Make yourself comfortable. Looks like this is going to be your new home for a while. I'll go to the store tomorrow and stock up on a few things," he said playfully, adding, "If you're a good girl, maybe I'll let you go shopping with me. You can pick out the groceries you want." He smiled, and teasingly winked at her.

"Umm...A good girl, huh?" She returned his smile, standing up and going back to the bar. "Are you ready for another drink, detective?"

"Sure. As long as you're going to have one." He handed his glass to her.

"Tell me, Nouri, are you ready to finish telling me the events of your past week?"

She rolled her eyes. "All work and no play, detective," she playfully responded, handing him his shot of Cognac.

"I have a job to do. Remember?" His expression was serious.

"So it seems. And you take your work very seriously, I might add," she said, slightly brushing her finger across his hand.

He swallowed hard. "Behave," he ordered blushing, when he noticed her mischievous grin.

"Ready to begin?" he asked, stretching his arm across the back of the sofa, almost touching her shoulder.

He looked into her mesmerizing eyes and melted again. Shaking himself back to reality, he quickly removed his arms and squirmed uneasily in his seat.

"All right detective, if you insist. What do you want to know?" She sighed, as though she were bored with it all, while taking a sip of her drink. She glanced at his handsome face, waiting for him to ask her a question.

"Tell me about your Friday night out in Mason, with your friend, Genna Matthews. That is her name isn't it?" he smiled.

"Oh, please detective, can't we do this tomorrow? It's been a very long day. Why can't we just have a few drinks, a little non-business type of conversation, take a hot bubble bath and call it a day?" she smiled.

"Oh, I don't know. I have a lot of questions that I need answered." He shook his head.

"Please detective," she pouted, placing her hand on his upper thigh without realizing what she had done.

His heart raced madly from her touch. *'Oh, please God! Don't let me get excited now'*, he thought, quickly removing her hand from his leg, and rising to his feet, making his way to the bar as fast as his long legs would carry him.

"Well, since you put it like that..." He smiled. "...I suppose a few drinks and a little casual conversation might be all right tonight, but I don't do bubble baths..." He smiled seductively. "... At least not by myself." He playfully wiggled his eyebrows at her, causing her to laugh.

"Thanks, Gabe," she said smiling brightly. "Make mine a double."

He shook his head playfully. "You and your booze," he playfully responded, glancing indiscreetly down at his trousers to make sure it was safe for him to return to his spot beside her on the couch.

'God, I need a cold shower', he thought to himself, handing her the drink.

"Thanks," she said softly, taking the drink from his unsteady hand. She smiled knowingly to herself.

"Oh, detective. You had another phone call when you went to the car to get my luggage." She glanced at him through the corner of her eyes, enjoying the look of guilt slowly sneaking across his face.

"Oh really. I imagine you overheard the message being recorded." He took a sip of his drink, trying to hide his nervousness.

She sat her drink down and slid slowly over to him, and seductively began to run her hand down his chest and across his muscular upper thigh.

"Oh Gabe darling… I'm sorry about the other night. It was my fault! Don't worry about Daddy… Mother will take care of him… I miss you darling. And I love you… Please call… Bye," she playfully recounted. "That message? Is that the one you're inquiring about, detective?" She grinned mischievously, as she gazed into his beautiful teal-blue eyes.

He swallowed hard, visibly moved by her caresses, blinking himself back from a dream state. He finally responded. "Very funny..." He cleared his throat in an effort to calm himself.

"… Did this apologetic little minx leave a name?"

"Ha!" She snapped, jealousy sliding back to her side of the sofa. "You must surely know the face behind a voice like that! After all, how many grown women do you date that still call their Father's 'Daddy'!"

"Excuse me. Maybe you would like to critique all of my personal messages. I believe I may have noticed several more calls lighting up on the machine..." He toyed. "… I rather enjoyed watching you act them out." His smiled lustfully.

"If it would keep your mind off business for a while, I'd love to." She glanced at him smiling.

Gabe sat in silence for a few moments, his curiosity getting the better of him.

'Are she and Charles having an affair? Why does he seem so interested in what happens to her? Is she the little Thief of Hearts that broke his heart all those years ago? Is she really through with Clint Chamberlain? Her Husband? Where does Charles fit into all of this? How many other men have had their goddamn hearts torn out over this five-foot five-inch, hundred and eight pound seductive temptress? Why am I so damn attracted to her? What kind of a spell has she got me under? God! She's masterful...'

"Hello. Is anybody in there?" she said teasingly, when she noticed the distant look on his face and in his eyes.

"Sorry, Nouri. I just have a lot on my mind right now. What were you saying?" He forced a smile, standing to his feet. "Want another drink?" He offered before going to the bar.

"Umm..." she replied, handing him her glass.

He reached for the Cognac bottle, emptying the remainder of the amber-colored liquor into his glass, then circled the bar to get another bottle.

He sat down on a bar stool, as he removed the burgundy and gold colored foil snuggly sealed around the tip of the bottle. Reaching for a corkscrew, his mind drifted again.

'God! It isn't fair. How can one woman be that damn beautiful...intelligent...incredible'! he sighed.

'She's too good to be true. She's got to have at least one flaw... I couldn't begin to imagine what that flaw might be... That is except for her poor choice in men. Her husband is an unimaginable pervert. Her fiancé a goddamn skirt-chasing prick, God... I can't believe she fell in love with that damn jerk... not once, but twice For Chirssakes! And well, I'm still not sure about Charles, but he fits in her little red book of lovers somewhere, I'd bet money on it...

She's almost got to be that St. Charles chick. I'd bet big money on that too. Fuck this guessing game. I've got to know. I'll make her confess. She's got to be the same woman... That's the only thing that makes any sense! The not knowing is killing me. At least I could put all this shit behind me and quit thinking about it, if it is her. I've got to know...'

"Detective." She was saying, as she pulled out a bar stool to sit beside him. "I was lonely. Do you mind?" She smiled seductively, quite aware that his mind was on other things. But what, she thought, as she waited for him to say something.

She intentionally brushed up against him, as she sat down on the barstool. He noticed, but was so flustered wondering about the next course of action he was going to take with her. He needed to know about her and his friend and he needed to know now.

"You like to play games, don't you Nouri?" he said in response to her intentionally brushing up against him and trying to excite him.

"We've been over this, detective...Remember?" she said smiling.

"Yes. I have an incredible memory, as a matter of fact. You, as I recall, said that with me, and I quote, 'I just can't seem to help myself', unquote. Is that correct?" He smiled faintly.

"Yes. I believe that is what I said, all right." she nodded, agreeing.

"But, you do like to play games, right?" His expression was one of confusion to her.

"It depends detective," she said shrugging her shoulders in response.

"On what?"

"On what kind of game we're playing...and who I'm playing the game with."

"I see. Well then…" he paused briefly. "It's a game I like to call 'fill in the blanks'. It's a game where I get to dazzle you with my professional intelligence," he smiled. "…And, of course, it's a game that you will be playing with me. Want to play?" he smiled, causing her to grow weak in the knees.

She swallowed nervously. "All right detective. I'll play your 'fill in the blanks' game. Go ahead and dazzle me. It's been a long time since I've been dazzled," she playfully remarked. Glancing into the handsome detective's eyes, she melted.

"Oh really? What about your two night sex-a-thon with Clint Chamberlain? It sounds to me like he did an admirable job of dazzling you, Nouri." His tone was one of jealously.

"Cute, detective," she replied, reaching for the Cognac bottle.

Gabe removed the liquor bottle from her hand and glanced at her before pouring himself a full glass and quickly swallowing it in one long drink, before pouring himself another shot, as well as one for her. She stared at him curiously, waiting for him to speak.

"I needed that," he finally said after catching his breath. "Shall we go to the sofa? It's more comfortable there," he smiled, leading the way with his drink in tow.

He sank down on the sofa, patting the spot beside himself. "Why don't you join me?" he said, continuing to surprise her with his sudden odd behavior. "Are you ready for me to dazzle you with my professional ability to fill in the blanks?" He leveled his eyes to her wide-eyed ones.

"Yes, but I'm afraid I don't understand what blanks you're talking about, detective." She took a sip of her Cognac.

He smiled, setting his drink down on the coffee table. His confusing manner was making her more nervous by the minute.

"You have had a very interesting week, to say the least, Nouri. I've decided that we can pretty much finish up a lot of the details of what I need to know, if you just let me help you fill in a few of the blanks." He shifted his weight and crossed his leg over the other one.

A sudden expression of disappointment crossed her face. "But, I thought you said that we could..."

"I know I did. But there are a few things that I really do need to know tonight." He sighed.

"All right. Let's just get this over with, for chrissakes!"

"It appears to me, Nouri, that you have left out quite a bit of your week's activities, haven't you?" His tone was serious.

"I don't know what you mean, Gabe?" She shook her head knowingly.

"I don't believe you've told me all the details pertaining to you and Charles Mason."

"Oh, really. What kinds of details would that be, detective?" She rolled her eyes with annoyance.

"Intimate details, actually," he said without batting an eyelash.

"I see. Then maybe you wouldn't mind explaining to me just how my intimate relationship, if I indeed had one with Mr. Mason, could help you in your quest to solve the Lambert Murders?" she snapped.

"I suggest that you let me be the judge of that," he barked back sharply.

"I'd rather not discuss my sex life...or lack of it, pertaining to Charles Mason with you, Gabe. I... I have my reasons, if you don't mind," she responded nervously.

"You have your reasons, Nouri, and I have mine. Will you continue to explain your relationship with Charles, or shall I start filling in the blanks?" His tone was more jealous than professional. He quickly added, "And while you're at it, I'd like a confession!"

A surprised expression quickly covered her beautiful face. "A confession? What kind of confession?" She stared at him with her wide-eyes.

"An admission of guilt, I believe is what I'm asking for."

She was confused. His expression looked serious, but his tone was almost teasing.

"Guilt!" She shouted heatedly. "I don't have a clue as to what you are talking about, Gabe," she said, beginning to wonder what type of game his so-called fill in the blanks game entailed, exactly.

He uncrossed his leg from the other, stretching his muscular arm along the back of the sofa, and gently patted her shoulder, sending shivers up her spine.

He smiled, knowing he had her both excited and angry at the same time. He watched her squirm before replying. "You know, I'm very good at getting confessions out of guilty people. As a matter of fact it's one of the things that I seem to do best." He smiled invitingly, driving her mad with confusion.

Beginning to wonder where his silly game was headed, she responded. "Oh really, detective." She met his searching gaze.

"You know, I have ways of making guilty people, much like yourself, confess." His tone was insistent and sure.

"Oh, I just bet you do, detective," she said suddenly realizing what it was that he obviously wanted her to confess to. '*The ball in this game is in my court now*', she silently thought after realizing the homicide detective wanted her to confess to being the *Thief Of Hearts* that had broken his partner's heart seven years earlier. After all, that's all it could be. She knew that he didn't suspect her involvement with the two Lambert Murders. She smiled to herself winningly.

"Oh, I do indeed," he said continuing to seductively stare into her eyes.

She smiled to herself as the pictures of the words she was about to say to him suddenly popped inside her brain. She almost giggled out loud.

"Just exactly what do you do, detective, handcuff your suspects to a bed and sexually torture them?" she smiled. "Or perhaps you cuff them to a bed post and offer them a thorough tongue lashing." She giggled, not being able to control herself any longer.

"Umm... Those are both delicious idea's to consider, I must confess." He gently touched her shoulder, adding, "I've never thought of those tactics. They certainly deserve some consideration... for possible future use," he said, smiling, causing her heart almost takeoff in flight. He slowly withdrew his hand from her shoulder and picked up his drink.

The pictures behind the descriptive words she had just so deliciously described to him suddenly began to take on a life of their own inside his brain. He felt himself quickly getting hard again.

Rising to his feet before she had a chance to notice his hardening condition, he quickly walked across the floor toward the bar. With his back to her, he asked her if she would care to join him for another drink.

She suspected why he had jumped to his feet so quickly and headed to the bar.

"I suppose I may as well, detective. I remember reading something about confessions one time. And from I recall, it could take a very long time to get an admission of guilt out of someone," she said enjoying herself, watching the sexually frustrated detective humorously try and calm himself down a bit. She giggled.

He overheard her giggle. "Is there something that you find humorous, Mrs. Sommers?" He said, suspecting why she was giggling.

"You, detective. I just can't seem to help myself. Are you all right?" She giggled again.

Crossing the floor to join her, he gazed into her eyes, as he handed her the drink. "I'm fine. Thank you very much. Nothing a cold shower couldn't fix I assure you, ma'am." He blushed, but his tone was cocky.

After he sank back down into his cozy spot on the sofa, Nouri leaned over and seductively whispered into his ear. "Pity."

Pulling herself away from his ear, she added, "I could have suggested a more satisfying approach."

Gabe sighed, silently praying that the lower region of his trousers would give him a break this time... It was too much to hope for. He felt himself getting hard, yet again. He tried not to draw attention to himself, as he crossed his legs again, one over the other.

'*This woman is going to be the death of me... I just know it*', he silently thought, getting angry with himself for having such little self-control around her. '*Damn it! Get a grip*', he scolded himself, anxious to get back to the issue at hand, which of course, was getting her to confess that she was the same woman that had broken his friend's heart seven years earlier.

"Well, I suppose I'm going to have to fill in the blanks for you, huh Nouri?" he said after much thought.

"You know, Gabe. Your 'fill in the blanks game' is beginning to bore me. Why don't you just come out with what we both already know, and be done with it?" She said, rising to her feet to stretch.

"All right then, confess!" he said sharply

"Not until you confess first!" she snapped back.

With a stunned expression across his face, the police detective sharply responded. "To what? What the hell have I got to confess to?"

"Gabe, You know damn good and well what I'm talking about... Admit it!"

Suddenly realizing that she was trying to make him admit that he was attracted to her, he rose to his feet, and without saying a word, walked over to the fireplace and tossed on another log.

After a few moments of silence, he walked back to the sofa and sat down.

"Nouri, all I care to know about this moment is..." He swallowed hard. "... I need to know if you are the same woman that destroyed my friend seven years ago. Are you?" He closed his eyes already knowing the answer.

She slid close to him and gently touched his face, causing him to open his eyes and look at her.

"Gabe... I didn't mean to hurt Charles. I was only nineteen at the time. My God, Gabe! He was a grown man, fourteen years older than myself. I wasn't ready to settle down with a man that had already lived a full life, when I had only begun to live one. I love Charles. I always have... and always will. He knows that. I'm just not in love with him. Do you understand?" She released a frustrated sigh.

Gabe looked at her, not wanting to understand, not wanting to forgive her so easily, not wanting to feel the knife that was jabbing him in the heart.

He shook his head, disbelievingly, and released a deep sigh.

"How many other men have you destroyed, Nouri?" His tone was sharp, his words cruel!

She fought back her tears. "Oh, I don't know, detective. Maybe several hundred or so by now... What do you think? Does that sound about right to you?" she snapped in response reaching for her drink and nervously downing it.

"That was real mature, Nouri."

"Listen, Gabe. You're making me crazy. I don't know what you want from me. What is it? Tell me!" She swallowed hard again struggling hard not to cry.

"All right, damn it... I'll tell you what I want! I want to know why you slept with Charles last night. Wasn't it bad enough that you destroyed him once? You had so much fun doing it the first time you thought you'd do it again. Is that it?"

"Oh, you jackass! You wouldn't understand it if I were to try and explain it to you!" she cried.

"Okay, I'll give you this much, Nouri... I don't like what you did to Charles seven years ago, and for along time, I thought that I even hated you for it. But, after what you said to me on the beach earlier tonight, I suppose I can almost understand your side of it..." He swallowed, and rubbed his chin with one hand thoughtfully. "...But, why did you have to go and get him all hot and bothered all over again?" He nervously pulled a cigarette from his pack and lit it, quickly releasing a puff of smoke.

Nouri shook her head in disbelief. "And is this why you're so upset with me? Because I slept with Charles last night?"

"I'm just trying to understand, that's all, Nouri. Do you really care for Charles? Or is it Clint Chamberlain that you're still in love with? How about your husband? Does he know about Clint or Charles?" He shook his head in dismay. "Tell me, what were you thinking while you were making love to Charles? Were you thinking about him...Clint...or perhaps your elusive husband? I don't know...maybe there's someone else you haven't told me about...Is there?"

Nouri angrily jumped to her feet and heatedly put her hands on her hips. "This conversation is over, detective!" She clicked her heels together attempting to turn, almost falling to the floor.

Gabe quickly reached for her stopping the fall.

"Are you all right?" he asked, softening his tone to her. She angrily jerked herself free from his hold and stormed out of the room, running upstairs as fast as her legs would carry her.

She threw herself across the bed and began to cry. Nouri didn't know if she was crying over her argument with the handsome detective, his obvious rejection, Charles Mason falling in love with her all over again, Clint Chamberlain cheating on her all over again, her husband disappearing into thin air, the two murders in Lambert, or a combination of everything.

Gabe stood frozen in front of the sofa where he had rushed over to stop Nouri's fall, still in shock from the emotional outburst she had just unleashed on him.

Several moments later, he managed to pull himself from the invisible frozen spot that had been holding him prisoner.

He shook his head in disbelief, throwing himself down on the sofa. "Get a goddamn grip on yourself Baldwin, you stupid jerk." he mumbled to himself, as he laid his head back on the sofa, realizing the unwarranted, unprofessional, and hurtful actions he had just forced Nouri to endure, especially after the horrible week she had just gone through.

"What the hell is with you, Gabe?" He scolded himself, after not being able to explain his uncontrollable streaks of jealously over this woman that he had just met the day before. He opened his eyes and sighed hopelessly, glancing down at his watch.

Gabe knew he had to go upstairs and apologize to Nouri, but did he dare? Would he be strong enough to walk away from her this time if she came running back into the comforting safety of his strong arms?

Gabe suspected that Nouri had let Charles make love to her the night before because she needed to be held, possibly even feeling a little betrayed by Clint Chamberlain.

'*Makes sense*', he continued to think. '*A beautiful woman like that...married to a man like Ethan Sommers for the past two years...it seems like he was sexually satisfying every woman in Boston instead of his own incredible wife. That's probably why she let Clint Chamberlain back into her life...feeling ignored and neglected by her dumb-ass husband... Made her an easy target for her skirt-chasing ex-lover*'. He sighed unconsciously.

'*She finds him cheating on her again, right after he had promised to marry her after her divorce from Ethan...Feelings of rejection...betrayal? Probably add a touch of revenge laced with a lot of booze. Enter Charles Mason, her childhood protector, teacher, and powerful lover. It all makes sense. Except for one thing. Why lead the man on again? What did she have to gain? Is he aware that she's not in love with him? Or does he even care? Is he so blinded by her beauty that he can see no reason? Yet she says she truly cares about him. Does she? I know Charles. He has no intention of letting her go that easily this time. And me. Where do I fit into her little scheme of things? Am I willing to take the number four and wait in line? It would be the end of my relationship with Charles. Is she worth it*'? Gabe sighed again.

Would I ever be able to look at him in the eyes again? I know she wants me...As much as I want her...Admit it, damn it! That's what she's longing to hear. Am I strong enough to continue rejecting her'?

His mind raced on…

'*You know, Gabe. She may not be a murderer, but she is dangerous! Truly a thief of men's hearts! Look at yourself... Less than twenty-four hours after you first met her, and she's been nothing but a constant distraction for you. You can't stay focused. All you do is think about her... Her incredible body...Her beautiful face. My God, Gabe. Is it lust? Love? Or just plain insanity? Whatever the feeling is, it has got to stop! It can't continue. She'll only destroy*

you just like she did Charles. Look at the poor bastard...
Seven years later....Just look at him! He honestly believes
he still has a shot of winning her back. Poor smuck! No
woman should come between friends. You have to cut her
loose, Gabe. The fantasy must end...'

Gabe thoughts were suddenly interrupted when he heard Nouri let out a scream.

He jumped to his feet, grabbed his revolver, and ran up the flight of stairs taking them three at a time.

With his gun ready to fire, he kicked the bedroom door open and quickly darted inside the room- only to swiftly lower his gun when he realized she had been screaming in her sleep. After scanning the room, he quickly went to the bed to wake her.

Laying his gun down on the nightstand, he put his arms gently around her shoulders. "Nouri..." He said softly, gently shaking her. "You're having a bad dream...Wake up, everything is all right. Do you hear me?"

"Oh, God! Gabe, it was awful...just awful." she cried, reaching her arms up to his neck and hugging him tightly.

He swallowed hard, softly patting her back. "It's all right, Nouri. It was only a dream. See?" he said, as his touches grew more sensual than he intended.

She moaned softly, brushing her lips across the flesh of his throat.

"Oh, God Gabe... Please, just hold me... I need to be held."

He tightened his embrace and let his face fall to the side of her neck. "Nouri," he whispered helplessly, closing his eyes.

"Please don't say anything, detective...Just hold me for a while. I'm so afraid." She sighed, burying her face between his throat and his shoulder.

Gabe could feel himself getting aroused again. Nouri was driving him insane with desire for her. He swallowed hard again gently freeing his arms from around her.

"Nouri... Sit up, please." He reached for a pillow. "Here, let me put this across my lap. You lie on it and I'll massage your back until you go back to sleep, okay," he said, longing to join her in a more intimate way.

"No, Gabe...I...I need for you to lay with me and hold me close. I promise I'll behave. I just need to feel your strong body touching mine. I'm too afraid to sleep alone." she whined childishly.

'God this woman is going to be the death of me... I just know it'. He thought, before responding. "All right, Nouri. But you have to promise me. No more games tonight. I'm fighting a lot of issues within myself right at the moment. And God help me...I'm only human, okay?" he said in a shaky voice.

"I promise, Gabe. Sex is the last thing on my mind right now." She bit her lower lip nervously, sliding her body around on the bed to allow enough room for him to lie beside her.

He went to the fireplace and started a fire, as Nouri watched. She was still visibly shaken. He glanced over at her, admiring her beautiful face in the glow of the dancing golden flames of burning embers.

'God help me', he thought, walking back to the bed.

"Don't you want to take off your clothes?" he asked, not intending the way his words came out.

She shook her head. "No. Just come and lay beside me," she said softly, watching the incredibly sexy stranger slide into bed beside her. He propped his pillows up to the point where he was almost sitting, and pulled her close to him protectively.

"Nouri," he said her name softly glancing down at her, as she tightly molded her body to his, her head resting comfortably on his powerful chest, her arms clinging tightly to his waist and her right leg coiled over his left one.

"Umm," she whispered hoarsely, slightly raising her head to look at him.

"I'm sorry about tonight. I had no right…"

She interrupted him. "It's okay, Gabe. I'm a little confused myself," she said smiling understandingly.

He gently began to stroke the soft, thick, long strands of hair that were running down past her shoulders.

"No it isn't okay, Nouri. I'm sorry. It was very insensitive of me…not to mention my timing being so inept considering the week you've just endured. My behavior was way out of line," he said. "Unforgivable." He shook his head.

Understanding the obvious confusion that the handsome detective was experiencing about his attraction to her, being apparently a victim of the same dilemma herself, she smiled and nodded, stretched, yawned and cuddled her body back into the masculine mold of his.

He pulled his right arm up and placed it behind his head, as he continued to gently caress her shoulders and back until she finally dozed back off into a safe, sound sleep.

As Gabe laid beside the beautiful stranger that was so contently snuggling next to him, he smiled knowing that for reasons he may or may never be able to explain, he would go to his grave if he had to in order to keep her safe and out of harms way. He closed his eyes and soon fell asleep.

Chapter 27

The continued loud banging of the shutter outside the bedroom window of the cabin jarred Gabe from a rather light sleep. He opened his eyes and glanced down at the beautiful woman that was still so snuggly wrapped around his body. He smiled longingly, as he gently uncoiled his body from hers.

Sliding out of bed, he went to the window to see what the ruckus was all about. He smiled when he opened the window and noticed a couple of raccoons playing together in the large, solid, oak tree only a few yards away. He inhaled deeply; letting his lungs fill with the crisp, clean air.

Gabe could smell the rain in the air even though it hadn't started yet. The way the wind was whipping around, he knew it wouldn't be long. He leaned half-way out the window to fasten the shutter that had been jarred loose from its lock. "There, that ought to do it," he said pulling his body back inside the window.

"Are you attempting suicide, or is that how you keep that manly body of yours in shape?" Nouri said, smiling lustfully as she continued to cuddle with the detective's pillow tightly clutched in her hands.

"I'm sorry. I didn't mean to wake you," he chuckled. "The shutter had apparently pulled free from its lock," he replied, turning to face her.

"You didn't wake me. I went to reach for you. I'm a cuddlier," she explained quickly adding: "...but you were gone. It startled me." She smiled.

Gabe swallowed hard. "Nouri... I..."

She interrupted. "Please come back to bed with me," she said softly patting the spot beside her on the bed, causing the frustrated detective to swallow hard again.

"I do wish you would watch how you phrase things, Nouri. I keep telling you, I'm only human." He smiled nervously walking back to bed.

Before he had time to slide back in bed there was a loud knock on the front door. Gabe stopped in mid-step and turned to face the bedroom door. He glanced over at the nightstand to make sure that his gun was still where he had put it.

He walked over to get the gun and shoved it in the back of his trousers.

"You stay here. I'll see who it is," he said, glancing at his watch and quickly leaving the room.

Nouri jumped out of bed, too curious to stay in bed, like she was told. She quietly tiptoed down the hallway and stood at the top of the staircase, hoping to be able see or hear who it was that knocked on the door and what they wanted.

Gabe cautiously opened the front door with one hand on the doorknob and the other hand behind his back ready to pull his gun if he had to.

Nouri saw Gabe slowly remove his hand from behind his back when the person on the other side of the door pushed her way past him. "Hi neighbor. Remember me?" Her voice sexy and her mission obviously *SEDUCTION!*

"Huh," Nouri whispered under her breath jealously when see saw a woman wearing a long, sparkling-red, evening gown with a slit, up to her hip throw her arms around the detective's neck and passionately kiss him.

Gabe, too stunned to do anything, just stood there while his beautiful neighbor, Celina Sawyer, ravished his lips.

Finally coming up for air, Gabe took a step back. "Celina. What brings you out so late?" He glanced at his watch nervously again, already quite aware of the time.

The sexy woman laid her arm on one of his shoulders and smiled. "I was at a party earlier and on my way home tonight. I noticed the smoke coming out of your chimney, so I thought I'd bring you a little something to sort-of warm you up," she said seductively in response, waving a bottle of champagne in front of the nervous detective's handsome face.

Gabe swallowed hard, tempted to take Celina into the living room and toss another log on the fireplace. But the voice of reason cautioned him when he spotted Nouri peeking at him and Celina from atop the staircase. He smiled amusingly to himself and ushered his sexy neighbor to the front door instead.

"I'm sorry Celina, this is not a good time for me. Can I phone you tomorrow?" He asked nervously glancing at Nouri, again from out of the corner of his eye.

His sexy neighbor pouted. "Sure I can't change your mind, detective? After all, the last time you were here, you did say it would be my turn to bring the champagne next time you…"

Gabe quickly interrupted her knowing from the looks of it, his spirited houseguest was about ready to storm down the stairs, and God only knows what she might do or say to embarrass him with one of her silly games.

"Celina, as tempting as all this is…and I do appreciate the gesture, I'm afraid your timing is a little off tonight. Like I said, I'll call you tomorrow. Okay?" he said, smiling and walking her to the door.

"But Gabe, darling this isn't like you," his sexy neighbor protested as he ushered her out to her car.

"Huh!" Nouri snapped jealously, as she began to mimic Celina's last few words to the sexy detective.

"But Gabe, darling… This isn't like you." She stopped mumbling to herself and quickly ran back into the bedroom and jumped into the bed, when she heard Gabe shut the door and start back up the stairs.

He smiled to himself, knowing Nouri would most probably pretend that she had been in the bedroom the whole time. He opened the door, determined to tease her a little.

He walked into the bedroom, deliberately pretending to be up to something. He nervously began to pace back and forth, glancing at his watch every few minutes or so, acting as though he were trying to think of an excuse to get out of the house for a while.

"So, who was at the door?" she asked in a jealous tone of voice.

He continued to act as though he were nervous about something. "Huh? Oh, just a neighbor. It was nothing, really." He forced a smile, glancing nervously at his watch again.

"What's the matter, detective? You're acting as though something is on your mind, something to do with your neighbor? Is... Is he all right?" She studied his face for a reaction, trying to catch the good detective in a little white lie.

"Oh... Ah, my neighbor is ah...ah...fine. I think," he said glancing at his watch again. "...Listen Nouri, I was just thinking...maybe I'd better run out and try to find a grocery store open or a twenty-four hour mini-mart...or, something before the storm starts. I don't think there's much to eat around here. I shouldn't be too long...Oh, maybe several hours or so...you'll be fine until I get back. It should be light in a couple of hours," he said smiling and walking to the door.

Nouri jumped out of bed and quickly whirled the detective around to face her. "Listen detective! I think I'd rather go to the store with you. If you don't mind." She smiled suspiciously, suspecting she knew what he was up to.

He smiled to himself, finding her jealousy rather amusing. He leveled his gaze to hers after glancing at his watch again. "Oh, you would, would you? I'd rather you stay here and hold down the fort while I'm gone." He smiled and turned to leave.

She quickly ran around him and blocked the doorway, holding one arm up against the frame of the door and her other hand on the door knob.

She smiled stubbornly, looking into his eyes, melting the very core of his being. '*God, how I want to pull you into my arms and have my way with you*' --Is what he wanted to say, but instead he remarked, "What? Does this mean you don't want to stay here and hold down the fort?" His tone was playfully curious.

"Yes, detective. You are not leaving this house without me. Understand?" She removed her arms from the doorway and placed them determinedly on her hips.

The turned-on detective was dying to pick her up into his arms and playfully toss her into the bed. But he knew if he would even touch her in anyway what so ever, he wouldn't be able to stop this time.

"All right. Then maybe you should go with me then," he said, surprising her by how little he was going to argue with her about it.

"Yeah! You mean it? It's okay if I go?" she said smiling, surprised at how easily he let her come between him and his sexy neighbor.

He smiled the ever so sexy smile of his, responding in an amused tone. "Sure. You can help me pick out a few things to tide us over for a few days."

"Oh, wait a minute. Maybe I should change." She bit her lower lip, as she started to walk past him.

Gabe reached out and grabbed her by the hand. "No. It's going to start raining soon. We'll take a shower and change when we get back. Okay?" he said, playfully pulling her through the bedroom door.

"All right, detective. But wait a minute…" she remarked, pointing down at her bare feet. "Don't you think

I should at least put some shoes on?" She smiled running back into the bedroom.

"Okay, but hurry. I'll be downstairs waiting," he shouted, running down the stairs.

Chapter 28

"So, Nouri, what do you think you might like to fix us for breakfast this morning?" Gabe asked, teasingly turning the corner of aisle two with their empty grocery cart.

She laughed. "Me, detective! Surely you must be joking," was her surprised response.. "I can do a lot of things good... quite good, actually. But cooking? You have no idea." She shook her head. "If someone were to hand out awards for the world's worst cook, I'd take home the gold." She laughed again.

"I see. And when was it exactly that you discovered...shall we say, to be kind of course, your lack of ability in the kitchen?" he mused, passing aisle three and four, not paying attention to where they were going.

Nouri smiled mischievously. "Let's just say, detective, that after they kicked me out of home economics class after my first week of school...I believe it was the ninth grade..." She looked thoughtful for a moment. "Yes, it was the ninth grade...anyway, that was pretty mush my last lesson in the kitchen." She smiled mischievously.

"Poor baby. Can't boil water, huh?" He chuckled, shaking his head in amusement.

She shrugged in agreement. "Pretty much so, I'm afraid," she said, as they continued to pass a few more aisles.

"Well, lucky for you, I'm not just another pretty face. I, my dear lady, can... not only cook the best three-egg scrambled omelet in Boston, but I can also clean...and sew, as well," he mused adding, "That is...only if I'm forced to." He smiled, glancing at her.

"A three-egg scrambled omelet? One doesn't scramble omelets does one, detective?" she giggled, looking at his handsome face.

"This one does ma'am," he laughed. "I put everything but the kitchen sink in my omelets. One of a kind...I can assure you." He laughed again, passing aisles five and six with the grocery cart still empty.

"Umm. I can hardly wait, detective," she mused as they rounded the last aisle.

"So you don't cook, or clean house, and you don't sew. Is that right, ma'am?" He playfully leveled his eyes to hers.

"No. I'm afraid not, detective. But I do other things pretty well." She seductively toyed, licking her full, thick lips sensually and biting her lower lip, with a naughty expression plastered across her face.

The excited detective swallowed hard, shaking his head in an attempt to clear his brain of his lustful thoughts of his sexy assignment, while he pushed the cart past aisle four and five again. "I just bet you do, ma'am," he said in response to her last suggestive statement, which caused him to break out in a cold sweat. Just the thought of her beautiful, full lips, and what he passionately longed to do with them... Oh, God! he thought, clearing his throat.

"What's the matter, detective? You look rather flushed all of the sudden," she smiled knowingly.

"Behave," he whispered nervously heading for aisle one, yet, again, with their grocery cart still empty.

"Behave! Why, detective. What ever do you mean?" she teased, playfully batting her eyes.

The *detached* detective responded with a grin, glad that he finally seemed to be able to keep his excitement under control, for the moment anyway.

"So we're going to have scrambled egg omelets for breakfast...and bloody Mary's, of course." She grinned when he shook his head at her. "And, what... pray tell, detective- do you plan on feeding me for dinner tonight?" She smiled seductively, melting his heart again.

He paused for a moment and sighed. "Well, I've already told you what I cook best." He raised eyebrows teasingly and shrugged his shoulders.

Nouri laughed. "Omelets again, detective? Oh, please!" she giggled.

Suddenly a short, round man with a bald head and horrible mustache that needed trimming very badly, stopped the distracted couple, as they were getting ready to pass aisle four for the fourth time.

"Excuse me. Is there something I might be able to help you with?" he asked nervously.

Nouri and Gabe looked at one another, suddenly realizing that they had been going around in circles for over an hour and still hadn't put one grocery item in their cart.

Sensing the clerk's nervousness, Gabe reached for his badge and flashed it, hoping it would calm his uneasiness towards them.

The manager released a sigh of relief and nodded. "Thank goodness! I'm here, all alone tonight. We were robbed a few nights ago by a man and woman. I guess I must still be a little spooked. I hope I didn't appear to be rude to you, sir," he said apologetically, wiping the sweat from his brow.

"No. I can't blame you for being cautious. I probably would be, too," Gabe said in response, nodding. "Say, did they catch the couple that held you up?" he asked curiously.

"No. But I'm sure they will, sir," the clerk sighed.

"I'm sure they will, too. Well, I guess we'd better get our groceries and be on our way. Sorry if we frightened you," the detective smiled.

The spooked grocery clerk returned Gabe's smile and went back to the front of the small grocery mart and gas station

'See what you do to me, Nouri. I turn to mush. I can't stay focused when I'm around you', Gabe thought, as he smiled at her.

"Well, guess we'd better grab a few eggs...some cheese, peppers, mushrooms, ham, sausage, bacon, and milk. What else do you like in your omelets?" he smiled, as he looked around for the dairy aisle.

Nouri laughed, shaking her head. "That should pretty much cover it...I would think, detective." she smiled adding, "Don't forget the V-8 Juice for our Bloody Mary's."

Gabe stopped walking long enough to shake his head. "You and your booze," he said teasingly. "What ever am I going to do with you?" he smiled, heading for the dairy section.

Chapter 29

"Here, Nouri, you take this one. It's the lightest bag. I think I can manage the rest of them," Gabe said, pulling the bags out of the car.

"Looks as though we bought the entire store out just for breakfast!" she said, amused, as they walked up to the front door of the cabin.

"I guess you'll have to reach into my pocket for the key," Gabe said reluctantly. "I haven't had a chance to put the spare key back into the plant holder yet."

Nouri couldn't resist toying with the frustrated detective every time she got an opportunity to do so.

"Why, detective Baldwin. I can't believe you're actually asking me to put my hot little hands inside your pants," she smiled lustfully.

'*This woman is going to be the death of me. I just know it*', he thought before asking her to, "behave."

She giggled mischievously, as she put her hand inside the detective's trousers, her eyes gazing lustfully into his the entire time she was trying to fish out the keys.

"Whoops!" she whispered seductively when she accidentally brushed the side of his huge bulge, causing him to become instantly aroused.

He swallowed hard, almost dropping the overstuffed grocery bags. "Just open the damn door," he groaned in frustration, causing Nouri to giggle.

In frustration, Gabe stormed into the kitchen, needing to put immediate distance between the two of them for a few moments.

"This damn woman..." he was mumbling, as she entered the kitchen behind him.

"This damn woman, what?" she remarked teasingly. "What were you going to say, detective?" lnowing the

311

detective was probably less than a heart beat away from losing all self- control.

He looked at her still flushed faced. "Whew!" he sighed, shaking his head. "You have no idea what it is that you are…"

He suddenly stopped talking and turned his back to her. "Listen, I'm going to run upstairs and take a quick shower. You put the things away and I'll start the omelets when I come back down." He quickly left the kitchen without waiting for her to comment.

She smiled winningly, knowing she was driving the poor detached detective mad with desire for her.

'*I have nothing but time… It will happen*', she silently thought before shouting to the detective, "Be sure to save some hot water for my bath, detective." She giggled, wondering if Gabe was going to come back at her with one of his short fused replies.

She didn't have to wonder long. He instantly responded. "Oh, they'll be lots of hot water left ma'am, I only intend to use the goddamn cold!"

She giggled mischievously as she began to put the groceries away.

Once inside the bedroom, Gabe threw himself across the bed, shaking his head in frustration. He put both hands over his face, muttering to himself.

"This is without doubt the damnedest case I've ever worked on since joining the force nineteen years ago. It's confusing…frustrating…aggravating…yet exciting! Never a goddamn boring minute around her. Whew!" He said, releasing another frustrated sigh forcing himself to sit up.

'*She's going to be the death of me… I just know it*'! he thought again, walking to the bathroom to take a cold shower, struggling within himself between honor, and loyalty between friends, his duty being a cop, and his fiery desire for a woman who's touch alone completely disarms him.

Lust! He was an expert of, but, with this woman, it was different! She seemed to be able to do things to him no other woman has ever been able to do before. And yet, he doesn't know her, nor, had he kissed her, though God knows he had wanted to ravish her lips from the very moment he laid eyes on her.

Could this be love at first sight? Is it possible? Does something like that really exist between two people? It's more than lust. It's almost magical. He continued to search for the voice of reason inside himself as he let the cold water beat against his fiery hot flesh.

Suddenly, another voice entered his brain and it wasn't the voice of reason. It was the voice of the woman that had caused all his confusion and frustration to begin with.

He shook his head with annoyance. "I'll be out in a minute. Is everything all right?" he asked, quickly darting into the bedroom-- attempting to wrap a towel around his manly waist.

Her eyes eagerly traveled the length of his gorgeous body. She swallowed hard, trying to fight her impulse to rush into his arms.

"Ah...ah..." She swallowed again, trying to pull herself together. "I'm sorry to disturb your shower, but, while I was making a batch of Bloody Mary's, you had an ASAP message from a Captain Mark Bauer with the Boston Police Department. He said it's extremely important that you phone in immediately...If you get the message." She released a nervous sigh, checking his manly frame out again, as she waited for him to say something.

"Thanks..." he said half dazed. "...Listen, while I'm brushing my teeth and taking a quick shave would you get me something out of the closet to wear?" He motioned to the closet. "There should be some shirts in there, too." Without thinking anything of it, he added, "My socks and underwear are in the dresser...Thanks." He darted back into the bathroom, leaving the door open, but not meaning to.

Nouri smiled, but not knowing why. It just felt good to have a man, not just any man, but the sexy detective ask her so nonchalantly, as though it were the most normal thing in the world for her to do, to help her man get dressed. It sort of made her feel as though they might have been a couple. It felt nice.

She smiled as she walked to the closet to choose a suit for him, then to the dresser to get his socks and underwear.

"Boring!" she mumbled under her breath when she pulled out a pair of white cotton boxers.

Nouri selected a dark gray suit with a pale blue shirt and a tie that seemed to match perfectly. She laid everything down on the bed, except for the suit jacket, which she was still holding in her hands when Gabe walked out of the bathroom, still wearing a towel.

"Oh, damn," she groaned quietly in protest, after having her heart set on a sneak peak of his entire body. "Gabe, I hope the things I selected are okay," she smiled excitedly, hoping he wouldn't come to his senses too soon.

Not really paying much attention to anything, being lost in his own thoughts, he nodded and smiled, dropping the towel from his waist. "Oh thanks, Nouri that will be just..." He suddenly stopped talking and quickly reached for his towel again when he realized that not only was his babysitting assignment still in the room, but how easily he had asked her to do something personal for him. Not only was she a stranger, but a woman like her, you just don't ask a woman like Nouri Sommers to get your underwear out of a drawer.

"Oh, my God!" He cringed when he finally put it all together. "Nouri, I'm so sorry... I was lost in thought..." He blushed.

She quickly interrupted him. "Hey detective, I didn't mind. It was...well...it was sort of fun for me. I've never been asked to help dress a grown man before." She smiled lustfully when she saw him nervously holding the wadded bath towel in front of his manhood, not realizing his behind was exposed.

She giggled mischievously. "All right. I'm leaving, detective," she said, admiring his perfectly contoured body... '*My lord the detached detective looks pretty amazing to me*', she thought, walking toward the door.

The still flushed-faced detective replied, "Hey, thanks...I like what you picked out. I usually don't pay much attention to what I wear unless I'm going out on a date or something," he went on, still aware that Nouri's wide eyes had not left his muscular body.

She smiled. "Somehow detective, I thought so."

He chuckled. "So, you didn't like the suit I had on yesterday?"

"Oh God, that's an understatement! If I were you, detective, I'd burn the damn thing as soon as possible," she teased.

Gabe shook his head. "What! And hurt my poor aunt Marsha's feelings? She got that suit as a birthday present, oh...about seven...no, make that eight years ago," he lied teasingly.

Nouri rolled her eyes in disbelief and shook her head, as she started toward the door. Again glancing back over her shoulder, she playfully remarked, "Oh, by the way, detective...you did save me some hot water, didn't you?" She smiled and opened the door.

Gabe quickly responded, "Oh, yes, ma'am. But, if I were you, I'd consider a cold shower as well. After all, you keep forgetting that we are going to be joined at the hip for God only knows how long...and it might be to your advantage to try and remember that...after all, I am only human." He smiled lustfully, causing her to suddenly feel weak in the knees.

She cleared her throat and leaned against the door, aware that the detective had just deliberately disarmed her with that seductive smile of his. She released a sigh, unable to speak. She just simply returned his lustful smile with a seductive smile of her own, and backed out of the doorway, slowly closing the door behind her.

'*That woman is going to be the death of me... I just know it*', he thought, reaching for his boxers.

Nouri went to the bar and poured herself a Bloody Mary. She decided to stay at the cabin and let Gabe take care of his police business himself. She wanted to take a long, hot bubble bath, but suddenly found herself, wondering if Mai Li had packed her favorite brand for her. After all, everything the night before had happened so quickly. And since arriving at the cabin, she hadn't had the time to unpack yet.

"Well Nouri, are you ready to go? We better hop to it." Gabe was saying, as he entered the living room.

She smiled approvingly. "Wow! Look at you, detective. You look very dashing, I must say."

He blushed, playfully spinning himself in a circle. "Glad you approve. I'd hate to have to burn this suit, too." He smiled that incredibly sexy smile of his again. "So, are you ready?" he asked, fidgeting with his tie.

"No, Gabe. You go and take care of your police stuff. I want to stay here and take a long, hot bubble bath...that is, if Mai Li didn't forget to pack my bubble bath," she sighed.

"Well, if she didn't, I think there might be some upstairs somewhere," he said knowing he would get a reaction out of her for that statement.

She jealously looked at him. "Oh really, detective! I thought you said you don't do bubble baths."

He grinned mischievously at her responding, "No. Actually, what I said was…that I don't do bubble baths alone." His eyes still locked to hers.

"Umm. So you did, detective." She held her drink up to salute him before taking a sip.

He smiled, knowing he had made her jealous again. "Play time is over, come on…put your shoes on; we have to go now. I think it's about a forty-five minute drive to the station from here. I have to check in with the chief first, and then they'll probably give me an office to use for a while. Our DA will then have to…"

Nouri quickly stopped him from talking. "No. You go on. I'll be fine. I haven't had a shower since yesterday afternoon, and I just want to relax. I'll just stay here, take my bubble bath, have a few drinks, and wait for you to come home and feed me," she smiled.

"Umm. Wait for me to come home, huh?" he smiled. "We're starting to sound more and more like an old married couple, aren't we?" He shook his head, amused.

She giggled. "Yeah, and after laying out your boxer shorts, I'm starting to feel like an old married woman as well," she playfully mused.

Gabe turned an amazing shade of red. "God! I'm sorry. I have no excuse…"

She interrupted him again. "Tell me Gabe, have you asked your sexy neighbor, Celina, to lay out you underwear, yet?" A devilish grin curled her lips, causing him to turn an even deeper shade of red.

"Very funny, Nouri. All teasing aside, I'd feel much better if you would come with me. If you want to take a quick shower first, I can wait. I just don't think it's a good idea to leave you alone right now." He sighed thoughtfully. "I'm fairly certain we weren't followed last night, but you never know." He shrugged.

She released a sigh. "I don't want to go. I'll be fine. And I promise I'll leave the door locked, and I haven't forgotten... don't worry, I won't answer the phone..." She paused, biting her lower lip. "...But detective, I didn't say I wouldn't listen to your entertaining messages." She giggled mischievously.

He shook his head, smiling. "All right. But I'll take both keys. If anyone knocks on the door, don't answer it! Especially if it happens to be my sexy neighbor, Celina," he playfully responded, knowing his remark would drive her nuts.

"Huh!" she jealously snapped. "Don't worry about Celina and I--I'm sure we could find something in common to talk about," she teasingly returned.

He blushed again, as he nervously glanced at his watch, not really wanting to leave his feisty house guest. "Oh, yeah. Like what exactly?"

That mischievous grin circled her lips again. "Oh, I don't know, detective. Maybe we could discuss your boxers, for starters." She giggled, not being able to help herself.

Gabe blushed, shook his head, and started to cross the floor. "I'll see you in a few hours or so. If you get too hungry before I get back...I know you say you can't cook, but you can make yourself a ham and cheese sandwich, right?" he chuckled playfully.

"What? And ruin my appetite! Oh, no...I have my mouth set on tasting your..." She paused teasing, "...Ah...your, ah..." She bit her lower lip seductively again- deliberately toying with him. "...Oh yes, your scrambled egg omelet." She smiled lustfully, knowing she was getting the detached detective excited yet, again.

He smiled, shaking his head, as he opened the front door. "You're an amazing woman, Nouri Sommers. I'll give you that much...Lock the door behind me."

Nouri wanted to wrap herself inside the detective's big, strong, protective arms, and kiss him goodbye. But instead, she waved goodbye, and slowly shut the door behind him.

Chapter 30

"God, help me!" Gabe was mumbling to himself, glancing at his watch, as he ran up a short flight of stairs leading to the front door of the Connecticut Police Department.

He was having difficulty believing how quickly the time seemed to go by when he was in the company of the very beautiful but distracting Nouri Sommers. But what puzzled him even more was the fact that he could hardly wait to return to her again.

After filling Patrick Murphy, the Chief of Police in on the situation surrounding Nouri Sommers, he was given a small office with a secured phone line to go about his investigation during his stay in their city.

Gabe glanced at his watch, wondering just how long it might take Nouri to finish her bubble bath. He wanted to leave a playful message for her on his answering machine, knowing she liked to eavesdrop on his personal calls. He smiled at the remembered thought of her listening and then acting out his message from his ex-fiancee, Lisa Clayborne.

Deciding to give her a little more time to finish her bath, he dialed the number to the Boston Police Department to speak with his boss instead.

"Yeah, Mark. I got your message. What's up?" He asked curiously scratching his head.

"The DA is having a cow! That's what's up For Christsakes, Gabe!"

"Calm down Mark, and tell me what she's so damn upset about," Gabe sighed, pulling a cigarette out of his pocket and lighting up.

"She wants Charles Mason's head on a silver platter!" The captain cringed at the thought of district attorney's anger towards the famous P.I.

Gabe rolled his eyes. "Damn it, Mark! I told you what to say to her. What happened?"

"Hell, Gabe. You know Tonya. She's still jealous over Mason. I think she suspects there's something between Mrs. Sommers and him, especially, since he wants her so well protected, even though she never actually said so," the police captain said reaching for the folder in front of him.

"You mean Charles wanting me to babysit her?" Gabe asked shaking his head in disbelief.

"Partly, and, dragging you away from the murder investigation without her permission."

"Just tell her Charles said he understands that he owes her big for this one. And that he wants to take her out to dinner when he gets back from France, to that new French Restaurant...what the hell is the name of that damn place?" he sighed.

"*Le Massionette's*...I had to take Bev there last week for our big twenty-fifth wedding anniversary, remember?"

"Yeah, I remember...that should put her in a better mood, don't ya think? Mason said for me to be creative. What do ya think? Think that's creative enough, Mark?" Gabe chuckled as he lit his cigarette.

"I think Mason will kick your goddamn ass when he gets back." Mark laughed amusingly at the thought.

Gabe chuckled at his boss. "I doubt it. And anyway, Mark, I personally think Charles belongs with Tonya. I don't understand why she won't tell him about little Chucky. After all, he is his son," Gabe sat back in his chair and propped his legs on the desk.

The captain released a sigh. "I don't know, Gabe. I guess she must have her reasons." The police captain began to scan the papers in front of him.

"Yeah, maybe so...But if I had a son out there somewhere, I'd sure as hell would want to know about it. Wouldn't you?"

"True enough," the captain agreed, scratching his head thoughtfully. "Is there anything about this Sommers broad Mason isn't telling us? Is he involved with her?"

"Well Mark, there's definitely some history between them...but I can honestly say I don't know what his future plans with her are. He hasn't told me anything about her except to say she's a long time friend," Gabe sighed, as he pictured his friend's face.

The captain laid the file he was glancing at on the side of his desk. "Oh shit, Gabe! I've seen the woman. She's something, all right. Breathtaking! I should've known with Mason's reputation involving beautiful women and all. If I were you, Gabe, I'd keep it in my goddamn pants. As I recall, you have the same reputation," Mark said quickly adding, "You *are* keeping it in your pants...aren't you, detective?" He released a sigh of concern.

"I'm stunned, Mark. You of all people should know me better than that! My friendship and loyalties come first, at least when it comes to other friend's women. Charles knew he could trust me with her. Why do you think he asked me to personally watch her?" The detective nervously reached for another cigarette.

"Yeah...I know, Gabe. But..."

"But what, Mark? Lets just change the damn subject, all right?"

"You're a little touchy this morning, aren't ya, detective? What's the matter? The beautiful Mrs. Sommers isn't getting to you already, is she?"

"Mark, This conversation is over. I know my damn job. And I know what's expected of me, okay!" he snapped sharply.

"Ouch! She *is* getting to ya, huh?" The captain mused. "Well, if you ask me, Gabe, you should've taken a few men with you. It would've not only looked better for everyone concerned, but just maybe, it would've cut down on a little temptation. Don't you think?" he sighed.

"For the last time, captain, I don't need you or anyone else to tell me how to do my goddamn job. Nouri Sommers hasn't gotten to me. She's just another assignment. Nothing more. So just drop it, okay?" he lied, hoping his captain would believe him.

"Fine detective. Have it your way." Mark shook his head hopelessly.

"So, what was so damn important that you needed me to phone you ASAP?"

"To tell you about Tonya's hissy fit for one thing. Shit Gabe, I didn't know what to say to calm her down." He shrugged his shoulders helplessly.

"Yeah, and what else? So, what was the other?" Gabe released a frustrated sigh when Nouri Sommers face flashed inside his mind again.

"We finally heard from forensics. The lab boys and the medical examiner, Gabe."

"Great. After you fill me in, put Ballard on the phone. I have a little leg work for him to do for me."

After the captain filled Gabe in on all the medical reports and the scientific findings on the two Lambert murder victims, and after he spoke to his young partner, Al Ballard, Gabe quickly dialed the telephone number in France that Charles Mason had given him.

"Hello Charles. It's me."

"Gabe. Thanks for calling. I've been awfully worried about Nouri since talking to Mai Li last night. How's she doing?" He released a sigh of relief.

"She's fine, Charles. She was pretty shaken last night, though." Gabe lit another cigarette.

"Do you think it was the same bastard that had called earlier in the day and the night before?" Charles reached for his coffee cup.

"Yes. I believe he's the same man," Gabe said, exhaling a puff of smoke.

Charles nervously swallowed. "Any leads yet?"

"Ballard said it's dead so far. But the F.B.I. are still on it, of course."

"Swell," Charles sighed. "Are my men still at the estate?"

"Yes. I had Ballard ask them to stick around for a few days, just in case." Gabe glanced at his watch and wondered if Nouri was finished with her bubble bath, yet.

"We don't have anything at all to go on, Gabe?" Charles asked with disappointment.

"Well, we are working on some things. We have the tapes surrounding the outside of the estate, as well as the estate grounds, for starters. When the mystery caller phoned while I was there, he told Nouri that he saw the delivery truck pull inside the estate grounds, so, for him to be able to know that, he would have to be close. The videos are all in color and the date and times are recorded on each frame. Then, of course, we have the actual calls that he made, being taken apart as we speak. On the taped phone call that he placed at midnight, there were a few back ground noises we might be able to pin point something."

"Good work. Did the Feds think of that?"

"Everyone is working as a team on it. I'm not sure whose idea going over the tapes were."

"What else is being done?"

"Well, Charles, we're having the backgrounds of all the estate employees being looked into. Anything else you can think of that we should be doing right now?"

"Yeah, get Nouri the hell out of town for a while." Charles said, pouring himself another cup of coffee.

"I've already done that, Charles. We left last night."

"Good. Where are you going to be keeping her hid?"

"Now. Now, Charles, you know better than that," Gabe said amusingly.

"Yes. Of course...you're right. Who's protecting her with you?" Charles took a sip of his coffee.

Gabe nervously reached for another cigarette. "Just me. Do you have a problem with that, Charles?" he asked, not meaning to add the later.

"No, of course not, Gabe. I don't have a problem with you being alone with her. Do you?" The jealous P.I. asked in an uncertain tone.

"No, of course not, Charles. She's just an assignment. Not to mention a friend of yours," the police detective said feeling himself getting mad for having secret feelings for her.

"Just watch yourself, Gabe. She can be quite a little charmer when she wants to be," he teased.

"Meaning what? Is there something about this chick you want to tell me, Charles?" Gabe's tone was jealous, but knowing, he was hoping his friend would stop playing games and confess to him who Nouri Sommers really is.

"Listen Gabe, you sound stressed. Are you sure you're all right?"

"You didn't answer my question about Mrs. Sommers, Charles. Is there something between the two of you or not?"

"Truthfully, I'm not sure, Gabe. It's a long story and I don't really have the time to get into it right now." He sighed nervously.

"Well, if I may give you a suggestion before you get too involved with your heart again, old friend. Before you make any long-term commitments with her, I'd at least talk to Tonya one last time. I had to promise her that you would take her to dinner at that new French Restaurant when you return from France." He chuckled.

"You what! You son-of..."

Gabe quickly cut in. "Ah, ah, ah, Charles. You told me to use my imagination if I had to. And guess what, partner...I had to."

"So, now I'm stuck with taking her out to an expensive dinner?" Charles teased in response.

"I'm afraid so. Anyway Charles, there are a few unresolved things between the two of you that need to be settled once and for all, and you know it as well as I do."

"What the hell are you talking about?"

"I can't say. But, you will be pleasantly surprised, I'm sure. At least I would be if I were you, Charles." The detective released another sigh.

"You sound as though you know something that I don't. What is it that you aren't telling me, Gabe?"

"Hey man, it's none of my business what went on between the two of you, but..."

"There are no buts, Gabe. I told you, it's over between us."

"Okay, Charles, have it your way. But, I think you stopped seeing her because you were afraid of what was happening to you. You were falling in love with her. Admit it!"

"Gabe, I stopped seeing Tonya...well, because..."

Gabe finished his statement for him. "Because you were actually falling in love with her, and you weren't ready to give up that old flame of yours. Does that sound about right, Charles?"

"Listen Gabe, I know you mean well, but I have no intention of saying the *I DO* words to anyone except..."

"Don't tell me. I know, the woman of your dreams, the same woman who stole your heart seven years ago, right?"

"Yes. That's right, Gabe. We can't help who we fall in love with." He shrugged his shoulders hopelessly.

"Well, that maybe true enough, but, what if she doesn't love you back? Then what?" Gabe questioned with growing interest.

"But, what if she does, but just doesn't realize it yet?" Charles returned.

"Charles, loving someone and being in love with someone are all together different. Maybe this dream woman of your does love you, and for the sake of argument, she may always love you, but maybe she just isn't in love with you. What then, Charles? Here you have a shot with Tonya, a woman that is in love with you…One that actually wants to bear your children, and you're willing to let it go for a love that may never be possible…One that just might only be in your head. I just don't get it, Charles." Gabe shook his head in disbelief.

"What the hell is with you today, Gabe?"

"All right, Charles. I want to share something with you- something quite unnerving, actually. But you have to promise me that you won't pull me into it. This information did not come from me. Is it a deal?" the detective asked nervously.

"If it will calm you down and get you off my case, then yes, I won't say anything." Charles reached for his pack of cigarettes and nervously lit one.

"Charles, first you have to be honest with me, and admit to me that you were falling in love with Tonya and that's why you stopped seeing her. If the answer is no, then forget me mentioning anything, I'll have no more to say on the subject, all right?"

"All right, Gabe. I'll admit to having feelings for her that scared me, but love? I don't know. I'm not sure that I will ever be able to give any woman that part of me, that is except for one woman."

"Charles, why do you think Tonya is still so damn angry with you?"

"Hell, I don't know, Gabe. I thought it was because I just couldn't force myself to make a commitment with her. Why?" Charles asked with growing annoyance.

"What would you do if I told you that you have a son that she didn't want you to know about?"

Charles was stunned for several quiet moments before he pulled himself together. "If it were coming from anyone but you, Gabe, I'd call them a goddamn liar!" he barked in response.

"Well, it's true. You have a little boy named Chucky. He's three, a real little heartbreaker. Just like his old man. Charles, this wonderful child deserves to know who his father is," Gabe said excitedly.

Charles shook his head in disbelief. "Why didn't Tonya tell me?"

"She tried to tell you hundreds of times at first, but you never returned her calls. And after awhile, she got tired of trying, but, I do know one thing, Charles, she's still very much in love with you."

"That's strange. I heard through the grape vine she was considering a marriage offer from that big shot lawyer of hers...what's his name?" Charles remarked jealously.

"Christopher Graham."

"Yeah, that's it." Charles sighed.

"So, what are you going to do about it?"

"Nothing. What can I do?" Charles sighed again.

"You can stop acting like Tonya means nothing to you, at least talk to her before it's too late. And maybe, you might even want to meet your son."

"Goddamn it!" Charles shouted, slamming his coffee cup up against the living room wall of his hotel suite.

"Charles, I just thought you had a right to know. At least now you can put all your cards on the table."

"What the hell does that mean for chrissakes, Gabe!" Charles snipped with an attitude.

"I just mean you have a shot at a real life for a change, one with a woman that truly loves you, one that has already given you a son. Why throw your life away on a broad that isn't in love with you?"

"Gabe, why didn't you tell me this before I left for France?" Charles asked nervously.

"I wasn't sure if I was going to say anything to you at all, even now." Gabe answered in response standing to his legs to stretch.

"So why did you?"

"Because I just saw the paper this morning, where Tonya had made the rumored engagement official. The wedding is scheduled for next month." He shook his head in disbelief.

"Swell," Charles remarked sarcastically. "Well, I can't imagine her ever wanting to talk to me now. Now that she's officially engaged to Graham."

"That's not true, Charles. You ought to have seen Tonya's eyes light up when I told her that you wanted to take her to dinner at that French Restaurant." Gabe lied knowing his friend would be better off marrying Tonya Daughtery than wasting his time carrying his torch for Nouri Sommers.

"Well, I don't know, Gabe. My friend, you are certainly full of surprises this morning. I'm sorry, and I do appreciate your concern, but I have a lot of things on my mind. I don't have the time to think about any of this right now. I'll have to deal with it later. Of course, I'll want to financially take care of my son. And if she will agree to it, I'd even like to see him when I get back, but, as far as anything else...I'll just have to digest it when I have the time," Charles said in a confusing tone.

Confusion--Gabe could certainly relate to that. He had been thrown into his fair share of it overnight. "Okay, Charles. Let's get back to business. Do you want to hear the official reports on the Lambert Murders first, or do you want to share what you have found out about Ethan Sommers?" He asked, wondering if he had done the right thing about telling his friend about the son he shares with the District Attorney of Boston.

"I'll go first. It's even better than I had originally thought," Charles said, shaking his head in disbelief.

"I can hardly wait," Gabe replied, sinking back down into his chair, and propping his legs back on top of the borrowed desk.

"Well, it appears that our elusive Mr. Sommers is definitely a heavy hitter. He's sleeping with the Red Devil, all right. Hell, they own his ass. He's in so deep with the Chinese Mob, the only way out would be through death, I'm afraid."

"In what way, Charles?"

"Ethan Sommers and his half-brother, Steven Li, together share one of the largest total revenues of most countries in the goddamn world. Yes, including ours."

"I don't understand, Charles," Gabe remarked with uncertainty.

"Crimes of this nature used to be labeled, as you know, *White Collar* or *Suit Crimes*. Today governments are labeling them, *Crimes in The Suites*. They have gone from the boardrooms to the bedrooms." The P.I. sighed.

"I'm still not following you, Charles." Gabe sighed.

"Ethan Sommers has been buying up the major corporations as fast as he can get his greedy little hands on them. The number of companies in one corporation varies, depending on many different things. Anyway, for example, he has recently made a bid to take over a company called the Medallian Corporation. It's the project that he is currently working on for the Chinese Mob. The Medallian Corporation alone consists of three connecting companies with assets exceeding Two-hundred-fifty- billion dollars and that's just the tip of the iceberg."

"Okay, you have my complete attention. Go ahead...I'm listening," Gabe said, reaching for his cigarette lighter.

"Ethan Sommers is one clever son-of-a-bitch...brilliant, actually. Through these corporations...and, Gabe...he's all over the damn globe, they're fronts and are used for foreign payoffs, misuse of economic power, influencing and shaping our foreign relations with China and other countries…" Charles paused for a moment and then continued. "… Manipulating public opinion through the media, affecting the stock market, decreasing dividends to millions of stockholders…You see Gabe, only large corporations like the Medallian Corporation deploy the requisite capitol. It alone can mobilize the requisite skills. The capital resources of the large corporations enable them to adapt and change technology on the massive scale. They can set excessive prices in the areas where a few can dominate an industry. These bastards can even jeopardize the democratic process through illegal political contributions, Gabe. It goes on and on!" he said excitedly.

"Now what, Charles?"

"Well, rumor has it that a billion dollars of the Asian Mafia's money has somehow strangely disappeared overnight. Meaning, Ethan Sommers was the last known person to have the billion dollars in his greedy hands. The Mob gave it to him for a down payment to use in the negotiations for the Medallian Corporation. It was deposited one day and then the next day it was gone without a trace, just like Sommers himself."

"Is that like one billion with a" B"?"

"Yes, like with a "B." But it doesn't make sense. A billion dollars is chump change to a man like Ethan Sommers."

"Yeah, probably so. But if you take a billion-dollars from the Chinese Mob, they will find your ass. It won't matter if you have taken five dollars or a billion bucks, these red brothers…"

"I get the picture, Charles. So you think they might be trying to get to Nouri to hurt her husband?"

"Maybe. But, it still doesn't feel right to me. There is something more. I just haven't been able to put it together yet. But I will. You can count on it," Charles sighed.

"I thought that slick, high- powered- attorney, friend of his...Clint Chamberlain, made all the bids to take over the corporations. Maybe he took the money and bolted?"

"Maybe. But the Fed's can't find the money trail suggesting it."

"Maybe a transfer in a new account somewhere. Maybe a new account in Switzerland under an assumed name or number?" Gabe offered as a suggestion, then adding, "Shouldn't be hard to find. We have the date the money was deposited, right? Well, your boys should be able to track a new deposit or transfer for a billion bucks a day or so later, right? My money says Slick-Clint has it in a Swiss account, just waiting for the right moment to make his move."

"Damn Gabe, that is impressive! Truthfully, I had never thought of that theory...yet, any way." Charles smiled to himself. "Why don't you quite the force and come join me? It might be nice having a partner I could trust and count on again." He smiled again.

"Umm...I may have to give your offer a little consideration one of these days," Gabe playfully teased. "So what is your next move?"

"I've tracked Clint Chamberlain down. I'll pay him a surprise visit later today."

"Good. Maybe he'll have a few leads, huh?"

"We can only hope, Gabe." Charles sighed, just as someone knocked on his hotel door. "Listen Gabe, can you call me back in about fifteen or twenty minutes, someone's at my door. I think it might be Franko. I had him run an errand for me."

"Sure. I need to make a pit stop and get a cup of coffee. I'll call you back shortly. See ya, Charles," Gabe said, hanging up the phone.

Chapter 31

Gabe rose to his feet and crossed the room, quickly jerking open the door to his borrowed office, scaring the attractive woman standing on the other side of the door.

"Oh, God!" she gasped, gently patting her heart with her right hand. "You scared me half-to-death, detective," she said still, a little shaken.

"I'm sorry. Are you all right?" he asked putting his arm around her shoulder in a concerned manner.

"I will be in a few moments." She smiled seductively, after noticing just how handsome the detective from Boston was.

He returned her smile. "My name is Gabe Baldwin. I'm just borrowing this office for a short time today. Is this your office, miss?" he inquired, turning to gesture around the room.

"Oh no, I was just going to pop my head in and see if you would like a cup of coffee or something. I just made some fresh," she smiled. "Oh, by the way, detective, my name is Isabella Bedaux."

"Well, Isabella Bedaux, it's nice to meet you. And yes, thanks...I'd love some of your fresh coffee, please. I drink it black...and call me Gabe." He smiled.

"Great, I'll be right back. Oh, you want a doughnut, too?" she asked, smiling.

"No thanks, Isabella. This is one cop that doesn't eat donuts, but thanks anyway." He smiled, nodded and went to make his pit stop, only to return to his borrowed office with the sexy female detective from France waiting anxiously inside for him.

"Hello, again," he said entering the room.

"Hi. Well, here's your coffee- black like you said," she offered, smiling. "So detective, how long will you be staying in Connecticut?"

"Gee, Isabella, I'm not quite sure just yet." He shrugged his shoulder, as his eyes admiringly traveled the length of the female detective's sexy body.

"I see," she said smiling. "Well, detective, while your in town, if you need someone to show you around, or, perhaps someone to have dinner with, I'd like to make myself available to you," she offered nervously, gazing into his incredible teal-blue eyes.

"That's very sweet of you, Isabella. But, unfortunately, I'm on a special assignment that keeps me pretty much tied up right now." He glanced at his watch, and after he noticed the disappointment suddenly cross her attractive face, he added, "If I'm still here at the station, maybe I can buy us a quick lunch today," he smiled. "How would that be?"

"Great. I'll check with you at noon, okay?"

"Sure, Isabella. Do you have somewhere special you would like to eat?" He seductively toyed, knowing that the ever so sexy, Isabella Bedaux wanted to have *him* for lunch!

And why shouldn't he give her what she so obviously wanted. After all, she was a very sexy woman...apparently available, and...

Suddenly the beautiful face of Nouri Sommers invited herself into his lustful thoughts.

"Shit," The detached detective protested, causing Isabella Bedaux to look at him strangely.

"What is it, detective? Is something wrong?"

"Isabella...I'm sorry. I just remembered something. I'm afraid I won't be able to have lunch with you today, but maybe you'll be kind enough to give me a rain check?" he asked in a frustrated tone of voice.

"Oh, that's all right, detective. I understand. Would you like my home number? That way you could phone me next time you're going to be in town," she offered, reaching for her pen.

Gabe eagerly nodded his head. "Great! And here's mine...when I'm in town, anyway. I just bought a cabin here, a few months ago, as sort of a get-away spot between cases. Know what I mean?" He smiled, handing her his phone number.

"Cool! Does your cabin have a fireplace? I just love fireplaces," she said lustfully, staring into his eyes. She swallowed hard in an effort to slow the pace of her heart beat down.

"Yes it does. But, Isabella, as much as I would love to sit here and chit-chat with you all day, I'm afraid I have a few more phone calls to make now. Do you mind?"

"Oh...no, of course not. I'm sorry, detective. Great...well, then...I guess I'll see ya soon. I hope anyway," she smiled. "Maybe I'll just call you later at your cabin...just to say hello. Would that be all right, detective?"

"Sure. That would be fine. But I may not be there. I'm out a lot. You can always leave a message though, okay?" he smiled.

"Okay then, I'll see ya...bye," she smiled, slowly walking out of the office door pulling it shut after her.

Gabe reached for the telephone and dialed.

"Hi. It's me. Is that you? Hope I didn't disturb your bubble bath. I should be home in about an hour. I have one more phone call to make. Believe it or not, Nouri...I miss you. Bye."

He mouthed the words, a little angry at himself for not putting his intended message on the machine. He reluctantly hung up the phone, wishing she had picked up the receiver. "God, you are so sad, detective. Get a damn grip, for chrissakes!" he mumbled under his breath, reaching for the phone again.

"Charles," The police detective said in a distracted tone of voice.

"Oh good, Gabe. I was beginning to think you had forgotten about me," Charles teasingly responded.

"I got tied up with some…"

"No, don't tell me…let me guess- a sexy, young woman? Am I close?" Charles chuckled.

"You're amazing, Charles." Gabe said, shaking his head.

"What was her name?"

"Isabella Bedaux…sexy, huh?"

"Whew! With a name like that, hell…she ought to be," the P.I. laughed.

"Want to get back to the Lambert Murders, Charles?"

"Yeah, what have you got?"

"It isn't pretty," Gabe sighed.

"Murder never is, Gabe."

"So I've been told," The homicide detective mused.

"Go ahead. What have you got?"

"The younger victim, Kirsten Kamel, was eighteen years old, apparently kidnapped from a ski lodge in Colorado, where she was on a weekend get away with her Mother and Step-father. She was originally assumed to have been killed during a snow storm at the lodge, but it was later noted someone remembered seeing her being forced onto a lift by two huge men."

"Only eighteen…how sad," Charles shook his head.

"Yeah, it looks like she had just turned eighteen shortly before her murder."

"That might explain the diamond necklace wrapped around her neck, huh?"

"Seems to be the theory they're working on."

"What else?"

"It's not clear how young Kirsten wound up in Lambert. Anyway, her family says she had been missing almost six months."

"Was the shooting the cause of death? Or was it the blow to her head?"

"The gun wound right through her heart was listed as the actual cause of death. The inside of her body was a mess, however."

"Right through the heart. Sounds like a crime of passion. Was she raped?"

"No, but apparently she had had sex many times before she died. There was significant expansion of the anal opening and fibroid scarring of the rectum- indicating a recent history of anal sex and vaginal intercourse. She was also three weeks pregnant. Now, this is where it gets a little surprising- apparently not the same blood type as Ethan Sommers. But she was..."

Gabe suddenly stopped talking, fighting back the impulse to be sick.

"Getting to you, huh?"

"Yeah, it's strange. But even after nineteen years on the force, I never seem to be able to stop myself from feeling sick. Speaking of sick, she was apparently with a real sick animal. She had been fucked so many times in a forty-eight hour period...well, you get the picture."

"Yes, I certainly do, Gabe." Charles released a sigh of disgust.

"Whose gun was she shot with?"

"Apparently Becka Chamberlain's. It was a .32 revolver. Becka Chamberlain was given a paraffin test on her hands...and the gunpowder still apparent on them was a match."

"So Becka Chamberlain killed young Kirsten Kamel... but why? And who killed Becka?"

"I'm not sure yet, but it's starting to look more and more like a love triangle- starring none other than Ethan Sommers."

"But you have no evidence involving Ethan Sommers...do you?"

"Maybe. Modern science is an amazing thing."

"So tell me about Becka Chamberlain. What was the cause of her death?"

"She was apparently choked to death by the whip that was wrapped around her lovely neck."

"Damn. What a way to go. What else did the reports say about her? I hear she was an incredibly beautiful woman."

"Well, the picture I'm currently looking at certainly doesn't suggest that. But there is another photo. She was a very beautiful woman, but what a psycho. Wonder how people wind up that way?" Gabe reflected, as he turned the page to the report that he was reading from.

"So, the report…what did it say?"

"Becka Adams Chamberlain…age twenty-six. Her fallopian tubes had been ligated recently- suggesting a recent abortion. She had been pregnant several times before. She had fresh cuts and bruises all over her body-most of which were caused by the same whip that she had been strangled with. She also had old scars and hidden, unhealed bruises, suggesting a long history of violent sex--teeth marks, hair, saliva and semen were found all over her. She, too, had had sex many times within forty-eight hours of her death."

"Anal sex?"

"Oh yeah. Scars going back as far as childhood," the detective sighed.

"Pity. A beautiful woman like that." Charles shook his head in disbelief.

"Yeah, isn't it?"

"Anything else?"

"Yeah. Both women had dangerous amounts of alcohol and drugs in their blood…And get this, Charles…both women had traces of an exotic Asian Oil on their skin."

"A Chinese connection, huh?"

"Seems to be under every rock that we pick up, lately," Gabe sighed.

"So it seems."

"Well, that pretty much does it on my end. I'll call you again in a few days."

"Sounds like a plan. Tell Nouri that I ..." The P.I. suddenly stopped talking.

"What were you going to say, Charles?"

Charles sighed. "Just tell her I said hello. And I'll talk to her in a few days. In fact, bring her with you next time you phone me." He paused. "Take care of her, Gabe," the private investigator said in a concerned tone.

"I intend to. Don't worry, Charles." Gabe responded shaking his head., "I'll talk to you soon."

Gabe reached for his cup of coffee, as his mind began to race into several directions at once. He sank down in his chair, trying to digest what Charles Mason had just shared with him about Ethan Sommers. The reports he had just received from his boss on the two Lambert Murders concerned him, and he was trying to make some sense out of his distraction, as well as, attraction to Nouri St. Charles Sommers.

What was it that was so special about this beautiful woman that was causing so much frustration and confusion, just twenty-four hours after first meeting her.

"It wasn't just her beauty, even though she was magnificent! It wasn't her incredible body, even though her body was perfect in every way, every curve, every strand of hair on her head. And those eyes...how very dangerous they had become to him.

He swallowed hard at the thought.

'*What is it about her that separates her from any other woman I have ever known before?* he thought, pulling a cigarette from his pack.

Suddenly, it dawned on him that Nouri was waiting for him to return and make breakfast for them. He jumped to his feet and flew out of the police station without even taking the time to say goodbye to the very sexy, Isabella Bedaux, who stood staring at him with a very disappointed expression plastered across her pretty face, as he ran out the door. "Call me." She whispered the words after the front door to the station slammed shut.

In a hurry to get back to his cabin, Gabe put the pedal to the metal, quickly jumping on the entrance to the freeway.

Chapter 32

Reaching for his cup of coffee, his cigarettes, and his 24 k. Gold lighter, the same lighter that Nouri Sommers had given him seven years earlier on his thirty-third birthday, Charles Mason, lost in thought, slowly walked to the bedroom of his luxurious hotel suite in France.

Other than a few faded photographs, his lighter was the only other tangible piece of evidence that he had left to remind him of the beautiful woman that had so effortlessly stolen his heart, and quite possibly his soul, as well.

That is, except for his treasured memories of her that had kept him company for the past seven years. Well, at least up until two nights ago, when the woman of his dreams re-entered his life, needing him more than ever.

Now the very real possibility of her wanting to be a part of his life again was more than he could ever have dreamed possible. Winning her hand at marriage this time? Who knows, but with her husband and Clint Chamberlain both out of the picture now, she needed him, and he knew it. There was no other man she could turn to. No other man around to stand in his way anymore.

Charles could hardly wait to clear Nouri's name in the Lambert Murders, help solve Becka Chamberlain's murder, and supply Nouri with enough evidence and information to get a divorce from her husband, Ethan Sommers, ridding her of him forever. She would then be free to marry him, something she should have done seven years earlier.

He released a puff of smoke, trying to organize his thoughts, mixed with a quick fantasy about his future with the woman of his dreams.

As far as he was concerned, he should've already been living his fantasy future with her. What could possibly go wrong now? For once, everything seemed to be going his way. All the past road blocks had suddenly being cleared away. All the emptiness he had felt since she had left him would soon be a thing of the past. And, his future-- looking brighter than he could ever imagined.

Yes, it was soon going to be payday for Charles Mason, that is, after he tied up a few loose ends for her, as well as, for himself.

Suddenly thinking about the conversation that he had with his friend, Gabe...he hit a brick wall.

"Oh shit, I'm a father! God, Gabe must think I'm the biggest jerk that ever lived for the lack of excitement over finding out that I have a son... Oh my God... I'm a father... I have a three year óld son named Chucky... How is this possible? How could I have let this happen to me again? What about Tonya? How could I have done that to her, and just walk out of her life like I did? Sure I didn't know, but that is no excuse! I should've at least returned her phone calls...Oh, my God! Why didn't I return her phone calls? Because I'm an idiot...Gabe was right about me...I knew I was falling in love with her, and was afraid to give in..." Charles stopped mumbling to himself, as he walked over to pick up his lighter.

"It doesn't matter, Charles, you moron! The point is, you didn't give Tonya an opportunity to tell you, but that doesn't matter now, either... Like it or not, Charles Mason, you are a father! And some other man is about to raise your son!" He scolded himself, walking over to his bed and sitting on it while he lit his cigarette.

Suddenly, the face of another woman that he had once shared a similar situation with flashed inside his head. He swallowed hard, trying to fight back the tears of the painful memory of the woman who had gotten pregnant by him, but chose not to have his baby, just to hurt him. He had wanted her to have the baby. He wanted to be part of its life. He would've been happy to support the child, but marriage to a woman like her, well it was just out of the question. He shook his head, as he continued to feel the pains from his past.

The woman from his past robbed him of his child by having an abortion. Now it appeared as though Tonya Daughtery was about to try and rob him of another child, a son that very much exists.

'No... Hell no! Not this time. This time it was going to be different. Chucky is my son and I have every right to be a part of his life'! he thought heatedly, releasing a cloud of cigarette smoke.

Out of curiosity, and suddenly feeling as though he needed a million questions answered by his former lover, he reached for the phone, but put it back down just as quickly as he had reached for it.

"No, Charles...this isn't the way. Not over the telephone like this," he said, agreeing with the voice of reason whispering to him inside his head.

Uncomfortable feelings of mixed emotions, excitement, and confusion suddenly began to surge throughout his body, forcing him to rise to his feet and walk over to look in the mirror. He wanted to look at the reflection of the man that had just been told he was a father!

"I should've been there for her," He released a deep sigh of regret. "Charles, you selfish bastard!" Shaking his head in disgust, he walked back to the telephone and placed a call to his office in Boston, asking his private secretary, Tess, to send the District Attorney of Boston, three dozen, long-stem red roses...each dozen representing one year of his young son's life.

"Tess, I want the card to read: Congratulations on your engagement...I think? I'm hoping to wind this case up before you walk down the aisle with What's His Face...I'm sorry I was such a fool...I have no excuse...I'll phone you for that dinner I owe you when I return...That is, if you will join me. I look forward to seeing you soon. P.S. Please bring my son. I 'm dying to meet him. Always, Charles."

Charles chuckled when he overheard his secretary gasp for breath, noticeably stunned to learn that he was a father, and how shocking that the mother of his Son was none other than the DA of Boston. How Scandalous!

"But...but..." his secretary stuttered the words, unable to complete her sentence.

"Yeah, I know what ya mean, Tess," he said teasingly, shaking his head in disbelief. "Can ya believe it, Tess? I'm a father!" He chuckled proudly before hanging up the phone.

He pulled out his wallet, and hidden behind a faded photograph of Nouri Sommers was another photo, one of Tonya Daughtery, busy at work decorating their first Christmas tree together. He loved the surprised look on her pretty face when he snapped the picture. He smiled fondly at the remembered thought, gently outlining her smiling face with his index finger.

"You should have told me," he whispered, studying her face for several long moments.

His thoughts were suddenly forced on hold when someone loudly knocked on his hotel door. He slid Tonya's picture back inside his wallet and put his wallet back into his trouser pocket, as he went to answer the door.

"Hi stranger," the beautiful Lacey Alexandria Bonner- STAR of STAGE, SCREEN, and TELEVISION said, quickly adding, "I heard you were in town."

Too stunned to speak, Charles shook his head in an effort to focus his eyes more clearly.

"Charles, if this is a bad time..." she asked, sounding disappointed.

"Oh God, no...please, come in, Lacey," he offered, smiling, backing up against the door to gesture her in.

She turned to face him. "I was beginning to think..."

"Stop right there, Lacey. Don't even think about saying another word until you…'

"Is this what you had in mind, Charles?" she said, anxiously running into his arms, where they passionately embraced and kissed.

"Oh, God, Charles. I can't believe it's really you," she breathlessly whispered, showering his face with hundreds of tiny little French Kisses.

"Shhh…Lacey, we have unfinished business that we need to attend to immediately," he whispered urgently in response, outlining her beautiful full lips with his finger.

He lifted her up into his arms and carried her into the bedroom where they spent the next several hours making love, time and time again. He urgently needed her body.

"God! How I've missed you, Charles." Lacey breathlessly panted, still whirling in the after glow of it all.

"I've missed you too, Lacey. Too much, I'm afraid," he said, pulling her body close to his again, and lowering his head to kiss her.

"I can't believe it's been a whole year. What happened, Charles? You were supposed to…"

He put his finger to her full, seductive lips. "Shhh…Lets not open that old wound again. Just hold me, Lacey. I had almost forgotten how wonderful you feel," he reflected, smiling, as he continued to gently caress her soft, curvy body.

"Well Charles, we're going to have to talk about it sometime," she replied propping herself up on his strong manly chest.

"Yes, I know we do. But not now, okay," he sighed softly, gently patting her on her shapely bottom. "Come on baby, let's have a drink," he said getting out of bed and offering his hand.

"Charles, you are going to be able to make my opening celebration party after the show tonight, aren't you?" She smiled, extending her hand to him.

"You just try and keep me out!" he teased. "Why don't you have a car pick us up here about seven?" He kissed her hand, leveling his eyes to hers adding, "On second thought, better make that eight." he smiled lustfully.

"Oh, Charles... I adore you. You know that, don't you?" She threw her arms snuggly around his neck after he picked her up into his arms. She wrapped her legs tightly around his waist and kissed him passionately, as he continued to stagger playfully into the living room.

After he poured them a drink, he made a few necessary phone calls and turned his full attention back to the incredibly sexy, and very, hot-natured Lacey Alexandria Bonner--French Star of Stage, Screen and Television.

Chapter 33

Gabe Baldwin swiftly pulled Nouri's Mercedes into the gravel driveway leading to his cabin, in a hurry to fix breakfast for himself and the beautiful woman that was patiently waiting inside for him to return.

After sliding out of the car, he noticed the door to the cabin had been left open. He was immediately engulfed with a surge of panic. A feeling that was So Strong and So Powerful, that it made him actually feel sick to his stomach. "Oh, my God!" he whispered, quickly reaching for his revolver.

In a matter of seconds, he was inside the cabin, holding his weapon in a position ready to fire at a moment's notice. After swiftly scanning the kitchen and living room, he quietly darted up the stairs, taking them two at a time. Standing in front of the bedroom with his ear pressed against the door, he could hear a man's voice speaking heatedly in Chinese.

Without any further hesitation, the police detective forcefully kicked the door open, causing the intruder to impulsively jump to his feet and dive out the closed window, head first.

Gabe quickly ran to the window, firing several shots, after the shadow of a man he saw running away from the cabin in record breaking speed.

"Son-of-a-bitch!" The detective shouted angrily at his failure to stop Nouri's attacker from getting away. Suddenly remembering her, he glanced in the direction of the bed, repulsed by what he saw.

He ran to her side, quickly freeing her from her current state of bondage, releasing her wrists from the red silk scarf that held her captive, and gently removing the ugly gray tape that had been so tightly placed around her beautiful, but swollen lips.

"Oh, my God! Are you all right?" he asked nervously pulling her into his arms and reaching for the sheet to wrap around her.

Crying hysterically, she somehow managed to answer. "I...I don't know, Gabe...I think so." She threw her arms around his neck and hugged him tightly, her tears now running down her face to the side of his.

"Did he rape you, Nouri?" he asked as a tear fell down his worried face. He gently stroked her hair and shoulders.

"No, thank God!" she cried. "He was about to just as you entered the room...Oh, God, Gabe! I'm so thankful you came in here when you did," she cried, still clinging to him tightly.

He pulled her to him even tighter. "Oh, baby. I'm so sorry I left you alone. Can you ever forgive me?" he whispered against her ear, choking back his tears.

"I'm just so thankful you came in when you did." she said trying to fight back her tears of fear, too upset to notice that he had just called her baby.

"Do you want to go to the hospital? I think it's a good idea. Let the doctors make sure that you are okay. What do you say?"

"No. I...I'm fine... I think...just shaken...maybe a few cuts and bruises...that's all."

"Let me see," he said turning her to face him and examining her face and arms. "Yeah, around your wrist and your mouth a little, anywhere else?"

"I don't know. I don't think so. I'm very sore though. That creep was a real beast, very rough with me. But I think I'm okay."

"Come on, baby, let's go downstairs and have a drink. It might make you feel better." He gently patted her on the back and tried to loosen his hold on her.

"No, I just want you to hold me. I'm too frightened to move," she replied, still shaking inside his protective embrace.

He apologetically whispered, "I'm with you now. You're safe. I swear no one will ever get that close to you again. Come on, Nouri, a drink will help calm you down."

"All right, but, hold me close, okay?" She looked at him, trying to force a smile.

He returned her smile, rising to his feet, and helping her up. He was much too worried about her to notice her naked body when she stood to her feet.

After helping her to the sofa, he crossed the floor and went to the bar, anxious to get a drink or two in her, hoping to calm her down enough for him to ask her about specific things pertaining to her attack.

"Here baby. Drink this," he said, handing her a shot of brandy. Once again, he wasn't aware of the fact that he had called her a pet name.

'*Baby... Did he just call me baby*'? She thought, as she snuggled close to his protective body again.

"Better?" he asked removing the glass from her trembling hands. "Nouri, I know this is going to be very difficult for you, but I need for you to tell, me word for word, and action for action, what happened here this morning. It's very important that we do this now, so you don't have time to forget anything. Do you understand?" He turned her chin up with his curled index finger, gently encouraging her to look into his eyes.

"But..." she objected.

"Nouri...please. If we didn't have to do this now, I wouldn't ask you. Timing is important in matters like this."

She released a sigh of hopelessness and nodded in understanding. "All right, Gabe. Lets just get it over with, okay?" She forced a smile.

"Good girl. Now take a deep breath and be brave, okay?" he encouraged.

She nodded again, sucking in a deep breath and slowly releasing it. "All right...I'm ready," she said bravely, closing her eyes as though she were trying to recall every detail. "After my bubble bath, I went downstairs, still in my robe. I made a batch of Bloody Mary's and was getting ready to poor myself one, when I heard someone calling my name from outside. At first, I thought it was you, so I ran to the front door and opened it. After glancing around outside and not spotting the Mercedes, I started to come back inside. That's when I heard someone call out my name again." She opened her eyes and swallowed hard.

"Yes Nouri, you're doing fine. Go on," Gabe said gently massaging her back and shoulders, without realizing what he was doing.

"I don't know what I thought or why I even did it, but when I heard my name being called out again...I began to walk in the direction of the voice that was calling out to me. I still hadn't seen anyone by the time I reached the pond, so I looked around for a few moments...and began to walk back to the cabin. Suddenly I heard footsteps behind me, but I still couldn't see anyone, so I panicked and began to run..." She paused to catch her breath.

"The footsteps sounded as though they were getting closer and closer behind me. Fear engulfed me...forcing me to run faster. I stumbled, scraping the palms of my hands and knees on the gravel driveway. I tried to get up but he was standing over me by then...I froze. I couldn't think or speak...my words seemed to stay lodged in my throat. He was dressed completely in black...sort of like a ninja or something, is what he reminded me of. Anyway, he grabbed me forcefully and tossed me over his shoulder. The more I tried to struggle to free myself, the more my legs would cramp. So after a short period of time, I stopped struggling- just to ease the pain in my legs." She closed her eyes for a moment, revealing her fear.

"Please don't stop, Nouri. Let's just get this over with, okay?" He smiled comfortingly.

"All right..." She took another deep breath. "He was so strong...so powerful...and his laugh was so...I don't know...evil maybe? It was almost as terrifying as his brutal hold on me." She swallowed hard before continuing.

"Just before he entered the cabin, he pulled out a gun...I don't know what kind." She shook her head, adding, "I don't know anything about guns. Anyway, after checking out the cabin, he ran upstairs with me still draped over his shoulder. Then he threw me on top of the bed...slapped me in the face really hard- mumbling something in Chinese and then tied my wrists to the bedpost with that red scarf," she said gently rubbing her wrists at the remembered thought.

"Before taping my mouth shut, he kissed me. It was a horrible kiss... so brutal and demanding. When he forced my mouth open with his tongue, I bit him as hard as I could, hoping I had bit his tongue off!" She cringed. "He slapped me...then started cursing at me in Chinese, while he was taping my mouth shut...I could hardly breathe. As I continued to struggle, he savagely ripped my robe from my body. I kept trying to turn my body away from his, but he was too strong. It didn't do me any good. He held my legs down with one arm and seemed to enjoy knowing that I was watching his every move...He tore off my panties and tossed them to the floor...Just as he was getting ready to have his way with me, my prayers were answered. You came busting into the room and frightened him away before any real damage was done. Thank God, Gabe!" she said excitedly, trembling all over in fear.

"Nouri, it's all over. You did just fine. I have to ask you a few questions and then we can put it all behind us, okay'"" He smiled, arising and heading to the bar to get her another shot of brandy.

"All right, Gabe...then, will you feed me! I'm suddenly starving half to death." She smiled and patted her stomach.

He smiled handing her a drink. "Starved, huh? I'm rather hungry myself. Let's get these questions over with, okay?"

She smiled, nodding and picked up her shot of brandy and took a sip waiting for the detective to ask his questions.

"Nouri, did this man speak any English?'

"No...only Chinese." She shook her head and sighed.

"Are you sure?"

"Yes." She nodded.

"Did you understand anything that he said to you?"

"She nodded. "I recognized my name several times. And, knew that he was cursing at me in Chinese. That's pretty much all I can remember."

"Do you remember anything else? Anything at all?"

"No Gabe. I don't think so," she said shaking her head.

"Are you sure you don't want me to take you to the hospital?"

"No, I'll be fine. I'm still just a little frightened...a few scrapes and bruises, nothing serious, I don't think."

"As long as you're sure. If something would have happened to you, I don't know what I would've done," he said, shaking his head.

"Gabe, you're shaking. Are you okay?" she asked, wrapping her arms around his neck.

"God...If anything would've happened to you, I..." He stuttered. "...I would've died," he said pulling her into his protective embrace.

She returned his hug and laid her head between his neck and shoulder. "Gabe..." She swallowed before continuing. "You feel it, too, don't you?" Her tone was soft.

"Yes, Nouri. God...help me," he whispered.

"What are we going to do?" she asked, looking up at his handsome, but worried face.

Reaching for a loose strand of soft, curly hair that had fallen across her cheek, he gently wrapped his finger around it, as he gazed longingly into her wide, curious eyes. "Nouri, what I'd like to do about it..." He paused thoughtfully. "...And what I intend to do about it, are two completely different things," he said with regret, releasing his finger from around her strand of loose hair. He went on speaking softly. "Nouri, if it wasn't for Charles, you wouldn't be able to pry me off you right now." He shook his head adding, "But..."

She quickly stopped him. "No Gabe. I told you...I love Charles, but I'm just not in love with him. He understands that, why can't you?"

He released her from his embrace and sank back on the sofa hopelessly. "Nouri, it's just not going to happen. It would be a *forbidden* kind of love between us." He shook his head. "I just couldn't do that to my friend. If I were to make love to you right now...and God knows I want to...I...I just don't think I could look myself in the mirror tomorrow morning. Do you understand?" he sighed.

Nouri snuggled her shivering body up against his again. Pulling his arms around her, she wrapped her arms around him. "I don't understand, Gabe," she said shaking her head in protest. "So we're what...just going to continue to be joined at the hip...and not do anything about it!" she remarked in confusion.

"Nouri, please. This is difficult for me..."

She quickly interrupted him. "This isn't just about Charles, is it? You think I'm still in love with Clint Chamberlain, don't you?" she said, raising her face up to his.

He pulled his head free from her touch. "This isn't about the many loves of Nouri Sommers!" he snapped. "I don't give a damn about Clint Chamberlain, or your husband. This is about someone that I do care about…It's about Charles! He's like a brother to me, and like it or not, I do care about him…his feelings, and his heart…

"Something you obviously never cared about!" he barked. "Hurting him is a price I'm not willing to pay! Do you understand now?" he questioned, jumping to his feet heatedly.

Gabe was hoping his heated outburst would finally put a wedge between them, a large enough wedge to end the confusion and desire for her. But his heart knew it was far from over.

"Gabe," Nouri whispered, softly walking up behind him. "I'm sorry. I can see how much you love your friend, and no matter what you think, I love Charles too. He's just not the man for me." She released a sigh. "I was hoping, in all honesty, that maybe I had been mistaken about my type of love for Charles in the past. I was hoping we might be perfect for one another this time around." She swallowed hard. "But sadly, my feelings haven't changed for him. They're the same today as they were seven years ago." She sighed regretfully.

Gabe handed her another shot of brandy and poured himself one of her pre-made Bloody Mary's. "What are you trying to say?" he asked, as he walked back to the couch and sat down.

She followed and sat down beside, him clinging tightly to her sheet that was still snuggly wrapped around her.

"When I first met Charles…" She smiled fondly and took a sip of her brandy. "…I was only nineteen. It was love at first sight for him, and lust at first sight for me. Charles was my first real man." She released a sigh of remembered bliss. "He really is a wonderful man…" She suddenly stopped talking. She sat quietly, running her finger nervously around the rim of her glass.

"Why did you stop talking?" Gabe asked titling her chin up to look at him.

"You don't want to hear this." She shook her head.

"Yes, I do. For reasons I'm not sure of just yet, I feel as though I need to know about everything between you and Charles." He sank deeper into the sofa, and crossed his legs. "Please...go on. I believe you were saying Charles gave you your first real climax. Is that right?" His tone became jealous.

She smiled. "Detective...was that envy or jealously in you tone of voice?" She leveled her eyes to his.

Without batting an eye, he replied, "I don't know, Nouri...maybe a little of both. Please go on." He gestured with a wave of his hand.

She swallowed hard, fighting the impulse to kiss his sexy, full lips. "All right, Gabe..." she nodded. "...I have never...not even once, regretted having a relationship with Charles Mason...He's an incredibly sexy man... and explosive lover. I've never had anyone that could make my toes actually curl the way he has...and, by the way detective, the old myth that a woman's toes curl *up* during an orgasm isn't true, take my word for it, they turn *under* during one!" She paused and pretended to fan herself from the memory of sex with Charles, just to drive the detached detective crazy with jealousy. She smiled, knowing she had done just that.

"After you pull yourself together, maybe you'd like to continue?" he remarked sarcastically.

She smiled again, as she began to speak... "Charles was... I mean is, a wonderful man- but, a little too fatherly... a little too bossy... and a little too smothery to suit me. Oh, sure we had many talks about our problems together, but he couldn't seem to help himself when it came to me. He tried to tell me what to eat...what to wear...how to fix my hair. He's even tried to help me with my homework from school, For Chrissakes! He wanted to know what I was doing every second of the day. I was allowed no breathing space, no room to grow. Ya get the picture?" she smiled.

"I'm beginning to. Go ahead."

"I was hoping Charles had learned to lighten up a little, you know, learned to mellow out..." She shrugged her shoulders. "...But if anything, he's becoming more-- well, you know. Right?"

Gabe nodded understandingly.

"I do need Charles, just not like he wants me to need him. Like the other night for instance. I needed for him to hold me, not come running back into my life, trying to run it again." She shrugged her shoulders helplessly... "I guess it's all my fault. You were right to say what you did last night. It's my fault he's all hot and bothered all over again. I should've never let him make love to me again." She shook her head and sighed.

Gabe silently thought for a few moments before responding. "It was only once, wasn't it?" He watched a surprised expression suddenly mask her beautiful face.

Nouri couldn't help herself. She laughed amusingly. "I'm sorry, Gabe. You have never made love to Charles." She giggled teasingly. "Charles is a very heated lover. He can go for hours at a time. Time and time again." She smiled lustfully just to toy with him.

"So your saying you let him make love to you more than once?" He shook his head in disbelief.

"Well, it was only the one night, and, of course, the next morning. But technically, we made love only..."

The jealous detective jumped to his feet. "Just forget it! I get the goddamn picture!"

"Well, I'm sorry, Gabe. But I didn't even know you then," she said in defense.

"I said just forget it! And by the way, yes you did. We had been formally introduced the day before, remember?" he childishly responded.

"Well, forgive me to all hell and back, detective!" she playfully snapped, causing them both to start laughing hysterically.

"Let's go eat. You can keep me company in the kitchen, while I fix us breakfast," he smiled.

"Fine, but first I need to change into a little something less comfortable, okay?" she said smiling, gesturing to her body wrap.

"Will you go upstairs with me while I take a quick shower and change? I'm still a little jumpy to be upstairs alone." She smiled nervously.

Gabe returned her smile and in an understanding tone, he told her that he would fix the broken bedroom window while she was getting dressed.

After entering the bedroom, she turned to face him. "Tell me, Gabe..." She swallowed hard, as she glanced nervously at the broken window.

"What is it?" He noticed the nervousness in her tone.

"How did my mystery caller know where to find me?" She trembled at the thought.

He pulled her to him with his hands on her shoulders. "Nouri, are you saying that you think the man that attacked you today was the same man that threatened you?"

"Oh no, Gabe...I don't *think* it was him... I *know* it was him."

"How can you be so sure?" he asked with growing interest.

"It was his evil laugh. It was the same man, all right." She swallowed nervously.

Gabe released his hands from her shoulders and backed up a step. "I don't get it," he said shaking his head. "I can usually tell when I'm being followed," he remarked putting his hands nervously on his hips, as though he were going to be lost in thought for a while.

Before he had a chance to drift away, she quickly jumped in. "What is it, Gabe?"

He glanced at her. "I'm just trying to figure out how he found us so quickly. I know we weren't followed." He shook his head. "Maybe your suitcases might have a tracking device placed on them? Maybe your car." he suggested glancing at her. "You didn't make any phone calls, did you?" He leveled his eyes to her, when he suddenly remembered how long she had been in the ladies room at the seafood restaurant. He suspected she had placed a phone call then. After all, she couldn't have combed her hair or freshened her make-up, because he had locked her purse in the trunk of the car with the rest of her luggage before they had even left the mansion. So, he knew she had lied to him at the restaurant.

She bit her lower lip nervously. "Gabe..."she said softly. "...There's something I need to tell you, but you have to promise that you won't be mad at me, okay?" She glanced at him waiting for his response.

He shook his head in disappointment, already knowing she had placed a call to someone. "Who did you call, Nouri?" He leveled his eyes to hers.

She swallowed hard before answering hoping he wouldn't yell too much. She was already upset to begin with. After all, her phone call had nothing to do with the attack on her. It was to her best friend in the world, Genna Matthews.

"I phoned my friend Genna Matthews from the seafood restaurant...and again when you left this morning," she cringed.

She looked so pitiful standing there, shaking with confusion, Gabe didn't have the heart to yell at her again. Instead, he pulled her into a tight embrace.

"God, what am I going to do with you? Baby, don't you understand this is no game that were playing?" He released a frustrated sigh, not aware that he referred to her as baby again. "I'm trying to save your life, Nouri. Someone out there wants to hurt you, possibly even kill you. Don't you understand? Even though your motives were harmless enough…" He released a sigh of frustration. "…You may have now put your friend in danger, too. The people we are dealing with are not only smart and well financed, they are very dangerous. They're not playing games here."

"I don't understand, Gabe. How can you know so much about this person all ready? After all, we don't even know who he is yet." She released herself from his hold and took a step back so she could look at him.

"Nouri, to be able to locate you so quickly, they would have to either be informed somehow, or well financed. It takes a lot of money to have someone found that doesn't want to be found. Especially, when no one in Boston even knows about my cabin! That is except for a very few of my police pals! Perhaps your luggage is bugged…maybe the car? I'll have them checked for any listening or tracking devices. In the mean time…no more phone calls! I mean it! Okay? And while I'm fixing breakfast, you can tell me more about your girlfriend Genna Matthews, all right"

Nouri nodded and walked into the bathroom for a quick shower.

Chapter 34

"Nothing you can say could tear me away from my guy...my guy – Nothing you can do cause I'm stuck like glue to my guy...my guy – He may not be a movie star, but...dadi – dadi – dadi – dadi – dadi – dadi – There's not a man today who..."

Genna Matthews was singing and dancing playfully, as she stood on top of a foot ladder inside her wealthy Oil-Tycoon-husband's library, listening to her long time favorite radio station, playing the oldies but goodies that she and her friend, Nouri Sommers loved so much.

A few moments later, there was a gentle knock followed by the door opening. Genna glanced in that direction.

"Yes, Mr. Hoskins...come in. What is it?" She sang out teasingly when he entered the library. She cleared her throat. "Would you turn off the radio, please? I think I've found the book I was looking for," she said, climbing down the ladder with a small book clutched against her bosom.

"Yes, madam. There is someone to see you. He's waiting in the study, Mrs. Matthews." The butler said in a sharp condescending tone.

"Who is it, Mr. Hoskins?" She faked an angelic smile.

"A mister Steven Li, madam," he said, turning to leave.

"Umm..." Genna sighed. "All right Mr. Hoskins, tell him I'll be there in a few moments," she responded walking to her husband's desk and opening a drawer.

"Very well, madam," Mr. Hoskins replied, humoring her.

Genna pulled out a pack of cigarettes she had hidden there, and lit one up, inhaling deeply and quickly releasing a few small circles of smoke.

Crossing the floor of the library, she swiftly opened the door and went to the study to attend to some business that she had with Ethan Sommers half-brother, Steven Li.

After entering the study, she shut and locked the door behind her.

"Steven..." she nodded nervously.

"Ah...Genna," he responded, walking toward her leveling his eyes to hers.

"Well, Steven... Are you going to make me wait all day?" she asked, sharply tapping her foot impatiently.

When he didn't respond right away, she stopped tapping her foot and glared at him. "Is she or isn't she dead?" She nervously took a puff of her cigarette.

Steven shook his head. "No. That goddamn detective came back too soon," he said in a huff.

"What do you mean?" she barked.

"Well, I couldn't help myself...She's so goddamn beautiful. I wanted to fuck her before I killed her. It would have been a terrible waste to kill her before..."

Genna angrily interrupted. "You son-of-a-bitch! You mean to tell me that you blew it just because you wanted to have sex with her before you killed her? I don't fucking believe it! You fucking moron!" She threw her hands up in the air.

"Calm down, Genna. I told you I'd kill her...and I will." Steven shrugged defensively.

"Yeah, just like you were going to kill Otto Lambert and Ethan Sommers. Well, I'm still waiting!" She began to nervously tap her foot again as she took another hit off of her smoke.

"Don't worry, baby. We still have time. It's not like we have to burn them this very instant," He sighed, roughly pulling her into his arms.

"True Steven, but damn it! I want the bitch dead! I'm tired of waiting...do you hear me?" Genna huffed, jerking free from Steven Li's tight hold.

"What's the matter, baby? Jealous because I wanted to fuck your best friend?"

Genna angrily shook her head and sighed.

"What? Me jealous of a dead woman? Don't be ridiculous." She mused. "I should've killed her seven years ago when I had a chance to."

Steven shot her a heated glance. "All over some prick named Mason...Get a goddamn grip, Genna. You don't need that bastard anymore...you have me, remember? And just as soon as I kill my brother, I'm going to make you the wealthiest woman in the world. So, see...you don't need this Mason asshole anymore." He pulled her into his arms again.

"She laughed coldly. "Listen, you fucking idiot. I don't need Charles Mason. I never have. I want him. There's a difference. He was mine before that goddamn bitch stole him from me. After all, he wanted me to have his child, remember? I told you that." She barked as memory entered her brain.

"If you wanted Mason so goddamn badly back then, why did you shoot him seven years ago? And if he was so much in love with you, as you claim, then why did he have you comm..."

She quickly interrupted him. "Steven, just shut the fuck up! I don't want to talk about it anymore. I just want the bitch dead. Got it! And after you whack her, then do Lambert, then your goddamn, fucking, animal brother!"

"Calm down, Genna. Come on, baby, give me what I came for before your old man gets home," he prodded, glancing down at his wristwatch, and pulling her into his tight embrace again.

He began to unbutton her silk blouse, as he kissed her neck. She unzipped his fly.

"So what now, Steven?" she asked pulling his jeans down to the floor, then his underwear.

"We wait. When Nouri phones you again with her new location…then I'll pay her another visit. This will be the last face she will ever see again. I promise, baby. I can hardly wait! I owe her big now, after biting my tongue half-off I've got something really special in store for the bitch!" He unfastened her bra and tossed it to the floor beside her silk blouse.

"So you think the detective will move her again?"

"He has too. He knows that we know where she is now. For her safety, he'll have to move her again. But don't forget, baby, she'll call you and let you know where she is being taken to. After all, you *are* her best friend, remember?" He laughed wickedly, as he sat on the floor pulling Genna down with him.

"What if Ethan finds out what we're up to?" she asked nervously, as Steven removed her undees.

"Relax baby, he won't. I've got him hooked on the heavy shit again. Remember how he gets when he's on that shit?" He chuckled, as he began to caress her soft curvy body.

"Yeah, the poor sick bastard! He can't stay out of the bed long enough to do anything, anything constructive, anyway," she said coldly.

"Yeah, if John Q. Public knew what he was doing to the young non-suspecting teenagers of the world, they'd probably kill him before I had a chance to," he said pushing her back against the floor.

Genna eagerly opened her legs wide anticipating Steven's next move. "Yeah, him and that fucking Otto Lambert," she said pulling Steven Li on top of her.

"Speaking of fucking, Genna …How about shutting the fuck up for a few minutes!" he demanded savagely plunging himself deep inside her body, causing her to cry out screams of painful delight.

"Rough, Steven!" she panted excitedly, opening her legs wider still begging for more.

Without commenting, he continued to slam his body inside hers, time and time again, as the nosy butler continued to eavesdrop against the study door.

Chapter 35

"Today is another beautiful day on the island paradise of Lambert. Highs reaching in the mid to upper eighties with tonight's low a very mild seventy-five... Now back to you, Dave."

"Thank you, Rheeann. Now for today's headlines..."

Otto Lambert walked behind the registration desk and turned the radio down. "Good afternoon, Olivia," he said to his lovely wife.

"Good afternoon, darling," she responded, offering her cheek to him for an afternoon kiss. "I see Mr. Jarett standing over there. I believe you said you needed to speak to him today," she said, pointing in the direction of where Kirt Jarett was standing.

"Good. Thank you, Olivia." He smiled, kissing her on the cheek and swiftly walking out from behind the counter. Crossing the lobby floor, he made his way to where Kirt Jarett was busy chatting with Stacy Gullaume, the beautiful wife of Stuart Gullaume, another, Billionaire-Oil-Tycoon.

He quietly walked up behind him, touching him on the shoulder. "Excuse me, Mr. Jarett..." He leveled his eyes to his. "... I need to see you if you have a moment." Otto's tone was insistent.

A frown crossed Kirt Jarett's handsome face. "Sure thing, Otto," he responded with agitation, turning his attention back to Stacy Gullaume. "I'll call your suite later," he said, glancing at his watch. "... About three this afternoon?" He raised his brow, waiting for her to give him a nod of approval.

After receiving her approval, he followed Otto Lambert outside.

"Let's have a walk along the beach...shall we, Kirt?" Otto gestured towards to ocean.

After several moments of uncomfortable silence, Otto Lambert began to speak. "Ethan Sommers shipped us a group of kids from France," he said, hanging his head and putting his hands inside both of his pockets.

"Yeah…well, what's that got to do with me?" Kirk sharply replied.

"I need you to take the kids back to France." Otto released a deep sigh.

Staring at him coldly, Kirt snapped, "I thought you told me to stay the hell away from the kids, Lambert!"

Otto's tone shifted from insistent to serious. "If I were you, Jarett… I'd save the attitude for your lady friends. Let's not forget just who you're talking to…Understand?"

Kirt turned away from Otto and began kicking the sand, as he walked. "You know, Lambert…I'm not afraid of you or your threats anymore… Hell, man…as far as the goes, I'm not afraid of your weirdo friend and partner in slime, Ethan Sommers, either!" he responded angrily.

Otto chuckled. "I see…and would you mind elaborating a little more on that statement of yours?" He smiled wickedly.

Kirt stopped walking and turned to face him. "Sure old man. It's over…I'm sick of you…this place…and all the shit you have put me through for the past ten years of my life! I'm leaving, and this time you're not going to stop me!"

Otto coldly stared at Kirt. "Oh, so you want to go out in the world…all on your own now? I suppose you have saved up enough money to afford to live the luxurious life you have grown accustomed to for the past ten years. Is that it, Kirt?" He sighed, shaking his head. "You can afford your fifteen-hundred -dollar a day habit…plus food, lodging, expensive cloths and that Jag I gave to you for your birthday last year?"

"I've made some friends that are willing to help me out," he huffed in response nervously kicking at the sand.

Otto chuckled. "I see...and what happens a year or so from now when, suddenly, you realize that you have been replaced by a younger whore! Then what? Why do you think I cut you loose and replaced you with Thomas? People enjoy youth, Kirt- not some has-been knocking thirty... Get the picture? That's why we break the kids in here...and after a few years we start putting them in some of our other establishments. There's a lot of fucking money in youth, Kirt."

Kirt angrily laughed. "Who the hell do you think you're kidding, old man? You didn't replace me with Thomas because of my age. You replaced me with Thomas because of Kirsten Kamel...admit it! You knew that I was in love with her and you were jealous! You couldn't stand the thought of me falling in love with someone else! That's why you turned her exclusively over to Ethan Sommers. You wanted to hurt me...admit it, goddamn it!" he shouted waving his fist in the air.

Otto leveled his eyes to Kirt's angry ones. "All right...I admit it. I know what an animal Sommers is and that he would want her for himself...and after he was tired of her, if she were still alive...I knew I would have to ship her somewhere else." He stared coldly into his eyes.

Kirt turned red in the face. "You sick fuck!" he shouted grabbing the resort owner by the shirt collar and doubling up his fist to hit him...but, suddenly-swallowed hard, forcing himself to release Lambert from his hold. "This is what you want me to do, isn't it? You want me to get mad, beat the hell out of you, and then fuck your goddamn brains out. That's it...isn't it, Otto? What's the matter, old man...your new boy toy isn't man enough to satisfy you?" He sarcastically laughed.

Otto Lambert turned red in the face and tightly closed his eyes. "Yes, it's true..." he sighed. "...I miss you,

Kirt. I hated Kirsten for stealing you away from me. After all, I was your first lover, remember? You were only seventeen when I first…"

Kirt heatedly interrupted him. "Yeah…yeah…yeah. I was there…I remember. I don't need to go down memory lane with you. You know, Otto…I still have mixed feelings about you." He shrugged his shoulders. "Both love and hate…I suppose. One minute I want to fuck your brains out…and the next minute I wish I'd never see you again," he said in a confused tone, shaking his head.

"You know I own you, Kirt. I'll never let you leave me. Don't you understand that?" Otto grabbed his face, forcing the young man to look at him. "That's why I let you have more freedom around the Island than the rest of my whores…do what you want to do…go where you want to go…supply you with everything you need and want." He released his hand from Kirt's face. "You're free to sleep with anyone you want, that is, as long as you don't form any goddamn emotional bonds with them. As long as you don't fall in love with someone else…and as long as you behave yourself and do what you're told, and…of course, you still find time for me…" He placed his hand on Kirt's shoulder. "…I don't see why we can't work things out between us. You know, Kirt…it really would break my heart if I would have to go to your funeral," he said in a threatening manner.

Kirt laughed. "I told you, Otto. If I decided to stay it will be because I want to stay. I told you I'm not afraid of your threats anymore. Since Kirsten's death, I really don't give a damn for much of anything… Did you know that she was pregnant by me? I really did love her, Otto." He sighed, hanging his head sadly. "Since her death, I've been fucking your new boy toy. Does that bother you?" he asked trying to hurt him.

"Well. Well. Well. I suppose we'll have to do a threesome, sometime." The old man snapped. "How did you know that Kirsten was pregnant?"

"She told me a few hours before Becka Chamberlain shot her to death." A tear rolled down his cheek.

"And that's why you…"

"Yeah… me and Thomas." he said without remorse.

"I need you to take the kids back to France, Kirt. The cops are still snooping around here and will be for quite awhile," he said changing the subject after realizing how upset Kirt was getting over Kirsten.

"All right, Otto, but, I don't want anymore goddamn lectures about leaving them alone. I have needs and urges that I can't seem to control, thanks to you, you sick fuck! Now see what you've gone and done, Otto! You've gone and pissed me off! Get your ass over there and take off your goddamn clothes…I suddenly have an urgent need to hurt you real…real bad!" he commanded, gesturing towards a secluded area on the beach, quickly removing the belt from his blue jeans.

Kirt joined Otto behind a large rock along the secluded area of the beach. After Otto removed his clothes, Kirt began to beat him with his belt, causing the sick old man to soon cry out in pain mixed with perverted pleasure.

Kirt's anger quickly turned into rage, as he began to hit Otto more violently. The force of each blow to his body soon forced Otto to the ground, hitting his head on a large rock, rendering him unconscious.

Panic surged throughout Kirt's body, forcing him to kneel to the ground beside the unconscious monster that he both loved and hated.

After his tears stopped flowing, Kirt dressed Otto and ran back to the hotel for help.

Chapter 36

Clint Chamberlain jumped out of the shower and finished dressing in record time, at least for him it was record-breaking time.

"Now, what in the hell did I do with her phone number?" he mumbled under his breath, searching threw the dresser drawers in his posh hotel suite.

"Ah...there it is," he said, smiling while picking up the card. He eagerly walked to the bar and poured himself a shot of scotch, then sat down on a barstool, reaching for the phone.

After two rings the phone was answered. "Hello, Renea!" he said anxiously.

"Sorry, sir...you must have the wrong number." The voice on the other end replied.

"Is this 0033 1247?" Clint asked.

"Yes, but there is no one here by that name, sir."

"No Renea Chandlier?"

"I'm sorry, sir."

"Thanks anyway," he said, disappointedly replacing the receiver.

"Huh." he mumbled reaching for the telephone again.

"Good afternoon. Milford's of London...how may we be of service to you today?"

"Yes, I need to speak with Renea Chandlier, please." Clint said in response reaching for his drink.

"We have no Renea Chandlier that works here, sir."

"You're sure?" he huffed sitting his drink down.

"Yes, sir...no one by that name. May I connect your call to someone else?"

"No thank you. Sorry to trouble you," he said putting the phone down.

"Shit! What the hell is going on here?" he mumbled under his breath, reaching for his suit jacket and slamming the door.

After he exited the lobby he hailed a cab, not noticing the private investigator arriving just as his cab was pulling off.

"Where to, sir?" The taxi driver asked after turning on his meter.

"Here...take me to this address, please." Clint handed the driver Renea's business card.

Fifteen minutes later, the cabbie pulled into the driveway of an old French Villa-Style Mansion

"Shall I wait for you, sir?" the driver asked, glancing in the rearview mirror.

"Yes, I won't be long, thanks." Clint hopped out of the cab.

He swiftly walked to the tall, iron gate and glanced around for an intercom, but he couldn't see one. Scratching his head in puzzlement, he leaned up against the gate. Surprisingly, the gate wasn't locked, and pushed open the moment he touched it.

He jogged to the front door and rang the doorbell. The door was immediately opened by an older- but none-the-less, attractive French woman.

"*Bonjour*," she greeted glancing at him.

"Hi...I mean *Bonjour*," he smiled. "*Je cherche* Ms. Renea Chandlier (I'm looking for...)."

The mature French woman shook her head. "*Excusez – moi, non* Renea Chandlier here (I'm sorry, no...)."

All right... Maybe I have her name wrong. She's a very attractive woman...middle twenties...about a hundred and ten pounds or so...Five feet five...deep auburn hair."

"*Non*."

"*Merci* (thank you)," he said nodding his head disappointedly.

As Clint turned to leave, he glanced back over his shoulder hoping he might spot Renea peaking out of one of the windows or something but, of course, he didn't, largely because she wasn't there.

"I've obviously been dooped," he mumbled, walking back to the taxi. *'But why'*? he thought as he climbed inside.

"Where to, sir?"

"I need to speak with a doctor Schaffer at the State Hospital Bouclcaut. How far is that from here?" he asked glancing at his watch.

"About twenty minutes, I think."

"Fine...but I want you to wait for me there as well." Clint swallowed angrily.

"All right, I can wait, sir."

A few moments later, Clint Chamberlain shouted out, scaring the hell out of the poor taxi driver. "Ethan Sommers. You, rotten son-of-a-bitch!"

The driver slammed on his brakes and stared into the rearview mirror with a worried look draped across his face.

"What's wrong, sir?" The taxi driver asked nervously.

"I'm sorry..." Clint apologized after noticing the poor man trembling in fear. "...I've changed my mind about going to the hospital. Take me back to the hotel, please.

"Yes, sir...right away," the cabbie responded, stepping on the gas, happy to get his crazy fare back to his hotel and out of his cab.

"How could all of this be happening to me? How does Ethan do it? The rotten bastard is a genius... How could he have known I'd be on that goddamn flight to France? Where did he find Renea Chandlier? Did he have her face altered to look like Nouri just to fool me? Why would he'? Clint continued to be lost in thought, as the driver pulled in front of the hotel.

"Here we are, sir." Clint snapped himself back to reality.

"Here. This should cover it." Clint tossed a fifty-dollar- bill on the front seat of the taxi. "Sorry if I frightened you," he said, smiling and sliding out of the cab.

"No problem," The driver returned the smile, quickly retrieving the fifty-spot.

Clint continued to search for answers to the many puzzling questions that seemed to be surrounding him. Why did Ethan want Renea to have sex with me? How did he know I'd let here seduce me so easily? The answer suddenly dawned on him- "Tape! The son-of-a-bitch has been taping me and Renea," he was angrily whispering to himself, when he suddenly bumped into Charles Mason, who was stepping off of the elevator.

"Mason. What the hell are you doing here?" he snapped, forgetting about their conversation the night before.

Charles shook his head amusingly. "What's the matter Chamberlain...all the strange booty you been getting from Renea Chandlier been affecting your brain or what?"

"Mason, you fuck! What have you been doing, filming my ass, too?" he huffed, stepping away from the elevator.

"Oh, so you know about the hidden video and listening devices I uncovered inside your hotel suite."

"I didn't until a few minutes ago." He sighed, shaking his head.

"Your boss?" Charles remarked suspecting as much.

"That's my guess, Mason."

"What's that you asked me to tell Nouri over the phone for you? Oh, yes...I remember," he said deliberately trying to provoke him. "Tell her what she's thinking about me and some other woman..."

Clint quickly interrupted him. "Fuck you, Mason...and the fucking Feds that are with you!"

"Come on, Chamberlain- get a goddamn grip! Let's go to the bar. We need to talk," the P.I. said, motioning in the direction of the cocktail lounge in the lobby of the posh hotel.

"Sure...why not?" Clint heatedly agreed, taking the lead.

"I'll have a double bourbon on the rocks, please. Chamberlain, what will you have?" Charles said to the bartender and then motioned to Clint.

"The same will be fine," Clint sighed, sitting on the barstool next to Charles.

"So, Chamberlain...where's Ethan Sommers?"

"I don't know. I haven't had much luck finding him yet," Clint reached for his drink.

"Maybe if you'd keep it in your pants for a little while..."

"Fuck you, Mason," Clint snapped, setting his drink down on top of the bar.

"What's the matter, Chamberlain? Had to spend a few hours by yourself for a change?"

Clint shook his head. "Cut the shit, Mason. I'm in no mood for it." He glanced angrily at him.

Charles chuckled. "All right. So you say you just found out that Sommers has been taping your every move inside your suite?"

"Yeah. I finally figured it out when I tried to find Renea. I phoned the numbers that she gave me...neither one was her real number. So, then, I stopped by the address she gave me- a family mansion she was supposed to have inherited." He released a deep sigh.

"I see. Any other ideas where she might be?" Charles asked, reaching for his drink.

"No, she's probably somewhere fucking Ethan by now."

"I'll have the F.B.I. check all the tapes in and around the hotel. We might get lucky. Maybe she hopped in a car or something. The license number on the car may show up." He shrugged his shoulders.

"She's been driving a yellow Jag," Clint offered.

"Yeah, we know. Stolen tags, though." He shook his head.

"Great! Now what?"

"I've got a plan…but I'll need your cooperation, Chamberlain."

"I told you, Mason. I'm not working with you."

"And I told you…you have no choice. If you don't play nice, I'll just have to tell Daddy on you!" he chuckled.

"Very funny, asshole. I suppose your daddy means the Feds?"

"Yes, that's right, Chamberlain. You can either help us, or you can get ready to phone your attorney. You're going to be charged in your wife's murder."

"That's a bunch of shit, Mason, and you know it. I had nothing to do with Becka's death…or, the Kamel woman's death!"

"Maybe. All I know for sure at this point is that I was informed early this morning that your wife pulled the trigger on the Kamel woman."

"Becka killed Kirsten?" A stunned expression quickly covered the attorney's face.

"Yes…that's right." Charles nodded.

"Son-of-a-bitch! I wonder why?" Clint remarked in disbelief.

"Who knows? A lover's triangle, maybe? From what I've found out so far, your wife was pretty fucked up in the head…pity really. A beautiful young woman like that."

"Yeah, so I've recently been told."

"You had no idea before her death?"

"Oh, sure. I knew she was nuts…if that's what you mean… But as far as kinky sex and stuff…no. I didn't

380

know. I honestly didn't . Lately, her anger was getting worse and a few times she would drive me to the brink of actually wanting to hit her...but I could never bring myself to do it. Though in all honesty, God knows I wanted to. You would've had to know her to understand, Mason." Clint reached for his drink.

"Have you ever hit a woman, Chamberlain?"

"No Mason, I never have. I'm a lover of women...not the other way around," he said, smiling, holding his empty glass up for the bartender to see.

"So I've been told, Chamberlain." Charles said, pushing his empty glass to the side and picking up his fresh one.

"Shit! Who are you trying to bullshit, Mason? You're no goddamn angel. I've seen your pictures in the newspapers, on television, and...shall I go on?"

"No I'm not on trial here. It's your goddamn head on a platter that Nouri wants, not mine," Charles chuckled.

"Speaking of Nouri...how is she?" Clint leveled his eyes to Mason's.

"As well as can be expected, I suppose." He sighed. "Did you know someone sent her a death threat?"

A shocked expression quickly crossed Clint's face. "Oh, my God! I'm going to get on the next damn plane out of here, and..." he said almost jumping to his feet.

"Whoa! Back up Jack! She's in hiding. Not even I know where she's being kept at the moment." Charles motioned for him to sit down.

"Who's protecting her?" Clint asked jealously.

"A detective friend of mine. His name is Gabe Baldwin. He's my ex-partner at the Boston Police Department. He's one of the best. He'll protect her with his own life. She'll be fine with Gabe."

"But you said he's one of the best. Why can't she have the best? I want her to have the goddamn best..."

"Whoa... She can't have the best, because I'm here with your ass," Charles chuckled.

"Very funny, asshole," Clint snipped with an attitude.

"All right, Chamberlain. Take it easy. I was just trying to lighten the mood around here, for chrissakes."

Clint released a sigh of frustration. "So, do they know who's threatening her?"

"Maybe her husband. They're not sure yet." Charles shrugged his broad shoulders.

"Any other leads?"

"A few things they're working on. They'll get him. Don't worry, Gabe will look after her."

"Yeah. Well, Mason...who's going to be looking after good ol' Gabe?"

"Enough, Chamberlain! I trust my friend." Charles sharply snapped.

"Yeah, well I used to trust mine...and look where it's gotten me."

"Yeah, well my friend is a man of character. He knows how important Nouri is to me. Gabe knows his place. He wouldn't...I...I...mean...he couldn't..." His tone suddenly confused and uncertain.

Clint interrupted him. "Listen to yourself, Mason. Just exactly who are you trying to convince...me or yourself?"

"Shut your mouth, Chamberlain. Gabe is one of the finest men I've ever had the privilege of knowing. Got it?"

"Yeah. Sure...whatever, Mason. Now, what the hell do you need me for? Seems like you have everything under control...well almost anyway. You say Becka killed Kirsten, right? Then who killed Becka?"

"We have a few leads. Nothing sound enough to talk about yet, but we hope to lock onto something soon."

"So why are you here? You obviously don't think Ethan killed Becka anymore, right?"

"We're not a hundred percent sure of that, yet. And anyway, we want him for a lot of other shit."

"Like what, Mason?" Clint curiously glanced at Charles.

"Did I mention that the phones in your hotel suite were bugged... We listened in and retrieved your phone conversation with Ethan." Charles smiled knowingly.

"You son-of-a..."

"Now is that anyway to talk to someone that is about to help you out of a tight spot with the woman of your dreams?"

"What the hell are you talking about, Mason?" Clint questioned with interest.

"I want to make a deal with you, Chamberlain."

Charles motioned for the bartender to bring another round of drinks, and then pulled out a pack of cigarettes from his inside shirt pocket.

"What kind of deal, Mason?"

"It appears that our only lead in locating Ethan Sommers, at this point, is through Renea Chandlier. Right now both of them aren't aware of the fact that you know about the hidden camera's or bugs in your room, right?"

"I suppose," Clint sighed, downing his drink.

"We'll locate Renea Chandlier for you... You'll convince her that you didn't mean to hurt her feelings...kiss and make up. Sooner or later, she'll lead us to Sommers...and then we'll nail his miserable ass and you can go back to doing whatever it is that you do." He blew out a puff of smoke. "That is...as long as you aren't involved with any of Sommers' illegal activities," Charles added, flicking an ash in the ashtray.

Clint shook his head and sighed. "I'm not lily white if that's what you mean, Mason... However, the past few years, I've done everything I know how to do to make things right again. At least a few things from my past that I have been ashamed of... And part of that includes a few business transactions that I've been trying hard to clean up." The high-powered- attorney released a sigh of regret, reaching for his drink.

"That's the way it sounded when I listened to your conversation with Sommers."

"On the tape Sommers mentioned child prostitution, remember?"

"Yeah, Mason...It made me sick to my stomach." Clint shook his head in disgust.

"Yeah." The famous PI nodded. "But the F.B.I. have been in Lambert for a few months now. They got wind of it when some young kid managed to escape before the bastards had time to get him hooked on the heavy shit." Charles heatedly lit another cigarette.

"I'm glad. I was led to believe the hired help in Lambert were there because they were eighteen or older, and they wanted to be there doing what they do," Clint shook his head in amazement.

"Yeah, well Sommers and Lambert are going to pay for what they have done to those children...believe me. I want those sick fucks! I want them real bad!" Charles downed his shot of bourbon.

"You know, Mason...for the life of me I can't begin to imagine why Ethan has harbored such hatred for me the past fifteen years. I swear I never knew it."

"Well, it might have something to do with the young woman that Sommers was supposedly in love with at the time." Charles blew out a puff of smoke before continuing... "From the background investigation I ordered, my team of ex-agents have managed to dig up some interesting things about Ethan. Sommers... It appears that the young woman who fell down the stairs at the university and died from a broken neck, didn't just fall... It was suspected at the time that Sommers may have slapped her, deliberately causing her death in a fit of rage... It couldn't be proven at the time, largely due to his father's connections, money, and influences.... And, of course, there weren't any known witnesses... For the lack of evidence, there were no charges filed against him... Did I forget to mention the young lady was pregnant?" Charles leveled his eyes to Clint Chamberlain's. "That information wasn't made public." Charles waved his glass to get the attention of the bartender.

"Was it Ethan's child?" Clint asked nervously reaching for his drink.

"No. We figure that's what got Sommers so pissed off." Charles released a puff of smoke.

Clint began to turn red in the face. "Shit! No wonder he hates me. It was probably my kid."

"You didn't know?" Charles remarked curiously.

"No. Of course not... Ethan and I used to share chicks all the time back in those days... Hell, it could have been one of at least five guys... There were five of us that were as close as brothers... One for all and all for one – get the picture? ... Now that I think about it... Ethan was a little more touchy about her than most of his other chicks." The attorney sighed, downing his drink.

"What do you mean 'touchy'?" Charles asked with growing interest.

"Ethan would get moody after one of us kicked it with her. A few times, he even caught her sneaking out of my bedroom... You see, Mason...it was one of our rules, we could have sex with each other's chicks, if she was willing, mind you. We just weren't supposed to do it behind closed doors, so-to-speak... The guy whose chick it was, was supposed to be present... Watching was supposed to be part of the fun of it," Clint explained as reached for his drink.

"Pretty sick, huh?" Charles Mason remarked, reaching for the ashtray.

"Yes, Charles we were all messed up back then. But, Ethan did love this girl. I think he only went along with our club rules because he's the one that made them... He didn't know Legs at that time he made the rules... He met her about a year after we started our 'private club'."

"Legs?" Charles asked curiously.

"Yeah, that was Makus's nickname. We gave it to her because her legs were one of her best features... God, when she wrapped those long legs around your waste and reeled you inside her...Damn! She was pretty remarkable!"

"So, do you agree? Makus might be the reason that Sommers hates you so much today?"

"There's a strong possibility. Makus once told me that she loved me and not Ethan." Clint shook his head.

"Ouch! If Sommers knew that or even suspected it... Was he capable of the kind of rage it would take to knock someone down several flights of stairs?"

"Yeah. Ethan could...and did display some pretty ugly scenes with uncontrollable rage. Ethan enjoyed getting crazy, I think. Of course, he had to have a shot or two of false courage first."

"Alcohol?"

"Yeah and drugs... He could get pretty screwed up sometimes...When Ethan was like that, most people around him would shake with fear," Clint nodded, as the memory rushed through his brain.

"Were you afraid of him, Chamberlain?"

Clint laughed. "Hardly! I was probably the only one at the time who wasn't. I'd kick his ass." He shook his head. "And refuse to put up with his shit...I think that's one of the things he liked most about me...I sure as hell wasn't in his league when it came to family background or Papa's money... But, for reasons I've never really understood completely, Ethan seemed to need me... I don't care what he says now, he did love me like a brother at one time...At least before Makus died."

They ordered two more shots of bourbon.

"Well, hopefully, we've helped solved that mystery for you, Chamberlain. So, now maybe you will help us...What do you say?"

"First Mason I'm still waiting to hear how you can help me out with the woman of my dreams. I'm confused, it seems. I was under the impression that you were in love with her, too?"

"It's like this, Chamberlain. I need you to help us out. We need Renea Chandlier in order to locate Ethan Sommers. I'm willing to help smooth things over with Nouri for you by backing your lie to her, in return for your help. I figure if she really is in love with you, well, so be it... Who the hell am I to stand in her way? But, on the other hand, if she chooses me over you this time, you'll be asked to stand aside and leave her alone forever. Do we have a deal?"

"You know, Mason, I never thought I would ever be saying something like this to you, Hell, I don't even like you..." Clint said smiling. "...But you really are quite a man. Actually, you're much more a man than I could ever be when it comes to Nouri. I really do love her, Mason." He released a frustrated sigh.

"I believe you, Chamberlain- especially, after listening to your taped conversation with Ethan. But tell me this. What are you going to do if Renea Chandlier is pregnant by you? What are you going to tell Nouri? After all, you're supposed to be innocent of any wrong doings with other women, right?" Charles said, grinning sheepishly.

Clint shook his head in disbelief. "I guess I'll have no other choice but to carry out what I said, I was going to do." He released a frustrated sigh.

"And what was that, Chamberlain?"

"Blow my goddamn brains out! Then I won't have to worry about it," Clint responded with a sad look masked across his handsome face.

"I see your point. But suicide doesn't solve problems, it just creates confusion. I'm a firm believer that if something is meant to be, eventually it will be. There are certain things that we have no control over, and just as many things that we can't do anything about. So, why worry about them? If you are meant to be with Nouri it will work out. If you're not meant to be with her, then…" he suddenly stopped talking.

"What about you and Nouri, Mason?"

"I used to be a hundred percent certain that she and I would wind up together, someday. No matter how long it would take, we would eventually be together." Mason shook his head. "But now…" he paused…

"But now what, Mason?"

"Well, let's just say I'm only about eighty percent certain, and leave it at that." He grinned and blew out a puff of smoke.

"How come I get the feeling you're not telling me everything!"

"I can't believe I've even said this much to you, Chamberlain. After all, I don't really like you either," Charles grinned.

"Sounds like we need to tie on a good one, Mason," Clint said ordering two more double shots of bourbon.

Charles glanced at his watch. "What the hell, Chamberlain. I've got a little time on my hands this afternoon, but, first I need to know if we have a deal or not?"

"Sure… Why not?" Clint shrugged. "I've lost Nouri for sure if you don't help me. But I still don't quite understand what it is that you want me to do?"

"Actually, nothing… Just do what you have been doing, but instead of entertaining just one man on film, you'll have to entertain an entire crew," Charles chuckled, amused by it all.

"You still want me to, ah...ah..." Clint swallowed nervously as he turned red in the face.

"Exactly. That's what Sommers seems to paying her to do, right?"

"I suppose. But, I'm not sure I can get it up now that I know people will be watching me," The attorney chuckled.

"It'll be just like your old college days. Besides, after seeing you two together, let's just say I don't think you'll have that problem. Hell, Chamberlain, I got hard just watching the film of you two going at it!" Charles mused.

"Fuck you, Mason," Clint teased, returning the muse.

"All joking aside, Chamberlain, just keep doing what it is that you have been doing. Try to get as much info out of her as you can without making her suspicious. Also, see if you can find a way to give her a reason to want to sneak out and pay Sommers a visit. At the very least, she may call him. In the meantime, we'll replace the tapes and listening devices in your suite, okay?"

"All right, Mason. We'll try it your way. But, I still can't believe your going to lie to Nouri for me."

"Listen Chamberlain, I'm a selfish bastard. I'm not doing it for you. I'm doing it for me. Like I said, I can't wait forever for Nouri to get you out of her system. If she's still in love with you, well then I guess what I'm doing is just part of the price I have to pay to know for sure."

"You know, Mason, you really are an okay guy. Too bad I don't like you. We might have made good friends," Clint smiled, downing his drink.

"You know something, Chamberlain, I was just thinking the same thing about you." They both began to laugh.

Chapter 37

"One spicy Bloody Mary on the rocks," Nouri Sommers called out as she entered the country-style kitchen of police detective Gabe Baldwin's A-frame cabin in the woods.

"Great! I was beginning to think you had forgotten all about me," Gabe responded teasingly.

She smiled seductively. "I don't think so, detective."

He returned her smile with a lustful smile of his own, slowly brushing past her to pull out her chair. He smiled knowingly when he heard her softly sigh.

"Thank you," she replied, trying to act as though his closeness had zero effect on her. After all, what good would it do? He had all ready informed her that things between them just wasn't going to happen, because of his close relationship with his friend, and ex-partner, Charles Mason. Her efforts to seduce him had been in vain.

None-the-less, she couldn't seem to help herself. He wanted her as badly as she wanted him and she knew it. But his determination not to have his way with her out of loyalty to his friend made her want him even more.

She released an unconscious sigh.

"Is something wrong?" Gabe asked, knowing damn good and well what was bothering her.

She swallowed hard, trying hard to pull her emotions back under control. "No. I was just thinking of something." She forced a smile.

"Umm. You did a nice job on the Bloody Mary's...a little spicy, but not too hot. I like it." He smiled deliberately changing the subject. He knew she was sulking, and the sad part was he was *dying* to pull her into his arms and kiss her. But, he also knew that was one thing he was determined never to do. His friendship with Charles Mason was more important to him than any woman could ever be. His word was his bond, something he had never broken before, and he certainly had no intention of breaking it now, especially, now that he had gotten his emotions back under control.

"Do you like your omelet, Nouri?" he asked trying to lighten the mood.

"Yes, it's good...quite good, actually." She forced another smile, reaching for her fork again.

"Have you tried the toast yet?" he asked excitedly.

"No...why?" She glanced at him curiously, reaching for a slice of it.

"Taste it and tell me what you think?"

"Oh, it's wonderful! What's on it? Apple butter?"

"No. It's pumpkin butter, actually. My aunt Marsha sent it to me along with some other jams and jellies from a little town along the Kentucky-Tennessee border. A little Quaker town, I believe."

"You're aunt Marsha sounds like a caring Aunt," she smiled gazing into his beautiful teal-blue eyes.

As he gazed into her incredibly sexy, hazel- blue-green eyes, he felt himself wanting to rush over to her, and pull her into his arms.

'Oh, God! You have no idea what you do to me'! Is what he wanted to say, but instead he responded, "Yes, she is. Aunt Marsha is a lovely woman. I love her deeply." He smiled, reaching for his Bloody Mary- thinking, '*God I need a drink*'.

"Sounds like you have a really wonderful family, detective," she said nervously toying around the rim of her glass with her index finger.

"Yes, I do. But, I've told you all that I intend to about my family for now. It's your turn to tell me a little about yours, don't you think?" he smiled.

"Maybe some other time," Nouri softly answered, finishing her drink.

"Would you mind?" Gabe asked holding up his glass for a refill.

"Not at all," she answered standing to her feet and walking to the refrigerator. "I made extra."

"Good," he said walking over to help her. "If I had known I could have gotten it myself... sorry"

"No problem, detective."

"Nouri," Gabe said, gesturing her back to her seat.

"Thank you."

"After we eat, I suppose we'll have to find a new place to hide out. I'll have to talk to my captain and the DA about what happened today I'm afraid," he sighed.

"Oh, Gabe, I like it here at the cabin. Do we have to leave so soon?" She made a pouting face.

He released a frustrated sigh. "I'm afraid so. We aren't safe anymore." He shook his head. "The guy could come back and next time could bring others with him."

"Oh, Gabe. I'm sorry. Do you think it was my fault that he found us so easily?"

"It's hard to say. I just don't know. I hope not, but to be on the safe side we can't take any chances." He shook his head.

"What do you mean?"

"We'll have to change cars and have yours checked out for any possible tracking devices. We'll also have your suitcases checked out for the same...and I'm sorry, Nouri...please don't be mad at me, but I'm going to have your friend, Genna Matthews checked out, as well."

Nouri jumped to her feet and angrily folded her arms. "That's absurd! Genna has been my best friend for the past seven years, Gabe. You can't honestly think she would have anything to do with wanting to hurt me. Do you?"

"Please sit down, Nouri...I hope not, for your sake, anyway. As for me, I'm a cop. That's what I do. I'm sorry if that upsets you, but, that just the way it is."

"But, you're wrong. Genna just couldn't possibly be involved with anything like this. Why would she? What would she have to gain?" She swallowed nervously.

"All right, Nouri…just calm down. I'll tell you what…let's finish our breakfast and have a few more Bloody Mary's…and while we're eating you can tell me all about your friend. Maybe you can convince me that she's as wonderful as you think she is…deal?" he said, smiling

Nouri sat back down and nodded. "Okay, detective, but when this is over, and you catch the bad guy, I'll expect an apology from you about Genna…all right?" She leveled her eyes to his.

"Fine. Now tell me when and how you met."

"We met seven years ago at The Fine Arts Academy in Boston. We were in school together."

"And…"

"And we became friends immediately. Actually, detective, she's the one that introduced me to Charles Mason."

"Really?"

"Yes. Genna was dating a young cop at the time by the name of Mike Jones…did you know him?" She glanced at him, as she shoved her plate away from her.

"Is he the same Michael Jones that's now a *big wig* in congress?"

"Yes, that's him."

"No kidding? I understand he has some heavy hitters backing him." His tone was one of surprise.

"I'm sorry, detective, I don't know what that means," she shrugged.

"Never mind…go on, please."

"Michael had a friend that Genna wanted to fix me up with. That friend was Charles."

"Somehow I knew you were going to say that," the police detective teased.

"It was love at first sight for Charles and lust at first sight for me. Since she was responsible for introducing us, I just assumed they liked one another, but I was wrong." She shrugged her shoulders.

"What do you mean?"

"Well, one day I walked in on Charles and Genna, it was obvious to me that they had been arguing about something. Whatever it was, neither one would say. But it really must have upset her...she had tears in her eyes." Nouri paused thoughtfully for a moment. "I tried to comfort her, but she pushed me aside and ran out of the room. I asked Charles about it later, but he just shrugged it off. So I never thought anything of it, until Charles tried to tell me that he didn't want me hanging around with her anymore." Nouri reached for her drink.

"Did Charles say why he didn't want you hanging around her anymore?"

"No. He just said she wasn't the person that I thought she was. That was ridiculous, of course. Charles just didn't want me hanging around anyone. He was very protective of me."

"What happened after that?"

"Well, I didn't see Genna for a period of time right after that. She sort of disappeared. But then she came back around...just out of the blue and we have been best friends ever since."

"How long had she disappeared?"

"Oh, I don't remember...maybe a couple of months or so."

"Did she say where she had gone?"

"No, but she got pretty nervous when I asked her about it."

"What do you mean?"

"I don't know exactly. She just didn't quite seem like her old self. Does that make sense?"

"Maybe she was just having an off day?"

"Maybe. But it was more than one day. She seemed wilder...more nervous. She started smoking and doing drugs. She hated drugs and cigarettes before she went away. I don't know--she just seemed different."

"So which is it, Nouri? Did she disappear or did she just go away for a few months?"

"She disappeared. I just assumed she went away somewhere. I don't even know why I said that."

"What about Charles? Where was he while Genna was gone?"

"I don't remember. But I think he was gone for a few weeks. He was working undercover, I believe, why?" Nouri asked curiously.

"No reason," Gabe shrugged.

"There had to be a reason or you wouldn't ask, Gabe."

"No, honestly. I was just curious. Did you mention her disappearance to him when he got back?"

"I may have…I'm not sure," she shrugged.

"What else can you tell me about your friend?"

Nouri laughed. "My friend is the wildest person I have ever known. She loves the male strip clubs. She's always getting into trouble, sneaking into those places." She laughed again.

"Trouble? In what way?" Gabe asked with growing interest.

"She's married to a man who is as old as he is wealthy. And when he's away on business, she sneaks out to the clubs and usually winds up with one or two…" She suddenly stopped talking.

"One or two what?"

"Never mind, detective. Let's just say she enjoys herself…tremendously." She giggled, toying with the rim of her glass.

"Has Genna's husband ever suspected her of sleeping around?"

"At first, maybe. But they've been married for quite some time now. I think he just thinks she like's looking at their young well built bodies and shoving money down their... Well, you know what I mean, right, detective?" She smiled mischievously.

"Right. And how about you? Do you like looking at the young male stripper's well built bodies, too?" he asked jealously.

"Detective. The male strippers are my friend's things, not mine. I like more mature men myself." A seductive smile crossed her face.

"Would you care to define mature for me, ma'am?" he asked teasingly.

"Lets just say I like mature, well built men that at least know where their zippers are located," she giggled.

"So your saying what? That mature men are better lovers?"

His heart began to race madly at just the thought of making love to her.

"Oh, yeah!" she blushed. "That has been my experience. However, detective, I'm certainly no authority on the subject. I'm afraid I've only slept with four men in my life. And you seem to know three of them...The first young man in my life was a complete dud, to say the least...Shall I continue, detective?" She paused, just to drive the detached detective crazy with jealously.

"Oh, please continue," he said sharply, getting more envious by the moment.

"Why don't we go the living room, detective. It's more comfortable in there."

"Only if you finish telling me about the experience you had with your young lover," he teased.

"All right, detective. I can talk as we walk, if you're that interested," she playfully responded, brushing past him.

"I'm all ears, ma'am," he replied in response rolling his eyes.

"Like I was saying, my first lover wasn't a lover at all. He was too excited...Anyway, I was so hot and bothered after making out for about an hour…I thought I was going to die if he didn't do something…and quick." She laughed at the remembered thought.

"Don't stop now. I can hardly stand it!" he chuckled, as he sat down beside her on the couch.

"Oh, he did something all right. He did it before he could get his zipper down!" She shook her head in disbelief. "I couldn't believe it!" She laughed, reaching for her empty glass. "Shall we have another drink, detective?"

"Here, I'll pour us one," he offered, reaching for the picture of Bloody Mary's that he sat on the coffee table. "So your first lover didn't make love to you at all, then?"

"That's right detective." She nodded.

"So, Charles was truly your first real man, as you so eloquently put it?" A confused look crossed his face.

"That's right. He was my first real man, both making love to me, and, yes, giving me my first organism." She swallowed hard as the memory appeared in her brain. She instinctively blushed.

Gabe noticed her reaction and shifted uneasily in his seat. "And Charles didn't know you were a virgin?" he asked curiously.

She shrugged defensively. "No, I wanted him to think that I knew what I was doing."

Gabe shook his head and sighed. " I can't believe he didn't realize that…"

"It's okay. I didn't want him to know." She smiled nervously.

The detective shook his head in disagreement. "But, something like that is supposed to be so, so …"

She cut in. "What were you going to say, detective…So special. Is that it?"

"Yes," he said pointedly. "I'd certainly want to know something like that if I were …"

She interrupted. "Well, maybe he might've wanted to know," she conceded. "But, he just assumed I wasn't. I didn't see any point in telling him any differently." She swallowed and shifted uneasily in her seat. She went on... "And anyway- it wasn't like I didn't want him to make love to me. God!" She shook her head at the memory. "Believe me detective, I've never regretted letting Charles Mason make love to me. he was incredible!" She smiled, reaching for her drink. "You know detective, in my opinion, every young virgin should have a lover like Charles Mason, to be their first *real man*," she remarked, setting her drink down on top of the table.

"Lucky man. My friend and ex-partner," he smiled adding, "That was real nice, what you said about Charles, Nouri." He gazed longingly into her eyes.

She smiled appreciatively. "Can you imagine how much more protective of me he might've become had he have known that I was a virgin?"

Gabe shrugged unknowingly. "Well, if Charles was as possessive as you say he was, then maybe you were right not to tell him," he sighed. "But, had it been me, I would've wanted to know," he nodded, as he glanced at her.

She instinctively moved closer to him. "Why?" She asked curiously.

"I don't know. Maybe knowing it was your first time might've made Charles a little less aggressive. He might've been a little more romantic. Certainly he would've been a lot more gentler." A thoughtful expression covered his face.

She sighed. "All the things you said are true. And would have made my first time just as wonderful, I'm sure. But, the night Charles made love to me for the first time, my hormones were raging out of control. I was more than ready, my body was on fire! I was practically begging him for it, I swear, she giggled. "I told you, Gabe, for me, it was lust at first sight when I first met Charles," she said biting her lower lip unconsciously, almost driving the poor detective over the edge.

Gabe shook his head. "I still think if he had known he would've handled himself a little more carefully, wanting to make sure you were okay, and enjoying yourself," he said glancing at her.

"It's not like Charles was an animal or anything like that, for goodness sake, Gabe! That came later," she mused.

The detective rolled his eyes with irritation. "Very, goddamn funny, Nouri," he snapped jealously.

She fought back a chuckle, suspecting he was jealous of her first sexual experience being with his ex-partner and not himself. "What's the matter detective?" she asked coolly.

He rolled his eyes and released a frustrated sigh. "Not a goddamn thing, Ms. Hormones!" he replied sharply, causing her to chuckle.

"So, what now, detective? You want to hear about my other young lover?" She asked mischievously.

"I thought you told me that you had only slept with four men?" he asked with noticeable annoyance. He leveled his gaze to hers, and shifted uneasily in his seat.

She smiled. "Actually, what I meant to say was that- I've slept with three men that you know of and one younger man. I don't really count Mr. Zipper, because he got off before he could get it out of his pants," she giggled.

"Mr. Zipper? Cute, Nouri." He smiled in spite of himself at her colorful choice of words.

"I didn't sleep with him, but I did sleep with an artist around my own age before I started dating Clint Chamberlain."

"Well, thank you very much, Doctor Ruth, but I think I've heard more than I can handle already. I keep telling you, Nouri, I'm only human." He swallowed hard, as his eyes traveled slowly down her curvaceous body. He unconsciously licked his lips, before releasing a frustrated sigh.

"Something on your mind, detective?"

"Behave!" he whispered hopelessly, closing his eyes tightly for a moment. '*God, please help me*'! he silently prayed.

"Gabe," she whispered, sliding close to him, causing him to open his eyes. He swallowed hard again, quickly rising to his feet. He no longer trusted himself to be close to her.

"What's the matter, detective?" she asked knowingly, as she watched him cross the room and go to the bar, where he tightly clutched both of his hands on the padded railing.

Closing his eyes tightly again, he released a frustrated sigh. "Never mind." He swallowed hard again, trying to rid his thoughts of her and his ever-increasing need to make love to her.

She silently came up behind him and put her arms around his waist, pressing herself hard against his muscular frame. He glanced over his shoulder at her. She could feel him trembling when he turned to face her. His arms tightened around her, pulling her body to his. Without saying a word, he gazed longingly into here eyes. Her eyes sparkled with longing in return as desire quickly swept through her body.

His heart threatened to burst as he sensuously outlined her moist warm lips with his finger and thumb, aware his desire for her was dangerously close to entering the point of *NO RETURN*.

He moved his soft touch down her cheek tracing the outline of her beautiful face, neck, and arm. She could feel the heat from his touch scorching into her flesh.

She swallowed hard, closing her eyes anticipating his next move. She bit her lower lip when goosebumps trickled up her spine. Her heart began to race so rapidly that she thought it might somehow sprout wings and fly away.

He noticed the increase in her breathing, causing her breasts to erotically rise and fall beneath her satin blouse. He swallowed hard, trying to force himself to listen to the alarm that was going off inside his brain.

It was too late... '*He kissed her...*'

His urgent need to taste her FORBIDDEN lips...So Moist...So Tempting ...So Close...Too much temptation for any man to deny himself.

'*God help me*'! he silently thought, surrendering himself to the moment and his urgent need to kiss her.

He pulled her body against his, imprisoning her. She was instantly aware of his desire for her.

His mouth instantly on top of hers... Her lips Soft, Moist, Delicious... His kiss--Fiery Hot...

She gasped and her heart pounded out of control, as his kiss continued to take her *breath* away.

When he finally lifted his mouth from her beautiful, but swollen lips, she was completely disarmed, gasping, light headed, and weak in the knees. She closed her mouth and then her eyes, staggering back against the railing of the bar. She swallowed hard, attempting to get her emotions back under control. She inhaled several times...slowly releasing each breath.

Gabe regained consciousness and slowly took several steps away from her, not wanting to be accountable for what he might do next if he didn't put an immediate distance between the two of them. He swallowed hard and shook his head in an attempt to clear his mind.

"Nouri," he whispered breathlessly gazing at her, secretly enjoying watching her pull herself together after his *MASTERFUL* kiss. It made him happy to know he had such a disturbing affect on her. But then he had known that all along. His kiss only confirmed what he was already aware of.

She reluctantly opened her eyes, gently patting her chest, as though she were trying to slow her heart beat. She swallowed hard and cleared her throat. "Yes Gabe," she answered in a shaky tone.

"Are you all right? I'm sorry...I shouldn't have..." He shook his head and sighed.

She quickly interrupted him. "Sorry?" She shook her head in dismay. "Gabe Baldwin...How can you say that to me!"

He swallowed hard, not quite sure what to say next. A moment later, she flew into his arms, wrapping herself tightly around him.

"Oh God, Gabe!" she whispered. "Please don't tell me you don't feel it, too."

He quickly released himself from her tight embrace. Taking both of her arms, he slid his hands down to her wrists and cuffed them tightly, as he looked into her curious wide eyes. "You're going to be the death of me...I just know it!" he said hoarsely releasing one of her hands. He led her out the door where he quickly ushered her inside the car.

Chapter 38

After several moments of silence, Gabe reached down and put her hand inside his. Unable to speak, he pulled Nouri close to him. He gently kissed two of her fingers, as he continued to look at her beautiful face- that was now supporting a curious expression.

After several more moments of silence, he released her hand and glanced at her again. "Nouri…we have to go to the station. I need to report in with my boss and see what the District Attorney wants me to do." He smiled nervously.

She looked at him with her curious expression that slowly turned into an expression of disbelief.

'*I don't believe you Gabe Baldwin. First you kiss me like that, taking my breath completely away from me…then you pull me close to you and sensually kiss my fingers like that, once again stealing my breath away…and then you just act as though nothing has happened between us*'! she silently thought, still looking at him with her mouth wide open in dismay.

Still lost in thought, she found herself wondering just how long he would make her wait before he would pull her back into his arms and kiss her again with one of his fiery hot kisses that seemed to melt her very soul.

She had no idea how long of a drive it was to the Connecticut Police Department, but she was surprised to learn that she had traveled the entire distance with her mouth still wide open.

"Well, here we are," Gabe was saying to her, as he opened her car door, smiling as he intentionally brushed up against her. "Try and behave yourself in there, okay," he teased, jogging up the short flight of steps.

"What do you mean, detective?"

"There are quite a few good looking young cops inside the station. I just might get jealous." He smiled seductively, as his eyes slowly traveled the length of her body.

Her heart instantly began to race madly, as she tried to act as though she were under control. "Oh, really. Young and sexy...are they detective?" She returned his seductive smile with one of her own.

"I'm afraid so, ma'am." He teasingly leveled his eyes to hers.

"Umm." She sighed thoughtfully. "Well, then I'm not interested. I like my men to be..."

He interrupted her. "Yeah, I know...mature and sexy, right?" He playfully wiggled his eyebrows.

She smiled. "You forgot one thing, detective."

"Yeah...and what would that be?"

"Experienced!" She bit her lower lip, as she watched him melt.

"Is there something wrong, detective?" She coyly teased.

He leaned over and pulled her close to him before he opened the door to the station. He smiled longingly at her, gazing into her eyes. "You..." He paused for a moment. "...Just behave yourself. I don't think I can whip more than...oh, I don't know...maybe five cops at one time. So just watch yourself. Got it?" He smiled quickly, brushing his soft lips lightly across hers, causing her legs to almost buckle right out from under her. She gasped for air.

He knowingly smiled, opening the door. "Is there anything wrong, ma'am?" he mischievously returned, smiling.

She swallowed hard, longing to lean up against something, anything, to support her wobbling legs. 'Who's going to be the death of who, detective'! She silently thought before entering the police station.

As Gabe led Nouri down a brightly lit hallway of the Connecticut Police Department, sexy, female detective, Isabella Bedaux came running up to greet him, almost knocking him over with her eagerness to see him.

"Gabe!" she squealed with excitement, throwing her arms impulsively around his neck.

"Ah...uh...um..." he muttered reaching up to his neck to remove her arms. "Hi. Nice to see you again." His face reddened. "Listen, I'm sorry, but I have to speak with the chief on duty...and I have a few call to make, so..." Nouri mischievously interrupted them. "Aren't you going to introduce us, detective?" she asked darting a jealous dagger in his direction.

He nervously smiled and reached for her arm, and without saying a word quickly ushered her inside the office that was assigned to him earlier that morning.

"Nouri, I don't remember her name," he said, as they entered the office.

She chuckled sarcastically folding her arms angrily. "Yeah, so it would seem, detective."

"Honest. I just met her this morning. She told me her name, of course, but I just don't seem to remember it." He nervously swallowed.

"Yeah, right," she pouted, turning her back on him.

He walked up behind her and turned her around to face him. "Could be I don't remember her name, because I have something more important on my mind." He lowered his head to kiss her. when suddenly, the office door flew open, startling the two of them apart.

"The chief wants to see you immediately, detective!" Isabella snapped crisply, shooting Nouri an unpleasant look before huffing out of the room as quickly as she had entered it.

Gabe swallowed hard trying to reel his emotions back under control. "I'll be right back," he said, slowly running the palms of his hand down the length of her arm.

Unable to speak, she nodded and glanced around the room for the nearest chair.

Gabe returned to the tiny office thirty minutes later. "Quick...pick up line one. Someone wants to talk to you," he nervously prodded.

"Who is it, Gabe?" she whispered excitedly.

"Charles Mason." He forced a smile.

She walked over and eagerly picked up the receiver. "Charles...oh, God! It's good to hear your voice...yes...yes... I'm fine. Yes... Gabe is wonderful." She glanced at him and smiled.

"What? What? I don't believe it!" she said shaking her head.

"No. I heard what I heard, Charles! He can't be innocent! Charles, why are you telling me this? I thought you hated Clint?"

Gabe shot her a jealous look and sank down into the chair beside her.

"What! I said I don't want to talk to him, Charles. Stop it...Charles! Innocent? You're sure? All right...I'll talk to him," she said excitedly.

Gabe felt as though his heart had suddenly crashed to the floor. He couldn't bare sitting beside her- watching her face light up at just the mention of Clint Chamberlain's name.

"Goddamn it!" he jealously whispered under his breath, working himself up in a hissy. An instant later, he angrily jumped to his feet and without a word, he stormed out of the room, slamming the door to the office so hard he cracked the thick glass at the top of it.

Nouri was so completely involved in her conversation with Clint Chamberlain, that she barely noticed Gabe had left the room.

Printed in the United States
1267300002B/119

9 781588 515940